Praise for C.L. Taylor:

'*Black Narcissus* for the Facebook generation, a clever exploration of how petty jealousies and misunderstandings can unravel even the tightest of friendships. Claustrophobic, tense and thrilling, a thrill-ride of a novel that keeps you guessing.'
Elizabeth Haynes

'A gripping and disturbing psychological thriller: every bit as good as *The Accident*.'
Clare Mackintosh

'Fast-paced, tense and atmospheric, a guaranteed bestseller.'
Mark Edwards

'Haunting and heart-stoppingly creepy, *The Lie* is a gripping roller coaster of suspense.'
Sunday Express

'5/5 stars – Spine-chilling!'
Woman *magazine*

'An excellent psychological thriller.'
Heat *magazine*

'Packed with twists and turns, this brilliantly tense thriller will get your blood pumping.'
Claire Frost, Fabulous *magazine*

'A real page-turner, with two story lines: one of growing menace in the present, and a past narrative of a girls-only holiday that goes horrifically wrong. Creepy, horrifying and twisty. C.L. Taylor is extremely good at writing stories in which you have no idea which characters you can trust, and the result is intriguing and scary and extremely gripping.'
Julie Cohen, 2014 Richard and Judy Summer Book Club Pick

'*The Lie* is absolutely brilliant – *The Beach*, only darker, more thrilling and more tense. It's the story of a twisted, distorted friendship. It's a compelling, addictive and wonderfully written tale. Can't recommend it enough.'
Louise Douglas

'C.L. Taylor delivers another compelling read that'll keep you turning pages way too late into the night. Warning: may cause drowsiness the following day.'
Tamar Cohen

'My heart was racing after I finished C.L. Taylor's brilliant new book *The Lie*. Dark, creepy and full of twists. I loved it.'
Rowan Coleman

'C.L. Taylor is fast becoming the queen of psychological suspense. Read this: you won't be disappointed.'
Victoria Fox

THE MISSING

C.L. Taylor lives in Bristol with her partner and son. She started writing fiction in 2005 and her short stories have won several awards and have been published by a variety of literary and women's magazines. C.L. Taylor was voted as one of the Bestselling Adult Fiction Debut Authors of 2014 in *The Bookseller*.

Also by C.L. Taylor

The Accident
The Lie

C.L. TAYLOR

The Missing

avon

AVON
A division of HarperCollins*Publishers*
The News Building
1 London Bridge Street
London SE1 9GF

www.harpercollins.co.uk

A Paperback Original 2016

3

Copyright © C.L. Taylor 2016

C.L. Taylor asserts the moral right to
be identified as the author of this work

A catalogue record for this book is
available from the British Library

ISBN-13: 978-0-00-811805-1

Set in Sabon LT Std by Palimpsest Book Production Limited,
Falkirk, Stirlingshire

Printed and bound in Great Britain by Clays Ltd, St Ives plc

MIX
Paper from
responsible sources
FSC C007454

FSC™ is a non-profit international organisation established to promote
the responsible management of the world's forests. Products carrying the
FSC label are independently certified to assure consumers that they come
from forests that are managed to meet the social, economic and
ecological needs of present and future generations,
and other controlled sources.

Find out more about HarperCollins and the environment at
www.harpercollins.co.uk/green

To my late grandmothers Milbrough Griffiths and
Olivia Bella Taylor.

Thursday 5th February 2015

Jackdaw44: *Do you want to play a game?*
ICE9: *No.*
Jackdaw44: *Not sex.*
ICE9: *What then?*
Jackdaw44: *Questions. I'm bored. It's just a bit of fun.*
ICE9: *. . .*
Jackdaw44: *I take it that's a yes. OK. First question. Would you rather go deaf or blind?*
ICE9: *You really are bored, aren't you? Deaf.*
Jackdaw44: *Would you rather drown in a river or burn in a fire?*
ICE9: *Neither.*
Jackdaw44: *You have to choose.*
ICE9: *Drown in a river.*
Jackdaw44: *Be buried or cremated?*
ICE9: *I don't like this game.*
Jackdaw44: *It doesn't mean anything. I'm just trying to get to know you better.*

ICE9: *Weird way of doing it.*
Jackdaw44: *I love you. I want to know everything about you.*
ICE9: *Buried.*
Jackdaw44: *Be infamous or be forgotten?*
ICE9: *Forgotten.*
Jackdaw44: *Seriously???*
ICE9: *Yes.*
Jackdaw44: *I'd choose infamy every time.*
ICE9: *No surprise there.*
Jackdaw44: *Cry at my funeral or save your tears for private?*
ICE9: *WHAT?!! Stop being so morbid.*
Jackdaw44: *I'm not. I'm just preparing you.*
ICE9: *For what?*
ICE9: *Hello?*
ICE9: *HELLO?*

Chapter 1

Wednesday 5th August 2015

What do you wear when you peer into the barrel of a camera and plead for someone, anyone, to please, please tell you where your child is? A blouse? A jumper? Armour?

Today is the day of the second television appeal. It's been six months since my son disappeared. Six months? How can it be that long? The counsellor I started seeing four weeks after he was taken from us told me the pain would lessen, that I would never feel his loss as keenly as I did that first day.

She lied.

It takes me the best part of an hour before I can look at myself in the bedroom mirror without crying. My hair, cut in a short elfin style last week, doesn't suit my wide, angular face and my eyes look dark and deep-set beneath the new fringe. The blouse I'd deemed sensible and presentable last night suddenly looks thin and cheap, the knee-length pencil skirt too tight on my hips. I select a pair of navy trousers and a soft grey jumper instead. Smart, but not too smart, serious but not sombre.

Mark is not in the bedroom with me. He got up at 5.37 a.m. and slipped silently out of the room without acknowledging my soft grunt as I peered at the time on the alarm clock. When we went to bed last night we lay in silence side by side, not touching, too tense to talk. It took a long time for sleep to come.

I didn't say anything when Mark got up. He's always been an early riser and enjoys a solitary hour or so, pottering around the house, before everyone else wakes up.

Our house was always so noisy in the morning, with Billy and Jake fighting over who got to use the bathroom first and then turning up their stereos full volume when they returned to their rooms to get changed. I'd pound on their bedroom doors and shout at them to turn the music down. Mark's never been very good with noise. He spends hours each week driving from city to city as part of his job as a pharmaceutical sales rep but always in silence – no music, audiobooks or radio for him.

'Mark?' It's 7.30 a.m. when I pad into the kitchen, taking care to step over the cracked tile by the fridge so I don't snag my pop socks. Three years ago Billy opened the fridge and a bottle of wine fell out, cracking the tiles that Mark had only finished laying the day before. I told him it was my fault.

'Mark?'

The kettle is still warm but there's no sign of my husband. I poke my head around the living-room door but he's not there either. I return to the kitchen, and open the back door that leads to the driveway at the side of the house. The garage door is open. The *rrr-rrr-rrr* splutter of the lawnmower being started drifts towards me.

'Mark?' I slip my feet into a pair of Jake's size ten trainers that have been abandoned next to the mat and slip-slide across the driveway towards the garage. It's August and the sun is already high in the sky, the park on the other side of the street is a riot of colour and our lawn is damp with dew. 'You're not planning on cutting the grass now, surel—'

I stop short at the garage door. My tall, fair-haired husband is bent over the lawnmower in his best navy suit, a greasy black oil stain just above the knee of his left trouser leg.

'Mark! What the hell are you doing?'

He doesn't look up.

'Servicing the lawnmower.' He gives the starting cord another yank and the machine growls in protest.

'Now?'

'I haven't used it for a month. It'll rust up if it's not serviced.'

I don't know whether to laugh or cry.

'But Mark, it's Billy's appeal.'

'I know what day it is.' This time he does look up. His cheeks are flushed and there's a sheen of sweat that stretches from his thick, unkempt eyebrows all the way up to his receding hairline. He passes a hand

5

over his brow, then wipes it on his trouser leg, rubbing sweat into the greasy oil stain. I want to scream at him that he's ruined his best suit and he can't go to Billy's appeal like that, but today isn't the day for an argument, so I take a deep breath instead.

'It's seven-thirty,' I say. 'We need to get going in half an hour. DS Forbes said he'd meet us at eight-thirty to go through a few things.'

Mark rubs a clenched fist against his lower back as he straightens up. 'Is Jake ready?'

'I don't think so. His door was shut as I came downstairs and I couldn't hear voices.'

Jake shares his bedroom with his girlfriend Kira. They started dating at school when they were sixteen and they've been together three years now, sharing a room in our house for the last eighteen months. Jake begged me to let her stay. Her mum's drinking had got worse and she'd started lashing out at Kira, physically and verbally. He told me that if I didn't let her live with us she'd have to move up to Edinburgh to live with her grandfather and they'd never get to see each other.

'Well, if Jake can't be bothered to get up, then let's go without him,' Mark says. 'I haven't got the energy to deal with him. Not today.'

It was Billy who used to disappoint Mark. Billy with his 'I don't give a shit' attitude about school and his belief that life owed him fame and fortune. Jake was always Mark's golden boy in comparison. He worked hard at school, gained six A- to C-grade GCSEs and passed his electrician course at college with flying colours. These days it's phone calls about Jake's poor attendance at work that we're dealing with, not Billy's.

I haven't got the energy to deal with Jake either but I can't just shrug my shoulders like Mark. We need to present a united front to the media. We all need to be there, sitting side by side behind the desk. A strong family, in appearance if nothing else.

'I'm going back to the house. I'll get your other suit out of the wardrobe,' I say but Mark has already turned his attention to the lawnmower.

I shuffle back to the path, Jake's oversized shoes leaving a trail in the gravel, and reach for the handle of the back door.

I hear the scream the second I push it open.

Chapter 2

'Jake, give me that!' Kira's screech carries down the stairs and there's a loud thump from the bedroom above as something, or someone, hits the floor.

I kick off Jake's shoes and take the stairs two at a time, cross the landing and fly into his bedroom without stopping to knock. There's a flurry of activity as Kira and Jake jump away from each other. Barely five foot tall with blonde hair that falls past her shoulders, Kira looks tiny and doll-like in her pink knickers and a tight white T-shirt. Jake is bare-chested, naked apart from a pair of black jockey shorts that cling to his hips. His shoulders and chest are so broad and muscled he seems to fill the room. At his feet is a shattered bottle leaking pale brown liquid onto the beige carpet. There are shards of glass on the pile of weights plates beside it.

'Mum!' Jake leaps away from Kira, planting his right foot on the broken bottle. He howls in anguish as a shard of clear glass embeds itself in his sole.

'Don't!' I shout, but he's already yanked it out. Bright red blood gushes out, covering his fingers and dripping onto the carpet.

'Don't move!' I sprint to the bathroom and grab the first towel I see. When I return to the bedroom Jake is sitting on the bed, one hand gripping his ankle, the other pressed over the wound. Blood seeps between his fingers. Kira, still standing in the centre of the room, is ashen. I pick my way carefully through the broken glass on the floor, then crouch on the carpet in front of Jake. It stinks of alcohol.

'Let go.'

He winces as he peels his fingers away from his foot. The wound isn't more than half a centimetre across but it's deep and blood is still gushing out. I wrap the towel as tightly around it as I can in an attempt to stem the flow.

'Hold it here.' I gesture for Jake to press his hands over the towel. 'I need to get a safety pin.'

Seconds later I'm back in the bedroom and attempting to secure the makeshift bandage around my son's foot. There are dark circles under his eyes and the skin is pulled too tight over his cheekbones. Mark and I weren't the only ones who didn't sleep last night.

'What happened, Jake?' I ask carefully.

He looks past me to Kira who is pulling on some clothes. Her lips part and, for a second, I think she's about to speak but then she lowers her eyes and wriggles into her jeans. Downstairs the back door opens

9

with a thud as Mark makes his way back into the house, then there's a *click-click* sound as he paces backwards and forwards on the kitchen tiles. In a minute he'll be up the stairs, asking what the hold-up is.

I sniff at Jake. His breath smells pungent. 'Were you drinking that rum before I came in?'

'Mum!'

'Well? Were you?'

'I had a few last night, that's all.'

'And then some.' I pluck a large piece of glass from the carpet. Most of the label is still affixed. 'What the hell were you thinking?'

'I'm stressed, okay?'

'I haven't got enough for a taxi,' Kira says plaintively, reaching into her jeans pocket and proffering a palm of small change.

'Claire?' Mark's voice booms up the stairs. 'It's eight o'clock. We have to go. Now!'

'I need to leave,' Kira says. 'There's a college trip to London today – we're going to the National Portrait Gallery – and I'm supposed to be at the train station for half eight.'

'Okay, okay.' I gesture for her to stop panicking. 'Give me a sec.'

'Mark?' I step out onto the landing and shout down the stairs. 'Have you got any cash on you?'

'About three quid,' he shouts back. 'Why?'

'Doesn't matter.'

'Right.' I step back into Jake's bedroom. 'Kira, I'll give you a lift to the train station. And as for you, Jake . . .' There's no blood on the towel I've pinned around his foot but he'll still need the wound to be cleaned and a tetanus jab. If there was time I'd drop Kira at the station and then take Jake to the doctor's but it would mean doubling back on myself and I can't be late for the appeal. Why did this have to happen today of all days?

'Okay.' I make a snap decision. 'Jake, stay here and sober up and I'll drive you to the GP's when I get back. If you need anything, Liz is next door. She's not working until later.'

'No, I'm coming with you. I need to go to the press conference.' Jake grimaces as he pushes himself up and off the bed and hops onto his good foot so we're face to face. Unlike Billy who shot up when he hit twelve, Jake's height has never crept above five foot nine. The boys couldn't have an argument without Billy slipping in some sly jab about his older brother's stature. Jake would retaliate and then World War III would break out.

'Claire!' Mark shouts again, louder this time. He'll fly off the handle if he sees the state Jake is in. 'Claire! DS Forbes is here. We need to go!'

'You're not going anywhere,' I hiss at Jake as Kira pulls an apologetic face and squeezes past me. She presses herself up against the linen cupboard on the landing, pulls on her coat and then roots around in the pockets.

'Billy was my brother,' Jake says. His face crumples and for a split second he looks like a child again, but then a tendon in his neck pulses and he raises his chin. 'You can't stop me from going.'

'You've been drinking,' I say as levelly as I can. 'If you want to help Billy, then the best thing you can do right now is stay at home and sleep it off. We'll talk when I get back.'

'Claire!' Mark shouts from the top of the stairs.

'Mum . . .' Jake reaches a hand towards me but I'm already halfway out the door. I yank it shut behind me, just as Mark draws level.

'Is Jake ready?'

'He's not well.' I press my palms against the door.

'What's wrong with him?'

'Stomach upset,' Kira says, her soft voice cutting through the awkward pause. 'He was up all night with it. It must have been the vindaloo.'

I shoot her a grateful look. Poor girl, getting caught up in our family drama when the very reason she moved in with us was to escape from her own.

Mark glances at the closed door behind me, then his eyes meet mine. 'Are we off then?'

'I need to drop Kira at the train station for her college trip. You go on ahead with DS Forbes and I'll meet you there.'

'How's that going to look? The two of us turning up separately?' Mark looks at Kira. 'Why didn't you mention this trip last—' He sighs. 'Never mind. Forget it. I'll see you there, Claire.'

He hasn't changed his trousers. The greasy oil stain is still visible, a dark mark on his left thigh, but I haven't got the heart to mention it.

Chapter 3

Neither of us say a word as we pile into the car and I start the engine. The silence continues past the Broadwalk shopping centre and down the Wells Road. Only when I stop the car at the traffic lights by the Three Lamps junction and Kira pulls her iPod out of her jacket pocket do I speak.

'What was that all about?'

'Sorry?' She looks at me in alarm, as though she's forgotten I'm sitting next to her.

'You and Jake, earlier.'

'It was just . . .' She stares at the red stop light as though willing it to change to green. Without her thick black eyeliner and generous dusting of bronzing powder her heart-shaped face looks pale and the sprinkle of freckles across her nose makes her look younger than she is. 'Just . . . a thing . . . just an argument.'

'It looked serious.'

'It got a bit out of hand, that's all.'

'I'm guessing Jake didn't go to bed last night.'

'No. He didn't.'

'Oh God.' I sigh heavily. 'Now I'm even more worried about him.'

'Are you?'

I feel a pang of pain at the surprise in her eyes. 'Of course. He's my son.'

'He's not Billy, though, is he?'

'What's that supposed to mean?'

'Nothing. Sorry. I don't know why I said that.'

I wait for her to say more but no words come. Instead she reaches into her handbag, pulls out a black eyeliner and flips down the sun visor. Her lips part as she draws a thick black ring around each eye, then dabs concealer on the raised, discoloured patch of skin near her right temple. It looks like the beginning of a bruise.

The red light turns amber, then green and I press on the accelerator.

Neither of us speaks for several minutes. I glance across at Kira, at the lump on her temple, and my stomach lurches.

'Did Jake hit you?'

'What?'

'When you were fighting over the bottle. There's a bruise on your head. Did he hit you?'

'God, no!'

'So how did you get the bruise?'

'At the club last night.' She flips down the visor and examines the side of her head in the mirror,

14

prodding it appraisingly with her index finger. 'I dropped my mobile and hit my head on the corner of the table when I bent down to get it.'

'Kira, I know I'm not your mum but you're the nearest thing I've got to a daughter and if I thought anyone was hurting you—'

She slaps the visor shut. 'Jake didn't hit me. All right? He'd never do something like that. I can't believe you'd say something like that about your own son.'

I tighten my grip on the steering wheel.

'Sorry,' she says quickly. 'I know you're trying to look out for me but—'

'Forget it.' I slow the car as we approach the roundabout. 'Just tell me one thing. How long has he been drinking in the mornings?'

She doesn't reply.

'Kira, how long?'

'Just today. I think.'

'You think?' I can't keep the incredulity out of my voice. They spend every waking minute together. How could she be unsure about something like that?

'Yeah.' She zips up her make-up bag and gazes out of the window as the car swings around the roundabout and we approach Bristol Temple Meads. As I indicate left and pull into the station and park the car, I can't help but scan the small crowd of people milling around outside the station, smoking cigarettes and queuing for taxis. I can't go anywhere without looking for Billy.

'Do you think he's got a drink problem?'

'No.' She shakes her head as she unbuckles her seat belt and opens the door. 'He's not an alcoholic, if that's what you mean. He opened the rum when we got home from the club. He was wired and couldn't sleep.'

'Because of Billy's appeal?'

'Yeah.' She lifts one leg out of the foot well, places it on the pavement outside and gazes longingly at the entrance to the train station.

'Kira?' I reach across the car and touch her on the shoulder. 'Is there anything you want to talk to me about?'

'No,' she says. Then she jumps out of the car, handbag and make-up bag clutched to her chest, and sprints towards the station entrance before I can say another word.

Chapter 4

It's a small conference room, tucked away in the basement of the town hall with a strip light buzzing overhead and no natural light. It's a quarter of the size of the one where we made our first appeal for Billy, forty-eight hours after we reported him missing. Unlike that first appeal, when every single one of the plastic-backed chairs in the rows opposite us were filled, there are only half a dozen journalists and photographers present. Most of them are fiddling with their phones. They glance up as we file in with DS Forbes, then look back down again. A couple of them begin scribbling in their notebooks.

Mrs Wilkinson looks sombre in a pale grey jumper and trouser ensemble whilst Mr Wilkinson looks surly and distracted in a dark suit, the leg of his trousers stained with what looks like dirt or oil.

I have no idea if that's what they've written. I'll find out tomorrow, I imagine. I can't bear to read

17

the papers, particularly not the online versions with the horrible, judgemental comments at the bottom, but I know Mark will. He'll pore over them, growling and swearing and mumbling about 'the bloody idiot public'.

I didn't know what a double-edged sword media attention would be back when Billy disappeared. I was desperate for them to publish our story – we both were, the more attention Billy's story got the better – but I couldn't have prepared myself for the barrage of speculation and judgement that came with it. I looked *pale and distraught*, those were the words most of the reporters used to describe me during that first press conference. Mark was described as *cold and reserved*. He wasn't reserved – he was bloody terrified, we both were. But while I quaked, twisting my fingers together under the desk, Mark sat still, straight-backed, his hands on his knees and his eyes fixed on the large ornate clock on the opposite wall. At one point I reached for his hand and wrapped my fingers around his. He didn't so much as glance at me until he'd delivered his appeal. At the time I felt desperately hurt but later, in the privacy of our living room, he explained that, as much as he'd wanted to comfort me, he hadn't been able to.

'You know I compartmentalize to deal with stress,' he said. 'And I needed to deliver my appeal without breaking down. If I'd have touched you, if I'd so much as looked at you I would have crumbled. And I couldn't do that, not when what I had to say was so important. You can understand that. Can't you?'

I could and I couldn't, but I envied his ability to shut out the thoughts and feelings he didn't want to deal with. My emotions can't be shut into boxes in my head. They're as tangled and jumbled as the strands of thread in the bottom of my grandmother's embroidery basket. And the one thought that runs through everything, the strand that is wrapped around my heart is, Where is Billy?

'Claire?' DS Forbes says. 'They're ready for your statement now.'

A television camera has appeared in the aisle that runs between the lines of plastic-backed chairs. The lens is trained on my face. We decided some weeks ago that I should be the one to make this appeal.

'The public respond more favourably when the mother does it,' DS Forbes said. He made no mention of the horrible comments that had appeared online when Mark made the last appeal six months ago. Comments like: *You can tell the father's behind it. He's not showing any emotion* and *I bet you money it was the dad. It always is.*

'Ready?' DS Forbes says again and this time I sit up straighter in my chair and take a deep breath in through my nose. I can smell DS Forbes's aftershave and the faintest scent of motor oil emanating from Mark, who's sitting on the other side of me. I can sense him watching me, but I don't turn to look at him before I pick up the prepared statement on the desk in front of me. I can do this. I no longer need a hand on my knee.

'Six months ago today,' I say, looking straight into

the camera lens, 'on Thursday the fifth of February, my younger son Billy disappeared from our home in Knowle, South Bristol, in the early hours of the morning. He was only fifteen. He took his schoolbag and his mobile phone and he was probably dressed in jeans, Nike trainers, a black Superdry jacket and an NYC baseball hat . . .' I falter, aware that some of the journalists are twisting round in their seats, no longer scribbling in their notebooks. Mark, beside me, makes a low noise in the base of his throat and DS Forbes leans forward and puts his elbows on the desk. 'We all miss Billy very much. His disappearance has left a hole in our family that nothing can fill and . . .' I keep my eyes trained on the camera but I'm aware of a commotion at the back of the room. One man is wrestling with another in the doorway. 'Billy, if you're watching, please get in touch. We love you very, very much and nothing can change that. If you don't want to ring us directly, please just walk into the nearest police station or get in touch with one of your friends.'

The producer standing next to the cameraman taps him on the shoulder and signals towards the back of the room. The camera twists away from me and a shout emanates from the doorway.

'Get off me! I've got a right to be here! I've got a right to speak.'

Chapter 5

'What's Jake doing here?' Mark stares over the heads of the journalists and several flash bulbs fire at once, lighting up the corner of the room where Jake is remonstrating with a male police officer. 'I thought you said he was ill.'

'He was . . . is. Let me deal with this.'

'Mrs Wilkinson, wait!' DS Forbes shouts as I hurry across the room and shoulder my way through the circle of journalists that has formed around my son. I can just about make out the back of Jake's head. His fair hair is wild and tousled without a liberal application of hair gel. He disappears as a policeman steps in front of him, blocking my view.

'Excuse me. Excuse me, please.'

The TV cameraman hisses as I push past him but he's shushed by his producer. 'That's the mum, get her in shot.'

I push past a couple of council officials and

approach the policeman who's shepherding Jake towards the open doorway. Tapping him on the back of his black stab vest has no effect so instead I pull on his arm.

He doesn't so much as glance at me. Instead he keeps his eyes trained on Jake; Jake, who's a good six inches shorter, with his hands clenched at his sides and the tendons straining in his neck.

'Please,' I shout. 'Please stop, he's my son.'

'Mum?' Jake says and the police officer looks at me in surprise. He lowers his arms a fraction.

'He's my son,' I say again.

The policeman glances behind me, towards the poster of Billy affixed to a flipchart beside the desk.

'No, not Billy,' I say. 'This is Jake, my other son.'

'Other son? I wasn't told to expect any other relatives . . .' He looks at DS Forbes who shakes his head.

'It's all right, PC George. I've got this.'

DS Forbes has met Jake before. He interviewed him at length, the day after Billy disappeared, just as he and his team interviewed all our extended family and friends.

'Show's over, guys.' He signals to the producer to cut the filming and gestures for the journalists to return to their seats. No one moves.

'Jake!' A female journalist with a sharp blonde bob reaches a hand over my shoulder and waves a Dictaphone in my son's direction. 'What was it you wanted to say?'

'Jake?' The producer proffers a microphone. 'Did you have a message for Billy?'

My son takes a step forward, shoulders back, chin up. He glances at PC George and raises an eyebrow, vindicated.

'What happened to your foot, Jake?'

A short, balding man with hairy forearms that poke out of his rolled-up shirtsleeves points at Jake's trainers. The instep of his right shoe, normally pristine and white, is muddied with brown blood.

'Jake?' Mark says.

The room grows quiet as my husband and son stare at each other. They're waiting for Jake to speak. I wait too. I can feel Mark bristling behind me. This is his worst nightmare – our respectable, measured appeal transformed into a bar-room brawl.

I hear a *click* and a *whirr* from the camera to my left and I imagine the lens zooming in on Jake's pale, drawn face. He passes the heel of his hand over his damp brow and then, with only the briefest of glances at me, turns on the heel of his good foot and limps out of the room.

Monday 11th August 2014

Jackdaw44: *Fuck my life.*
ICE9: *Don't say that.*
Jackdaw44: *Why not. It's true. My dad is a hypo-critical wanker and my mum is fucking clueless.*
ICE9: *Have you talked to your dad about the weekend?*
Jackdaw44: *Are you fucking kidding?*
ICE9: *You should give him the chance to explain.*
Jackdaw44: *What? That he's weak, spineless, a liar and a lecherous bastard? No, thanks.*
ICE9: *Maybe it's not how it seemed.*
Jackdaw44: *You're taking the piss, right? You saw me. You saw what I did.*
ICE9: *That was stupid.*
Jackdaw44: *It was sick. I wish I'd seen the look on his face when he saw his car window. When he got home he told Mum that vandals did it. Ha. Ha. Ha. I'm the fucking vandal.*

24

Jackdaw44: *You still there?*
ICE9: *Yeah. Sorry. Bit busy.*
Jackdaw44: *No worries. Just wanted to say thanks for cooling me out. I would have totally lost my shit if you hadn't turned up.*
ICE9: *You did lose your shit.*
Jackdaw44: *Could have been worse.*
ICE9: *Hmm.*
Jackdaw44: *Anyway. Thanx.*

Chapter 6

'What the hell were you thinking?' Mark is standing in the centre of the living room with his arms crossed over his chest. He's loosened his tie and popped the top button of his shirt. The skin at the base of his throat is mottled and red.

'Sod this.' Jake moves to get out of his armchair, wincing as he puts weight on his bad foot.

'You'll stay where you bloody are,' Mark shouts and I grip the cushion I'm clutching to my chest a little tighter. 'This is my house and as long as you live here you'll do what I say.'

'Yeah, because that worked out well with Billy, didn't it?' Jake doesn't raise his voice but Mark stumbles backwards as though the question has been screamed in his face.

He seems to fold in on himself, then quickly recovers. 'What did you just say?'

'Forget it.'

'No, say it again.'

'Please!' I say. 'Please don't do this.'

'It's all right, Mum,' Jake says. 'I can take Dad.'

'Take me?' Mark laughs. 'Aren't we the big man now we've grown a few muscles? Steroids making you brave, are they, son?'

I stare at Jake in horror. 'You're not taking steroids, are you?'

'Dad doesn't know what he's talking about.'

'One more word from you,' Mark says, 'and you're out.'

'Please!' I say. 'Please! Please stop! Mark, he's your son! He's your son.'

A tense silence fills the room, punctuated only by the sound of my own raggedy breathing. I brace myself for round two. Instead Mark's shoulders slump and he exhales heavily.

'Always the villain,' he says, looking from me to Jake. 'I'm always the villain.'

I want to say something. I want to contradict him. To support him. But to do so would mean choosing between my husband and my son. It's like the night Billy disappeared all over again. My family is disintegrating in front of my eyes and there's nothing I can do to stop it.

'Mum,' Jakes says as the back door slams shut and Mark leaves the house. 'I can explain.'

'Later.' My throat is so tight I can barely speak. 'I'll talk to you later.'

Chapter 7

'Here you go.' Liz places a steaming mug of tea on the table in front of me, then pulls out a chair and sits down. A split second later she stands up again, crosses the kitchen and rummages around in the back of a cupboard bursting with tins, jars and packets of pasta and rice. It's the day after the appeal. I was going to pop in on Liz yesterday but, after everything that happened, I didn't have the energy.

'Ah! Knew I had some.' She brandishes a 100-gram bar of Galaxy at me and returns to the table. 'Hidden from Caleb and for emergencies only,' she says as she sets it in front of me. 'And days when I decide to skip Slimming World.'

'I'm not hungry.'

'Mind if I do then?' She runs a nail along the gold wrapper and snaps off four pieces. She bites into the chocolate, takes a swig of tea, then smiles broadly. 'That's better. Caleb was in a pig of a mood this morning, whingeing about the lack of clean socks in his drawer. Hellooooo, we both work and you're twenty. Wash your own bloody socks. I thought he'd make more of an effort with his personal hygiene now he's met someone. Did I tell you about the new boyfriend?'

I shake my head.

'He met him in a pub in Old Market. Eighteen, works in House of Fraser. I haven't met him yet. Caleb said he doesn't want to scare him off by introducing him to me. Cheeky shit. Anyway, sorry.' She leans back in her chair and folds her arms across her chest. 'How are you? I meant to watch the appeal but next door's cat got into the garden again. It was primed to take a shit on the lawn so I chucked some water at it. I thought I'd pop in after you got back but I spotted Mark storming out the back door looking really pissed off and figured it wasn't the best time.'

That's the thing I love about Liz; Billy's disappearance hasn't changed our friendship in the slightest. Whilst everyone else awkwardly avoids the subject or cross-examines me about the latest developments Liz is just Liz. You crave normality after something terrible happens. Everything reminds you of what you've lost – everything – and sometimes you just want to stop thinking about it. I love hearing Liz bitch about Lloyd. I enjoy her little rants about her son Caleb or Elaine, her boss at the supermarket where she works.

Mark compartmentalizes his life. He has the 'boxes'

in his head he escapes into. I don't. But at least I have Liz.

'So how was it?' she asks.

'Awful.'

I tell her about Kira screaming, the booze, the cut foot, Jake's interruption and the argument when we all got home.

'I'm just so tired,' I say as she swipes a box of tissues from the windowsill and pushes them towards me. 'I just want Billy to come home and for this to be over. I miss him, Liz. I miss him so much.'

'I know,' she says. 'I know you do.'

I pull a tissue from the box and dab at my cheeks. I hate that my default emotional reaction is crying. I wish I could shout and scream or punch something instead.

'Sorry,' I say.

'For what? If you can't snot all over your best friend's kitchen where can you?'

I try not to cry in front of Mark and Jake because I don't want them to worry about me but it's different with Liz. Her kitchen is a safe haven. We've known each other since Liz and Lloyd moved next door when the boys were little. They'd play in the back garden while Liz and I would sit on deckchairs and chat. It was a tentative friendship at first, as we sussed each other out, but it wasn't long before we started taking it in turns to do the school run and the odd bit of babysitting. The first time we went out for drinks we got so drunk we stopped being polite and properly opened up. We were both in tears by the end of the night. Since then we've been there for each other through everything – Lloyd walking out on Liz last year, my father-in-law's heart attack and now Billy.

'What you going to do now then?' she asks, snapping off another piece of Galaxy and popping it into her mouth.

'I need to get Mark and Jake in the same room as each other so they can sort out their differences.'

'Claire . . .' Liz reaches across the table and puts her hand over mine. 'I'm only saying this because I love you but maybe you should let them sort it out in their own time. You're going to make yourself poorly if you don't let go.'

'Let go of what?'

'Of them. You're not responsible for everyone else's happiness, sweetheart.'

'None of us are happy.'

'Least of all you.' She gives me a searching look. 'Mark and Jake are going to butt heads from time to time – you need to accept that.'

'They'll kill each other if I don't intervene.'

'They won't.'

'Jake will move out.'

She makes a soft, sighing sound. 'Would that be the worst thing in the world? He's nineteen years old. He makes a good living as an electrician. He could afford a one-bedroom flat.'

'What about Kira?'

'There'd be enough space for her too. They pretty much spend all their time in his bedroom as it is from what you've said. And they'd have more space.'

'But the house would be so empty without them. And besides, I want everything to be exactly the same as it was when Billy left. That way we can just go back to normal when he returns.'

My best friend gives me a long, searching look. She wants to comment but something is holding her back.

'What is it?'

She shakes her head. 'Doesn't matter.'

'Yes, it does. What were you going to say?'

'I just think . . .' She looks away and rubs her fingers over her lips. I've never seen her look this uncomfortable before. 'I just think that maybe you're putting your life on hold for something that might not happen. I think you should . . . prepare yourself for bad news. It's been six months, Claire.'

I stand up abruptly. 'I think I should go.'

'Oh God.' Liz stands up too. 'I shouldn't have said anything. Are you okay? You've gone very pale.'

'I'm fine.'

'I'll make us some more tea. Are you sure you won't have some chocolate? You look—'

'I'm going to be sick.' I sprint from the room, one hand to my mouth, and only just make it up the stairs and into the bathroom before my stomach convulses and I dry retch over the toilet.

'Claire?' Liz says from behind me. 'Are you okay?'

'I'll be fine. I just need some water.'

32

As I twist the cold tap something in the bin by the basin catches my eye.

'No!' Liz shouts as I reach for the newspaper. 'Claire, don't! Don't read that.'

I turn my back on her and angle myself into the corner of the room as I unfold the newspaper. Billy's name is on the front cover.

BRAWL OVER MISSING BILLY

There's a photo beneath the blaring headline: me, wide-eyed and frantic with Mark at my shoulder. I'm reaching across the journalists for Jake who has his head against the wall, his hands balled into fists on either side of his face.

Pandemonium broke out at the six-month appeal for missing Knowle schoolboy Billy Wilkinson yesterday when his mother, Claire Wilkinson (40), was interrupted during her message to camera as Jake Wilkinson (19), the missing boy's older brother, burst into the council offices. Wilkinson, who was visibly intoxicated, was heard to shout that he had a right to speak. His mother Claire and father Mark (42) abandoned their appeal to intervene and Mark Wilkinson was heard to exclaim, 'Get him out of here! Get him out of here!' Mrs Wilkinson looked visibly upset as the family was bundled out of the room. Bristol Standard reporter Steve James spoke to a neighbour who watched the appeal on the television. 'We've never had any run-ins with the Wilkinsons. They seem like a perfectly normal family but you have to wonder whether someone knows more about Billy's disappearance than they're letting on.'

'Claire!' Liz snatches the newspaper from my hands before I can read another word. 'It's all crap. They make stuff up to sell copies. No one believes that shit.'

She reaches an arm around my shoulders but I twist away from her, knocking her against the basin in my desperation to get out of the bathroom. It's unbearably hot and I can't breathe.

I take the steps down to the hallway two at a time and wrench open the front door. The second I step outside I run.

Chapter 8

I stand at the end of the bed with my feet pressed together and my arms outstretched and I tip backwards. The bedspread makes a delicious *floop* sound as I hit it and the bed springs squeak in protest. I can't remember the last time I felt this happy.

'No!'

I look to the right, in the direction of the voice, but there's no one beside me on the bed. I'm alone in the room. There must be someone in the corridor. A woman arguing with her husband perhaps, although I can't hear the low rumble of a male voice.

'No!'

The voice again, quieter this time but closer, as though someone has spoken the word directly into my ear. I sit up in bed and pull my knees in to my chest.

'NO!'

I clamp my hands to my ears but there's no blocking

out the woman's voice as she shouts the word, machine-gun fast – NO, NO, NO, NO, NO.

It's inside my head. The voice is coming from inside my head.

'CLAIRE!' it shouts. 'I AM CLAIRE. I AM CLAIRE.'

Claire? Who is Claire? I recognize the name but I don't want to. I don't want to know who Claire is. I just want to get back to the seafront. Back to the sunshine and wind and the café on the edge of the pier.

'I AM CLAIRE! I AM CLAIRE!'

The voice fills my brain, screaming and buzzing, and my head is vibrating and the light, happy feeling inside me is fading.

Dark. Light. Dark. Light.

My thoughts are dark and foggy, then brighter, clearer and then, just for a second – a split second – I know who Claire is, then the darkness returns and with it a confusion so disorientating my hands instinctively clench as I try to anchor myself to something, anything solid. There is something smooth and slippery soft under my fingers. Bed linen. I am sitting on a bed. But this is not my bed, this is not my room. There is a framed art print on the wall to my right: a faded Lowry, stick people milling around a town. There is a lone boy in the centre of the scene. He has his back to me. He's looking at the crowd of people spilling out of one of the buildings. Who is he looking for? Who has he lost?

A shrill sound makes me jump. A small black

mobile phone jiggles back and forth on the orangey pine bedside table to my right. A name flashes onto the screen. A name I don't recognize. But the noise hurts my head and I need it to stop.

I reach for the phone and press it to my ear.

'Mum?' says the voice on the other end of the line.

I want to reply but I can't talk. I can't think. I can't . . . it's as though my mind has shattered. I can't focus . . . I can't form coherent . . . what's happening to me?

'Mum?'

'Claire.' I say the word out loud. It sounds strange. Like a noise, a sound, an outward breath. 'Cl-airrrrr.'

'Mum? Why are you saying your name?'

My name?

'Cl-airrrrr.'

'Mum, you're freaking me out. Stop doing that.'

'Claire.' The word crystallizes inside my mouth. It tastes familiar. As though I've known it for a long time. Like buttered toast. Like toothpaste. 'Claire. Claire Wilkinson.'

'Oh Jesus Christ. Dad, I think she's having a stroke or something.'

My head . . . my head . . . my brain hurts . . . no, aches . . . but not a headache . . . foggy . . . and then a thought, breaking through the darkness and I grip hold of it as though it is a rock to tether my sanity to.

'Is my name Claire Wilkinson?'

'Yes, yes, it is. Jesus, Mum. We've been trying to ring you for hours. Where are you?'

Mum. I am a mum? The man on the phone sounds scared. Is he scared for me? Or of me? I don't know. Nothing makes any sense.

'Where are you?' says the voice on the phone.

'I'm . . . I'm . . .' There are gingham curtains at the far end of the room and a full-length mirror, smeared with fingerprints. Beneath me is a bedspread. Pink, satiny, puffy. I dig my nails into it and cling to it, rigid with fear. 'I don't know. I don't recognize this room.'

'It's okay, Mum,' the man on the phone says. 'Just . . . sorry, hang on a second . . .' There's a muffled sound like a hand being placed over the receiver but I can still make out the low rumble of his voice.

'Mum?' His voice is clear again. 'Is there a door or a window you could open? Tell me what you can see.'

I don't want to move from the bed. I don't want to open the pine door to my right or the closed gingham curtains at the far end of the room.

'Please, Mum. As soon as we know where you are we can come and get you.'

We? Who is we? Who is coming to get me? I'm in danger. I need to run but I can't move.

'Dad's here, Mum. Do you want to speak to him?'

'No,' I say and I don't know why.

'Are you sure?' the man says and an image appears in my mind – vivid and sharp in the gloom – of a young man with tousled fair hair, shaved at the sides, and broad shoulders, lying on a bench, pushing weights into the air.

'Jake?' I venture.

'Yes, Mum. It's Jake. I'm at home with Dad. Liz just came round, wanting to talk to you. That's when we realized you'd gone missing.'

I search for a memory, something, anything, to still my mind, to stop this terrifying free-fall sensation. Where is my home? Why don't I remember?

'Yes, I know, okay. Okay, Dad.' The man is talking to someone else again. 'I just asked her that. Mum, can you describe what you can see?'

I look back at the Lowry painting, at the boy standing right of centre staring into the crowd, looking for someone, then I look at the shiny pale pink bedspread, the mirror, the cheap pine table and the white tea tray.

'I think I'm in a hotel room.'

'Is there a phone? Can you ring reception to find out which hotel you're in? Or is there a brochure or room-service menu anywhere?'

I slide across the pink bedspread and press my toes into the worn pile of the beige carpet, then inch my way across the room, keeping one eye on the door, and approach the table near the mirror. There's a white china teapot on a tray and two cups and saucers. There's also a dish containing tea, coffee, sugar and tiny cartons of milk. There are no brochures, no menus, no phone. Nothing else in the room at all other than my handbag and boots, with my socks tucked into the top, on the floor by the bed.

I touch the edge of the gingham curtain and tentatively pull it back. Outside is a low railing, a balcony and a stretch of grey-brown sea with a lump of land in the distance, an island shaped like a turtle's back.

'Steep Holm,' I say and the darkness in my mind fades from black to grey at the sight of the familiar lump of rock in the distance. 'Jake, I'm in Weston-super-Mare.'

As he relays the information I feel a sudden desperate urge to throw open the window and inhale great lungfuls of sea air but when I yank at the sash it only opens a couple of inches at the bottom.

'Do you know which hotel, Mum?' Jake asks. 'If you stay where you are we'll come and get you.'

It's a small room: shabby but warm and clean. The floral wallpaper behind the bed is peeling in one corner and when I open the door to the en suite there are no branded toiletries, just a bar of soap in a frilled wrapper and a glass, misted with age, on the shelf above the sink. There is no welcome pack on the table that holds the tea and coffee things, no branded coaster or complimentary notepad.

'Reception,' I say. 'Need to find reception.' But then I spot a fire-evacuation notice pinned next to the door. It is signed at the bottom by Steve Jenkins, Owner, Day's Rest B&B.

'Day's Rest,' I say. 'I'm at Day's Rest B&B.'

'The one we used to stay in as kids,' Jake says and I have to steady myself against the wall as a wave of grief knocks the breath from my lungs.

Billy.

I have two sons. Jake and Billy. Billy is missing. He's missing.

'Mum?' The worry in Jake's voice bounces off me like a stone skimming the sea.

I snatch up my handbag, my boots and my socks and I reach for the door handle.

'Mum?' he says again as I yank open the door.

'Billy!' I scream into the empty corridor. 'Billy, where are you? Where are you, son?'

Friday 22nd August 2014

Jackdaw44: *You there?*
ICE9: *Yep.*
Jackdaw44: *Liv is a bitch.*
ICE9: *Who's Liv?*
Jackdaw44: *Girl I was seeing.*
ICE9: *I didn't know.*
Jackdaw44: *You wouldn't. I keep my shit private.*
ICE9: *OK . . .*
Jackdaw44: *But I'm pissed off today. Need to talk to someone. I know you can keep secrets.*
ICE9: *It's up to you to tell your mum what you saw, not me.*
Jackdaw44: *And that's why you're cool.*
ICE9: *Ha! I've never been called that before. So why is Liv a bitch?*
Jackdaw44: *She told Jess not to go out with me. She totally slagged me. Said I've got a small dick.*

ICE9: *Have you?*

Jackdaw44: *Go fuck yourself.*

Chapter 9

The man behind the reception desk jumps as I slam up against it.

'Is he here?'

'Is who here?' He's a tall man, over six foot with balding hair and an auburn moustache. The buttons of his shirt strain over his gut.

'My son. Billy. He's fifteen.' I raise a hand above my head. 'He's about this tall.'

'Did he check in with you?'

I don't know. The last thing I remember was running out of Liz's house. How did I get here and why don't I remember? Am I asleep? Unconscious? Did I trip and hit my head when I was running? But this feels real. The reception area feels solid under my fingertips. I can smell the musty aroma of old furnishings beneath the pungent scent of furniture polish. 'I've got no idea. Could you check to see if he's booked in? His name's Billy Wilkinson.'

The man runs a thumb along the length of his gingery moustache. 'And your name is?'

'Claire Wilkinson.'

He reaches for a clipboard on his desk. He raises it to eye level, then mutters, 'I can't see a thing without my glasses,' and replaces the clipboard and begins ferreting around in a drawer. I tap the counter as he searches. It's all I can do not to clamber over the top and snatch up the clipboard.

'There!' I point at a pair of glasses on top of a paperback book. 'Your glasses are there.'

'Ah, thank you.' It takes an age for him to clasp his fingers around them, for ever for him to unfold them and then, as he finally places them on his nose, he removes them again and wipes the lenses on the hem of his jumper.

'If you could hurry. Please. It's urgent.'

'All in good time, Mrs Wilkinson, all in good time.'

'Hmmm.' He hums through his nose. 'Room eleven, is that right?'

I hear the sound of footsteps on the stairs but it's a middle-aged man, not Billy, who steps into the reception area and raises a cheery hand at the man behind the desk. 'I don't know what room I'm in. I didn't look.'

The receptionist gives me a quizzical look, then says, 'I've got a Mrs Wilkinson in room eleven. Queen room. One occupant.'

I press a hand to my forehead but the fog in my brain remains. Somehow I booked myself into a B&B in Weston. I can't remember doing it, so either I did

45

check in and I don't remember or . . . nothing. There's a black void where my memory should be. 'Could Billy have checked into one of the other rooms?'

The man's lips disappear beneath the bushy arc of his moustache. 'I can't give out information about other guests. Guesthouse policy.'

A vision plays out in front of my eyes, of me ripping the clipboard out of his hands and smashing him around the head with it – *thwack, thwack, thwack* – and I have to close them tightly shut to make it disappear. When I open them again he's still pursing his lips, still staring at me.

'Billy is my son. He's missing. You have to tell me if he's here.'

'Missing? Goodness. Have you told the police?'

'Yes. Six months ago. Please! I need to know if he's here or not.' I lean over the counter and reach for the clipboard but he snatches it away, flattening it against his chest.

'I've got a flier.' I duck down and rummage around in my bag. 'Here!' I hold the appeal leaflet face out so he's eye to eye with Billy's photo.

The man gives the briefest of nods when he's finished reading and our eyes meet as I lower the leaflet. There. He's giving me the look. The 'you poor bloody woman' look I've come to know so well.

'I wouldn't normally do this but . . .' He presses his glasses slowly onto his nose, lowers the clipboard and dips his head. He trails a bitten-down fingernail along the list and my heart stills when his finger stops.

Has he . . .

46

Is it . . .

He shakes his head. 'I'm sorry. There's no Billy Wilkinson on this list.'

'Maybe he's using a different name?'

He places the clipboard on the desk and presses down on it with his palms. 'It's a small hotel, Mrs Wilkinson, just thirteen rooms. We've got a couple in with a teenage girl and half a dozen families with young children. I'd remember your son's face if I'd booked him in.'

'Does no one else take the bookings?'

There's sadness in his eyes now. Sadness and pity. 'No. I'm really very sorry.'

The tension that's been holding me upright for the length of the conversation vanishes and I slump against the desk, eviscerated. It's all I can do not to lay the side of my face on the cool wood and close my eyes.

'I'm so sorry,' he says again.

I look up. 'Did you check me in?'

He nods. 'Yes. One night, paid upfront. Don't you remember?'

'No. I don't remember walking in, or even how I got to Weston. One minute I was talking to a friend in Bristol and the next . . .' I can't explain what happened because I don't understand it myself. I came to but not in the way you do when you wake up after a nap or a long sleep. And it wasn't like the hazy slip into consciousness after a general anaesthetic either. I was awake but my mind was muddled, tangled in a jumble of sounds, images and thoughts

47

that gradually faded away. And then everything was sharp, in focus, as I became aware of my surroundings. And it was terrifying. Utterly terrifying.

'Boozy lunch, was it?' the man asks, the sympathy in his eyes dulling.

'No,' I say. 'We were drinking tea.'

'Sounds like you should get yourself to a doctor.'

'I will. Just as soon as I get home.' I crouch down and pull on my boots and socks. A drop of sweat rolls down my lower back as I haul the strap of my handbag over my shoulder.

'Thank you,' I say as I head for the door.

'No problem.'

I wrench the door open and then, as the sea air hits me, I turn back. The receptionist looks up, Billy's flier still in his hands.

'Can I just ask one more thing? Was I alone when I checked in?'

'You were, yes.'

'And did I seem frightened? Scared? Confused?'

'No. You seemed . . .' He searches for the right word. 'Normal.'

Chapter 10

The wind whips my hair across my face as I pull my handbag onto my knee and unzip it. There are five messages on my phone from Jake, each one more frantic than the last.

'Mum. Stay where you are. We're coming to get you.'

'We're half an hour away. I just tried to ring you. Could you pick up, please?'

'Mum, where are you?'

'Mum? We're in Weston. WHERE ARE YOU?'

'MUM, PICK UP OR WE'RE CALLING THE POLICE!'

I press the button to call him. Jake answers on the first ring.

'Mum?' I can hear the relief in his voice. 'Where the hell are you?'

'I'm on the seafront. On a bench just to the right of the pier.'

'Okay. Don't go anywhere. We'll be right there.' He stops talking and I wait for him to hang up, but then he speaks again. 'Promise me you won't go anywhere.'

'I'm not going anywhere, Jake. I promise.'

'Good. She's on a bench, on the right of the pier . . .' I listen as he relays my whereabouts to Mark and then the line goes dead.

It's the middle of summer but the wind cuts through the thin material of my top and I wrap my arms around my body, tucking my hands under my armpits. We used to sit on this bench with the boys when they were little. They'd eat ice creams and Mark and I would drink scalding-hot tea from thin paper cups. Both boys loved our visits to Weston-super-Mare. They adored the bright flashing lights and the *bleep-bleep-bleep*, *ching-ching-ching* of the amusement arcade; Mark standing beside them, pressing two-pence pieces into their reaching palms. I'd slip outside, ears ringing, and stand on the pier, breathing in deep lungfuls of sea air, relishing the sense of freedom and space that opened within me as I looked out at the horizon.

I was eighteen when I met Mark, nineteen when we got married, twenty-one when I had Jake, twenty-five when I had Billy. I slipped effortlessly from the family I grew up in, to the one I created with Mark. I never regretted that decision, not once, but there were moments when I envied my single friends. Especially when Mark was away on a training course and whatever activity I'd dreamed up to try and

50

entertain the boys had descended into chaos, fights and tears, and I couldn't even escape to the toilet without small fists pounding on the door, voices begging to be let in. What would it feel like to read a book without interruption, to nurse a hangover on the sofa with a film and a mountain of chocolate, or book a holiday and just go? What would it be like to have a career where people respected you instead of taking you for granted and to have a bedroom, all of your own, where you could retreat when you'd had enough of the world? Those thoughts were always fleeting and I would dismiss them guiltily, tucking them away deep in my mind where they wouldn't bother me. I knew how lucky I was to have a husband who loved me and two healthy children.

I press my lips together and run my sandpaper tongue against the roof of my mouth. I'm thirsty. God knows when I last had something to drink. There's a kiosk on the edge of the pier that sells soft drinks and tanniny tea but I can't risk moving from my bench in case Jake and Mark miss me. I unclip my handbag and rummage around inside. Gum will help with my dry mouth. I sift through papers, tissues, receipts and oddments of make-up. Long gone are the days when I'd find a small car in the base of my handbag or a half-empty packet of wet wipes scrunched up in a pocket, but my bag is still a mess. I clear it out every couple of weeks but, no matter how hard I try to be tidy, random crap still accumulates inside.

I shove a flier for a music event I'll never attend

to one side and something small and yellow catches my eye. It's a bundle of paper tokens from the arcade, five of them in a row, folded over each other. The machines spit them out when you successfully throw a basketball into a hoop, bash a mole or shoot a target. Billy was obsessed with these tokens. You need to accumulate dozens just to buy a small lollipop but he had his eye on a shiny red remote-control car and he vowed, aged eight, not to trade in a single token until he had enough to buy that car. Mark tried to explain to him that it would take years to collect enough, and cost us more than the price of the car just to play the games, but Billy was resolute. The car would be his. He never did collect enough and a year later, worn down by his dad's constant assertion that it was 'all a big con', he gave up. I bought him a similar car that Christmas but he barely looked at it, declaring that remote-controlled toys were 'for kids'. I hated that he'd become so disillusioned so young.

For a long time after Billy gave up on his quest I'd find tokens secreted under his bed, in his pockets, in the depths of his bag and squirrelled away in his sock drawer. I kept them in one of the cupboards in the kitchen, just in case Billy had a change of heart but one day, when I was looking for something else, I realized they'd gone. When I asked Mark if he'd seen them he barely looked up from his newspaper.

'I was looking for something and there was so much crap in that drawer I couldn't find it. I threw them away.'

That was four or five years ago. We haven't been to Weston as a family since. Jake and Kira have been a couple of times since they started dating but that doesn't explain why there are tokens in my bag now. I take a closer look, examining them for a date or time stamp but they're generic arcade tokens with the words *Grand Pier* printed in the centre. They're exactly the same as the ones Billy collected all those years ago. I found some more recently, a few months before he disappeared, stuffed into the pocket of his jeans when I was doing the washing. There was a receipt too, for a room in a hotel. A few days earlier the school had rung me to say he hadn't turned up for registration and, when I called him on his mobile, he wouldn't say where he was, just that he was fine and he was hanging out with some mates. It was a lie. He'd obviously skived school to come to Weston with a girl. He wouldn't say who and we grounded him for two weeks.

So where did I get these from? Could I have won them? In the six hours between leaving Liz's house and finding myself in a bedroom in Day's Rest B&B did I visit the arcade and play a game? Why?

I delve back into my handbag, pulling out wodges of paper, tissue packets, empty paracetamol blister packs and several red lipsticks. I remove my phone, my house keys and my make-up compact. In the bottom of the bag is a shell. It is tiny, no bigger than the pad of my thumb, pale pink with darker pigment along its scalloped edges. I went down to the beach then? Another memory comes flooding back, of me

53

walking hand in hand with Jake and Billy along the beach when they were very little – two and six years old. The tide was out and we had our shoes off, our toes squelching into the sludgy sand. Every couple of seconds one of the boys would dip down, dig around in the sand and then jubilantly offer me a shell, stone or bottle top. Anything they spotted would immediately become the most precious of spoils, thrust upon me until my pockets were full.

Now I turn the bag upside down, attracting the attention of strutting seagulls as I litter the ground with crumbs. There is nothing else inside, no clue as to where I have spent the last six hours or what I have done. Unless . . . I lift my purse from my lap and peer inside: £25 in notes, a little over £3.50 in change, various bank, store and credit cards, and a tiny laminated photo of the boys one Christmas. Nothing unfamiliar, nothing unexpected, apart from a train ticket tucked between my Tesco card and my credit card. It's dated today, with 13.11 as the time of purchase. Bristol Temple Meads to Weston-super-Mare, an open return.

'Mum?' Jake appears beside me, his hair flattened to his forehead, a sheen of sweat along the bridge of his nose. He's clutching my granddad's walking stick in his right hand. Mark is beside him. It's only been a few hours since I last saw him but I'm shocked by how drawn his face is, how dark the circles under his eyes.

'Claire? Oh, thank God.' He sinks onto the bench beside me, then glances down at my lap, where the contents of my handbag are piled beneath my hands. 'What's all this?'

'I was trying to understand how I got here.' I shovel everything back into the bag, including the arcade token and the shell, then zip it shut. Worry is etched into every line on Mark's face.

'We thought someone had taken you,' Jake says, leaning heavily on the stick. I gesture for him to sit down but he shakes his head. 'We spoke to Liz and she said you suddenly got up and ran out of her house like you were on fire. Then when we rang and you didn't know where you were . . .' He breathes heavily. 'I thought whoever took Billy had taken you too.'

Mark's lips part and I know he wants to contradict Jake. He wants to say that we have no proof that Billy was taken by anyone. We have no idea what happened that night.

'I did run out,' I say before my husband can speak. 'I remember that much but . . . after that . . .' I shake my head. 'The next thing I knew I was sitting on a bed in the B&B and then the phone rang.'

'How did you get here?' Mark asks. 'The car was still in the drive.'

'By train.'

'So you remember that much?'

I shake my head again. 'No. I found the ticket in my bag. Mark, I don't remember getting the train, I don't remember checking into the hotel. I don't remember anything other than leaving Liz's.'

'Did you hit your head or something?' He gently

55

moves my hair away from my face with his hand and my heart flutters in my chest. I can't remember the last time he touched me so tenderly. 'I can't see any swellings or contusions.'

I used to joke with the kids about Mark's 'medical speak' after he got a job as a medical sales rep. It was almost as though he'd become a doctor himself with all his talk of angina, stents and angioplasty. Apparently it's very unusual for someone without a medical background or degree to get a job selling pharmaceuticals to GPs and hospitals but Mark's never been one to let someone telling him he can't do something get in his way.

'We didn't realize you were missing until tea time,' Jake says and I have to smile. I don't imagine they would have. They'd have returned home after work and congregated in the kitchen, sniffing the air and peering into the oven and fridge. 'Dad said you were probably round at Liz's, pissed off with us for screwing up Billy's appeal.'

'Pissed off with who—' Mark starts but Jake interrupts.

'And then Liz came round and told us that you'd rushed out of her house and you weren't answering your phone. She was really upset. She thought she'd said something to upset you.'

Mark shifts away from me now his 'examination' of my head is complete, but his eyes don't leave my face. 'What did she say?' he asks.

I shake my head. If I tell him he'll only agree. Mark's told me over and over again that we should assume the worst about Billy. 'Six months is a long time, Claire.' It's become his mantra, his invisible shield against hope whenever I tentatively suggest that maybe, just maybe, Billy could still be alive.

'It doesn't matter what she said.'

'It does if it made you run off to Weston without telling anyone.'

I slip my handbag across my body, then stand up and rub my upper arms. 'Can we just go home? Please, I just want to go home.'

Mark stands up too. 'I think we should get you to a doctor first. Don't you?'

Chapter 11

It's warm in Mum's living room. Warm and ever so slightly musty. The top of the telly is grey with dust, the magazine rack is groaning under the weight of books and magazines piled on top of it, and there are dead flowers on the windowsill; green sludge in the base of the vase instead of water. Even the spider plant on the bureau, a plant so hardy that it could survive a nuclear attack, is wilted and yellow. Its babies, trailing on the carpet on long tendrils, look as though they've parachuted out in an attempt to escape. Mum would declare World War III if I offered to tidy up so I do what I can whenever she leaves the room; wipe a tissue over the surfaces when she goes to the loo or tip my glass of water in the spider plant when the postman comes.

I haven't had a chance today. She hasn't left my side since I arrived a little after 9 a.m. I haven't told her about my blackout yet; she thinks I'm here to talk about Billy's publicity campaign. Mark refused to go to work until I promised him I'd spend the day with her. He's terrified I'll go missing again.

He's not the only one.

The doctor doesn't know what's wrong with me. She ran a series of blood tests yesterday and said I'd have to wait a week for the results. It's terrifying, not knowing what caused me to black out. What if it's something serious like a brain tumour? What if it happens again? When I asked Dr Evans if it might she said she didn't know.

I didn't want to leave her office. I didn't want to step outside the doors of the surgery and risk it happening again. Mark had to physically lift me off the chair and guide me back outside to the car.

'See that?' Mum slides the laptop from her knees to mine and points at the screen with a bitten-down fingernail. 'That spike in the graph?'

I shake my head. 'I don't know what I'm looking at.'

'They're the stats for the website. We had a huge peak in page views the day the appeal went out. Over seven thousand people looked at it. Seven thousand, Claire.'

'And that's a good thing, is it?' Dad says, appearing in the doorway to the living room.

'Derek.' Mum shoots him a warning look. 'If you can't say something good—'

'It's okay, Mum,' I say. 'I know what Dad's thinking.'

'Your dad's not thinking anything.' Her eyes don't leave his face. 'Are you, Derek?'

His gaze shifts towards me and I feel the weight of sadness in his eyes. There's indecision too, written all over his face. He wants to tell me something but Mum's warning him not to.

'What is it, Dad?'

'Derek!'

'It's okay. You can tell me.'

Mum pulls at my hand. 'It's nothing you need worry about, Claire. Just a bunch of drunks in the pub speculating. We know no one in the family had anything to do with Billy's disappearance.'

I ignore her. I can't tear my eyes away from my dad who looks as though he might burst from the stress of keeping his lip buttoned. 'Dad?'

He shifts his weight so he's leaning against the door frame and bows his head, ever so slightly, finally breaking eye contact with me. 'They think Jake had something to do with it. I overheard a conversation when I was coming out of the loo in the King and Lion the other night. No smoke without fire and all that.'

'Absolute rot!' Mum snaps the laptop lid shut. 'Everyone will have forgotten all about it by next week and then, when the dust has settled, we'll ask the *Bristol News* to run a story about Billy and Jake as kids. If the *Standard* are going to shaft us we'll get them onside instead. We'll dig out some photos of the boys in their primary-school uniforms. The readers will see them when they were young and sweet and they'll forget about Jake's little outburst. It's all about the cute factor. You'll see.'

'Cute factor?'

'It's a PR trick to gain public sympathy. I read about it in a book I got out of the library, the one by the PR guru who was arrested for sex offences. Dirty bastard but he knew his stuff.'

I can't help but marvel at the woman sitting in front of me. Six months ago she didn't really know what PR meant never mind the tricks 'gurus' use to gain public sympathy for a client. Whilst I could barely speak for grief she went part-time at the garden centre and asked a friend's son to create the findbillywilkinson.com website so she could post a few photos of him and include the police contact details. Now there's a Facebook page and a crowd-funding site. She's read every book that's been written by the parents of other missing children and she spends hours on the Internet looking for the contact details of journalists who might be interested in covering Billy's story.

'So can you dig some out?' Mum asks. 'Some photos?'

I nod my head. 'Of course.'

'Are you all right, love?' Dad says. 'You look a bit peaky.'

I can't tell them what happened yesterday. I don't want to worry them, not until I know what I'm dealing with.

Waiting. My life has become one long wait. I've never felt more impotent in my life. Mark and Jake wouldn't let me help with the search after Billy went missing. They said I needed to stay at home. 'Someone needs to man the hub,' Mark said. I don't think that was the real reason he told me to stay behind. I think he was worried I'd break down if we found anything awful. He would have been right but I can't continue to sit and wait. I need to find Billy.

'I'm fine, Dad.' I force a smile. 'But I could do with some fresh air. Are those fliers up to date?' I point at the teetering pile of paper under the windowsill.

'Yes.' Mum nods.

'Could we go somewhere and hand them out? Maybe . . . the train station?'

Last week I went through Billy's things. I've been through them a hundred times since the police searched his room – the familiarity is comforting – and I found an exercise book at the bottom of a pile on his bookshelf. He'd only written in it twice. On the first page he'd half-heartedly attempted some maths homework and then crossed it out and written underneath, *Maths is shit and Mr Banks is a wanker.*

That made me smile. It was something I could imagine him saying to Mark when he'd ask how Billy was getting on with his coursework. Billy knew it would push his dad's buttons but he'd say it anyway because he liked winding him up. I'd tell Billy off for swearing but it was always an effort not to laugh. Poor Mark.

After I'd read what he'd written I found a pen and wrote underneath it, *No swearing, Billy.* The tightness in my chest eased off, just the tiniest bit. So I kept on writing. I wrote and I wrote until I had cramp in my hand. It was so cathartic, so freeing to be able to cry, alone, without worrying that my grief might upset Jake and Mark.

I almost missed the other thing he'd written in the book. I only spotted it when the back cover lifted as I put it down. He'd graffitied the inside and scrawled *Tag targets* in thick black marker pen:

– *Bristol T M (train?)*
– *The Arches*
– *Avonmouth*

I couldn't believe I hadn't spotted it before, not when I'd been through Billy's things so many times, and I immediately rang DS Forbes. He wasn't as excited as I was. He told me they'd looked at the CCTV at the train station when Billy was first reported missing and they'd checked out Avonmouth and the Arches as they knew he hung out with his friends there. But what if they'd missed something? Something only a mother could spot?

'Great idea.' Mum snatches the laptop from my knees and slips it behind one of the sofa cushions.

'Hiding it from burglars,' she says when I give her a questioning look.

'We'll have to be quick,' Mum says as she parks the car. 'We've only got twenty minutes before a traffic warden slaps a ticket on the windscreen.'

I clutch the fliers to my chest as we cross the road, passing a line of blue hackney cabs and a lone smoker pressed up against the exterior wall of the station.

Inside Bristol Temple Meads there's a crowd of people gazing up at the arrivals and departures boards and a stream of traffic in and out of WHSmith's. It's not as busy as it would have been if we'd got here at seven or eight o'clock but hopefully we're less likely to be brushed off by harassed commuters.

'We'll get a cheap-day return to Bedminster so we can get through the barriers,' Mum says as she heads towards the ticket machines, 'then we'll split up. You do platforms eight to fifteen and I'll do one to seven. Try and get the shops in the underpass to stick a poster in their window if you have time.'

'You okay?' she says, looking back at me as the machine spits out two tickets. 'You've gone very white.'

It's as though the earth has just tilted on its axis. That's the only way to explain how I feel. I was here yesterday. I bought a ticket to Weston. I crossed through the barriers. I got on a train. One of the staff, a man with fair hair and glasses, catches my eye as I glance across at the ticket counter and I look away sharply. Did he recognize me? Is that why he's staring? Has he been told to keep an eye out for me because of something I said or did?

'Claire?' Mum touches my arm. 'Do you want to go back to the car? I can do the leaflet drop if you're not feeling well. Or we can do it another day.'

'No.' I press a hand over hers. There's no reason to think I did anything strange during my blackout. Even when I'm drunk the worst I'll do is massacre a song during karaoke or embarrass Mark by firing off the most childish jokes I know. 'I'm fine. Honestly, Mum. Let's get this done.'

'You sure?'

'Yes.' I let go of her hand and pass a leaflet to the man waiting patiently for us to vacate the ticket machine. 'My son Billy is missing. Have you seen him? Do you recognize his face?'

We've barely passed through the ticket barriers when Mum's phone rings.

'Oh, bugger,' she says under her breath as she fishes it out of her handbag. 'It's Ben, the journalist from the *Bristol News* that I was telling you about. I'm going to have to take this, Claire. You okay to go by yourself?'

'Of course.'

Mum turns left towards the coffee shop while I continue down the stairs to the subway that gives access to the platforms. I approach a lady who's waiting for an elderly man to use the cashpoint and show her Billy's flier.

'This is my son, Billy Wilkinson. He's fifteen. Have you seen him?'

She looks down at his photo and, as her eyes dart from left to right, scanning his face, my heart flickers with hope. There are nearly half a million people in Bristol but all I need is for one person, just one, to say, 'I saw a boy who looks like him sleeping rough,' or 'I think I was served coffee by this boy yesterday.'

'Sorry.' The woman shakes her head.

I rush away before she can offer me any words of sympathy and thrust a leaflet at a man in a suit.

He raises a hand. 'No, thank you.'

'It's not a charity leaflet.' I rush after him. 'And I'm not selling anything—'

I'm cut off as he takes a sudden left and disappears into the men's toilets.

Undeterred, I approach a gang of foreign students, gabbling away to each other in Spanish outside the juice bar. 'Have you seen this boy? He's my son. He's missing.'

They exchange glances, then an attractive girl, with glossy black hair that reaches almost to her waist, steps forward and peers at the leaflet in my hands.

'Nice,' she says, looking back up at me. 'Nice boy. Handsome.'

'Have you seen him? You or any of your friends?'

She takes the leaflet from my hand, shows it to her friends and says something in Spanish. I can't understand a word they say in reply but I know what a head shake, a shrug and a pouting mouth signify.

'Could you put it up where you're studying?' I ask the black-haired girl. 'In your school? There's a contact telephone number and an email address at the bottom if anyone has seen him.'

She nods enthusiastically but I'm not sure she understands me. I don't have time to double-check. I need to move on. I need to get Billy's face in front of as many people as possible.

The barista behind the counter of the coffee shop in the middle of the subway tells me she can't put up Billy's poster without consulting her manager, and he's not in until 5 p.m. The queue at the sit-down coffee shop just yards away is too long to even contemplate talking to a member of staff, so I drop a pile of leaflets on the table nearest the door instead. As I hurry through the subway towards platforms thirteen and fifteen I scan everything I see – posters, free newspaper racks, walls, doors – but they're graffiti-free. If Billy did tag the train station he didn't do it down here.

I stop short when I reach the top of the stairs to the platforms. There's a wreck of a building on the opposite side of the tracks. It's the derelict sorting office, now little more than a rectangular slab of concrete with gaping holes where the windows used to be. As I watch, pigeons flutter in and out but it's not the birds that catch my eye. It's the graffiti daubed all over the building. There are high walls, topped with barbed wire, surrounding it but that wouldn't stop Billy, not if he was determined to put his mark on it.

'Excuse me, madam.' A hand grips my shoulder and I spin round to find myself face to face with a tall man in a luminous yellow waistcoat and a black peaked cap.

'British Transport Police,' he says, glancing at the bundle of paper in my hands. 'It's been reported that you've been distributing material to members of the public. Can I see your licence or badge, please?'

'Licence?' I step away from the yellow line on the platform edge as a train pulls into the station and the overhead announcer reports that the 11.30 a.m. train to Paddington is standing at platform thirteen. 'What licence?'

'You need a licence from the council to distribute leaflets at this station. There's a fixed penalty of eighty pounds or a court-imposed fine of up to two thousand five hundred if you haven't got one.'

'But . . . I . . . I don't know. I came with my mum. She's the one who got the leaflets printed and I'm sure she's got permission for us to—'

The doors to the carriages open and, as the passengers disembark, I'm distracted by a fracas further up the platform. There's a small crowd of people around one of the doors and a man is shouting at someone to stop pushing in.

And then I see him. Tall, slim, in a baseball cap and a black Superdry jacket, shoving his way to the front of the queue.

'Billy!' I fling the leaflets away from me and sprint up the platform. 'Billy! Billy, wait!'

The policeman shouts. A pigeon, pecking at crumbs beneath a bench, is startled and flies into the air. A woman gasps, the crowd parts and my lungs burn as I launch myself through the open door and sprint down the carriage.

'Billy!' I shout as he reaches an empty seat at the end and pauses. 'Billy, it's—'

The words dry in my mouth as he turns and I see his profile.

It's not Billy. It's not him.

Tuesday 26th August 2014

Jackdaw44: *Sorry.*

ICE9: *What for?*

Jackdaw44: *Telling you to go fuck yourself last week.*

ICE9: *No, you're not. You want something.*

Jackdaw44: *Ha. Ha. Spot on.*

ICE9: *So?*

Jackdaw44: *Just wanted to talk to you.*

ICE9: *You know where I live.*

Jackdaw44: *Ha. Ha. Am at school. Need advice.*

ICE9: *What about?*

Jackdaw44: *Girls. Why are they such bitches?*

ICE9: *What makes you think I know?*

Jackdaw44: *I fucking hate Liv. She dumped me so why is she trying to put Jess off me?*

ICE9: *Jealous? Maybe she still fancies you.*

Jackdaw44: *Yeah, right. She's fucking Ethan Thomas.*

ICE9: *Revenge?*

Jackdaw44: *What for?*

ICE9: *Did you cheat on her?*
Jackdaw44: [confused face}
ICE9: *That's a yes then.*
Jackdaw44: *I was drunk.*
ICE9: *Dick.*
Jackdaw44: *That's Mr Big Dick to you.*
ICE9: *Not according to Liv.*
Jackdaw44: *Fuck off. (Not sorry.)*

Chapter 12

'I'm not sure this is a good idea,' Mum says as I turn the key in the lock. 'I don't feel right leaving you here alone. Not after what happened. He was decent though, wasn't he, that policeman? In the end. I knew he wouldn't fine us, not when we told him about Billy. You saw the look on his face when he told us he had a son of about the same age. Kind of him to say he'd keep an eye out and help spread the word.'

She follows me into the kitchen, hovering in the middle of the room as I drop my handbag onto a chair and open the fridge.

'Are you okay?' Mum asks. 'I know you feel embarrassed about what happened on the train but you mustn't let it get to you. Imagine if it had been Billy and you hadn't gone after him. You'd never have forgiven yourself.'

'I thought I'd do a casserole for tea,' I say. 'I know

it's the summer but everyone likes a sausage casserole, don't they? I drop two onions, five carrots
and two packs of sausages onto the counter. 'Twelve
sausages – that'll be enough, won't it, although God
only knows Jake could probably finish off the lot
himself.'

'Claire, talk to me, sweetheart. You haven't said a
word since we left the station.'

I take a knife from the block on the counter. 'The
onions haven't had long enough in the fridge to chill
the juices. I always cry if they're too fresh.'

'Claire.'

'I'm going to need swimming goggles. I think Billy's
got some in his room. I'll just go up and—'

'CLAIRE!'

Mum slips around me, blocking my exit from the
kitchen.

'Claire, sit down.'

'I can't. I need to put the dinner on. I need to—'

'Claire, please. Please sit down, love.' She gazes up
at me, pain etched into her soft, lined skin. 'Talk to
me.'

'I can't. If I do I'll cry.'

'And?' Mum rubs her hand up and down my upper
arm.

'And I don't know if I'll ever stop.'

'Oh, sweetheart.'

'I thought I'd found Billy,' I say as she wraps
me in her arms and I slump against her. 'I thought
the nightmare was over. But it's not. It just carries
on.

She squeezes me tightly. 'We'll find him, Claire. We'll bring him back home.'

Mum left an hour ago. She was going to stay until Mark or one of the kids got back but then Dad rang to say that his car battery had died and he was stuck at B&Q and could she collect him. She told him to get a taxi and they'd sort out the car later but I insisted she go to his rescue. I reassured her that I could go over to Liz's if I was feeling wobbly. She left, begrudgingly, and gave me an extra-long squeeze at the door.

My phone bleeps. It's a text message from Mark.

Are you still at your mum's? How are you feeling? I'm going to try and get home a bit earlier than normal. Text me if you feel unwell.

I text back.

Just got home. I went to the train station to hand out some fliers.

My phone bleeps almost immediately.

With your mum?

Yes.

Who's with you now?

No one. I'm fine though.

Don't go anywhere. Jake or Kira should be back soon and I'm on my way.

There's no need to hurry, I type back. The last thing we need is for him to put his foot down and end up having an accident. *Honestly. I'll be fine.*

I met Mark in a nightclub in town. I was eighteen, he was nineteen and he crossed the dance floor to talk to me, shoulders back, all South Bristol swagger with an attitude to match. He told me he was going to become a policeman. 'I've passed the competency tests, the fitness test and the medical. I've just got the second interview to go and I'm in.'

For months, joining the police was all he could talk about. He'd turn up the radio whenever there was talk of an assault outside a nightclub or a drugs bust out in a disused barn in the countryside. He read true-crime book after true-crime book, piling them up on his bedside table like badges of honour. And then he had his second interview and I didn't hear from him for a week. My calls went unanswered. When I went to Halfords where he'd been working while he completed the application process he took one look at me, then turned on his heel and headed straight for the nearest staff-only door.

I thought it was me. I thought that now he was a big-shot policeman he didn't want anything more to do with me. He was going places whilst I was a receptionist at the Holiday Inn. He'd probably met some fit, ambitious policewoman during celebration drinks and didn't have the guts to tell me we were over. I went to his house. Twice. The lights were on both times and I could see the TV flickering through the thin curtains but Mark didn't come to the door, even when I kept my finger glued to the doorbell and screamed at him through the letterbox.

The truth came out three weeks later when I ran into one of his mates in a pub in town.

'Mark not with you?' I said, two large glasses of wine and the encouragement of a friend giving me the nerve to approach him. 'Teetotal now he's a copper, is he?'

'Mark's not a copper.' He raised his hand and waved at a group of lads over by the bar.

'What?' I grabbed his arm as he turned to go. 'What did you say?'

'He didn't get in, did he? He wouldn't say why, secretive little bastard. I reckon it's because his uncles have done time. Anyway, Mark's at home sulking.' He shrugged me off. 'Why don't you go and give him a blow job? Cheer him up a bit.'

I swore at him under my breath as he made his way through the crowded bar but relief flooded through me. Mark hadn't dumped me for someone else. He was hiding and licking his wounds. All the plans he'd made, all the hopes he had. Gone. I couldn't help but feel sorry for him but I was angry too. How dare he cut off all contact with me just because he'd failed to get into the police? I deserved more than that.

Two weeks later I found a note on the doormat when I got home from work.

I've been a twat and I'm sorry. Meet me for a drink so I can explain. Please.

I didn't reply. Six weeks he'd kept me hanging. Let's see how he liked it.

I told Mum to tell Mark I was out if he rang, which he did – the next day. He didn't leave a message.

Ignoring his calls was torture. I nearly caved in several times but I ripped up the letters I'd spent for ever composing before I could send them. Then he turned up at my door.

'I thought about bringing flowers or wine or something but you're worth more than that, Claire. Please,' he added before I could respond, 'just hear me out. You can tell me to fuck off after I've said what I need to say. Can we go to the pub? We can sit outside if you want.'

I listened for an hour as he explained how he'd struggled academically at school after his mum died, going in during the holidays for extra help with his coursework and scraping five low-grade GCSEs. He told me how his dad had said he'd never amount to anything and his best bet was to join him in the family's building-supplies firm so he could learn about running a business. His dad had laughed when he'd told him he didn't want to do that – he wanted to be a policeman – and had called him a grass. Two of Mark's uncles were in prison, one for aggravated assault and one for fraud, and he knew his own dad wasn't beyond taking a few backhanders and passing on stolen goods.

'I wanted to better myself,' Mark told me. 'Everyone on our estate thinks my family is dodgy. People cross the street when they see me out with my uncle Simon. The family thinks it's respect but it's not, it's fear, and I don't want that kind of life for me and my kids. Because I want kids, you know, Claire. I want a family.'

Kids. His eyes shone as he said the word, just as they had when he'd talked to me about joining the police.

'I want to be respected. I want people to look up to me because I've achieved something.'

And then he told me about what he called the 'boxes' in his head. It was his way of compartmentalizing his life. He couldn't get in touch with me after he'd been rejected by the police because he was trapped in that box in his head. He had to process what had happened, then shut the box and get back on with his life. If he'd rung me he'd have taken a lot of his anger and resentment out on me and he didn't want that. He didn't want me to see him at his lowest.

'If you'd seen me like that you'd have lost all respect for me. I'd have lost you.'

'Maybe you already have?'

He hung his head then, chin tucked into his chest, as he swirled a small puddle of lager around the base of his glass. I said nothing.

'Fuck it!' He gripped his hair with his fingers and covered his face with the palms of his hands. 'I've screwed everything up, haven't I?'

There are some decisions that alter the course of your future; pivotal moments in life where you find yourself standing at a crossroads. Go left and you're off down that path and there's no turning back. Same if you go right.

'Bollocks.' The wooden picnic table shook as Mark got to his feet. 'I'm sorry, Claire, you're better off without me.'

He strode across the patio with his hands in his pockets and his shoulders hunched forward.

'Mark!' My throat was too tight and his name came out as a whisper. 'Mark!'

I had no choice but to go after him.

'Mark!' I grabbed hold of his arm. 'Don't you dare walk away from me. Don't you dare!'

He stopped walking but said nothing.

'Is that it?' I said. 'You tell me you had a shit childhood, then you walk away? You're not the only one who had a rough time, you know, but you don't see me feeling sorry for myself and—'

He grabbed me around the waist and pressed his lips so hard against mine that our teeth clashed and my neck cricked as he leaned his weight into me.

'Give me another chance,' he breathed as he pulled away. 'Give me another chance and I swear I'll never let you down again, Claire. I love you. I don't want to lose you.'

I didn't have to think twice. I was eighteen years old. I was in love.

Now the back door clicks open and I catch the briefest glimpse of a baseball cap before it ducks back outside and the door slams shut.

'Wait!' I jump up from my chair and sprint across the kitchen. 'Come back!'

Chapter 13

'Jake! Wait! We need to talk.'

My eldest son ignores me. He reaches into the pocket of his jeans and pulls out a key. He stoops to place it into the lock, wincing as he shifts his weight onto his bad foot, then turns the handle and yanks the garage door open.

He hobbles inside, swears at the pool of oil puddled around Mark's lawnmower, then fiddles with the dusty stereo on the shelf at the back of the garage. Pounding rock music fills the room as he straddles the weights bench and shuffles onto his back. His fingers wrap around the silver bar and his biceps tense as he lifts the dumbbell off the bar.

'Jake! Are you ignoring me?'

He doesn't reply. Instead he grunts as he dips the bar down to his chest and then presses it into the air.

His interest in lifting weights began about six

weeks after Billy disappeared. I welcomed it initially – Jake lifting weights was preferable to Jake spending every waking moment in the pub – but he became obsessed. An hour after work in the early evening became two hours and then he added another two hours in the morning. The *bleep, bleep, bleep* of his alarm at 5 a.m. drove Mark to distraction. Jake began spending less and less time with Kira and the family and more and more time in the garage. If he did deign to join us in the living room he'd be lost in the pages of *Lifting* or *Power Grunt* or whatever magazine he couldn't get his nose out of. Kira would sit beside him, *tap-tap-tapping* into her phone, nodding politely as he'd explain how he was going to increase his deltoids by doing a certain combination of lifts.

Kira's always been a quiet girl but she shrank into herself during the height of Jake's obsession. The bigger he grew the smaller and more silent she became. Shortly after she first came to live with us she told me how our home was like a breath of fresh air. We weren't the perfect family by any means but I could see why our living situation was preferable to the one she'd escaped. But then Billy disappeared and everything fell apart. We fell apart. Poor Kira. She'd swapped one screwed-up, dysfunctional family for another.

'Jake.' I take a step towards him. 'You need to tell me what's going on.'

'I'd have thought –' his face contorts as he presses the bar into the air – 'that was obvious.'

I stride across the room and switch off the stereo.

A muscle twitches in my son's cheek as he stares up at the corrugated roof. The barbell wobbles above him and for one horrible moment I imagine it slipping from his hands and pinning him to the bench but then he grunts and lowers it onto the rest.

'Sorry.' He sits up and runs a hand over his face.

'You need to talk to me,' I say softly as I crouch on the edge of the bench.

He reaches for the sports bottle on the floor and takes a swig, grimacing as he swallows. Jake is almost the spitting image of his dad. Whilst Billy inherited my dark hair, Jake is fair like Mark with the same small eyes, prominent nose and thin lips. His is a masculine face; strong and angular with a wide expanse of forehead. Billy's features are more refined. He has my large brown eyes, a smaller nose and fuller lips. Dad always used to go on about what a pretty boy he was when he was little. 'Angelic,' Mum called him. I've always been careful never to comment on the way my boys look – they're both beautiful in my eyes – but the world isn't so circumspect. I lost track of the number of times old ladies would nod at Jake, then gaze at Billy in the buggy and announce, 'He's going to be a right heartbreaker that one.' The comparison wasn't lost on Jake. 'Why don't me and Billy look the same?' he'd ask when he was nine and Billy was five. 'Arrogant bastard,' he growled when Billy was twelve and the letterbox rattled with cards for Valentine's Day; only one of them was for Jake (and that was from me).

81

Jake replaces the sports bottle on the floor and his gaze flickers towards me. 'I'm just stressed, that's all.'

'About what?'

His pale blue eyes are unreadable. 'Everything. Work, Kira, Dad, this house, Bill.'

'Is that why you've started drinking again?'

'What do you mean, again?' he says but he knows what I mean. After Billy left I lost track of the times he'd stumble into the house at night, crashing into the kitchen table, swearing at the coat hooks as his hoody hit the floor, stumbling up the stairs and into bed with Kira. I confronted him about it but he said he wasn't doing anything that other nineteen-year-olds didn't do and if he went to work every day and he paid me my rent then what right did I have to hassle him about it?

What could I do? It was obviously his way of dealing with the loss of his brother. But I can't stick my head in the sand any more. I can't stand idly by as he destroys himself. We need to talk.

'Jake, we need to discuss what happened on the day of the appeal. I know everyone's been worried about me, but I can't just forget about the fact that you were drinking at seven o'clock in the morning.'

He takes off his cap and runs a hand through his hair. 'I just had a bit of a session, okay? We got back from the club at three and I kept drinking because I was pissed off.'

'What about?'

'Oh, for God's sake, Mum. Do you have to be such a control freak?' He shifts position to stand up but the sudden movement is too much for his foot and he's forced to sit back down again.

The accusation stings and it takes everything I've got not to retaliate. Instead I take a steadying breath.

'Sorry. That was out of order.' He puts a hand on mine, his palm sticky with sweat. 'Look, if you really want to know, I was pissed off because some bloke started chatting up Kira while I was in the loo.'

'He was probably just trying his luck.'

'Yeah, I know. But she looked really happy. She was laughing and playing with her hair, like she did when we first got together.' He shrugs. 'And I was shitting myself about Billy's appeal. So I kept drinking to try and block it all out. That's all there is to it.'

I want to tell him that I understand, that it's been longer than I can remember since his dad looked at me that way too, but this isn't about me. And it certainly isn't about Mark. This is about my son opening up to me for the first time in a long time.

'Oh, Jake.' I wrap my arms around his broad shoulders and pull him in to me. His body feels hard and unwieldy in my arms. 'I understand. Really I do. She'll look at you like that again. I promise. You and Kira have been to hell and back, we all have. When Billy comes home everything will go back to normal. I promise you.'

Jake stiffens and it's as though I'm hugging rock.

Thursday 25th September 2014

Jackdaw44: *I saw you in town today.*
ICE9: *Shouldn't you be at school?*
Jackdaw44: *Skiving.*
ICE9: *I'll pretend I didn't hear that.*
Jackdaw44: *Liv was stirring shit with her mates at lunchtime. I've fucking had it with girls. I left before I hit her.*
ICE9: *You can't hit girls!*
Jackdaw44: *Duh! That's why I left.*
ICE9: *Why do you keep texting me?*
Jackdaw44: *I like talking to you. You got a problem with that?*
ICE9: *Wow, so aggressive!*
Jackdaw44: *Fuck this shit. You're a piss taker like everyone else.*
ICE9: *No, I'm not.*
Jackdaw44: *You look down on me. You think I'm a stupid kid.*

ICE9: *a) I don't look down on you and b) You're cleverer than you let on.*
Jackdaw44: *Fucking Stephen Hawkins, me.*
ICE9: *You know what I mean.*
Jackdaw44: *Yeah. Don't tell anyone though.* 🐑
ICE9: *Your secret is safe with me.*
Jackdaw44: *If you ever need to share a secret you know where I am.*
ICE9: *I'll bear that in mind.* 😊

Chapter 14

'DS Forbes speaking.' For a split second his clipped tones make me question my decision to call him. It's Monday morning and he sounds stressed but I can't ignore what I saw at the train station. Not if it takes us a step closer to finding Billy.

'It's Claire Wilkinson. Billy's mum.' I don't know why I added that last bit. He knows perfectly well who I am but a lifetime of introducing myself at the school gates, talking to the kids' teachers or ringing the doctor's surgery has drummed it into me. Claire Wilkinson, Mark's wife. Claire Wilkinson, the boy's mum. I can't remember the last time I introduced myself as Claire.

'What can I do for you, Mrs Wilkinson?'

I can hear noises in the background, keyboards clacking and snatches of conversation.

'I was at the train station on Friday,' I say. 'Temple Meads. I was on platform thirteen and I was . . .' I falter. How do I explain the surety I felt that the ugly building I must have passed a thousand times holds a vital clue to my son's disappearance? 'I was wondering if you've searched the disused sorting office. There's a lot of graffiti on it and Billy did say in his diary that he wanted to tag the station or one of the trains. Maybe he went there instead. Maybe he's still there.'

DS Forbes doesn't respond immediately. Someone in the same room shouts, 'Yes!' and there's a smattering of applause.

'DS Forbes?' I say. 'Did you—'

'Yes, still here.'

'Do you think it could be a lead? Do you think he might be squatting there? Sleeping rough.'

He makes a low humming sound. 'I doubt it. That place is completely open to the elements. It's basically a couple of floors on stilts. You'd be better off sleeping in a doorway.'

'But he could be there?'

'Billy could be anywhere, Claire. That's the trouble. There are a thousand places in Bristol where he could be sleeping rough. Unfortunately we don't have the time or resources to search them all. I'm still hopeful that we'll get a lead as a result of the appeal. It's still early days.'

'But you'll look? You'll get someone to check it out.'

Another pause.

'I'll see what we can do.'

* * *

There is no way I can get into the old sorting office. Even if I was fifteen years old I still don't think I'd be able to make it over the barbed-wire fence, even with a leg-up, and the double gates are securely padlocked. I wasn't going to come here, not after I called DS Forbes this morning, but I wanted to get a glimpse inside, just to set my mind at rest. Cattle Market Road is a busy street, with cars whizzing backwards and forwards, but most of the shops are boarded up, long since abandoned. There is a red sign affixed to some railings just outside the gates warning the general public that it's private property. The sorting office is clearly visible through the grey metal bars of the gates. It looks even bleaker from here than it did from the train station opposite. DS Forbes wasn't joking about it being open to the elements. There are no longer any walls or partitions inside, just a series of concrete columns separating one floor from the next. Even if you could get over the barbed wire why would you shelter here? I've spent months wondering where I'd go if I was sleeping rough. I'd want to squirrel myself away from the world so I wouldn't worry about being robbed or attacked as I slept. I'd go to a women's shelter if I could or, if I didn't want to be found, I'd settle down for the night in a shed in the allotments off Talbot Road and take my belongings with me each morning to avoid discovery. We've already checked the allotments, and posted up signs in BS4 and BS3 asking people to check their sheds. We've searched everywhere and anywhere we could think of – the river-bank near Marks & Spencer at Avonmeads, the local parks, the Downs. Everywhere.

Well, not everywhere. Or we'd have found him.

I look down at the notebook in my hands and Billy's thick, black scrawl:

– *Bristol T M (train?)*
– *The Arches*
– *Avonmouth*

The Arches. I'll go there next. It's a railway viaduct – ripe for tagging – on the edge of Gloucester Road. It's on the other side of Bristol but that never stopped Billy, not if he wanted to see his friends. He'd set off on his bike and cycle the eight and a half miles it takes to get there from our house. Billy was always secretive about who he was going to see. 'Just mates, Mum,' he'd say. When the kids were little and went to a local primary school I knew who all their friends were. We seemed to spend half our lives going to birthday parties and playdates and ferrying the kids to and from sleepovers. But when the boys started secondary school on the other side of town their friends, scattered all over Bristol, became a mystery to me. Jake told us that Billy's Gloucester Road friends weren't from school at all. He said they were older guys, in their late teens and early twenties, who lived in a squat. I was horrified. I imagined drugs and squalor and crime and I told Billy I didn't want him to have anything to do with them. He told me I was narrow-minded and brainwashed by Mark. His friends weren't down-and-outs, they were artists who refused to become wage monkeys to line some capitalist landlord's pocket. Why shouldn't they live in an abandoned building? They weren't doing any harm to anyone. I didn't know what to do. We couldn't keep him locked in the house all weekend. The alternative was to ferry him into town in the car if he was going to the cinema with friends and then pick him up afterwards but what was to stop him from getting a bus to Gloucester Road the second we dropped him off? Mark said we should take Billy's bike off him for a bit, until he learned some responsibility. I suggested that Billy take me to the squat to meet his new friends but my son said he'd rather die than do that.

'Did you introduce your parents to all your friends when you were fifteen?' he asked me and I had to admit, to myself anyway, that I hadn't. There were countless boyfriends who I met at night after sneaking out of the house. Lots of older brothers and sisters of my mates who'd go into the Co-op to buy us bottles of White Lightning and Thunderbird to drink in the park. One of my male friends had to go to the hospital to get his stomach pumped after we got stupidly drunk and he was someone I'd known since childhood. I didn't end up in A&E. I'd already puked into a flower bed.

I was torn. Billy was fifteen years old. He was stretching his wings. He was a good boy. He was sensible at heart and I trusted him not to do anything stupid. And then he got into trouble at school for graffitiing the science block and Mark said that was that, he was grounded for two months and he was going to take away Billy's bike. Only we couldn't find it. And Billy refused to say where it was.

Now I jump as the gate clangs open and a man and woman in neon yellow vests with lanyards around their necks step through the gap.

'Excuse me,' I say as the man closes the padlock. 'My name is Claire Wilkinson. My son is missing. He's called Billy, he's fifteen. I'm worried that he might be sleeping rough and—'

'Not here he's not,' the woman says. She's mid-forties with a half-inch of grey roots showing through her curly red hair. 'Bristol Council.' She gestures towards her lanyard. 'We're redeveloping the place. Waterside offices and homes. There's twenty-four-hour security in place.'

'You're quite sure there's no one sleeping rough inside?'

The man pulls on the padlock. 'Not unless he's a pigeon. And we'll be getting them out ASAP too.'

I glance through the gates and try to imagine the building coming back to life – with glass in the windows and families sitting on sofas in front of their tellies and office workers wheeling back and forth in front of computer screens – but I can't see it.

'Thank you,' I say. 'I don't suppose you know of any squats in Gloucester Road, do you?'

But they've already wandered off.

I am a couple of hundred feet away from the Arches and stuck in traffic when I see him, a heavyset man with a bushy beard. He's riding a yellow-and-black BMX bike with distinctive blue-and-white tyres. He slips into the bus lane and undertakes me, his white trainers pumping the pedals as he speeds down Cheltenham Road. He looks almost comical with his large body balanced on top of the small bike and his thick knees spread wide. I remember how Jake laughed and said Billy looked like a circus monkey when he rode his Mafia BMX. It was a kid's bike, he said. And he looked like an idiot.

Just like the man in the hoody.

It's Billy's bike. It has to be. I've never seen one like it, not with the same combination of colours.

I don't think twice. I indicate left and pull into the bus lane. A horn sounds behind me and the driver of the 3A bus shakes his head at me in my rear-view mirror. Startled by the sound, the man on the bike glances back. I wave frantically but he either doesn't see me or he doesn't want to stop because his head drops and he begins to pedal even faster. He turns left onto Zetland Road just as the lights change and I'm forced to stop.

I drum my fingers on the steering wheel as he zips across the road and jumps off the bike outside a kitchen-and-bathroom shop and then hammers on the panelled wooden door of the building next to it, on the corner of the street. There are curtains at the window and a large piece of white card or wood – at least twelve feet by six feet – propped up inside, obscuring the view. As the traffic light turns green the door opens and the man disappears inside, taking the bike with him. It has to be the squat Jake told me about.

There's a space outside a tile shop on the opposite side of the road so I park quickly, half mounting the pavement in my desperation to get out of the car.

I have to wait for one, two, three cars to go past before there's a gap in the traffic and I can sprint across the road.

'Hello!' I knock on the door and then wait.

A young mother walks past, pushing a red-faced, squalling baby in a pram. Her eyes are fixed on a spot in the distance, as though she's willing herself to . . . just . . . get . . . home. She doesn't so much as glance at me.

I knock again and walk around the corner and tap on the window.

Nothing happens. No one comes to the door and the curtains don't twitch.

'Hello?' I lift the letterbox and peer inside but it's lined with nylon bristles and I can't see a thing. 'Hello! I know you're in there. I just saw you go in with the bike.'

'They're all drug addicts, you know.' An elderly man, with a walking stick in one hand and a blue plastic bag in the other, pauses beside me. 'If they've stolen something of yours you need to call the police.'

I instinctively touch my handbag, slung across my body. I should call the police. Or at least Mark. But adrenalin's coursing through me and I can't stop myself from shouting through the letterbox again as the man continues his amble up the road.

'My name's Claire Wilkinson. My son Billy is missing. I think you might know him.'

I reach into my handbag and pull out a flier, then shove it through me and go round the corner to the window again. The curtain twitches, just at the edge of the frame, and I catch a flash of pale pink flesh before it vanishes again.

There's a creaking sound and I rush back to the door. It opens an inch or two and a male voice hisses, 'Keep your voice down would you? The neighbours hate us as it is.'

The door opens wider. 'Well, are you coming in or not?'

Chapter 15

I'd expected syringes and drug paraphernalia on the floor, or at least the stench of weed, mixed with urine and shit. I'd also imagined piles of rubbish, fast-food boxes, split bin bags, dirty walls and stained mattresses. Instead the walls are white – grubby but not soiled – and decorated with posters and murals. Mark would call it graffiti. There's a frayed sofa too, an armchair and a low table holding what looks like some kind of screen-printing equipment. A guitar is propped up in the corner of the room along with several piles of books and half a dozen blank art canvases. Two men are sitting on the sofa. One's reading a book about Andy Warhol; the other's asleep, his head tipped back and his mouth wide open. I should be terrified, shut in a room with three men I don't know, but I'm too shocked to feel fear. I thought I was about to walk into a drugs den and instead it's as though I've walked into a student flat.

'He was up late working,' says the large man in the red hoody who hissed at me to come in. 'He's off to a festival soon. T-shirts,' he adds, gesturing towards the screen-printing equipment. 'He does them all by hand.'

I feel myself gawp. 'Squatters work?'

'We all work,' says the man with the book, looking up, and my cheeks burn. Did I just say that aloud? 'Jay busks and—'

'You don't work,' says Red Hoody who must be Jay. 'You're a student.'

'I use my brain,' says the man on the sofa. 'It's work, believe you me.'

'I'd offer you a cup of tea,' says Jay, 'but the council shut off the electric last week. We've still got water though, if you want some?'

'No, thank you.'

He's holding Billy's flier, crumpled up in his hand, but no one has mentioned my son since I walked in. And there's no sign of the bike.

'Have any of you seen Billy?' I gesture at the flier.

Jay shakes his head. The art student shrugs. Sleeping man snorts in his sleep and wakes with a start. He stares at me through glassy eyes, then seems to jolt into himself. 'Who are you?'

'Claire Wilkinson. Billy's mum. I think you might know him.'

'Billy?' He scratches his head. 'I know a Will Turner. Is that him?'

'No. His name's Billy Wilkinson. He's fifteen. He disappeared over six months ago. I know he had friends near Gloucester Road.'

'Never heard of him, sorry.'

'You must know him then.' I turn back to Jay. 'You let me in.'

He runs a hand over his ginger beard, finds the end and tugs on it. 'You were shouting through the letterbox. What else was I supposed to do?'

I feel myself grow hot under the scrutiny of three pairs of eyes.

'But the bike . . .' The door is open on the other side of the living room revealing a dark hall or passageway.

'What bike?'

'I saw you on a bike. A BMX. Distinctive. Yellow and black.'

'And?' Jay crosses his arms over his broad chest and takes a step back, as though to get a better look at me.

'Could I . . .' I take a step towards the hallway. 'Could I have a look at it?'

'It's not for sale.'

The atmosphere in the room has changed. When I entered the house they were amused and curious. Now they want me to leave.

I hear a sound from beyond the open door, the *squeak-squeak-squeak* of rusty bed springs and a low groan. Jay and the art student exchange a look. The student hides a smile behind his book. Why are they looking at each other like that? Is Billy here? Are they hiding him?

'All right, lady.' Jay puts a hand on my arm. 'I think it's time for you to go now, don't you?'

There's another sound from beyond the hallway. A moan of pain. The art student sniggers.

I snatch my arm away from Jay and, before he can react, I dart round him and run across the living room towards the open door. It's dark in the hallway but I can just make out a bike, propped up against the wall. There are several rooms along the length of the corridor. All the doors are open apart from the one at the far end of the hallway. As I sprint towards it a hand grabs my shoulder and I'm yanked backwards, but not before I've kicked out a leg and made contact with the door with the heel of my boot.

It swings open.

There's a gasp and a grunt and my breath catches in my throat as two men, naked and flushed, spring away from each other. The thinner and paler of the two men, standing at the base of the bed, grabs an item of clothing from the floor and presses it to his crotch. The other man, still on the mattress, shouts, 'What the fuck?' and picks up a shoe. He stares at me as though deciding whether or not I'm a threat, then launches himself off the bed and slams the door shut. 'You can fuck off too, Jay,' he shouts as his flatmate, still standing behind me with his hand on my shoulder, roars with laughter.

'Come on, mad bird. Time for you to leave.' Jay moves his hand to the small of my back and manoeuvres me out of the hallway, back into the living room and across to the front door.

'Please.' I twist away from him as he reaches for the door handle. 'Please just tell me where you got the bike from. Is it stolen? I won't tell the police. If it is Billy's bike it could be a clue, it could help us—'

'It's not stolen.' Jay glances back at his friends but they aren't on the sofa any more. They've moved to the other doorway, where they're nudging each other and laughing as they peer into the hallway. 'It's Rich's bike, the guy in the bedroom. He hates us using his stuff, particularly me. Says I'll buckle the frame.' He laughs drily.

'But you saw me, in my car, and you sped up.'

'What car?' He looks genuinely confused. 'I was trying to get the bike back before Rich got up. Look –' his expression softens as he opens the door – 'I'm sorry your son's missing. We'll stick the leaflet up in the window, okay?'

'Thank you,' I say, even though it is no longer in his hand. It's in a crumpled ball under the table.

'All right then. You take it easy.'

'Wait! Are there any other squats around here? My son—'

The question hangs in the air as the door is shut in my face.

Chapter 16

'Oh, crapping hell, missus.' Liz squeezes me tightly, then holds me at arm's length so she can look me up and down. 'I've been so worried about you. Where the hell have you been?'

I open my mouth to reply but my best friend gets there first. 'Come in and tell me everything. Do I need to lock the front door this time? Because if you do a runner again I swear I'll rugby-tackle you to the ground. I've eaten a metric fucking tonne of chocolate in the last few days so I'm packing a few pounds!'

We've been sitting at Liz's kitchen table for ten minutes. I've been talking non-stop since I stepped into her house. When I finally pause to take a breath Liz stares at me, her eyes large and round. 'And all this has happened in the last few days?'

I nod.

'Why didn't you come round? I mean, I appreciated

the text you sent saying you were okay but Jesus, woman, you only live next door. You could have popped in. When Mark and Jake came round to say you'd disappeared I totally freaked. I thought it was my fault. That bloody newspaper.'

'I know.' I reach across the kitchen table for her hands. 'I'm so sorry. I should have come round earlier but it's . . . it's all been so . . . I feel like I'm going mad. That's the only way I can explain it. I'm literally losing my mind.'

'Of course you are, bab. Anyone in your situation would be. But I'll tell you something for nothing – don't you be going to any more places on your own. You need to let the police do their job. Anything could have happened to you in that squat. They could have robbed you or worse.'

'They weren't like that.'

'And you know that for sure, do you? People turn, Claire. You need to be a bit less trusting.'

'I'm not too trusting.'

'You bloody are.'

'But I need to find Billy. If Caleb went missing you'd do everything you could to get him back. I've waited six months for the police to find him but I can't keep doing that. I need to find him. I can't just sit at home doing nothing. But I've started to see him everywhere I go. Everywhere . . .'

I snatch my hands back from Liz's and rest my forehead on my curled fists, suddenly exhausted. I don't know what to think any more. Or what to do. Each time I think I'm one step closer to finding Billy

I get my hopes up. Only for them to come crashing back down again.

'Deep breaths.' I hear the squeak of Liz's chair on the kitchen tiles and then her hand on my back. She rubs circles over my shoulders with the palms of her hands, just the way I'd do to the kids when they were little and upset. 'Take deep breaths, Claire.'

I close my eyes as she continues to rub my back but the darkness behind my eyelids is too dense, too deathless, and I open them again.

'Maybe what you need,' Liz says softly, 'is a bit of normality. Let me finish,' she adds quickly. 'I know there's no normal – I know life can't be normal until you get Billy back – but what I mean is maybe you need a routine. You've got too much time on your hands, Claire. Too much time to think and brood. Have you thought about going back to work?'

'Oh God, no.'

'I thought Stephen was a good boss?' Her voice softens as she says my brother-in-law's name. I think she's always had a bit of a soft spot for him, not that she'd ever admit it. 'He let you take six months off after Billy disappeared. I'm sure he'd be glad to have you back.'

'I know, but it's complicated.'

'How is it complicated? You loved your job at Wilkinson & Son. You were always telling me about the banter you had with the customers on the phone and how you and Stephen had a laugh.'

'Loved is a bit strong and anyway, what about Mark?'

'What about him? You went back to work after the argument, didn't you? And he didn't give you any grief.'

Mark and his stepbrother Stephen fell out a year ago. It was my birthday and we were having Sunday lunch in a local pub when Billy and Jake came to blows in the garden. They never revealed what started it but there was a lot of name-calling and insults thrown about before Jake landed the first punch. Mark intervened, heavy-handedly, and Stephen made a comment about Mark's parenting skills.

He said it jokily but Mark bit back, asking what the fuck Stephen knew about bringing up children. It was a low blow. Stephen and his wife Caroline can't have kids. They've tried everything, all the tests you can get. 'Unknown fertility issues,' the consultant said. Caroline got pregnant once, after ten years of trying, but she lost the baby in the second trimester. They never discovered why. She was broken by it and so was Stephen. I thought Mark was completely out of order for what he'd said to him and I let him know as much. I went back to Wilkinson & Son the next day, as though nothing had happened. Mark didn't give me grief about it but I could tell by the offhand way he greeted me that evening that he was secretly smarting. Where was my loyalty? Why hadn't I sided with him and told Stephen to stick his job? Because I was angry with him, that was why. Between him and the boys they'd completely ruined my birthday.

Mark and Stephen haven't spoken since their

argument, other than a few brusque words during the search for Billy, but I know Mark misses his stepbrother. He's just too proud to admit it.

'And – don't mind me saying this, Claire – but it's not as though you couldn't do with the money.'

Liz is right, again. Every spare penny we've managed to save over the years has been spent on publicizing Billy's disappearance. There's nothing left. Mark suggested cancelling our Sky subscription and giving up a few other luxuries he thinks we could live without but why put everyone through that when I could go back to work for a bit? I could deal with a few hours a week, at least until Dr Evans gets back to me with the result of the blood test.

'So?' Liz stops rubbing my back and slaps me square between the shoulder blades. 'Are you going to give it a go? Give Stephen a ring and arrange to go back to work. You only have to do a few hours, see how it feels.'

I twist round in my chair and smile up at her. 'And if I don't?'

She winks. 'I'll run you over and put you out of your misery myself.'

Chapter 17

I feel sick as I indicate right and turn the car into
the yard of Wilkinson & Son builder's merchants and
park. It's been three days since my conversation with
Liz about going back to work. Nothing has changed
since the last time I was here. The yard is still full of
fork-lifts, vans and lorries. There are empty pallets
stacked high in one corner. The sign – a yellow and
blue logo that looks like a triangle made out of bricks
– dominates the side of the warehouse. Inside, and
in the larger yard beyond the building, dozens of
builders and tradesmen will be perusing the timber,
bricks, pipes, paint and power tools. Mark's dad John
will be on the shop floor, making sure the customers
and staff are happy. And Stephen, Mark's younger
stepbrother, will be in the office: a phone in one hand,
a stained coffee mug in the other. I used to be the
office manager – a fancy title for what basically
involved answering the phone, printing and mailing

invoices, organizing the cleaners and running ads in the local press.

The good thing, if it can be called that, about working for members of your family is that I didn't have to explain my absence when Billy disappeared. John and Stephen didn't go to work either. They spent the best part of a week driving around Bristol, plastering posters of Billy's face onto lampposts, hoardings and billboards. Our house was a hive of activity, every room crammed with friends, neighbours and family. Mark was the epicentre, taking charge and instructing people where to search and flypost. He took down the mirror above the fireplace and replaced it with a huge map of Bristol which he stuck pins into – red for areas the police had searched, green for the places we'd be combing.

He ran everything by DS Forbes. 'That's the correct terminology, isn't it, DS Forbes?' 'It's important we have a chain of command, right, DS Forbes?' 'What's the latest, DS Forbes?' I was proud of him, assuming control, role-playing the career he'd so desperately wanted but part of me felt like screaming, 'This shouldn't be happening. Why is this happening? What did we do to deserve this? What did Billy do? No one should feel this kind of fear.'

Now my mobile phone bleeps impatiently in my bag and I snatch it up.

'Claire Bear!' I hold the phone a bit further away as Liz's voice booms into my ear. 'Are you at work?'

'Nearly. I'm parked up outside.'

'You don't have to go back, you know. I know it was my idea but—'

'It's all right. I can do this.'

'Did you tell Mark you were going back to work?'

'Yes, this morning.'

'And?'

'He said, "Do what you need to do, Claire." Then he walked out of the bedroom.'

'Supportive. Oh, shit. Sorry, lovely, early shift today and I'm due back on the tills. I'd better go. I'll give you a ring during my next break, okay?'

'Thanks, Liz.'

'Good luck. You'll be fine.'

The line goes dead.

I look at the screen. 9.25 a.m. It's not too late to text Stephen to say I won't be in after all.

A thumping sound on the driver's-side window makes me jump.

'Claire!' Stephen makes a 'wind down the window' gesture. 'Good to see you!' he shouts. 'You coming in?'

The second I step through the wide double doors, every pair of eyes in the building swivels in my direction.

'All right, Claire!' Wendy, one of the cashiers, raises her hand. Her smile is tight, nervous.

'Good to see you back, Mrs W.' Tony, the timber specialist. He gives me a nod, but it's short and sharp. The kind of nod you give someone at a funeral – nice to see you but not in these circumstances.

'Morning!' One of the regulars, whose name I don't know. He glances away before I can acknowledge him.

'Stephen, could you excuse me for a second.' I sprint away before he can object and head for the ladies' loos.

When I emerge from the cubicle I am shocked by the reflection that stares back at me from the tarnished mirror. My hair is wet with sweat around the hairline and my cheeks are flushed. This wasn't how I imagined coming back to work. Not that I've given Wilkinson & Son much thought since Billy left but this place has always represented normality. I come in, I do my job, I banter with my colleagues and the regulars. We swap stories about the weather and the traffic and how we spent our weekend. Will I ever be able to do that again?

I tidy myself up the best I can with my comb and the pressed powder I find in the bottom of my bag but it's a losing battle and Stephen's eyebrows twitch upwards in surprise as I walk into the office. To his credit he doesn't ask if I'm okay. Instead he pulls back the chair from my old desk and points at the steaming cup of coffee to the right of the keyboard.

'Milk, one sugar. Just how you like it.'

I sit down, wrap my hands around the mug and gaze about the office: same furniture, same carpet, same tea-stained countertop, same JCB calendar on the wall. Over six months have passed since I last sat at this desk and the only thing that has changed is me.

Stephen plonks himself into the chair on the other side of the room and picks at the top button of his shirt, sighing as it finally comes free. He is about the same height as Mark, but he's heavier and he looks as though he's put on even more weight since I left. He gave up smoking when he and Caroline were trying for a baby and she would pack him off to work with a Tupperware box full of carrot sticks and celery to crunch on. These would mount up in the fridge, box piled upon box, until the end of the week when Stephen would tip the contents into the bin, hiding the packets of Maltesers he'd demolished instead.

'So,' he says. 'What . . . uh . . . what prompted the decision to come back to work then?'

'Liz suggested it and it didn't seem like such a terrible idea.'

'Right. Right.' He nods. 'And how is Liz? Did she ever find out if Lloyd was having an affair?'

I almost laugh at how out of the loop he is but then I remember, we've barely spoken since Billy disappeared.

'They haven't spoken in a while. Last thing I heard he was still denying there was anyone else involved.'

'But she found texts on his mobile, didn't she? Explicit ones.'

'Yeah.'

'And she never rang the number?'

'She did but it went straight to voicemail. It was the generic one. You know, the one that your phone's set up with.'

'Ah.' Stephen shifts in his seat. His lips part, then he closes them again. I think he's run out of small talk. 'Okay, cool. So, I'm not going to throw you in at the deep end today. There's a bit of invoicing to be done and a stack of orders in the in-tray. We've taken on a contractor for the cleaning since you were last . . . since . . .' He pauses to swipe at the bead of sweat that trickles down the side of his face. 'Anyway, the cleaners were cutting corners so we got some new ones.'

'I'll do a bit of invoicing,' I say. 'Thank you.'

The tinny radio in the corner of the room plays pop songs as Stephen and I fall into companionable silence. The first order form I pick up takes me for ever to turn into an invoice because I can't remember my password for the computer or which buttons to click to make the accounting software add everything up. But then, like riding a bike, it becomes instinctive and I complete invoice after invoice and the fraught thoughts that have been whizzing around my brain like angry bees grow silent.

'Another coffee?' Stephen asks and I'm surprised when I look at the clock in the bottom right-hand corner of the screen. Half an hour has passed since I turned on the computer.

'Please.'

Stephen cracks his knuckles, stands up and crosses the room to turn on the kettle. It bubbles and then whistles as he unwraps a packet of biscuits. Out of the corner of my eye I watch him put two into his mouth in one go. He chews quickly, crumbs falling from his lips in his haste to eat them.

'Any news after the appeal?' he asks as he turns his back to pour the boiling water into two mugs.

'No, not yet.'

He says nothing. The spoon clanks against the mugs as he stirs the coffee. His hand shakes when he adds the sugar and half of it ends up on the countertop. Is he uncomfortable with me back in the office? Is that why he seems so twitchy? Or is it because we're talking about Billy?

He was distraught when Billy disappeared. He kept asking me, over and over again, to tell him what had happened the night he'd disappeared. Billy was always his favourite out of his two nephews. They both shared a love of Formula 1 and Billy would spend every Sunday at his house when it was racing season. Jake went along too the first few times but he said it was boring, watching cars whizz round and round the track, and he asked to stay at home instead. When I pressed him he said he thought Uncle Stephen was weird. He said he didn't like the way he hugged him – he squeezed him too tightly. Jake's never been keen on physical affection but his comment made me nervous. I started quizzing Billy about his visits to Stephen's house, and I looked for abnormal behaviour like lying or bed-wetting or night terrors, but Billy seemed fine. If anything, he seemed happier on leaving Stephen's house than he had been when he went in. I needed to be sure, though, so I went to pick him up an hour early once, just so I could peep through the window before ringing the bell. There was nothing worrying going on. Just Billy and Stephen sitting beside each other on the sofa with a can of Coke each, a tub of Roses chocolates between them, the TV blaring in the corner of the room and Caroline sitting at the table reading a magazine.

I still thought it was odd, the way Stephen had bonded with one of the boys and not the other, but there was no denying how much they had in common. As well as Formula 1 they both adored *Top Gear*, *The Gadget Show* and anything to do with robots. Stephen said he could relate to Billy more than Jake, being a younger son too. He said he saw a lot of himself in Billy, even though they weren't related by blood. He tried not to show his favouritism but you could see it in the presents he bought for the kids. Billy's were always more expensive, something he'd 'desperately wanted' whilst Jake's were generic 'boy's toys' that you might give to one of the kids' friends for their birthday. I hated seeing the hurt look in Jake's eyes so I started putting his Christmas card from Stephen in a different envelope, along with a tenner from my purse. I had to stop when Jake thanked his uncle for the money and Stephen said he didn't know what he was talking about.

Billy's visits to his uncle's house increased when he started getting into trouble at school. He said Uncle Stephen understood what it was like to be the black sheep. I told him that was rubbish. If Stephen got on so badly with his family why was he working for his stepdad? I tried to get Billy to open up about what he and Stephen talked about but he refused. 'Aren't I allowed to have any secrets, Mum?'

112

'And how's Jake?' Stephen asks now. He texted me to ask if everything was okay after he saw the appeal on TV. I didn't have the energy to get into what happened so replied obliquely, saying Jake hadn't been feeling well.

'Yeah, he's fine. Doing well with his apprenticeship and his weights. He's quite big now, muscles on top of muscles.'

'He'll get that from Dad. Size of a house he was, even as a teenager. I was a pipsqueak compared to him.'

'Yeah, Mark said.'

Stephen's back stiffens at the mention of his brother's name.

'And how's Kira?' he asks.

'Still living with us. She's still at college, doing well on her photography course by all accounts.'

'She took a few photos of me last year, can't remember why. Some project or other.'

'Yeah, she's always got her camera to hand. She took a lovely one of Mum on her birthday. You know she got her tongue pierced a few months ago. Kira, not Mum.'

He doesn't laugh. 'Tongue piercing, eh? She'll be getting a tattoo next. What is it with girls these days? It's like they're desperate for attention. Tits out, lips plumped, skirts barely grazing their arses. You're a very trusting woman, Claire Wilkinson, that's all I'll say.'

'What's that supposed to mean?'

'Well –' he continues to stir the coffee – 'it's temptation, isn't it?'

113

'What is?'

'Letting a nubile young thing like that into your home.'

My jaw drops. Nubile? Just the sound of the word makes my skin crawl, never mind the flash of damp tongue as he rolls it around his mouth.

'Look –' he holds up his hands – 'if you're comfortable with Kira parading around your house half-naked in front of your husband then good for you. There aren't many women who'd be so trusting.'

My horror switches to amusement and I laugh. Has he been saving that one up since he fell out with Mark this time last year? Oh, I know. I'll put the boot into my brother by implying that he's been leching over his son's girlfriend.

'Is that some kind of joke?'

'No.' He shakes his head, genuinely confused, then the mist seems to clear. 'Oh, I get it. You think I'm having a dig? I'm seriously not. Ask Caroline. She said there'd be no way she'd let a young woman live with us, wandering about in a towel and so on.'

'And you agree with her, do you?'

'Yeah—' He stops abruptly as he realizes what he's just said.

'Well, if you can't trust yourself . . .' I leave the sentence hanging and smile sweetly as I get up from my chair. 'Do you know what, Stephen? I think perhaps I made a mistake coming in today. I'm not ready to go back to work just yet. I need to be with my family and I've got a mountain of laundry to wash. I think Kira had a shower this morning. I'd

114

better get her towel in the machine before I catch Mark sniffing it.'

I stroll across the office, reach for the door handle, then turn back. 'Bye, then!'

Stephen doesn't reply. He's slouched back in his seat, gawping at me, his mouth a perfectly formed 'o'.

I slip into the car and take my phone from my bag. I can't believe I ever sided with Stephen over my own husband. Mark always said Stephen was jealous of him and I thought it was his ego speaking. But Mark was right. For Stephen to keep taking pot shots at him, this long after their argument, and with Billy missing too, he must be seriously screwed up. I won't let him draw me in. Not any more.

My thumb slides across the screen as I tap out a text.

Mark. I'm sorry. Going into work was a mistake. Can we talk when you come home tonight? Maybe go out for dinner, or to the pub?

I'm just about to start the engine when the phone bleeps in my hand. But the text isn't from Mark, it's an answerphone message. I must have missed a call when I turned my phone to silent before I went in to work.

'*This is a message for Mrs Claire Wilkinson. This is Hartfield Road Surgery, just ringing to let you know that your test results are in. If you could give us a ring back on—*'

I stab my index finger onto the green phone icon to return the call.

'Hello, this is Claire Wilkinson. I'm ringing about my test results. Yes, I'll hold . . .'

Chapter 18

'Cheers, son,' Mark says as Jake picks up his empty dinner plate from the table beside his armchair and adds it to the pile of dirty dishes he's carrying.

Kira follows in Jake's wake, collecting up the glasses before they both disappear through the living-room door. Thirty seconds later I hear the clunk of the dishwasher door being pulled over and the *clash-clang* of plates, glasses and saucepans being roughly stacked. Since Mark and Jake's argument they've pretty much avoided each other. They've been cordial but any warmth between them has gone.

'Good dinner, love,' Mark says as the stairs creak under the weight of Jake and Kira's steps as they disappear up to their bedroom.

I wait until the sound of footsteps on the landing fades away before I speak.

'Mark?'

He grunts in reply. Neither of us has mentioned

the fact that I went to Wilkinson & Son earlier today. When he got in from work I was peeling veg in the kitchen. He gave me a perfunctory kiss on the forehead and then, just as I was about to tell him about my day, he went upstairs to get changed. We haven't had a moment alone since.

'I heard back from the doctor's today.'

His eyes remain fixed on the flickering screen directly in front of him. 'Did you?'

'The test results are back. From my blackout.'

The programme he's watching freezes onscreen as he hits the pause button. 'Oh?'

'The receptionist couldn't tell me whether they're good or bad, just that I need to discuss them with the doctor. And I've got to wait until next week for an appointment.'

'Next week? Bloody hell. Well, it can't be anything serious. I'm sure they'd see you quicker than that if it was something to worry about.' He studies my face. 'You're worried, aren't you?'

'I'm scared it'll happen again.'

'Oh, love.' He grunts as he pushes himself up and out of his armchair. I half-rise, hoping he'll give me a hug. Instead he slumps onto the sofa beside me and rests a heavy hand on my knee. 'You haven't said anything about it so I assumed you were coping.'

I almost smile. It won't have crossed his mind to ask me how I feel about what happened. Once the A&E doctor gave me the all-clear and Mark realized I was in no immediate danger he filed the experience away in a box in his head marked *Claire amnesia episode* and then went to work the next day. Because I haven't mentioned it since there's been no need for him to reopen the box. It must be so nice to live in his black-and-white world where you only have to react when people tell you there's something to react to, when you don't spend your whole life second-guessing how the people you love feel.

'I didn't want to worry you.'

'You should have said something.' He tightens his grip on my knee. 'I do care, Claire. You know that, don't you?'

'Yes.' I place my hand over Mark's and meet his gaze. He doesn't look away and, as the TV glows in the corner of the room, something – sadness, hope, regret, I can't be sure – swells in my chest. I used to be able to read Mark's emotions as though they were my own but I have no idea what is going on behind his eyes. All I can see is my own concerned face reflected back at me.

'Can I talk to you about something else?' I ask.

He tenses. He thinks I'm going to mention Stephen. I can just tell.

'Can you make things up with Jake? Please.'

His hand slips from my knee and he leans back into the sofa. 'Do we have to do this now? I've had a hell of a day at work and I just want to relax.'

'But he's not happy, Mark. We had a chat the other day, in the garage. He's worried about his relationship with Kira and I know he's hurt by the things you said last week.'

'Jake's hurt?' He shifts across the sofa and angles

himself towards me. 'Seriously, Claire? He gets pissed and causes a scene at the press conference and you're having a go at me? What did you expect me to do – pat him on the back?'

'We could have handled it differently. Instead of flying off the handle we could have—'

'Done what? Sat down and had a nice chat? Taken him to a counsellor? Because that worked out well for you, didn't it? You stopped going after three weeks.'

'Why are you having a go at me, all of a sudden?'

'Because you're the one that's brought it up! Jake is a nineteen-year-old man, Claire. He's not a kid. I'm not going to mollycoddle him. He needs to hear it how it is.'

'You squared up to him. You goaded him. And you're supposed to be the parent. You're supposed to—'

'Don't tell me what I'm supposed to do!' He leaps off the sofa and glares down at me.

'All I'm saying is that, if you'd have listened to me in the first place – if you toned it down instead of exploding whenever you get angry – then we wouldn't be in this position.'

'What position?'

'Billy wouldn't be missing.'

Mark freezes, hands still clenched at his sides, eyes fixed on mine, his lips moist with saliva. It's as though someone has pressed pause on our argument.

'I'm sorry.' I can't get the words out fast enough.

'I didn't mean it. I was angry. I'm not saying it was your fault. Mark! Mark!'

I continue to shout his name as he walks out of the room. Seconds later I hear the back door slam.

Tuesday 7th October 2014

ICE9: *I am having a shit day. How about you?*
Jackdaw44: ☹
ICE9: *You're sad?*
Jackdaw44: *Cos you're having a shit day. What's up?*
ICE9: *Arguments.*
Jackdaw44: *Relationships suck. You should be single like me. No women. No drama. Result!*
ICE9: *No drama? What about the graffitiing at school? (Tell me to fuck off and I'll never text you again.)*
Jackdaw44: *Fuck yyyyy . . . (Just kidding!) Bollocks to the graffiti. I'm expressing myself. No bastard understands that.*
ICE9: *You can express yourself without doing it on school property.*
Jackdaw44: *Don't you start!*
ICE9: *You brought it up.*
Jackdaw44: *Actually, you did. Anyway, forget that shit. Do you want to go for a beer?*

ICE9: *Ha! Ha!*
Jackdaw44: *What's so funny?*
ICE9: *a) It's 3pm and b) You're 15.*
Jackdaw44: *a) It's never too early for a beer and b) I look 18.*
ICE9: *Well b) is true.*
Jackdaw44: *So? 🍺?*
ICE9: *You're at school.*
Jackdaw44: 😒
ICE9: *Skiving again!*
Jackdaw44: *Yeah, and I'm bored. Come to the pub with me.*
ICE9: *I'm busy.*
Jackdaw44: *No, you're not. You're having a shit day.* 😩 + 🍺 = 😊
ICE9: *Look at you, the emoticon mathematician!*
Jackdaw44: *It's all true. So is that a yes then?*
ICE9: *Oh, sod it. What harm could one beer do?*

123

Chapter 19

There's a cold space on the left of the bed, where the warm imprint of Mark's body should be.

I didn't chase after him when he left last night. Instead I sat on the sofa with my arms crossed and the TV still on pause and reran the argument in my head. How had we gone from me asking him to have a word with Jake to me implying that he was responsible for Billy going missing? Because he'd pushed my buttons, that's why. He'd gone straight on the offensive, bringing up my failed sessions with the counsellor and implying that I didn't know what I was talking about. I hadn't even mentioned getting counselling – just that he should talk to his son. What was so wrong with that?

I rehearsed what I'd say when Mark came back from the pub. I had it all word perfect. Only he didn't come back. There was a space in the street outside the house, where his silver Ford Focus had been parked. He'd taken his jacket too, and his briefcase from the hall. Wherever he'd gone he was planning on staying overnight.

I rang him several times but his mobile went straight to answerphone. I sent text after text.

I'm sorry. I don't think it's your fault.

Please, Mark. Let's not fall out. We need to stick together. I'm sorry.

Please. Please talk to me.

And then, after an hour of silence, I got angry.

You've made mistakes. You've said things you didn't mean in the heat of the moment and I've always forgiven you. Just talk to me, let's sort this out.

OK, fine. Ignore me. Because that makes everything better, doesn't it?

I'm going to bed.

Any anger I felt towards him has evaporated overnight. I'm pissed off with myself now. I was an idiot for taking my stress out on him. He didn't deserve it.

I glance at the bedside clock. 8.30 a.m. With any luck he'll be sitting in his car outside an appointment and I'll catch him before he goes in.

Mark. I'm sorry. Please. Just send me a text to let me know you're OK. I know you're angry. But please. Just let me know you're—

A noise from downstairs makes me jump. I heard Jake and Kira clattering down the stairs at least half an hour ago so it can't be them. And Mark should be on his way to work. Unless he's come back. Maybe he's decided to take the morning off and sort things out?

I push back the duvet and swing my legs out of bed, then cross the bedroom and take the stairs one at a time, treading quietly. Logically I know I'll find Mark sitting at the kitchen table, or standing by the sink, looking moodily out into the street, but there's still a tiny part of me that hopes that it's Billy. And if it is, if a miracle has occurred and he's home and he's tired and he's dirty and he's traumatized, I don't want to be the one who scares him off.

But it's not Billy bent over the kitchen table with his head bowed low. It's Kira, an ear bud in one hand, a camera lens in the other, her tongue stud clacking against her front teeth as she flicks her tongue forwards and backwards in her mouth. It's a habit she's developed since she had her tongue pierced a few months ago.

Clack-clack-clack.

She looks deep in thought, totally focused on wiping every last smear and streak from the glass.

I swallow my disappointment and step into the kitchen. 'You'll damage your front teeth if you keep doing that.'

She jumps at the sound of my voice and gathers her camera equipment to her chest.

'Sorry I startled you. I thought you were at college. Cup of tea?'

'No, thanks.' She stands up and begins replacing lens caps and zipping lenses and camera bodies into their cases. 'I've got a couple of free periods this

126

morning so I thought I'd clean my kit before I head into town to take some photos.'

'Don't mind me. This is your home too.' I've lost track of the number of times I've told her that. When she first moved in she could barely look me in the eye. I don't know if it was because she was shy or if the way her mother had treated her had left such a terrible imprint that she was intimidated by older women. She's been living with us for eighteen months now and she's still not comfortable being alone with me. If anything she's worse. A small, possibly foolish, part of me thought that we might develop a mother-daughter type relationship after she moved in. I thought we'd go to the cinema to watch romcoms or to the nail bar in town to get manicures but you can't force a relationship where there isn't one. Some people need time to settle in to new situations, to get used to people, to trust them. I genuinely care about Kira. I worry about her, almost as much as I worry about my own sons, but she's still not ready to let me in.

She continues to shovel her belongings into a large carry case at breakneck speed, her blonde hair covering her face. 'It's okay, I was pretty much finished anyway and I really should get—'

'Don't go. Please.' I approach the table, my hands wrapped around a steaming cup of tea. 'I'd like to have a chat with you.'

She peers at me through the curtain of hair that hangs over her face. 'What about?'

'About you, and how you're doing.' I pull out a chair and sit down. We haven't really had a conversation since my blackout in Weston. I've barely seen her to talk to, but I imagine Jake will have filled her in. Whenever I pass their room on my way to bed each night the low rumbling of their hushed conversations creeps from beneath the door.

'I'm fine.' Her gaze flits towards the kitchen window and the driveway outside and I instantly understand. She thinks I want to have another chat about her relationship with Jake and she wants to escape.

'Can we chat later?' She glances at the kitchen clock. 'I really need to get into town. I'm taking photos of someone and she's got to go to work at half past nine.'

'Okay, don't worry.'

I watch as she crosses the kitchen, her body sloped to the right under the weight of her camera bag and her battered trainers squeaking on the kitchen tiles. Her long, thin legs look pale and mottled despite the fact that it's the middle of summer.

'Kira!' I call as she reaches for the doorknob.

'Yes.' She turns back.

'Has Stephen – Jake's uncle Stephen – has he ever said anything inappropriate to you?'

She frowns. 'Like what?'

'About . . . I don't know . . . the way you dress?'

'The way I look?' She glances down, at the black T-shirt that clings to her body, the denim skirt that ends mid-thigh and the faded purple Converse on her feet. 'Why would he comment on that?'

'I don't know. I just wanted to check that he's never said anything to upset you?'

'No.' She shakes her head. 'Never. He's always been really nice to me.'

'And no one else in the family has ever made you feel uncomfortable? You don't feel uncomfortable being around Mark . . .'

'No!' She glances down at her outfit again and I feel angry at myself for paying attention to what Stephen told me. I've made her feel self-conscious about the way she dresses now. As if her self-esteem wasn't fragile enough anyway.

'No,' she says again, more softly this time. When she looks back up I'm startled to see tears shining in her eyes. 'Of course not. You've all been lovely to me. I'd be on the streets if you hadn't taken me in.'

'I'm sure that's not true.'

'It is. I don't know what I would have done if you hadn't said I could live here. Mum was . . . Living with her could be difficult and Jake knew that. He rescued me. I know we've had our problems but I do love him. He's everything to me and I'd die if I lost him. Actually die.'

'Oh, Kira.' I cross the room, arms outstretched, but she twists away before I can hug her.

'Please don't, Claire.' She fumbles the back door open and squeezes through the gap, knocking her camera bag against the wall in her haste to escape.

Wednesday 8th October 2014

Jackdaw44: *Yesterday was cool.*
ICE9: *Until your mates turned up.*
Jackdaw44: *What's wrong with my mates?*
ICE9: *They're immature.*
Jackdaw44: *And I'm not?*
ICE9: *Would I have been having a drink with you if I thought that?*
Jackdaw44: 😎
Jackdaw44: *Hey?*
ICE9: *What?*
Jackdaw44: *We should do beers more often. I like talking to you. Feel like you get me.*
ICE9: *Maybe that's because I do.*
Jackdaw44: 👊
ICE9: *Why are you punching me?*
Jackdaw44: *That's a fist bump, you twat!*
ICE9: *Ha. Ha!*

Chapter 20

I am sitting on the floor on the upstairs landing, photo albums scattered around me.

Mum's text arrived half an hour after Kira left.

Don't suppose you've had a chance to find those school photos of the kids yet, have you? Ben from the Bristol News said he'd run the feature but he needs them NOW. Can you have a look and let me know.

I still hadn't moved from the kitchen. There was a part of me that could relate to Kira's outpouring of emotion. I'd felt the same way about Mark when I was her age. Your emotions are so big when you're a teenager, so powerful. It's as though they're a violent storm, sweeping you from one day to the next. My worst fear was that Mark would realize that he could do better and dump me. I want to shake my eighteen-year-old self now. That wasn't fear. It's not until you have children that you truly know what fear is. After

131

Jake was born I had to stop watching the news because the world seemed so terrifying. What chance did I have of keeping my tiny baby son safe when there was danger around every corner? How the hell was I supposed to protect him from that?

I've found the album with Mickey Mouse on the outside that's full of photos of us and the kids at Disneyland Paris. I've also found the blue, slightly battered album with photos of Jake as a baby, crammed full of images of his tiny, soft shape, taken from every conceivable angle. There's Jake and me in the hospital bed, Jake in the pram for his first walk, Jake having a cuddle with Granny, Granddad hanging Jake upside down by his ankles, Jake in the bath, Jake going down a slide. It's as though we captured every waking moment of the first year of his life.

There's a similar album for Billy, with a pale green cover, but there aren't as many photos. I swore we wouldn't be one of those families that take fewer photos of the second child but, with Jake to look after too, I didn't have the time to luxuriate in Billy's first smile, his first word, his first step. Now I wish I'd recorded every single second of his life.

All the photo albums are here apart from the one I'm looking for, the grey album crammed with the children's school photos: staged poses and watery backdrops, the only way to distinguish one year from the next the number of teeth showing in Jake and Billy's rictus grins.

Where is it?

Perhaps Mark took it? The police requested photos

of Billy after we reported him missing but I was in no state to help so he took charge.

I try ringing him but it goes straight to answer-phone. Do I keep looking or wait until he gets home? That's if he does come home.

I throw open the door to Mark's bedside cabinet and scoop coffee-stained paperbacks onto the floor, then flip onto my stomach and haul two dusty suit-cases from underneath the bed. I rifle through them. Then I search through the wardrobe and chest of drawers. I search every last centimetre of our bedroom but there is no sign of the album.

Maybe Jake took it? Maybe he wanted to show photos of the two of them as kids to Kira and—

Kira. Photography. Film Studies. Billy. Photos.

And there it is, a memory, sparked into life – Billy, telling me about a project he was doing at school in his media class. His teacher wanted them to make videos and he'd been inspired by something he'd seen on Facebook about a man who photographed his daughter every day of her life and then put the pictures together into a time-lapse video.

'You literally see her grow from a baby to an eighteen-year-old,' he said. 'And you've got all those photos of us at school. I want to do one about how school changes you.'

I barely even registered the request the first time he made it. I heard the word, 'Mum!' and auto-matically pointed him in the direction of the fridge.

Now I take several deep breaths before opening the door to his room. It is not how he left it. It's not

133

a mess of clothes flung onto the floor, empty crisp packets jammed down the side of the bed and exercise books and pens strewn all over the floor. It's tidier than it's been since he was a baby and I made him the most lovely nursery room with framed photos of Winnie-the-Pooh on the wall and soft toys lined up on the dresser.

The police searched every inch of his room after we reported him missing. They took away his computer, his games console and all of his books, comics and sketchpads. I stayed downstairs, in the living room, and listened to the floorboards creak under the weight of their footsteps. When they left I ventured back upstairs. I cried when I saw the room. Not because they'd left it messy – they hadn't – but because it was as though all traces of Billy had been wiped from the room. All that remained was his bed and his posters of graffiti, rap stars and skateboarders.

His belongings were returned a few weeks later. A forensic examination of his computer had revealed nothing apart from the fact that he spent a lot of time surfing for information on his favourite graffiti artists and watching YouTube videos of skateboarders. And accessing hardcore porn.

'It's increasingly common for young males to access this kind of material,' DC Forbes told us. 'It can become quite a compulsion for teenage boys. It becomes addictive. I'm not suggesting this was in any way connected with Billy's disappearance but it has been noted in his file.'

Mark wanted to know what kind of hardcore porn Billy had been watching and DC Forbes was quick to reassure us that it was nothing illegal but it was quite extreme.

'What about his mobile phone?' I asked. 'Have you found it?'

He shook his head. 'GPS tracking failed to reveal anything and triangulation showed that it was last used in this house or street. We haven't located it yet, I'm afraid.'

'So nothing in his room has given you any clues what might have happened to him?'

'No, Mrs Wilkinson, I'm sorry.'

I push open the door to Billy's room and inhale deeply but all trace of him is gone. I used to tell him off for piling up his stinking trainers behind his bedroom door because you could smell them from the landing. There were other smells too: unwashed clothes, half-eaten burgers sweating in their white polystyrene boxes shoved under the bed, and the pungent chemical scent of his thick-nibbed marker pens.

I rifle through Billy's bookcase but there's no sign of the missing photo album amongst the neatly stacked comic books, graphic novels and the incongruous pile of Harry Potter books we used to read together before bed. When he turned eight he told me that being read bedside stories was babyish but he still insisted on Harry Potter each night. We made it all the way through the *Deathly Hallows*. I like to think he did that for me.

As I yank open the drawer to his bedside table the sketchbooks that are piled up on the top spill to the carpet. I pull one onto my lap and flip through it. Unlike reading, Billy's interest in drawing has never faded but it's been a long time since he's drawn robots, dinosaurs and flying cars. For the last couple of years he's done nothing but scrawl graffiti tags over every available surface.

Fliy – that was the tag he came up with first, but he changed it to DStroy when Jake teased him that he wanted to be called Fliy because he made a lot of noise and was dirty and annoying.

And here it is, page after page of thick black scrawl. *DStroy*. *DStroy*. *DStroy*. The letters becoming more and more illegible, turning into a spiky dark hieroglyphic as he worked on his design. He made no attempt to hide the fact that he was DStroy – that's why it was so easy for the headmaster to identify him as the culprit behind the graffiti at school.

The first time we were called into Mr Edwards's office Billy tried to explain that graffiti was his way of leaving a mark on the world. He might not be remembered for winning a trophy for sport or drama but everyone knew who DStroy was. DStroy didn't care how tall a building was or how risky it was to tag it. DStroy thought his teachers and the police were sleepwalking sheep carrying out the orders of hypocritical politician scum. Who were they to say he couldn't express himself the way he wanted? Tagging wasn't vandalism – it was art.

Mark called him a fucking idiot. He said respect

was earned by working hard, not by scribbling on school property, and he was ashamed to call Billy his son. I saw Billy flinch just for a second before he muttered, 'You're one to talk about respect,' under his breath. Mark didn't hear him and I wasn't about to ask Billy to repeat himself.

I hoped it was a phase, the graffiti and the defiance. I fell out with my own mum when I was about the same age as Billy. I felt so grown up and independent and I struggled with the fact that my parents still had so much control over my life. If Mum insisted Dad pick me up from a party at 10 p.m. instead of letting me stay until 11 p.m., or confiscated a lipstick I'd bought because it was 'tarty red', I'd argue back as though my life depended on it. I knew what was best for me, not her. Didn't she know how pathetic it made you look in front of your friends to be picked up before all the others? Didn't she remember how important it was to have the same shade of lipstick as everyone else?

I wasn't soft on Billy when he got in trouble with the school. I backed Mark one hundred per cent when he told him he was grounded for a month, but I felt it was important to talk to Billy too, to understand why he'd done what he'd done so we could prevent it from happening again. Mark accused me of molly-coddling Billy but I wouldn't back down. Shouting and screaming at him would only widen the gulf between us and I didn't want to be a stranger in my own son's life. But he wouldn't let me in.

I turn another page of Billy's sketchbook and dab

at the tear on my cheek but I'm too slow and it drops onto the paper. The ink escapes from the edge of the design and creeps, frond-like, through the fibres of the page. I never should have spent the night at Mum's house. If I'd just been stronger. If I'd held my ground and told Mark to get out instead then Billy would never have disappeared.

I would have woken up. I would have heard him creep down the stairs. I would have told him that we loved him, no matter what he did.

The police say there was no evidence of forced entry that night. And no sign of a struggle. Billy wasn't smothered in his bed and carried out of the house. He left of his own free will. Did he come to Mum's to look for me, then carry on walking when there was no answer at the door? Did he head for a friend's house and run into trouble en route? Did someone offer him a lift and then—

I drop the book and press my hand to the side of my head as a dark thought creeps into my brain.

'No.' I say the word aloud, to try and block it out. 'He's not dead.'

Billy's alive. He ran away because he felt ashamed, unloved and rejected. He's hiding out with a friend. He's seen the TV appeals but he's still angry, still hurt. Or he's sleeping rough and hasn't seen the appeals. He thinks we don't care enough to come after him. But it's been six months. Surely after this long he'd have got in touch? He knows how much I love him. He wouldn't put me through this kind of torment. The only reason why I haven't heard from him is because—

138

'No!' I say it again. 'No! No!'

'Claire?'

'No!' I won't believe that. I won't.

'Claire?' The voice is louder this time and I screw my eyes tighter shut.

'No! No! No! No!'

'Claire!' I feel a heavy hand on one shoulder. 'Claire, stop it! Stop it! Stop shouting.'

Mark is crouched in front of me. He's wearing his suit trousers and a white shirt. The top button is undone and his chin is speckled with stubble. 'What are you doing? Why are you shouting?'

I stare at him as his lips continue to move but I can't make sense of the words that come out. It's as though someone has woken me from a nightmare and there is a glass wall between me and reality.

'Claire. Oh God, Claire.' He pulls me into his arms and the scent of his aftershave fills my nostrils; a sharp citrus note against the stench of cigarette smoke. Mark hasn't smoked for years. He must have started again on the sly. 'Claire, I'm sorry.' He runs a hand over my hair, then does it again and again; firm strokes from the crown of my head to the nape of my neck. 'I'm sorry we argued last night. And I'm sorry I didn't reply to your texts. I was so angry and I needed to cool down.'

I wriggle my arms from where they are tightly pressed against my chest, then slip my hands around his back and press my palms to his shoulder blades. His shirt feels cool and soft.

'I'm sorry too,' I whisper, then I pull away so he

can see my face but I don't let go. Holding on to him makes me feel real. Grounded. If I let go I'll drift away. 'I don't know why I said that. I've been feeling so guilty and—'

'Claire, there isn't a single day I don't feel guilty about what I said to Billy that night. You were right when you told me to be a parent and keep control of myself. You'd have thought I'd have learned that by now. I've already lost one son.' He glances away, his teeth clenching as he tries to hold back tears. I pull him in to me, cradling his head with my hands.

His body judders against me as he cries silently. Then he coughs, takes a deep breath and pulls away, reaching for my hands, wrapping them in his.

'I'm just so angry with myself. I swore that I wouldn't be like my dad. I wouldn't laugh at my kids' ambitions. I wouldn't tell them that a job in a builder's yard was the best they could hope for in life. I was going to tell my kids that they could be anything they damn well wanted to be.'

'You did. You've always said that to the boys, ever since they were little enough to have ambitions. Remember when Billy said he wanted to be an astronaut? You said there was no reason he couldn't be if he just worked hard at school. You'd save up to take him to the NASA space centre in Florida if he passed his maths GCSE, remember?'

'Claire, he was eight!'

'But you told him you believed in him. You made him think he could achieve anything.'

'So what went wrong?' The light dulls in his eyes. 'Why throw it all in my face? Why skive off school? Why turn to vandalism? Shoplifting, for God's sake. I don't think my dad did a great job bringing me up but I turned out okay. What did I do so wrong?'

'You didn't do anything wrong. Billy's fifteen. It was a phase. He would have grown out of it.'

'Would he? What if he'd started dabbling in drugs next? Or stealing cars? Claire, some of those kids he was hanging out with were dropouts. Eighteen years old, living off benefits, graffitiing bridges and running from the cops. He looked up to them and thought I was the arsehole!

'Anyway –' he shakes his head as though trying to clear it – 'I'm sorry we argued. I was stressed and I took it out on you. I thought the appeal would result in some new information and then Jake—' He stops abruptly. 'Let's not go there again.'

'No.'

'I'm glad you came home early,' I add as Mark takes my hand and eases me up off the floor.

As he leads me towards the doorway I glance back at the sketchpads on the floor. 'Mark? You haven't seen the photo album, have you? The grey one with the pictures of Billy and Jake at school?'

'Nope.' He gives my hand a small tug. 'It'll turn up. Nothing's lost for ever.'

Chapter 21

I can't watch a TV programme all the way through any more. I can't sit still for that long. I need to do something instead – tidying, cleaning, chatting or surfing the Internet. I don't know if it's because motherhood and sleep deprivation have wrecked my concentration span or because I've forgotten how to relax. I miss being able to turn off my brain and lose myself in a film or TV drama. We used to watch *The X Factor* or *I'm a Celebrity* as a family when the boys were younger. We'd sit on the sofa, Mark and I book-marked on the ends with the kids squashed between us in the middle. We'd order pizza, drink thick, sticky Coke and pass comments on the acts or the celebrities. Mark and I would exchange looks at some of Ant and Dec's more risqué jokes and then burst out laughing, prompting confused stares from the kids and a chorus of, 'What? What's so funny?' I'd give anything to turn back time and do that again. Anything at all.

Mark went upstairs to do some work half an hour ago and Jake and Kira disappeared into their room after tea so it's just me sitting in front of the TV, half-watching a programme about adoption, half-reading the magazine on my lap. I can't stop thinking about the art pad I found in Billy's room earlier with *DStroy* scrawled over every page. DS Forbes still hasn't got back to me about the disused sorting office although I'm no longer convinced that's where Billy is. And I can't go driving around Gloucester Road knocking on the doors of squats. That just leaves the last place on Billy's list – Avonmouth. There's a pub near the river, the Lamplighters. I could suggest to Mark that we go for a walk along the riverbank and then grab a pint.

I take the stairs two at a time. The door to our bedroom is ajar. The curtains are still open and Mark, lying on the bed with a file on his chest and his mouth slightly open, is bathed in soft light. A snore catches in his throat before he falls quiet again. I gently fold the duvet over him, then retreat back out onto the landing. I can't wake him, not if he's this tired. He works so hard.

I glance at my mobile phone. It's just after 7.30 p.m. If I want to get to Avonmouth before the sun sets I need to leave now. I cross the landing to Jake and Kira's room and stand silently outside the door. Tinny dialogue drifts through the cracks. A second later Jake and Kira roar with laughter. The sound is so foreign, so wonderful, it makes my heart leap. They sound so happy. I can't ask them to come and look for Billy with me.

143

I return to the living room and call Liz. She picks up on the second ring.

'You all right?'

'Yeah. I was just wondering if you fancied coming to the Lamplighters in Avonmouth with me.'

'Now?'

'Yes.'

'Oh, sorry, mate. I'm in town. I'm meeting Caleb and his new boyfriend for a drink.' She practically squeals the words 'new boyfriend'.

'He's letting you meet him?'

'I know! I'm under strict instructions not to do, or say, anything that might embarrass him so that's basically me sitting mute in the corner for the whole night but yes, can you believe it?'

'That's great news, Liz.'

'We could go for a drink tomorrow if you like? Why do you want to go to Avonmouth anyway?'

'It doesn't matter. I'll tell you tomorrow. Enjoy your night.'

'I will. Take it steady!'

I put down the phone and drop back into the armchair. The documentary has finished and a weight-loss programme has started. I flick through the channels. Images flash up on the screen and then vanish – a woman in the throes of labour, a father and son playing football, a pregnant woman, a family having dinner, a teenager in a hospital bed. I turn off the TV. The sudden silence makes my ears ring.

I pick up my magazine.

Put it down again.

I pick up my mobile and scroll through Facebook.

Pictures of cats. Pictures of food. Pictures of sunsets. Gripes about bad days at work, leaking showers, annoying neighbours and the government.

I close the app.

My foot *tap-tap-taps* on the floor as I look around the living room – at the photos of Jake and Billy on the mantelpiece, at the DVDs and books in the bookcase, at the framed print I bought Mark for our first anniversary.

Tap-tap-tap. Tap-tap-tap.

I can't just sit here and do nothing.

I can't.

Liz's voice rings in my ears as I park the car and walk down the lane towards the Lamplighters pub.

'*Don't you be going to any more places on your own. You need to let the police do their job.*'

I block her voice out.

There isn't a single empty table outside the pub. Everywhere I look there are men and women in T-shirts and shorts, vest tops and dresses; all drinking, smoking and chatting and enjoying the last vestiges of summer. The sun is low in the sky, the clouds striped amber and red. It's warm but I still shiver in my thin cardi, maxi dress and sandals. I should have changed before I left the house.

I take a right outside the pub and weave through the gate into Lamplighters Marsh, the pathway that follows the river Avon. It's been a long time since I was last here. It was before the kids were born, back when

Mark had a motorbike and we'd go off on adventures, discovering parts of Bristol we'd never visited before, spending hours nursing pints of shandy (him) and glasses of Martini and lemonade (me) as we learned everything there was to know about each other.

Spiky bushes and dense bracken flank me on both sides, obscuring the view of the river and the city. In the distance is the Avonmouth Bridge, a grey metal slash cutting through the sky. A seagull circles overhead and then dips down towards the ground and disappears from view. I continue on towards the bridge. If Billy was going to tag anything around here that would be his target.

For several hundred metres I can still hear the laughter and chatter from the pub behind me and then it is gone, replaced by the rush of a wind that seems to come from nowhere and the low drone of cars speeding across the bridge. The path winds and curves as I continue to walk and the sun dips lower in the sky. I cross paths with a solitary dog walker. He raises a hand in greeting and then he too is gone. I continue along the path for five, maybe six minutes more and then discover a break in the bushes and a lone green bench on the edge of marshy riverbank. I pause as I spot something floating on the surface of the water. Something black, voluminous, like an item of clothing puffed up with air. When Billy first disappeared there was talk of dredging the river. I couldn't bear it. I had to leave the room.

I stand stock-still, with one hand pressed to my chest as the river carries its hoard closer, closer and then air rushes from my lungs as it turns in the water and the twisted knot of a torn bin bag appears on the surface. It's a bag. Just a bag.

As I turn away my toe catches on something and I look down. There's a patch of burnt grass beside the bench with stones at the edges and three or four charred logs in the centre, where a fire must have been. I dip down and hover my hand above them. Cold. Whoever started the fire is long gone. But there was someone here, someone who needed to light a fire to keep warm. The sound of voices cuts through the wind's whistle and the roar of the traffic and I freeze, my hand still stretched towards the logs. The voices are too close to have drifted up from the pub. And they're male voices, young male voices. My walk becomes a jog as I rejoin the path, then a sprint as I realize that the sound is coming from directly below the bridge.

I slow to a halt as I get closer: I can still hear the voices but there's no obvious way of getting to them. The foliage is thicker here with bushes and trees reaching way above my head. And then I spot it, a disturbance in the bracken and a stamped-down path leading directly under the bridge. The voices grow louder as I crash through the undergrowth and then someone shouts, 'Whoa,' as I burst into a small clearing on the riverbank. Four teenagers, sitting cross-legged around a fire with their bags and bikes scattered around them, stare back at me. There's a shocked silence, then one of them giggles. He stares at me, his eyes big and round, then tips backwards, his arms wrapped around his body as he explodes with laughter.

'Naz, you dick!' The boy to his right picks up a can of lager from beside his friend's head and turns it upside down. 'That was the last of my beer.'

'Lost your dog?' says another of the boys. He dips his head and takes a puff on the spliff hidden in his curled hand.

'No, I . . .' Behind the boys is a concrete column. Even in the dim light I can make out the swirl and curve of the graffiti at the base.

'Graffiti fan, are you?' says the boy with the spliff as I take a wide circle around the group to take a closer look. In two places someone has written the initials *DBK* in thick orange paint. There are some nonsensical letters sprayed in purple along the centre of the column. *CNSCS*, that's all I can make out. *ZYNK* is written in black spray on the lower strut of the column and there's something in a white bubble shape with black edging. I can't read a word of it.

'Do you . . .' I turn back to the boys. 'Do any of you do graffiti?'

'"Do you do graffiti?"' Spliff Boy repeats, totally deadpan, and Laughing Boy howls with amusement.

There was a time when I would have found a group of young lads like this threatening. I'd have crossed the street rather than risk attracting their attention but I've stopped being scared. I don't care if they think I'm old and embarrassing and uncool.

I rest my hand on the column. It feels cold and

damp under my palm. 'Do any of you know Billy Wilkinson?'

'Why?'

'He's my son. He's been missing for six months.'

'I know him,' pipes up the smallest boy in the group. It's the first thing he's said since I appeared in the clearing but I've seen him watching me, tracking me with his half-closed eyes.

'Shut up, Gray. We don't know who this woman is. She looks like police.'

'Undercover mum,' says Spliff Boy.

The lad with the beer can swipes him round the head. 'Don't be a dick.'

'This is Billy.' I unfold the flier I carry everywhere with me, and take a step towards them. It's very nearly dark now, the last of the sunlight is fading away and they peer through the firelight at the image of Billy's face. 'He's fifteen. He does . . . he's really into graffiti. Have you seen him? Recently, I mean?'

My question is met with shrugs and glazed looks.

I step around the group and crouch down next to Gray. The air surrounding him is thick with the scent of woodsmoke, weed and beer.

'You said you knew him. How?'

He inches away, pressing up against the boy sitting next to him.

'I know of him,' he says as he's shoved away. 'I heard of him.'

'How?'

'From the news, like.'

'Are you sure?' I look him straight in the eye but

he's unable, or unwilling, to meet my gaze and he fiddles with the laces of his trainers. 'Please, it's important. I know he's been here before. I know he wanted to tag the bridge. Have you seen or heard anything unusual?'

'Naz's face is unusual,' says Spliff Boy and they all laugh. Everyone apart from Gray who is twisting a lace round and round the index finger of his left hand. He's hiding something from me. If the others weren't here he'd tell me the truth. I feel sure of it.

I dip my head down to his and lower my voice. 'Could I just talk to you? Alone? Just for a minute?' I touch his shoulder and he jumps away from me, as though electrocuted, narrowly missing the fire as he scrambles to his feet.

'Whitey alert!' shouts Naz as Gray runs towards the river, then drops to his knees and pukes all over his hands. My heart sinks. He wasn't hiding anything from me – he was trying not to be sick.

I get to my feet, unsure whether I should check if he's okay or just go. Then, out of the corner of my eye, I notice Naz whispering something in Laughing Boy's ear. He stops talking the second I turn my head.

'What is it?' I say. 'It's Billy, isn't it? You know something about him?'

There's a sound from the bushes behind me. The sound of someone crashing through the undergrowth, snapping off twigs and scraping past branches in their desperation to escape.

*

'Billy?'

Bushes and brambles scratch at my chest, arms and hands as I force my way through them, following the sound. My dress catches on a brier. It rips as I tear it free and continue to run.

'Billy, stop! Stop!'

He's fast, so much faster than me. My smooth-soled sandals have no traction on the gnarly ground and I trip several times as I scramble through the near-darkness. The sound of laughter follows after me. Thorns tear at my palms and something sharp whips me across the cheek as I pick myself up and stumble after my son. He's been in the bushes the whole time, watching me, listening to me talk to the boys. Why would he run? Why?

'It's Mum! Billy, it's Mum!'

And then it stops. Almost as suddenly as it began, the noise of crashing and snapping stops. The only sound is the *thud, thud, thud* of my heartbeat pounding in my ears.

No, I can hear footsteps too. The faint pad of someone running. He must have made it onto the pathway.

'Billy, wait!' I wrap my arms over my head and plough through the bracken in the direction of the sound. My foot hits something solid, the path.

'Billy, it's—'

A hand grasps my wrist and a concerned face peers into mine. It's a woman's; she's roughly the same age as me, with her hair tied back in a ponytail. She's dressed in a neon vest, shorts and running trainers.

'Are you okay? I heard screaming and shouting coming from the bushes and—'

'Did you see him?' I look up and down the path but all I can see is near-darkness, stretching away from me in both directions.

'See who?'

'My—' Something brushes against my ankles; a border terrier with its tongue hanging out and bits of twig woven into its thick fur.

'Have you lost your dog?' the woman asks, following my line of vision. 'I thought a dog would be a great idea. He can come on runs with me, I said to my husband, but I think I'll have to start leaving him at home. He's a bugger for disappearing off into the bushes. I wouldn't have heard you shouting if I hadn't run back to see where he'd got to.' She crouches down and picks a piece of bark from his fur. 'You're a bugger. Aren't you? A little bugger.'

Chapter 22

I don't recognize the woman looking back at me from the bathroom mirror. She has dark circles under her eyes, sallow skin and two deep ridges between her brows where, only six months ago, there were light frown lines. But when I gently tap my fingers against my cheekbones, checking for pain or tenderness, the woman in the mirror does the same.

I covered myself in Savlon and arnica before I went to sleep and the scratch on my face has faded overnight, leaving behind the faintest of red marks along the length of my right cheekbone. There's a bruise on my collarbone too, where a branch smacked me straight in the chest, but it's mercifully small. I apply make-up to both areas, dabbing concealer onto the purple blemishes, and set it with powder. There's no disguising the deep scratches on my forearms – I look as though I've been in a fight with a wildcat – so I change out of the long-sleeved pyjama top I put on when I went to bed last night and pull on a pale blue shirt. Mark didn't comment on my injuries when he slid out of bed this morning. My right cheek was buried in the pillow and the rest of my body was hidden by my pyjamas and the duvet.

I attempt a smile and the woman in the mirror curves her lips in response but it doesn't reach her eyes. She looks tired and uneasy. I feel the same. I was an idiot for going out alone last night. I was lucky it was a group of teenage boys that I stumbled upon under the bridge, and not someone more dangerous. And what if I'd had another of my black-outs? No one knew where I'd gone. Anything could have happened to me.

The woman in the mirror shakes her head.

Liz was right. I need to stop looking for Billy and let the police do their job.

I reach for my phone, on the closed toilet lid, and reread the texts I missed when I was asleep.

Mum. 11.35 p.m.:

Hope this doesn't wake you. I don't suppose you found the photos, did you? The journalist is threatening to pull the story if we don't get them to him soon. Some crap about his work schedule and dead-lines. Want me to come and help you look?

Liz. 7.10 a.m.:

Don't suppose I could borrow your sonic screw-driver again, could I? I've got blisters on my blisters from trying to put together a bastard flat pack book-case.

Stephen. 7.15 a.m.:

Claire, there's a reason I said what I did. We need to talk. Give me a ring please. S.

The text from Stephen makes me feel twitchy. I still haven't told Mark what happened when I went back to work. I keep meaning to, but I can't find the right moment. Our relationship is so fragile I'm loath to bring up anything that could cause another argument.

I tap out my replies to Mum and Liz:

Hi Mum, I had a look the other day but I can't find it. Will another photo do? We've got lots of the two of them playing in the garden or on holiday. X

Course you can, Liz. It's in the garage somewhere. Are you still on lates? I'll drop it round in a bit if so.

I deliberate over Stephen's text. Do I want to reply? No. Do I want to talk to him? No. Do I care if he sacks me and I have to find a new job? Definitely not. He's a shit-stirrer and a troublemaker. No job is worth that.

Jake and Kira are in the kitchen. She's in a towelling dressing gown, munching on a piece of toast, whilst he's making the tea, already dressed for the day in his trademark uniform of scruffy jeans, sweatshirt and trainers. They remind me of me and Mark, pootling around in the kitchen of our first home, excited to have escaped from our parents' houses, joking that we were playing at being grown-ups.

I watch from the bottom of the stairs as Kira finishes her toast and drops her plate in the sink.

Jake watches as she turns on the tap, then abandons his tea-making and crosses the kitchen. He presses his body into hers and wraps his arms around her, then ducks down to kiss her on the side of the neck. She jolts in surprise and half-turns, the sweetest smile on her face, as she tilts her head to kiss him. Jake's hands move to the neckline of her dressing gown. He eases it down over her shoulders and I catch a glimpse of a bruise or a birthmark at the top of her spine.

I take a step backwards, suddenly embarrassed to be watching such a tender, intimate moment between my son and his girlfriend.

'Jake, don't!' Kira's shout is like a whip crack that cuts through the air and I knock into the table in the hallway, sending a plant crashing to the ground.

'Mum!' Jake turns round and Kira twists away, hugging the dressing gown around her neck.

'I'm sorry.' I crouch down to pick up the pot. It was plastic and hasn't broken but there's soil all over the carpet. 'I didn't mean to intrude – I was just . . .' I feel my face flush red. 'Sorry, I—'

'It's okay, Mum.' Jake glances at Kira, then shakes his head. 'It's cool. I'm off to work anyway.'

He reaches for his tool belt and straps it around his waist, then retrieves the dustpan and brush from under the sink and sweeps up the soil at my feet.

'You okay?' he says as he straightens up.

'I'm fine.'

'Cool. I'll see you later then, Mum.' He doesn't so much as glance at Kira as he crosses the kitchen. 'Oh –' he stops as he reaches the back door and looks back at me – 'I'm on a late-night job and I won't be back until eight at the earliest. Don't bother making me any tea. I'll grab a burger or something.'

As the back door clicks behind him Kira makes her escape.

'Sorry,' she mutters under her breath as she squeezes past me and thunders up the stairs, two at a time. 'I'm really sorry, Claire.'

I pick my way through the garage, sidling sideways past Jake's weight bench, stepping over the patch of lawnmower oil that Mark still hasn't cleared up, and approach the shelves. They're piled high with gardening and DIY paraphernalia: tins of assorted screws, half-empty pots of paint, crusted paintbrushes, rusty shears, trowels, netting and plastic plant pots.

I shift things around as I search. I find the drill and several ratchet and wrench sets the kids gave Mark for his birthday one year, but not the black plastic box containing the electric screwdriver that Liz wants to borrow.

There are several cardboard boxes crammed with clothes on the floor. We've been meaning to take them to the charity shop since we decluttered the house a year ago but no one's got round to doing it yet.

I open the flaps of the box nearest me and root around inside but it's all clothes, mostly mine. I open a second box and dip my hand inside, searching for anything hard and plastic, but my delving only reveals more clothing. My heart catches in my throat as the arm of a bright red football hoody rises to the surface.

It's Billy's. Mark bought it for him when he was twelve after a Bristol City match one weekend. We couldn't get Billy out of it. He wore it on top of his uniform on his way to school and over his T-shirt at the weekend. He continued to wear it even when his wrists poked out of the sleeves and he could no longer zip it up over his broad chest. He said he'd keep it for ever and then pass it on to his own kids. I couldn't believe it when I found it in one of the black bags during the declutter. I thought it was a mistake and put it back in his wardrobe.

'Mum,' he shouted, a couple of hours later. 'Why is this in my room?'

He dangled the top over the banister when I came out of the living room.

'Because it's your favourite top.'

'No, it's not. I hate football.'

He'd always been the first out of the door on match day, woolly hat on his head and scarf wound round his neck regardless of the weather, but he hadn't been to a City match with Mark and Jake for a while. He didn't even bother to shout goodbye to them when they left.

I tried not to read too much into it. Kids' passions can be fickle. When I was little I wanted to be a ballet dancer one year and an air hostess the next and I'd lost count of the number of toys that the boys had been obsessed with for months and then tossed aside, never to be played with again; but football was the one thing that bonded the three men in my life. It was their shared obsession. And then suddenly Billy didn't want to go any more. I didn't know if someone at school had teased him about his shrunken hoody or if his love of computer games had superseded his love of football but whenever I tried to talk to him about it he'd close like a clam.

As I yank on the arm of the hoody, something else rises to the surface of the box. The corner of a grey photo album. The one I was looking for. I tuck Billy's hoody under my arm and flip it open.

There's Jake and Billy at primary school, Jake aged nine proudly displaying his big teeth, Billy aged five, with his dark hair sticking up at ridiculous angles. I turn the next page, smiling at the memories and trying to ignore the sick feeling in my stomach. When I get to the middle of the book the school photos end. On the next page are photos of our last family holiday. Billy was thirteen. Jake was seventeen. We went to Weston for the day, then drove down to Bude in Cornwall to stay in a caravan for a week. There's a photo of the two of them sitting on the wall near Weston beach, both staring down at their mobiles. It was an awful holiday. The weather was terrible and with all of us cooped up together in a tiny caravan, the bickering reached new levels; Jake wound Billy up, calling him a little kid, and Billy bit back calling Jake a boring arsehole. Mark cracked before I did. He packed up the car after three days and said we were never going on another family holiday for as long as he lived.

I turn the page, wondering what's next.

My breath catches in my throat.

There's a photo of Mark and Jake having a beer under the awning as the skies opened. One of Billy and Mark messing about in the pool. Another one of us sitting around a table in the 'entertainment hall', giving the thumbs-down as we listened to the world's worst comedian. There are more recent photos too: of Mark and Jake when he graduated from college. Me, Mark and Kira with our arms around each other's shoulders, valiant after winning a game of bowling against the two boys.

Only Mark isn't in the photos any more. He's been blacked out, his face and his body obliterated by thick black marker pen. And there are words scrawled over the top of each photo – *WANKER*, *TOSSER*, *DICK*. I turn over page after page after page but they're all the same; Mark has been blanked out from each and every image. It's as though he no longer exists.

Friday 10th October 2014

Jackdaw44: *Hey.*
Jackdaw44: *Hello?*
Jackdaw44: *You there?*
Jackdaw44: *I know you're reading these messages.*
Jackdaw44: *Oi!*
Jackdaw44: 😮
Jackdaw44: 🙁
Jackdaw44: *You suck. Just like everyone else in my life. I thought you were different.*

Chapter 23

Why is Mark blacked out in every photo in the album? Who did that? And why hide it at the bottom of the charity box? It doesn't make any sense.

Pain rips through the side of my head and I screw my eyes tightly shut to block it out.

Did Billy do it? But why? What could Mark possibly have done to make him that angry?

CLAIRE!

I jolt at the sound of my name and smack my knee against the driving column but there is no one sitting next to me in the car. The windows are still wound tightly shut. No one is knocking on the glass. No one is outside the car looking in. The street is still quiet. And the keys swing back and forth in the ignition. Back and forth. Back and forth.

Did Mark come back from the pub early, drunk and angry? Did Billy say something awful? Something so awful that Mark lashed out? Is that why Billy defaced his photos? Because his dad hit him? But why would he hide the album in the garage? Why not destroy it?

The pain spreads across my forehead and I clutch my hands to my head. My brain is in a vice that's being wound tighter and tighter and tighter. I can hear it. The vice. It makes a high-pitched squeal, like metal on metal. I plug my fingers into my ears but the sound gets louder.

'CLAIRE! I AM CLAIRE!' The voice cuts through the metallic screech but I keep my eyes closed. I need to think. If I could just think clearly I could work out what this means.

Did Mark threaten to hit him again? Is that why Billy fled? Is that why he didn't take anything with him? He was afraid and he ran. Or was he taken? Did Mark hit him too hard? Did he panic? Did he try and get him to a hospital and then . . .

'*Mum? Help me, Mum!*'

The scream goes through me, cutting through the whine and whirr of the vice. Brakes squeal. Something flies through the air, hurtling towards the car, and I bury my face in my arms. There is a thump as something hits the bonnet and the whole car shakes. A loud crack follows and I am showered with glass.

And then silence.

A silence that seems to last for ever.

Whatever just happened was so terrible, so traumatic, I know that there is no way I can have survived it.

Silence.

The traffic doesn't roar. The road doesn't shake. The birds don't sing and no one speaks.

I peel myself from the steering wheel and raise my head.

A body lies slumped across the bonnet, one arm twisted behind its back, the other reaching for me. I can't see a face, just the back of a head, the dark hair slick with blood. The face is angled away from me, towards the doors of the doctor's surgery.

My hands shake as I fumble with the seat belt. Glass shards fall from my thighs and tumble into the foot well as I grip the steering wheel and ease myself up.

'Billy? Billy is that—'

I clutch my hands to my head as a pain unlike anything I have ever known tears through my brain. And then everything goes black.

There is something hard and leathery under my fingertips. Curved, solid. I grip on to it as my vision zooms in, zooms out, zooms in, zooms out. Focused, blurred, focused, blurred. The windscreen – clean apart from a dribble of bird shit, a street, a building, a road, the windscreen. Why do I keep looking at the windscreen? An image flashes through my mind, of Billy's lifeless body on the dashboard. I thought I'd run him over but I can't have. There's no glass, no blood and the windscreen is still intact. A wave of nausea courses through me. It's so powerful, so sudden, that I vomit over the dashboard, the steering wheel and my hands. The world spins and I squeeze my eyes tightly shut as the car fills with the stench of puke.

A voice whispers, 'It was another blackout. Oh God. Not again.'

My voice.

My name is . . .

I search for a name, for something solid to hang my identity on, but my mind is so muddled, so grey. There is nothing behind my eyes but inky darkness.

Who am I?

My chest tightens and I gulp air into my lungs. Breathe slower.

Claire!

I open my eyes.

Claire. My name is Claire Wilkinson. There is a gold band and a sparkling engagement ring on the third finger of my left hand, smeared with bile. I am married to Mark. I have two sons. Jake and Billy. Billy!

I undo the seat belt and open the driver's-side door. There is a flash of colour, a squeal of brakes and someone swears loudly.

'Fuck's sake!' A face in a bicycle helmet looms towards me, a man's face, his eyes wide with anger, his lips twisted into a snarl. He waves in front of my face, slicing his hand through the air. 'Watch what you're fucking doing. You nearly had me off my bike.'

I am so shocked, so terrified, I swing a leg out of the car and kick out at him. My shoe connects with his knee and he jumps back, doubling over, one hand pressed to his knee, the other wrapped around the handlebar of his bike.

I slam the door shut before he can recover and

turn the key in the ignition. I press my foot to the accelerator and the car lurches forward. Somewhere behind me someone presses their horn. The sound reverberates in my head as I speed away, the cyclist shaking his fist at me in my rear-view mirror. There's a woman standing beside him, a white Vauxhall Astra pulled up behind her. She's got her phone in her hand.

I drive down street after street. I don't know where I am or where I'm going. There are no thoughts in my mind, just an angry buzzing as though my head is a hive, crammed with bees.

There's a light, blinking red on the dashboard. I'm running out of petrol. I need to stop. I need to find a garage. The buzzing in my head dims as I pull in to a large Tesco but, instead of parking by one of the petrol pumps at the service station, I drive into the car park and turn off the engine. I pull a packet of wet wipes out of the glovebox and wipe my hands, the steering wheel and my jeans. I work methodically; wiping, then dropping the used wipes into an empty plastic bag until I am clean. Then I reach for my bag. It's on the passenger seat. Underneath it is a photo album and an A4 diary, opened at today's week.

Mark's appointment book.

Why have I got Mark's appointment book? He normally keeps it on his desk in the corner of the living room. Did I take it? He's methodical about diary-keeping, entering everything into this book as well as his phone, just in case his phone dies or is stolen. I open it and run a finger down the appointments he's got listed for today:

9.45 a.m. – Fallodon Way Medical Centre, 3 Fallodon Way, BS9 4HT

10.45 a.m. – Nevil Road Surgery, 43 Nevil Road, BS7 9EG

11.45 a.m. – Horfield Health Centre, Lockleaze Road, BS7 9RR

2 p.m. – Gloucester Road Medical Centre, BS7 8SA

Where am I? I open my handbag and take out my phone. It's 2.30 p.m., Friday 14th August. Five hours have passed since I went into the garage to look for the screwdriver set and . . .

I see an image in my mind of a photo album, the photos defaced and scrawled on, but that's it. That's all there is.

I must have gone back into the house and picked up Mark's diary but I don't remember doing that. Or getting into my car and driving. Oh my God. I could have killed myself. Or someone else.

I look back at the phone and open Google Maps. The red location dot blinks several times, then the map comes into focus. Tesco Lime Trees Road. So I am still in Bristol. I enter one of the postcodes from Mark's diary into the app and a tiny red line appears, connecting my location with the address I've just entered. It's three minutes' drive away. I zoom in on the location and turn on street view. That's where I was just parked, outside Gloucester Road Medical Centre. Did Mark ring me and ask me to bring his diary to him? It's the only logical explanation but it only takes twenty-five minutes to drive from Knowle to Gloucester Road. What else have I been doing in the last five hours?

I exit the Google Maps app and I'm just about to ring Mark when I spot the WhatsApp icon at the top of the screen. Someone's sent me a message in the last five hours. I tap on the icon and Liz's name appears on the top of the list. Three new messages:

Where is that?

She's replied to a photo of a row of houses I must have sent her. One of them has a sign outside that says *Fallodon Way Medical Centre*.

Why have you sent me a picture of a doctor's surgery? Do you need me to pick you up or something?

Then there's another image. One I must have sent. It says *Nevil Road Surgery* above the door.

Claire? Is that Mark? Who is he with?

I look closer at the photo. Yes, it is Mark and he's standing outside Nevil Road Surgery with a willowy blonde. His hand is on her arm. I zoom in on the image. It takes me several seconds to work out who she is. It's Edie Christian, Billy's form tutor. And she looks worried.

Friday 24th October 2014

Jackdaw44: *Why have you started ignoring me?*
ICE9: *I haven't. I'm busy.*
Jackdaw44: 💩
ICE9: *What's that supposed to mean?*
Jackdaw44: *Bullshit. You're not busy.*
ICE9: *OK. Truth. This feels a bit weird.*
Jackdaw44: *What do you mean?*
ICE9: *Us. Texting all the time. Sneaking off for secret beers. It feels . . . weird.*
Jackdaw44: *We're not doing anything wrong. Just talking. Nothing wrong with talking.*
ICE9: *It feels dangerous.*
Jackdaw44: *How?*
ICE9: *You know what I mean.*
Jackdaw44: 👻
ICE9: *So you do know what I mean.*
Jackdaw44: *I know nothing. I like hanging out with you. End of.*

ICE9: *I still feel weird about it.*
Jackdaw44: *There's a cure for that.* 🍺!
ICE9: *Not today.*
Jackdaw44: *You suck.*

Chapter 24

'Claire?' I jump as Liz knocks on the window of the car. Her hair is tied up in a messy topknot and there's a smear of eyeliner smudged into the creases beneath her right eye. She looks as though she's just woken up from a nap.

'Can you open it?' she mouths, signalling for me to wind down the window. I turn the handle.

'Oh my God, Claire.' She reaches through the gap and wraps her arms around my head, pulling me up against the door as she attempts to hug me. 'I can't believe it happened again.'

She lets me go, glances at the keys dangling in the ignition and holds up a hand as though warning me not to touch them. 'I'm coming round the other side.'

She skirts around the front of the car, opens the passenger door, picks up my handbag, the photo album and Mark's diary and plonks herself into the seat.

'Are you okay?' She sounds breathless from her run across the car park. 'You're not hurt or anything?'

'I'm not hurt.'

She looks me up and down as though she can't quite believe what she's seeing. 'You drove all the way across Bristol and you can't remember it? Fuck, Claire! That's really scary.'

'I know.'

'You can't remember anything at all?'

'Nothing.'

'Right.' She gives me a long look. I can tell she's freaked out, even though she's trying hard not to show it. 'I think I need to get you to a doctor. Are you okay to drive? Silly question. I'll drive the car. Caleb can pick mine up later.'

As we head back to Knowle I tell her everything I can remember, about the photo album, about finding myself parked in a street I didn't recognize, about the guy on the bike, speeding off, running out of petrol and checking my phone. I don't tell her about seeing Billy's dead body on the bonnet of my car.

'And then I rang you,' I say.

'Fucking hell, Claire.' She presses her foot to the accelerator as the traffic light turns green. 'I don't know what to say. When you WhatsApped me that first photo I thought maybe you'd taken it by accident or pressed the wrong button or something but then you sent a few more and I thought you were having a laugh but I didn't get the joke.'

She gives me a sideways look. 'Who's the blonde in the photo with Mark?'

'Edie Christian, Billy's form tutor.'

'Why did you take a photo of them? Is he having an affair or something?'

'I don't know. I can't remember anything. Oh my God.' I cover my mouth with my hands as the cars in front slow to a near halt and a cyclist overtakes us. 'What if the cyclist has reported me to the police for kicking him? The woman who stopped her car had a phone in her hand. She probably took a photo of my numberplate. The press will have a field day if they find out what I did.'

'It's okay.' Liz taps me on the leg, then puts her hand back on the steering wheel. 'You're ill. You didn't know what you were doing. Is that the photo album you were on about?' She glances at the two books on my lap. 'Can I see it?'

'Of course.' I open a page and hold it up so she can see. The traffic in front of us is still at a standstill.

'Jesus Christ, Claire. Who did that?'

'Billy, I think. The writing looks like his and it's the same sort of thick black marker he uses.'

'But why?'

'I don't know.'

'I thought the police searched the house?'

'They did, but only places they thought he could be hiding. Then they took his laptop and his Xbox from his bedroom but they didn't go through our stuff. They didn't go anywhere near the garage.'

'It's pretty macabre.' She runs a finger over one of the blacked-out figures and her eyes meet mine. 'I think you should tell them. Don't you?'

Monday 3rd November 2014

ICE9: *I can't do this any more.*
Jackdaw44: *Oh FFS. Not this again.*
ICE9: *No, not this. My relationship. I feel claustrophobic and trapped. I'm not happy.*
Jackdaw44: *So leave.*
ICE9: *I can't.*
Jackdaw44: *We could get a place together. I fucking hate living at home.*
ICE9: *You live on another planet.*
Jackdaw44: *What's that supposed to mean?*
ICE9: *It's a ridiculous idea.*
Jackdaw44: *Why?*
ICE9: *I'm miserable and you're not helping.*
Jackdaw44: *Sorry.*
Jackdaw44: *Let's both sneak out and go for a beer.*
ICE9: *OK. Meet you at the Victoria at 9 p.m.*

Chapter 25

Every seat in the waiting room has been filled and the air is ripe with coughs, sneezes and the occasional wail from a bored toddler or hungry baby. Liz had to do battle with the receptionist to get me an appointment. I would have given up after the initial 'There are no appointments left' but she wasn't deterred. Not even when the receptionist suggested that perhaps we would be better off going to the walk-in centre if I was having a 'psychiatric episode' as Liz put it. The poor woman eventually relented when Liz mentioned that I'd had my bloods taken at the surgery and that, if anyone knew what was wrong with me, it would be the doctor who had those results on her computer. We've been here over forty minutes so far and, during that time, my best friend has asked me twice if I'd like her to ring Mum or Jake and four times if I'm 'having another funny turn' because I look 'weird'.

'Look, here.' She jabs a nail at an article in the magazine she's reading. 'This is Tinder, that app Marco told me about.'

'Sorry?'

'The dating app. The one for straight people. I don't know why Caleb lied to me about meeting him on Grindr. I don't care if he met him in a pub or online. Just as long as he's safe.'

'Right.'

For the last ten minutes Liz has been filling me in on her night out with her son and his new boyfriend. According to Liz, Marco was an absolute scream and she couldn't have picked someone better for Caleb herself. Her exact words were, '*Marco's young, dark and fit. If he wasn't gay I might have gone for him myself.*'

She nudges me. 'So do you think I should download it then? Give it a go?'

'Sure, why not?'

'What's up?' She closes the magazine and twists round in her seat so she can get a better look at me.

'I was just . . .' I lower my voice. 'Just trying to decide what to do about the photo album.'

'Do you want me to drive you to the police station, after we're done here?'

I shake my head. 'I need to talk to Mark about it.'

'Are you sure that's a good idea?'

'No, but what if there's a completely innocent explanation for it? Mark's always going on about how he's the villain and if I go straight to the police that's exactly what I'm doing, isn't it? Painting him as the villain without giving him the chance to explain. I don't even know if it was Billy who blacked out the photos.'

'Who else would do that?'

Kira, I think, but don't say. I hate myself for even considering what Stephen said about Mark and the fact that there's a young girl who walks around our house in various states of undress but it's there – it's rooted in my brain and it's not going away. I am ninety-nine per cent certain that Stephen made that comment because he's a shit-stirrer, but what if I'm wrong? What if Mark did say or do something inappropriate? I don't want to believe it. I won't let myself believe it but someone vandalized those photos and I need to see the look on Mark's face when I show them to him.

'Mrs Wilkinson?' Dr Evans sticks her head around the door.

'That's me!' I gather up my bag and cardi and hurry towards her.

'This is my friend Liz,' I say as I draw closer. 'Is it okay if she comes in with me? For moral support?'

'Of course.' Dr Evans gestures for us to follow her into her office. 'We're in here.'

As she rounds the desk and Liz sits down in one of the patient chairs the words spill out of me like water from a dam. 'Thank you so much for fitting me in, Dr Evans. I know you're busy and my appointment wasn't for a couple of days but I had another blackout and—'

'One second.' She holds up a hand and glances at

her screen. 'Mrs Wilkinson. Claire. Can I call you Claire?'

I nod.

'Sorry for interrupting, Claire. I just want to get up to speed.' She twists round to face her computer, frowning as she scrolls down the screen. 'Okay.'

She turns back. 'So you're here for the results of your recent blood test, is that right? You had an amnesiac episode on the sixth of August?'

'Yes, eight days ago, that's right.'

'Okay. So . . .' She leans forward, resting her weight on her elbows, and I instinctively press my back into my chair, bracing myself for the verdict. 'The good news is that all your tests have come back clear.'

Liz squeezes my hand. 'Well, that's good news.'

'Yes, it is.' Dr Evans's eyes don't leave my face. 'I would like to refer you for a CAT scan though, just to be sure.'

'You think it's a brain tumour?'

'I think it's more likely that it's stress-related, but I wouldn't be doing my job if I didn't rule out every possibility.'

'How long will I have to wait for an appointment?'

'A few weeks. Maybe five or six.'

'Six weeks!' Liz says and I shush her.

'The thing is, Dr Evans, it's happened twice now. I had another one today. A couple of hours ago. I'd been driving and I can't even remember getting into my car. I can't wait six weeks. What if it happens again?'

Dr Evans's expression becomes grave. 'I see. Okay.'

She glances towards the window and taps her nails against her teeth. 'Claire, have you had any other unusual thoughts or seen any other unusual things?'

'What kinds of things?'

'Things that wouldn't normally be there?'

'Like a hallucination?'

'Yes.'

'During my last blackout I saw . . .' I can't tell her that I imagined running over my son. 'I saw something that wasn't real.'

Liz gives me a sideways look but says nothing.

'I see,' Dr Evans says. 'And have you ever seen anything you've attributed special meaning to?'

'I don't know what you mean.'

'Have you ever interpreted something you've seen as some kind of sign, some kind of special message, aimed at you?'

Liz sits very still, looking intently at me, and I tug at the sleeves of my shirt. I haven't told her that I went looking for Billy last night.

'There have been a couple of occasions when I thought I saw Billy,' I say quietly, wishing I hadn't brought my best friend in with me. I hate her seeing me like this. She must think I'm cracking up. 'Billy's my son who's missing. I saw someone on his bike and I went after him.'

'Hmmm.' Dr Evans's frown deepens. 'And have you ever heard voices, Claire?'

'No.' I shake my head, suddenly agitated. 'I'm not schizophrenic. I'm not mad. I just . . . I just don't want to black out again.'

'No one's saying you're mad, Claire, but you have been under a lot of stress recently and I think a referral to the community mental-health team might help.'

Mental-health team? That sounds scary. Liz leans forward in her chair. 'How long's the waiting list?'

Dr Evans grimaces.

'Worse than the CAT scan?'

'I could make it an urgent referral. They might be able to see you in the next few weeks.'

I grip the arms of the chair. Anything could happen to me in the next few weeks. 'Is there no one else I could see? We can't afford to go private but I could borrow some money.'

Dr Evans gives me a sympathetic smile. 'I'm sorry, Claire. It's as frustrating for me as it is for you and I wish there was some way of speeding things up but the NHS is stretched to—'

'I'll pay!' Liz says. 'I've got a bit put away, from when Mum died. It's yours, Claire.'

'No.' I shake my head. 'I couldn't.'

'Think of it as a loan if that makes you feel better. You'll go back to work eventually and, when you do, you can pay me back.'

Dr Evans looks from Liz to me and presses her lips together.

'If you're desperate to see someone you could Google Bristol-based psychotherapists who specialize in stress and anxiety disorders. I'm afraid I can't recommend anyone specifically but make sure they've got proper accreditation. And in the meantime I'll put in the referrals for you. I'll do

181

everything I can to get you seen sooner rather than later.'

'There you go then,' Liz says, half-rising from her seat. 'Everything's going to be fine. Isn't it, Claire?'

'Yes.' I force myself to smile.

I'm not sure who I'm lying to. Her, or myself.

Chapter 26

Kira sniffs the air as she shuffles through the back door, bent almost double under the weight of her camera equipment, but there is no chicken in the oven, no spaghetti bolognese bubbling away on the stove. There are no knives and forks laid out on trays. No cookbooks propped open on the kitchen counter with a spoon. It's been half an hour since I left Liz's house and came home. We spent what was left of the afternoon together, sitting in her living room watching old episodes of *Friends* and drinking tea. She said she wasn't going to let me leave until Jake came home so I lied and said he was getting back early today. The truth was I needed some time to myself, time to just think.

'Oh.' Kira pauses in the entrance to the kitchen and glances up at the clock. Her pale skin looks almost translucent under the glow of the spotlight, her hair loose around her shoulders, a black silk lily clipped behind her left ear. 'Did I miss tea? I'm sorry I'm late but the bus was delayed and—'

'We're not having tea tonight.'

'Oh.' She carefully lowers her camera equipment to the floor and rubs at her right shoulder with the heel of her left hand. 'Takeaway, is it? Or would you like me to cook?'

My right foot judders up and down on the lower bar of the stool I'm sitting on. *Shake-shake-shake. Shake-shake-shake.* I focus on it, willing it to stop and it does just for a split second before starting up again.

'Could I ask you a favour, Kira?'

'Of course.' She shuffles from foot to foot. She reminds me of a horse, edgy, quick to startle, unpredictable. She needs careful handling, a deft, confident hand, and I'm not the right person to do it. I've never ridden a horse in my life. Never raised a daughter either. Not that Kira's mother did any better. It angers me how much damage that woman did to her own child.

'Is there a friend you could go out with for a few hours? I can give you some money for the pub or the cinema or something.'

'When?'

'Now.'

She glances out of the kitchen window, her lips part ever so slightly and then there's the distinctive *clack-clack-clack* of her tongue stud against the back of her front teeth. 'Where's Mark?'

Why is she asking where he is? Does she feel uncomfortable being alone in the house with me? Or is she hoping he's not home?

'Mark's still at work,' I say. 'But he'll be back soon.'

'Right. Okay, then.' She crouches down, grabs the strap of her photography bag and hauls it back onto her shoulder. 'I'll just dump this lot upstairs and get changed and then I'll—'

'Kira.' I stand up. 'There's something I need to ask you.'

'Oh God.' She lowers her head, cringing into herself.

'It's not about what I saw this morning,' I say quickly. 'In fact, I should apologize to you. I know you and Jake don't get much privacy in this house and—'

'Don't worry about it.' She tries to move past me.

I step to my right, forcing her to stop. 'Hang on a second.'

'What is it?' There's a pained expression on her face now. It's the same one I'd see on Billy's face whenever I asked him if we could have a chat about school or whether he had a girlfriend.

'Do you know anything about that?' I point at the photo album on the kitchen table.

'What is it?'

'A photo album.'

She shakes her head. 'Should I?'

'Some of the photos have been defaced. Do you know anything about it?'

'No.' She stares at me with huge, round, uncomprehending eyes. 'Why would I? I'm a photography student – I take photos. I don't destroy them. That goes against—'

'Okay.' I reach out to touch her, to reassure her, but my hand falls back to my side before it makes

185

contact with her arm. 'I'm not accusing you of anything. I was just wondering if Jake or Billy or –' my throat is so dry it hurts to swallow – 'Mark said anything to you about them?'

Again she moves to step around me and reaches for the album.

'Please don't.'

She snatches back her hand. 'Why?'

'I'd rather you didn't.'

She inches forward, her eyes trained on the photo album, her slender body rigid apart from the fingers of her right hand which twitch against the thin denim of her skirt.

'What's in it?'

'Just family photos. The boys at school, family holidays, that sort of thing.' I move so I am standing between her and the album, the stool pressing against the backs of my thighs. As Liz pointed out earlier, if it is evidence then we've already contaminated it by touching it. The police will want to take fingerprints. That's if I do give it to the police.

'You said they'd been defaced,' she says. 'How?'

'I've said too much, Kira. I'm sorry. I don't know what any of this means. I only found the album this morning. I'm still trying to decide what to do.'

Her eyes meet mine. 'Are you going to take it to the police?'

'I don't know.'

Her gaze flicks towards the kitchen window again. The only car in the street is Liz's. 'Does Mark know about it?'

'Not yet. That's why it would be easier if we had the house to ourselves. Here –' I reach round for my handbag and pull out my purse – 'twenty pounds. Take it. It's the least I can do for kicking you out.'

Kira shakes her head. 'I don't want it, Claire. Honestly, it's fine.'

She returns to where she left her camera equipment, picks it up and heads for the hallway. She pauses at the entrance and glances back at me, then at the photo album, then her footsteps *thump-thump-thump* up the stairs as she heads for her room.

'So what do you think?' Mum asks and I have no idea what she's talking about. It's been half an hour since Kira left the house with a small rucksack over her shoulder and a resigned look on her face but I'm still standing at the kitchen window. I texted Jake after she left and explained that I'd had another blackout but that I was okay. No point telling him what I found in the garage or on my phone until I know what I'm dealing with. I didn't text Mark. I need to talk to him face to face about what happened. Seconds after I messaged Jake the phone rang.

'Sorry, Mum. I was miles away. What do I think about what?'

'About the psychic.'

'What psychic?'

She exhales heavily and the sound makes a hissing noise in my ear. 'The one I just told you about.'

'I'm sorry, Mum. I wasn't listening. I was . . .'

'You're not still worrying about the backlash after

the appeal, are you? I told you, I've got that in hand. I was telling you about the email I received from a psychic. I've got it in my handbag. Shall I read it out to you?'

I hear the sound of a zip being pulled, then a clattering sound, presumably as she tips the contents of her bag over the floor or table. Mum's predilection for filling her handbag with absolute crap is the last-gasp hoorah of a horrible hoarding habit that lasted until I hit my teens. When people ask me what my childhood was like I tell them that I shared it with my mum, dad, a dog, two cats and 'the clutter'. According to Dad the first house they bought together was clean and tidy for all of an hour. And then Granddad turned up in his battered van and brought out box after box of Mum's stuff. She moved everything in – her childhood toys, every book and magazine she'd ever been given, every drawing she'd done at school, dried-up make-up and empty toiletries bottles and a mountain of clothes. Mum's family were poor and she inherited the 'make do and mend' mentality from her own mother but, unlike Gran who'd actually mend and use the things she wouldn't part with, Mum kept everything; piling it all up in bin bags, filling the hall, the utility room and every available space in our bedrooms.

Mum and Dad argued a lot back then, about the mess, about the fact that Dad spent most nights down the pub. I was constantly afraid that my parents were going to split up. Now they seem happier than they've ever been. Maybe Dad got used to Mum's messy ways, or maybe she made an effort to change, or perhaps they just learned how to rub along together. They've been together for forty-five years.

I press a hand to the side of my head. 'Mum, I told you. No more stuff from psychics. Please.'

'But it says here that she's worked on some very high-profile cases with the police and they've helped retrieve the bodies of—'

'Mum!'

'They weren't all dead, mind,' she adds quickly. 'She's found runaways too. All she needs is something of Billy's, something he—'

'Wore or loved and touched frequently so she can tune in to his vibes. I know, Mum. We've heard it all before.'

She sighs. 'But she's provided a whole page-worth of testimonies from people she's helped.'

We were inundated with offers of hope from psychics after Billy first disappeared. I warily welcomed them into my kitchen and sobbed and sobbed as they consulted their cards or their runes or their stones or simply stood in the middle of the room with their eyes closed and told me how in tune they were with my distress and how the spirits would lead us to Billy. They told me that he was alive and well and living in a squat in Milton Keynes. They told me he was trapped in an underground cave in North Wales or held in a cellar against his will. They said he was in deep water, in the earth, across the sea. Alive. Dead. Alive. Dead. Hope. Despair. Hope. Despair.

I went from psychic to psychic, desperately hoping

that this time we'd find one that wasn't a fraud. I spent half the money we'd saved over the course of our twenty-year marriage paying for Jake to go to Wales, Milton Keynes and Dover to look for his brother. I went to seances. Dozens of them. Mark refused to come with me so I went with Liz or Mum instead. I was convinced that the next seance would be the one that would reveal Billy's whereabouts. And then a psychic told me that Billy had committed suicide. '*Why didn't you save me, Mummy?*' he wailed in the voice of a much younger child. '*You could have saved me, Mummy.*' I stopped going after that.

'Okay. All right.' I hear rustling as Mum shoves the piece of paper back into her bag. 'I understand. I don't mean to clutch at straws but it's been a while since we've had an email through the website. It's gone very quiet on the Facebook page too.'

I start at the sound of tyres on gravel. Mark's Ford Focus is pulling up outside.

'It's okay, Mum. I know you're trying to help and I'm sorry if I snapped. It's been a tough day today, you know?'

'Is there anything me and your dad can do?'

'You're doing so much already. I couldn't get through this without you, you know that, don't you?'

'We do, bab. We just wish that none of this had ever happened.'

'I know,' I say as the car draws to a halt and the engine noise dies. 'Can I give you a ring back tomorrow, Mum? Have a longer chat?'

'Of course you can.'

'I love you, Mum. Dad too.'

'Speak soon, love. Take it steady.'

As I press the end-call button, Mark walks through the door, his briefcase in one hand, his jacket thrown over his shoulder and the neck of his shirt undone.

'Everything okay? I saw you on the phone from the driveway—' His gaze flickers towards the kitchen table, and the photo album sitting on top of it. 'What's that?'

'One of our photo albums.'

We have been married for just over twenty years and, in that time, I have seen my husband's face register dozens of emotions – fear, regret, anger, happiness, sadness and pride – but there haven't been many occasions when I've seen him look the way he looks now, with the colour bleached from his cheeks.

He doesn't ask me where I found it or who I think put it there. Instead he puts down his briefcase on the chair by the door and folds his jacket neatly over the arm. He traces a finger over the edge of the album but he doesn't pick it up.

'You've seen what's inside, haven't you?' His question is little more than a whisper.

'Yes.'

'Have you rung the police?'

'Not yet.'

'"Yet" being the operative word.' He laughs drily.

A bead of sweat dribbles down my lower back. 'Tell me what it means, Mark.'

He laughs again. It's a low rolling sound in the back of his throat. 'Your guess is as good as mine.'

'Why are you laughing?'

His laughter halts and he presses his lips together but the edges turn upwards, his cheeks bulging as he smiles.

'Mark, talk to me. Tell me what you know about the photo album. Tell me what it means or I'll ring the police.'

His smile vanishes instantly. 'Go on then.' He nods towards the phone in my hand. 'Ring them.'

Why is he being so weird? I prepared myself for all kinds of reactions – denial, blame, shock, regret – but not this one. Not a smile and a strange, glassy stare.

'No, Mark, you ring them!'

He ducks as I hurl the phone across the kitchen. It smashes against the wall and then drops to the floor. The battery door scuttles back across the tiles towards me as the phone spins round and round before it finally lies still under the kitchen table.

'Jesus Christ, Claire!' Mark stares at me in shock and I'm pleased. Finally, he's acting normally.

'Tell me what you know about that!' My hand shakes as I point towards the photo album. 'Now. Or our marriage is over.'

'What's the point? You've already decided that I'm the villain of the—'

'Stop with the "villain" shit, Mark! What is it with you and that word? You throw it at me every time we have an argument and I'm sick of it.' I drop to my knees and reach under the table for the phone. 'If you won't speak to me maybe you'll speak to the police.'

'No.' There's a screech of wood on tile as he shoves a chair away from the table and reaches beneath it for my hand. His thick fingers are around mine before they can make contact with the phone. 'Don't.'

'Tell me what's going on.'

'Okay.' His grip softens. 'Okay.'

Tuesday 4th November 2014

Jackdaw44: *You kissed me.*
ICE9: *I was drunk.*
Jackdaw44: *Not that drunk.*
ICE9: *I fucked up. I'm sorry.*
Jackdaw44: *I can't believe you kissed me.*
ICE9: *Please don't tell anyone.*
ICE9: *Are you still there?*
ICE9: *Say something! I'm sorry.*
Jackdaw44: *You already said that.*
ICE9: *Please don't tell anyone what happened. I was drunk and lonely and I felt a connection with you. I made a mistake. It won't happen again.*
Jackdaw44: *Chill out. I won't tell anyone.*
Jackdaw44: *P.S. Now we both have a secret.*

Chapter 27

'I found the album in Billy's room,' Mark says, sitting forward on the sofa, his fingers interlocked between his knees. 'Before he went missing.'

I am sitting on the opposite end of the sofa, a cushion clutched to my chest. 'When?'

'A few months before he disappeared. It was a couple of days after Mr Edwards called us in to talk about the graffiti. The second time he called us in. I wanted to check Billy didn't have any graffiti pens or cans stashed in his room.'

'Where was Billy?'

'In town with you. It was a Saturday and you were getting him some new shoes for school.'

I remember the trip. I dragged Billy around shop after shop while he rejected every single pair of shoes I pointed out, telling me they were sad or gay, arguing that he should be allowed to buy the 'sick' pair of black trainers he liked because 'everyone else wears them' and anyway, 'clothes should express who you are'. Wearing the same uniform was enforced conformity, he told me. 'If I wanted that I'd join the fucking army.'

By the end of the trip we were both fed up and irritable. He refused to wear the shoes I bought him, preferring to slump around in his old knackered pair with the worn-down heels.

'I found the photo album under his bed, face down,' Mark says. 'I saw what he'd done to the photos.'

'And you didn't mention it when we got home? Not to me or Billy? It's not like you to avoid pulling him up on something like that.'

Mark exhales heavily. 'You're not the only one to get sick of the arguments, Claire.'

'I don't buy that. Not for one second.'

'My dad was still recuperating from his heart attack, work was a nightmare and we were arguing. I didn't need the stress. Neither did you. I thought the best thing to do was to hide the album until I had the time to go through the photos and take out the ones Billy had defaced and then put it back on the bookcase.'

'Why hide it in the boxes in the garage?'

'Because they were there. I just shoved it in the bottom where no one would see it. I didn't want it to upset you.'

'What if I'd taken the boxes to the charity shop?'

Mark shrugs. 'I didn't think. It was just a temporary thing. I was going to get it out again and then . . . stuff happened, life carried on and I forgot. I just forgot, Claire.'

I give him a long look. He was incredibly stressed a few months before Billy disappeared but Mark being Mark he refused to discuss it with me. Maybe finding the photo album was one step too far. 'But why would he do that? Why would he black you out of the photos and write those things?'

He unknits his fingers and gazes down at his hands, as though the answer lies in his cupped palms. 'Why did he stop wanting to go to football with me? Why did he start walking out of the room whenever I walked in? I don't . . .' Mark's voice cracks and, as he coughs to try and regain it, a well of sadness opens up within me. 'I keep telling myself that it's one of those things that happen between fathers and sons. I clashed with my dad when I was in my teens. I called him far worse things than "wanker" and "tosser" – never to his face though – and I told myself that would never happen with my sons.'

'It didn't happen with Jake.'

'No, it didn't happen with Jake. That's why I couldn't understand it. Imagine, Claire. Imagine if you opened up that album and saw what I saw but it was you he'd blacked out. Imagine if it was you Billy hated?'

Was it the Sunday lunch? Was that what sparked such anger in our younger son? When Mark tore the two boys apart, bellowing that they were an embarrassment to the family? Or was it when Mr Edwards called us in to the school to tell us about the graffiti incident and Mark said to Billy, 'What's wrong with you? Why can't you just toe the line and do what you're fucking told?' Mr Edwards was visibly shocked. He said he didn't think swearing and accusations were a helpful way forward, but I could see the effect Mark's words had on Billy. When he was younger he had such a strong sense of justice. Once, when Jake came home from school with a black eye, Billy was so upset that he burst into tears. Mark was horrified and kept telling him to pull himself together, repeating over and over again that only girls cried and he needed to toughen up if he wanted to be a man. Billy looked up into his daddy's face and fought to control his wobbling chin, swallowing back the tears that shook his little body.

'Good boy,' Mark said when he finally quietened. 'Proud of you.'

Billy's little face lit up and my heart twisted with pain. Why shouldn't he cry? He was only eight years old.

'You should have . . .' The sentence dries up on my tongue. I want to tell Mark that he should have talked to Billy about it, that he should have got to the bottom of whatever it was that upset him so much he felt the need to deface the photo album, but I can't bring myself to say the words. It'll just rub salt in the wound. It won't make him feel any better about it. If anything, it will make him feel worse. And it won't bring Billy back.

I slump back against the sofa, suddenly exhausted.

'Are you sure?' I say. 'Are you absolutely sure that nothing happened to make Billy do that to your photos? An argument you haven't told me about? A fight? A grounding I don't know about? Something you took from him?'

He frowns down at his hands, then turns his head to look at me. He blinks slowly, several times, and his frown deepens. 'What are you accusing me of, Claire?'

I don't know. Mark has never raised his hand to Billy; he's never hit either of the boys. He's lost his temper countless times but he's never done more than shout at them.

'You think I'm behind his disappearance, don't you?' he says. 'You meant what you said the other day.'

When I received the phone call from the school to say that Billy hadn't been in I assumed he'd skived off with some mates, something he'd done several times in the preceding few months. When he didn't return home that night I still didn't panic. He was sulking after the argument he'd had with Mark the night before, I told myself. He was hiding out at a friend's house, nursing hurt feelings and dented pride. But when he still wasn't home by half eleven I began to worry.

I went up to his room and looked through his things. His schoolbag was missing. His mobile phone too. I rang him several times but each time my call went straight through to answerphone. I tried texting him but there was no answer. I had the numbers for the mums of several of his old primary-school friends so I rang them and asked if their sons had seen Billy but none of them had.

When Kira got back from college and Jake returned from work, horribly hungover after a session in the pub the day before, Mark asked if either of them had heard from Billy. They both said they hadn't. Jake said we were over-reacting.

'This is exactly the sort of reaction Billy was hoping for,' he said. 'He's deliberately staying out late to make you worry. Then you'll be relieved, not pissed off, when he finally gets home.'

Jake's comment seemed to reassure Mark but I wasn't convinced. Billy wasn't that manipulative. There was no way he'd put me through the wringer to punish his dad and, as the living-room clock ticked from midnight to 1 a.m. I became increasingly frantic, insisting that Mark drive round with me to try and find him.

'I will fucking kill him when we find him,' he muttered as he fitted the keys into the ignition. 'I need to be up for work in five hours' time.'

We drove round and round, stopping at all Billy's known haunts – all the parks and the underpasses where he'd practise skateboarding with his mates – and everywhere else we could think of where a fifteen-year-old might shelter from the bitterly cold wind that had caught my skirt and wrapped it around my calves as I'd climbed into the car: bus stops, McDonald's restaurants, the train station and the doorways of the cinema and bowling alley in Avonmeads.

'I bet he's kipped down for the night on a mate's sofa,' Mark complained as I insisted we drive around

Knowle and Totterdown one last time. 'Probably one of those dossers he hangs around with. If he's still not home by morning we'll call the police.'

'And if he isn't?' I could barely bring myself to ask the question.

'Then the police will talk to everyone he knows and find out where he's hiding. Claire, he's fine. I guarantee it.'

He sounded so certain, so definite, that I agreed to ignore the knot of fear in my gut and go home.

Mark passed out the second his head hit the pillow. I lay awake beside him, ringing Billy's number over and over again, finally passing out somewhere around 5 a.m., the mobile pressed between my ear and the pillow.

'Is that a yes?' Mark says now. The sharp tone to his question makes me clutch at the cushion. 'You think I did something to Billy, don't you?'

I want to believe that my husband would never do anything to hurt our children but you hear that all the time, don't you, about men like that. 'He didn't look the type.' 'He was always so good with the kids.' 'They loved him.'

The police questioned everyone after Billy was reported missing: his friends, his teachers, his relatives, even Liz and Caleb next door. I spoke to Josh, one of his friends from school, who told me what they'd asked him. '*How long have you known Billy?*' '*When did you last see him?*' '*Do you have any idea where he might have gone?*' '*What social media does Billy use?*' The police spoke to his granny and granddads, his uncle Stephen, Mr Edwards and Miss Christian at the school.

Mark.

They spent a lot of time talking to Mark, with me and on his own. They asked him to talk them through the argument the night before, word for word, and asked him question after question about Billy's reaction and whether he thought what had happened might be enough to prompt him to run away.

A child doesn't disappear for no reason, that's what I kept telling myself. But there was never a reason. Not until I found the photo album. I don't . . . I can't . . . let myself believe that Mark would ever hurt Billy but I'd never be able to forgive myself if the truth lies between the covers of that grey album. I need to tell the police. I need to give it to them.

'For God's sake, Claire, say something!'

I force myself to look him in the eye. Then I tell him a bare-faced lie. 'No, I don't think you were responsible.'

'Thank God.' He sags into himself and runs his hands over his face. 'Thank God for that.'

Neither of us says a word for several minutes, then I reach into my pocket and pull out my phone. I turn it over in my hands.

'Mark?'

'Hmm.' He makes a low guttural noise from behind his hands.

'Did you run into anyone while you were at work today?'

His fingers slip from his cheeks and he twists his face towards me. 'What do you mean?'

'Did you bump into anyone we know?'

He closes his eyes and rubs the thumb and forefinger of his right hand over his temples as though it hurts to think. 'Yeah. I . . . I bumped into Billy's form teacher. Um . . .'

'Edie Christian.'

'Yeah. I bumped into her outside one of the practices. Nevil Road Surgery, I think. Why?'

I place the phone on the arm of the sofa. 'No reason, just wondered.'

'What is it?' He gives me a searching look.

'Nothing.' I glance at the photo album, propped up on the sofa between us. 'Nothing at all.'

We eat our dinner in silence, a defrosted shepherd's pie that I push around my plate with my fork as a game-show burbles away on the television in the corner of the room and we attempt to keep up the pretence of a normal Friday night. I keep glancing at the clock, hoping Jake will come home earlier than he said so there's someone else in the house. Not because I'm scared of Mark. I'm not. Never have been. I'm just scared I'm going to blurt out something awful if I stay silent a moment longer. When Jake turns up we can talk about normal things, like how hard his boss has worked him or how demanding the client is. As soon as he comes back I can stop imagining the look on DS Forbes's face when he turns the pages of the photo album.

My phone bleeps at me from the arm of the sofa. A text from Liz.

How are you?

I type back.

Tired. And my head is totally screwed.

I'm not surprised. Have you spoken to you know who?

Yes. He said he found the album in B's room and hid it in the garage so I wouldn't get upset. He says he doesn't know why B did it.

Do you believe him?

I glance across the room, at the plate on the side table beside Mark's armchair. He's barely touched the shepherd's pie, there's a lump of mash on his abandoned fork.

I don't know, I type back. *I think I'm going to take it to the police station tomorrow but I keep changing my mind. What if they call him in and it turns out to be nothing?*

Then you'll have peace of mind.

I look back at Mark, at the slight curve of his belly swelling beneath his shirt, the shock of white hair at his temples and the grey hue to his skin. He's aged so much in the last six months. We both have. I move my thumb over the keyboard on my phone:

It might mean the end of my marriage, Liz.

Would that be the worst thing in the world? (Don't hate me for saying that.)

I don't reply. Instead I stare at the phone and will myself not to cry. You read about it all the time in the papers, the number of marriages that don't survive a tragedy like a child going missing or being murdered. I don't want to be part of that statistic.

Is that my pride speaking or is it because I still love my husband? It felt as though we were drifting apart, long before Billy went missing. We were living in the same house and sharing the same bed, but so little else. I don't know if it was because we'd got to that stage in our relationship where we were taking each other for granted or if it was more serious than that. We clung to each other in the weeks and months after his disappearance but the gap between us has widened again. There are moments when I feel close to him but I'm so tired. So incredibly tired. The harder I try and hold this family together the weaker I become. I'm crumbling on the inside. If Mark is responsible for Billy's disappearance I think it will finish me off.

The mobile vibrates with a new text from Liz.

Have you told him about the blackout?

No.

So many things have been whirling around in my mind this evening but what happened to me isn't one of them.

Liz sends another text.

Do you want me to come to the police station with you tomorrow?

Thank you, I'd appreciate that. I'll knock for you at 9 if that's OK? Xx

I tap the phone's back button and look at the list of text messages I've been sent recently. Stephen's name is near the top. He'd be so unbearably smug if he knew about the photo album.

'I'm going to the pub,' Mark announces as he eases himself out of the armchair. He picks up his plate and then reaches for mine. He raises his eyebrows at my untouched food. 'You all right?'

All right? Isn't he the slightest bit worried about what I might do with the photo album? How can he have no idea what's going on in my mind?

'I'm not hungry.'

'About me going to the pub, I mean. Shouldn't Jake and Kira be back by now?'

Oh God. Kira. I'd completely forgotten I'd asked her to go out so I could talk to Mark. I need to text her and tell her it's okay to come back.

'Jake's working late and Kira has gone to a friend's house. You go to the pub.'

His gaze flits towards the photo album, still propped up on the sofa beside me. 'I'm sorry,' he says.

'What for?'

'Laughing. When you asked me in the kitchen if I knew anything about it. After everything we've been through in the last few weeks I didn't think anything else could go wrong. And then when I saw the album and the look on your face, I thought, here we bloody go again. I'm going to get accused of something I didn't do. And I laughed. Not because it was funny but because it seemed like a sick joke. I'm sorry, Claire. I shouldn't have laughed. It freaked you out.'

'I'm too tired to talk about this any more.'

'I know. That's why I'm going to the pub. Give us both some space.'

I nod. 'Yeah.'

'Okay then.' His gaze lingers on my face. 'I'll be back by ten. I've got an early start in the morning and—'

He's interrupted by the sound of the doorbell ringing.

I move to stand up but Mark shakes his head.

'It's okay. I'll get it.'

As he disappears into the hallway the chat-show host on the TV skips across the set as though the soles of his feet are on fire. I hear the clatter of plates in the sink and the low rumble of my husband's voice as he answers the door.

Seconds later a man appears in the doorway to the living room.

'Hi, Claire,' says DS Forbes, 'sorry to call round so late. Mind if I sit down?'

Chapter 28

DS Forbes knows what I did. I can see it in the grave look in his eyes and the tight set of his mouth. He's come to arrest me for assaulting the cyclist. They reported me, him or the woman in the car that stopped. I need to tell him about the blackout, the one I haven't told Mark about yet. I'll tell DS Forbes to talk to Dr Evans. And Liz. She knows what happened. She saw the state I was in when she picked me up. She'll testify that I wasn't in my normal state of mind.

'I didn't mean to hurt him.' The words fly out of my mouth before I can stop them.

'Hurt who?' DS Forbes takes a step towards me. Mark follows behind him.

'The cyclist. I didn't mean to knock him off his bike when I opened my car door. I genuinely didn't see him.'

'Claire.' Mark darts past DS Forbes and joins me

on the sofa. He wraps an arm around my shoulder and pulls me in to his side. 'DS Forbes is here to talk about Billy. He's got news.'

'Billy! Oh my God.' My hands fly to my mouth.

A cold chill runs through me and a thousand goosebumps prickle on the surface of my skin. It's bad news. I can tell by the look on DS Forbes's face. In his eyes.

'Do you mind if I sit down?' He lowers himself into Mark's armchair without waiting for a reply.

'Claire. Mark.' He glances at the TV, still flickering in the corner of the room. I can't remember him using our first names before. 'Do you mind turning that off?'

I hear the sound of Mark's voice but it's lost in the white noise that fills my head.

The TV goes black. DS Forbes clears his throat and then licks his lips, the pink tip of his tongue peeping out of his mouth as it moistens his upper lip. Each gesture, each tiny gesture he makes seems huge. I feel as though I'm looking at him through a TV camera that's zoomed in on his face. I want to press 'stop' and rewind him out of the room. Then I want to rewind my life back to the night that Billy left and skip past me storming out of the house, past the argument, past the visit to the police station to pick him up, past his first day of school and back to the moment he was born. When he was in my arms. When I wouldn't let him out of my sight, not even for a second. When he was safe.

'Claire. Mark. There's been a development in Billy's case and I'm afraid it's not good news.'

The image of Billy, safe in my arms, becomes grey and distorted as the white noise in my head closes around him and he vanishes. A voice in my head screams through the white noise. Stop! Stop that man from speaking. I don't want to hear what he's about to say.

'Does the name Jason Davies mean anything to either of you?'

Jason Davies? I close my eyes and search my memory for someone, anyone, I may have met with that name but all I can see are the faces of my friends and family, whirling around in the darkness.

'No,' Mark says. He nudges me. 'Claire?'

I feel paralysed but somehow I manage to open my eyes and shake my head.

'Should it mean something to us?' Mark asks.

'I've got a photo.' DS Forbes reaches down by his feet and retrieves a black attaché case. Did he have it in his hand when he walked in? I can't remember. I can't remember anything apart from the sombre expression on his face when he appeared in the doorway.

'Do you know this man?' He holds out an A4 sheet of paper.

The photograph quivers as Mark takes it from DS Forbes and then returns with it to the sofa, holding it tentatively by the edges as though it's a bomb, primed to go off. He rests it on his thighs. A man in his mid- to late forties gazes up at us. He has a long face with deep hollows under his cheekbones, heavily lidded eyes and wide, thin lips. His greying hair is thinning at the front and neatly cropped. His face is unremarkable. He looks like someone who might live next door, or work behind the counter at the garden centre, or play guitar in the pub on a Friday night. But it's his eyes I focus in on. They are blank, expressionless: cold grey pools with pinprick pupils. I want to look away before his face imprints in my mind but I can't stop staring.

'No.' Mark snatches up the photograph and hands it back to DS Forbes. I inhale, snatching air into my lungs. How long have I been holding my breath?

'Claire?' DS Forbes looks at me. 'Do you know him?'

'I've never seen him before. Who is he?'

He rubs a hand across his jawline, dark with stubble, and Mark reaches for my hand. I press my face into his shoulder and squeeze my eyes shut. Oh please, God. Please don't let him say—

'He has confessed to killing Billy. And while we don't yet have any evidence that he was responsible we have begun an investigation—'

A gasp catches in my throat followed by a wail of anguish that begins in my guts and works its way up through my body and out of my mouth.

No.

No.

No.

NO.

A roar fills the room – primal and terrifying. I clutch Mark instinctively but the sound is coming from him.

'Claire. Mark.' I feel a hand on my shoulder and DS Forbes's voice in my ear. Mark falls silent but I feel myself tense. I want the policeman out. I want him out of our house so I can drop to the floor and smack my head against the floor until I pass out.

'Mark.' The hand remains on my shoulder but the voice fades, ever so slightly. 'Mark, listen to me. At the moment it's just a confession. Jason Davies is in prison. He confessed to his cellmate that he was involved in Billy's disappearance and the cellmate was overheard discussing it with another inmate and—'

'So he might be lying?'

'That's a possibility, Mark. But we have to take confessions of this nature very seriously.'

'Has he done it before?' I can hear the fear and anger in my husband's voice. 'Is that why he's in prison? Has he hurt kids before?'

'I can't share that information with you, Mark, I'm sorry.'

'But you can tell me he confessed to killing our child!'

'Mark, I know this is difficult—'

'Difficult? You just told me someone has confessed to killing my son, our son, and you think it's difficult. I—'

'There's no easy way of doing this, Mark. I had to tell you about this development. We needed to know if you or Billy knew this man.'

I peel my face from Mark's shoulder. 'What are you suggesting?'

212

'It's a line of inquiry, Claire,' he says softly, 'and we need to follow it up.'

'Is he a paedophile, this Jason Davies?'

'Billy wasn't the only child he has confessed to abducting and killing. He mentioned some other names too.'

'Oh my God.' I press my hands to my face. My cheeks are wet beneath my fingertips.

Mark says nothing. He is staring at DS Forbes, his lips parted, his eyes flooded with fear.

DS Forbes rocks back onto his heels and looks from Mark to me. 'It's very important that you keep this development to yourselves and I'd urge you not to reveal it to anyone beyond your immediate family, particularly not the media, as it could hinder our investigation. You must not attempt to seek retribution or carry out your own inquiries as it could prejudice any future case we might file against this man. Do you understand?'

'Yes.' Mark's voice is little more than a whisper.

'Claire?' DS Forbes looks at me. 'Do you understand?'

'Yes.'

'We'll keep you informed about any developments and you should bear in mind that it may take some time. A few weeks at least.' He looks at Mark again. 'Have you got any questions? Bearing in mind what I said earlier about information I can't divulge.'

Mark shakes his head. He looks numb.

'Claire?'

'No.'

'Okay.' He eases himself up from the chair, groaning as he straightens his legs. 'I'll give you both some space now. I'm sorry I wasn't able to bring you more positive news. Don't get up,' he adds, even though both Mark and I are still rooted to the sofa. 'I'll let myself out.'

He crosses the living room in six large strides and disappears into the hallway. I grit my teeth and dig my nails into the palms of my hands but there's no holding back the tidal wave of grief building inside me and I howl with pain.

Chapter 29

Jake and Kira stumble through the back door at 11.12 p.m., giggling and shushing each other. There's a low thump, then a squeak of wood on tiles as though one of them has knocked against the kitchen table.

'Shit,' Jake shouts. 'I dropped my kebab.'

'It'll probably taste nicer.'

Their voices are dialled up to eleven and they bounce off the walls, joyful and drunken, as Mark and I sit side by side in the half-lit living room, holding hands. They must have met up in the pub after Jake finished work. My palm is tacky with sweat and my fingers are aching but there's no way I can let go of Mark's hand. A few hours ago I asked him to turn off the overhead light and put on a lamp instead. I feel like an exposed nerve. The noises in the kitchen are making my ears hurt. My throat is dry and my tongue feels too large for my mouth. I can't remember the last time I had something to drink.

'God, that thing stinks,' Kira says, her voice growing closer. 'The bedroom's going to smell like an abattoir.'

'Yeah, yeah. You love a bit of meat.'

'Jake!'

He laughs.

'Okay, fine,' he says. 'I'll eat it in the living room then. We can watch—'

He steps into the living room. Then stops.

'Ooph.' Kira charges into him. Her laughter catches in her throat as she peers round his shoulder. Her eyes catch mine.

'What is it?' Jake says. 'Mum, what's happened?'

'Sit down, kids.'

Jake doesn't move a muscle. A piece of wilted lettuce tumbles out of the box he's holding loosely in his right hand. It lands on the carpet.

'Mum?' Jake says again. 'What's happened?' He's still in his work gear, his jeans frayed at the bottom, his trainers dusty around the edges. His jaw is dotted with stubble, his fair hair swept back from his eyes. Behind him Kira's bottom lip is stained red with drink or the remains of her lipstick.

'Sit down,' Mark says again but there's no power left in his voice and no one moves. 'Jake. Kira. DS Forbes came round earlier this evening. He had some news about Billy.'

Jake sways on the spot and a thick slab of kebab

meat tumbles to the floor. For a second I think he's going to faint but then he regains his composure.

'Some nonce . . .' Mark says. 'Some piece of scum in jail told his cellmate that he abducted and killed Billy. He's confessed to killing other kids too.'

Kira is the first to react. She gasps and runs from the room, her bag bouncing against her shoulder as she sprints up the stairs.

Jake makes no move to go after her. Shock is etched into every line on his face.

'Mum?'

I want to tell him that it's not true, that it's the sickest of sick jokes. That Billy is in his room, in the hospital, at the police station. I want to tell him anything but the truth.

'Mum?' The word is loaded with fear.

'It's true, sweetheart.'

'The police are investigating,' Mark says. 'They said it might be a few weeks until we hear any more. We're not to share the news with anyone outside the family and you mustn't breathe a word on Facebook.'

The clock tick ticks in the corner of the room like a clockwork mechanism being wound inside my son. I brace myself, waiting for an explosion of rage and fury to burst from him.

None comes.

He bends at the knees and I feel sure that he's going to collapse but then he plucks the slice of meat and the shred of lettuce from the carpet and tucks them back into the polystyrene container. He closes it, his large hands fumbling the squeaky plastic lip back into the box, then he turns and walks up the stairs, taking them one at a time.

Chapter 30

Unlike the counsellor the police arranged for me to see after Billy disappeared, Sonia works from home. We're sitting in the back room of her terraced house in Bedminster. Not in an office block in town. It is a bright and airy room, decorated in shades of brown and beige with little touches of orange – the cushions on the sofa, the lampshade of the standard lamp in the corner of the room and a single white hydrangea in a vase above the black iron fireplace. On first glance it looks like a living room but it's too carefully arranged. There are no children's toys picking up dust under the sofa, no books propped open on the arm of the chair and no abandoned Diet Coke can on the table in the middle of the room. It's homely but there are no traces of Sonia's personality. I imagine that's deliberate.

Mark didn't go to work yesterday. Neither did Jake. I could hear him and Kira talking in low voices behind their closed bedroom door when I went to the bathroom a little after 7 a.m.

Mark and I stayed up in the living room for hours on Friday night. We both cried, taking it in turns to hold and console each other, whispering platitudes like, '*We've been through worse,*' '*We can get through this,*' and '*There's been a mix-up. Jason Davies has confused our son with some other family's child.*'

Neither of us wanted to go to bed but exhaustion gnawed at our bones and we dragged ourselves up the stairs a little after 1 a.m. I slept fitfully, waking on the hour, every hour, just as I had when Billy was little. Only it wasn't his tiny face, turned towards me in his cot, mewing for milk that jolted me awake. He was in my dreams, crying, screaming, reaching for me, begging for me to save him. When I woke up on Saturday morning I went straight from the warmth of my bed to the cold keys of the laptop. I Googled 'psychotherapist Bristol qualifications', as Dr Evans had suggested and Sonia's name came up first. Somehow I made it through the rest of the weekend. It's all a blur now. I rang Sonia yesterday morning, the second the clock in the living room chimed 9 a.m.

Sonia leans back in her chair and knits her fingers together in her lap. She gives me an appraising look but it's warm and sympathetic rather than cold and detached. I sobbed on the phone earlier, when I told her why I needed an urgent appointment, so she has some idea what she's let herself in for.

She's a few years older than me, late forties I'd

guess, but she has the tight, gaunt face of someone older. Her multicoloured kaftan-like dress is diaphanous but her impossibly tiny wrists poke out from the sleeves and her collarbones are so prominent I could pour water into the triangular hollows either side of her neck and it wouldn't dribble out. Her vivid red hair is piled on top of her head and secured with two wooden sticks. Chunky beaded earrings swing from her ears.

'Tell me how you're feeling, Claire.'

I have been asked how I am a thousand times since Billy disappeared and I still don't know the answer. I feel overwhelmed yet empty, frantic yet numb.

I shake my head. 'I don't know.'

'Okay. That's fine. Why don't you tell me what's happened instead. Take your time.'

It's a quarter past eleven when I finally stop speaking and take a sip of water. I've been talking, and Sonia has been listening and nodding, her eyes never once leaving my face, for over half an hour.

'Thank you, Claire,' she says as I place the glass on the coffee table in front of me. 'It must have been very difficult for you to relive that experience.'

I nod mutely.

'You've been through a lot recently, haven't you?'

My heart splinters. I don't want her pity. I want hope. But she can't give me that. No one can.

'We've got two issues here that we need to deal with,' she continues. 'The episodes of amnesia that you've been suffering, and the grief and pain you're going through as a result of Billy's disappearance. I'd like to tackle them separately, if that's okay with you. Starting with the amnesia.'

'Okay.'

'You're a private client,' she says, resting her elbows on her knees and leaning towards me, 'so I don't have access to your medical files but, from what you've told me about your visits to the doctor, it seems that the episodes of amnesia you've suffered are probably psychological in origin, rather than physical.'

'Dr Evans thinks they were caused by stress.'

'Yes,' she nods. 'Although I think what you've been through is more akin to trauma which has resulted in two episodes of psychogenic amnesia.'

'Psychogenic? Does that mean I was drugged?'

'No. It means the condition has a psychological origin rather than a physical one. It's also known as dissociative amnesia.'

Dissociative amnesia? I repeat the phrase over and over in my head but the words mean nothing to me. I thought I'd feel reassured, to finally receive a diagnosis, but all I feel is panic.

'Amnesia? But I didn't hit my head. Oh God, is it –' a thought occurs to me – 'is it early onset Alzheimer's?'

Sonia shakes her head. 'No, it's got nothing to do with Alzheimer's. It's a psychological condition that typically occurs as a result of a traumatic event – war, abuse or a highly stressful situation.'

'Can I stop it from happening again? Are there drugs I can get?'

222

'Not drugs, no. Although hopefully we'll be able to prevent you from having any more episodes by treating the root cause. The source of your trauma,' she adds.

'Dissociative amnesia.' I repeat the phrase back at her but it still sounds strange and foreign. 'I've never heard of it.'

'That's because it only affects a tiny proportion of the population. There is one well-known sufferer, though. It's commonly believed that Agatha Christie developed psychogenic amnesia as a result of her mother's death and her husband's infidelity. She travelled to a spa hotel in Harrogate and checked in under a different name. She said she was a bereaved mother from South Africa called Teresa Neele.'

'What happened to her?'

'Several of the guests at the spa recognized her so the police brought her husband up to Yorkshire to identify her. She returned home and never spoke of it again.'

'God. How long was she missing for?'

'Eleven days.'

Eleven days.

Sonia reads the fear on my face and holds up a hand. 'It's okay. Don't be scared. These periods of temporary amnesia, or fugues as they're often called, can last anything from hours to days to months. Sometimes people build whole new lives for themselves, just like Agatha did. And they have no idea who they used to be. That's why it's so disorientating when you come out of a fugue – your sense of identity completely changes.'

223

I clutch the ball of damp tissue in my hand. 'It was like waking up in a nightmare. I didn't know if I was awake or asleep. I was terrified.'

'Of course you were. Typically, someone who suffers from a fugue will feel distressed and confused and will develop feelings of shame, guilt, depression and anger after it ends. You mentioned briefly that you spoke to the receptionist at the B&B after you came round from your first episode. What kind of emotions did you experience then?'

I don't have to try very hard to conjure up his ginger moustache, straining shirt and the clipboard he kept just out of reach.

'It's okay, Claire.' Sonia stares at my hand, the skin stretched tight over the knuckles. 'I know it's hard, reliving those memories, but there's nothing you can't share with me.'

'I felt angry,' I say. 'Violent. I wanted to snatch his clipboard and beat him over the head with it because he was being so slow. I felt like he was doing it deliberately to stop me from finding Billy.' I pause. 'See, I knew you'd be shocked.'

Sonia's earrings sway from side to side as she shakes her head. 'I'm not the slightest bit shocked, Claire. Have you felt violent towards anyone else since?'

I look her straight in the eye. 'Yes.'

'Have you acted on those feelings?'

'I kicked the cyclist, the one I opened the door onto. I thought he was going to hurt me.'

She doesn't comment; instead she nods for me to continue.

'Could I . . .' I pause, unsure whether I can bring myself to ask the question that has been haunting me since my second blackout.

'What is it, Claire?'

'When I . . . when I came round the second time, I had a vision of Billy lying on the bonnet of my car. He was dead. I thought I'd run him over but I couldn't have. The windscreen wasn't shattered, the car wasn't damaged and there wasn't . . .' I swallow . '. . . there wasn't any blood.'

'And you're worried you may have had something to do with Billy's disappearance? You think you may have done something you can't remember?'

I press my fingernails into my palms to stop myself from crying and nod sharply.

'Claire,' Sonia says softly. 'You were at your mum and dad's house when Billy went missing.'

'But what if I had a blackout that I don't remember? What if I drove back to my house and ran Billy over?'

'Why would you do that?'

'I wouldn't.' I shake my head. 'I'd never hurt him. Ever.'

'Was your car damaged the day after he disappeared? Did you have to take it to a garage to get the windscreen repaired?'

'No, I . . . I drove to work and then back home at the end of the day.'

'I think,' Sonia presses the palms of her hands together, 'that the vision you had when you transitioned out of your fugue was more akin to a nightmare induced by feelings of guilt.'

'For going to mum and dad's the night Billy disappeared?'

She nods. 'I think the dream also manifests your worst fear.'

'That Billy's dead? No. He's still alive, I'm sure of it.'

'Okay.' She looks at me thoughtfully then leans back in her chair for the first time since I started speaking. 'In a minute we're going to do a few exercises to help you manage your anxiety but before we do I need to reassure you that what you experienced, what you felt and what you're still feeling as a result of your fugues is completely normal. And that the violent thoughts you've suffered are also normal.'

Normal.

The relief I feel is so sudden, so intense, that I burst into tears.

'Are you all right to continue?' Sonia asks as the tears abate and I slump back against the sofa, totally spent.

I nod. It takes every last ounce of energy that I have.

'What made you cry, just then?'

'Relief that I haven't turned into some kind of psychopath.'

She smiles sympathetically. 'You're not a psychopath, Claire. I'm ninety-nine per cent sure of that.'

I close my eyes and take a deep, settling breath. As I do so an image of Billy, lying on his bed with his headphones jammed onto his ears and his laptop on the bed beside him, pops into my head. He looks up, as though suddenly realizing I'm at the door, then winks. 'Only ninety-nine per cent, Mum? So that means there's still a one per cent chance you are a psychopath.'

My smile must have registered on my face because, when I open my eyes again, Sonia is looking at me curiously.

'What were you thinking about, Claire? Just then, when you closed your eyes?'

'About Billy. I was just imagining what he'd say if . . .' I tail off. Moments like that – happy thoughts that break up the unrelenting gloom – I need to hug them to my chest and hold them close. Sharing the image of Billy with Sonia would only dilute it.

'It's okay.' She smiles reassuringly. 'You don't have to share what you were thinking about if you don't want to. Now –' she crosses her legs and sits back in her chair – 'I'd like to move on from the amnesia if you're feeling strong enough, and talk to you about the development that DS Forbes shared with you the other day.'

'You want to talk to me about what Jason Davies said?'

'Yes.'

I take a deep breath and close my eyes. Only this time Billy is nowhere to be seen.

Saturday 8th November 2014

Jackdaw44: *Is it wrong that I want you to kiss me again?*

Chapter 31

I have no idea if my session with Sonia was effective or not. I haven't had another amnesia attack since I saw her six days ago but I still have terrible dreams. I dream that I'm driving around Bristol, looking for Billy, and then I see him – he's at the end of the road, baseball cap jammed onto his head, shoulders hunched against the driving wind and rain. There's a van, four cars in front of me, and it's going slowly, so slowly and I'm swearing at the driver to put his foot on the gas so I can get to my son before he disappears. Then the van stops. The passenger door opens and Billy gets in. I scream and pull at my door but it's jammed shut and I can't get out. The van drives off and I can't stop screaming.

Sleep deprivation has wiped my memories of the last six days. People have come and gone. Mum, Dad, Liz. There've been hugs, lots of hugs. And countless cups of tea. The days have run into each other as we all try and come to terms with what DS Forbes told us about Jason Davies. On a couple of occasions I've grabbed my car keys intending to go out and look for Billy, only to put them down again seconds later, unable to breathe.

Mark went back to work the day after my session with Sonia.

'I'll stay,' he said after the alarm bleeped and he reached out a lazy arm to turn it off. 'Claire, I'll stay if you need me to.'

I shook my head. He'd spent all of the day before pacing the house like a caged animal, settling for minutes in front of the TV and then up again, into the kitchen for a cup of tea, then out to the garage, then back in again. He spent a lot of time standing by the window, looking out at the park opposite our house. He reminded me of one of the tigers in Bristol zoo, stalking back and forth along the same patch of worn grass, eyeing the visitors beyond the glass wall. He could see what freedom looked like but he had no means of escape.

'No,' I said. 'You need to go to work. I'll be fine. Jake will keep me company.'

'If you're sure?' I could hear the conflict in his voice as he reached out his arms and pulled me close. I pressed my face into his hairless chest and inhaled his warm, sleepy, musky scent. 'Is Jake taking another day off then?'

'Yeah. He told me last night that he couldn't face going to work.'

'I'm worried about him. He spent all of yesterday in his room.'

'We'll go out. Take a walk.'

He stroked the hair back from my face and kissed me on the forehead. 'I think it'll do you both good to get some fresh air.'

We never did go for that walk. When I knocked on Jake's door he said he had a headache and maybe we'd go later. I rang Mum and we drove out to Chew Magna and walked around the lake together. She didn't mention the website, the appeal or the photos. Instead we held hands and we talked about Dad and his bridge games and the weather and the woman in the corner shop whose husband had been diagnosed with prostate cancer. Then Mum told me how worried she was about me.

I told her I'd started seeing a counsellor again but I didn't mention the amnesia. She squeezed my hand tightly and it struck me, not for the first time, how hard this must be for her and Dad. I am their child, Billy is their grandchild. They must feel the same sense of powerlessness that I feel. That's why Mum works so hard on the website. It's her way of helping, of showing she cares.

When I returned home just after eleven Jake was still in his room. At twelve I knocked on his door and offered him some lunch. He said he wasn't hungry. At tea time he asked if he and Kira could eat their meals in their room. Mark and I ate our steak, chips and peas in front of the TV. I can't even remember if it was on.

The next day I had a call from Ian, Jake's boss. He asked if Jake was over his stomach bug yet. I deliberated before answering, unsure whether to lie and say he was still ill or tell him that we'd had some bad news. Ian knows about Billy; Jake had only been working there for a few months when he vanished but I couldn't tell him the real reason Jake was off work. We weren't allowed to tell anyone outside our immediate family about Jason Davies. Ian didn't ask any questions when I said Jake was having a difficult time at the moment but he did agree to let him have a few more days off. I was grateful when he said goodbye.

This morning he rang back. Could I let him know whether Jake would be back at work some time this week as they had a big job planned and he needed to know whether or not to get someone else in? I asked him to hold on, then knocked on Jake's door. He opened it seconds later, in the same faded pair of boxer shorts he's been wearing for days, his eyes bleary, his jawline covered in stubble. Behind him, on the opposite side of the room, the curtains were still shut, the only light the blue haze of his laptop screen, the lid half-closed.

'Ian wants to know when you're going back to work.'

'Huh?'

'Ian. Your boss. He's got a big job on. He needs to know when you're going back or he's going to have to get someone else in.'

Jake shrugged. 'Whatever.'

'You'll lose your job if you don't go back soon, Jake.'

'Who cares?'

'You do. You love your job.'

'None of that shit matters any more.'

'Jake!'

'Mum –' he rubbed a hand over his face – 'I can't deal with this right now. Can you tell him I'll ring him back?'

He closed the door before I could reply. I stared at the knotted wood, grubby with semicircular grey patches – the remains of stickers he'd plastered on the door as a kid – and raised a fist to knock again, then remembered I'd left Ian hanging on the line and bolted back down the stairs.

'Hi, Ian. Is it okay if Jake rings you back this evening?'

He sighed. 'I like Jake. And I know he's got a lot of family stuff to deal with but I need to have a team I can rely on. If he doesn't call me in the next couple of hours I'm going to have to get someone else in. I'm sorry, Claire. Business is business.'

I can't help to find Billy but I can still look after one of my sons. I can still help Jake.

Chapter 32

It's almost impossible to find a parking space near the Bristol School of Art so I park at Trenchard Street car park and walk from there. Maybe Kira is the wrong person to talk to about Jake. Perhaps I should talk to a doctor instead. I watched as Liz slipped into a depression after Lloyd left her in January and I can see the same symptoms in Jake. He's irritable, he's got no energy, he doesn't show any interest in the things he used to enjoy and he spends all his time in his room. But antidepressants take weeks to kick in and he'll get worse if he loses his job too. He was so proud when he was offered his apprenticeship, so full of dreams about starting up his own business and getting a place for him and Kira. She knows him better than any of us. If anyone can talk him into ringing his boss, she can.

I glance at my watch as I approach the large brown front door of the Bristol School of Art: 1.03 p.m. It's

Monday, Kira's favourite day of the week because she only has a half-day.

Student after student files out of the building. None of them pays me, a frazzled-looking woman in her early forties in a pair of skinny jeans and a white shirt, the slightest bit of attention. As the crowd starts to thin so does my hope of running into Kira. What if she's decided to stay to work on her project?

I jump back as a lorry thunders down the road, its huge wheels splashing through last night's rainfall, and a flash of pink catches the corner of my eye.

'Kira!' I speed after her as she hurries down towards the Triangle. 'Kira, hang on a sec. I need to talk to you.'

She stops in her tracks and turns slowly, weighed down by the camera bag over her shoulder and the large, black portfolio dangling from her right hand.

'Claire?' She looks shocked. 'What are you doing here?'

'I need to talk to you about Jake. Could we grab a coffee?'

Kira pours hot water into the stainless-steel teapot, then dips a spoon into it and stirs. Her cheeks flush when she realises I'm watching her.

'I love vintage stuff like this. I would have loved to have been alive in the forties or fifties. Life was so glamorous back then.' She closes the lid of the teapot. 'Is Jake okay?'

I take a sip of my coffee. It's piping hot and I burn my lips. 'Has he said anything to you, about what DS Forbes told us?'

'Not really. But I know he's angry. He feels guilty too.'

'Guilty? Why?'

'He thinks he should have protected Billy. He thinks he's dead because of him.'

'He thinks Billy is dead?'

'I keep telling him that he's not. He's alive. I need to believe that, almost as much as you do.' Her fingers twitch on the tabletop and she glances away, towards the window and the busy street beyond the café. She's thinking about her dad. He died a couple of years ago. Cancer, I think Jake said.

'Sorry, Kira. I know this is hard for you too.'

'Mmm.' She presses her lips together.

I unzip my handbag and push a tissue across the table towards her. 'Here.'

'Thanks.' She dabs underneath her eyes, then takes a deep breath. 'I just wish . . . I wish none of this had happened. You're such a lovely family and you've been so kind to me and it kills me to see you all so unhappy. It's been awful watching Jake tear himself apart after Billy disappeared. Recently I felt like he was getting better. He was enjoying work and going out with his mates again but then the appeal brought everything back and—'

'DS Forbes turned up.'

'Yeah. I feel so awful for him but there's nothing I can do, nothing I can say . . .' Fresh tears take the place of the ones that have dried on her cheeks. 'Do you ever wish you could run away, Claire?'

I think back to my conversation with Sonia, when

she told me that my first fugue was my subconscious trying to run away from all the stress in my life. Kira might be nineteen but she's already gone through so much – dead father, alcoholic mother and now this. She's shouldering the weight of Jake's grief and I've been so burdened by my own pain I haven't considered that she might be suffering too.

'Maybe what you and Jake need is to get away for the weekend? Book a hotel, go to Bath or Weston for—'

She shakes her head.

'Okay, maybe not. Too close to home.' I force a smile. 'How about South Wales? Dad knows someone with a cottage there. I'm sure he'd do mates rates. I'll tell Jake not to give me any rent money this week. We can manage without it. What do you think? You both need a break.'

'I'm not sure Jake would come. I can't even get him out of bed in the morning.'

'That's because he's got nothing to look forward to but he'd do anything for you, Kira. You're his whole world. You know that, don't you?'

She nods dumbly, tears still glistening in her eyes.

'I want you two to be happy. I want you to get your own little flat and have some independence. That's why I came to meet you. Jake's boss was on the phone earlier. If he doesn't ring him this afternoon he's going to lose his job. If we can convince Jake to go in, just for a couple of days, then he can go away with you. It'll give him something to look forward to. What do you think?'

She reaches for the teapot and flips back the lid.

She closes it again, trapping the wisp of steam that attempts to escape. 'I don't know.'

'You don't have to make a decision now. Have a think about it on the way home.'

'Okay.' She looks back up at me. 'If you think it'll help him I'll ask.'

A wave of relief surges through me. 'I think it will. Are you going to drink that?' I point at the tea. 'Or shall we just go?'

'Go.' She nods decisively. 'Before I lose my nerve.'

We are halfway out of the door of the café when a crowd of teenagers surges up the pavement and forces us to step back.

'Sorry, sorry.' A harassed-looking blonde shoots me an apologetic look, then does a double-take. 'It's you, isn't it? Mrs Wilkinson, Billy's mum?'

It takes me a couple of seconds to place her face. 'Miss Christian?'

'Yes.' As she holds out a hand, half a dozen silver bracelets jangle around her wrist. 'I saw the appeal on TV a few weeks ago. Has there been any news?'

'No,' I say before Kira can interject. 'Unfortunately not.'

'Rosie!' Miss Christian releases my hands and waves at a woman further up the street. 'I'll catch up with you. Okay?'

I don't recognize Rosie but, from the way the teenagers congregate around her, she's obviously a teacher. I don't remember her from any of Billy's parents' evenings. She must be new.

'We're taking them to the open day at the School of Art,' Edie says, as though reading my thoughts. 'I'm pretty sure half the kids here aren't the slightest bit interested but it's a few hours away from school and . . .' She shrugs.

I scan the faces of the pupils surrounding Rosie but don't recognize any of them. One boy whispers something in another boy's ear. He's rewarded with a laugh and a punch to the shoulder. That's what Billy should be doing now, messing around with his mates, telling jokes and winding them up. Where is he? whispers a voice in my head. Where is he?

'Billy was a very talented artist,' Edie Christian says, drowning out the voice.

Is, I want to say. Billy is a very talented artist. But it's as though someone has placed a band around my chest that's stopping me from speaking.

Edie's gaze falls on Kira. 'Kira Simmons! My gosh, I haven't seen you since . . .'

'I left school three years ago,' Kira says. 'I'm doing photography up there.' She gestures towards her college.

'Yes, of course. Your GCSE project was about sport, wasn't it? BMXers and skateboarders?'

'Sort of. It was about perseverance.'

'That's right. Lots of images of scraped knees and jubilant air punches if I remember correctly.'

Kira slips her hand through the crook of my elbow. She tugs me, ever so slightly, away from Edie Christian. At the same time the two boys I've been watching

239

disappear into a crowd of people crossing the road and the band around my chest loosens.

'I didn't realize you two knew each other,' Miss Christian says, looking pointedly at Kira's hand on my arm.

'Kira lives with us. She's my son Jake's girlfriend.'

'I remember Jake. He was a hard worker. Oh!' She looks back towards the group of school kids on the other side of the road. 'I'd better be off. Good to run into you, Mrs Wilkinson. I know you're probably in touch with Mr Edwards but if there's anything I can do to help, then do let me know.'

'Miss Christian!' I call as she starts back up the street.

'Yes?' She turns back.

'You ran into my husband, Mark, near Gloucester Road.'

'Did I?' Her expression changes. It's the same worried look I saw in the photo. 'Yes, outside the doctor's. I remember.'

'How was he?'

'Um.' She looks confused. 'He seemed well. I'm so sorry, Mrs Wilkinson. I'm really going to have to go. Rosie isn't legally allowed to take charge of that many kids on her own and . . .' She raises a hand in goodbye, then speeds across the road just as the green man turns red.

'What was that about?' Kira asks.

'I don't know,' I say. 'What was she like – as a teacher, I mean?'

I'm interrupted by the muffled sound of my mobile

phone ringing inside my bag. DS Forbes said it could take weeks to follow the new line of inquiry. If the call is from him it can only be bad news.

A name flashes on the screen. I press 'end call' without picking up.

Tuesday 25th November 2014

ICE9: *We need to be careful. I thought I saw your mum at the window last night.*
Jackdaw44: *Probably wondering where Dad was.*
ICE9: *Where is your dad?*
Jackdaw44: *At a conference. If 'conference' is another word for fucking someone else.*
ICE9: *Do you really think he's cheating on your mum?*
Jackdaw44: *Hello?!*
ICE9: *Yeah. I know, but maybe what you saw was a one-off.*
Jackdaw44: *And you think I'm the naive one.*
ICE9: *I never said that.*
Jackdaw44: *You think I'm too young for you.*
ICE9: *Did I say that?*
Jackdaw44: *No, but I know you're thinking it.*
ICE9: *Mind reader are you?*
Jackdaw44: *You seemed a bit nervy last night.*

ICE9: a) It was freezing b) We were in the park opposite your house!

Jackdaw44: I like to take a risk.

ICE9: You're not kidding.

Jackdaw44: Exciting though, wasn't it? I know it turned you on, the risk that we might get caught.

ICE9: That wasn't what turned me on.

Jackdaw44: 💪

ICE9: I take back the comment about you not being immature!

Jackdaw44: I'm good though, aren't I? In bed.

Jackdaw44: *coughs*

Jackdaw44: *coughs louder*

ICE9: Yes, you are. You cocky bastard.

Jackdaw44: Let's go to Weston tomorrow. Get a hotel.

ICE9: I need to work and you need to go to school.

Jackdaw44: Skive!

ICE9: You live in a dream world.

Jackdaw44: And you need to have more fun.

Chapter 33

I keep expecting the phone to start up again on the drive back home but it sits silently on my lap the whole way. I should have known Stephen would eventually try and ring when he didn't get a response to his text message. If he's looking to kick everything off again I'm going to have to tell Mark what he said when I went into Wilkinson & Son.

I'm not surprised to see Jake's van still parked in the street but I am surprised to see Mark's car. If he comes home early it normally means one thing – he's off to a conference or training day and he's come back to shower, change and grab an overnight bag.

Sure enough, when I walk into the kitchen with Kira, Mark is sitting at the table, a mountain of paperwork piled up on one of the chairs beside him. He gets up when he sees me and pulls me into a tight hug before holding me at arm's length and looking into my face. He looks so tender, so loving, so like the man I fell in love with that all the concerns I had about him and Edie Christian flit from my mind.

'Good day?' he asks.

'Interesting.' I lower my voice as Kira slips past us into the hallway. 'I went to collect her from college so I could talk to her about Jake. Ian rang this morning. If Jake doesn't go back to work soon he's going to get someone else in.'

'Oh, for God's sake.' He raises his eyes to the ceiling, then sighs. 'Don't worry. I'm not going to go off on one. I just wish . . .'

'I know.' I reach a hand to the side of his face. 'We'll get through this, just like we've got through everything else.'

His eyes soften. 'You're a good woman, Claire Wilkinson. You know that, don't you?'

'Where did that come from?'

'I was thinking about you on the drive home today, about how strong you are. Sorry.' He suddenly looks embarrassed. 'I'm not very good at mushy stuff but I just wanted you to know how much I appreciate you, how much I love you.'

'It's not mushy. I need to hear it.'

'Then I should say it more often, shouldn't I?' He kisses me softly on the lips and one of his hands slips down to my waist. He pulls me against him as the kiss becomes deeper and I wrap my arms around his neck and kiss him back. I close my eyes as months of fear, frustration and exhaustion slip away and I lose myself in the embrace. His hands slide from my waist to the sides of my breasts and down to my bum. I tip back my head as his mouth travels from my lips to my neck and a low groan rumbles from the base of his throat.

A scream from upstairs makes us jump apart.

'What the fuck?' Mark leaves the room first, sprinting down the hallway and up the stairs, taking them two at a time as I tug my bra strap back over my shoulder and follow after him.

'Weekend break?' Jake shouts. 'You want me to go on holiday when some filthy pervert has done God knows what to my brother? How fucked up are you to even suggest that?'

'Jake!' I shout. 'It wasn't Kira's idea. It was mine. I – Kira!' I reach for her as she shoves her way past me on the stairs. 'Kira, wait!'

I run after her and grab her wrist as she yanks at the back door handle.

'Get off me!' She pulls away, her eyes red-rimmed. Streaks of black eye make-up reach down to her jaw. 'Please, Claire. Please. Just let me go.'

'Where are you going?'

'I don't know.' She pulls at the door handle. 'Everything's fucked up. I'm fucked up. Jake was right.'

'He's not. You haven't done anything wrong. You're a kind and thoughtful girl, a good girl.'

'No, I'm not.' Her hand falls from the door handle but she keeps her back to me. 'My dad used to say I was a good girl. He used to tell me every day how proud he was of me and how much he loved me. It didn't stop him from killing himself though, did it?'

All the hairs on my arms go up. 'Oh my God, Kira. I had no idea.'

'I'm going to Amy's house,' she says, her voice a monotone.

It takes me half an hour to talk Jake out of his festering pit of a room and down to the living room where Mark is sitting on the sofa with his head in his hands.

'Where's Kira?' Jake says, looking towards the kitchen. 'I need to talk to her.'

'She's gone to a friend's house.' I gesture for him to take a seat on the armchair. 'And you're going to have to do some serious apologizing if you want her to come back.'

'She's got nowhere else to go,' he says flatly as he slumps into the chair.

'Give her a ring after you've called Ian.' I hand him the cordless phone. 'Tell him you'll be back in work this week.'

'What if I don't want to?'

'What if you don't want to?' Mark jumps up from the sofa, his hands clenched into fists at his sides. 'Do you think I enjoy getting up at the crack of dawn so I can sit in traffic for an hour each day? Do you think I enjoy it when some sour-faced doctor's receptionist tells me the doctors can't make the meeting I scheduled three weeks earlier and drove halfway across town to make? Do you seriously think I'd rather go to work when I could stay here and look after your mother instead? Someone has to bring some money in. Someone has to feed this family and keep a roof over our heads.'

Jake claps his hands; a slow, sarcastic round of applause. 'Well, congratulations. The father-of-the-year award goes to Mark Wilkinson.'

'Jake, stop it!' I say.

'Stop what? It's all bollocks. All that shit about providing for the family. He doesn't do it for us. He does it for him. And if we don't toe the line we get it in the neck. He's not a father, he's a fucking dictator and he won't be happy until I'm dead and buried too.'

I put my hands on his shoulders and shout in his face. 'STOP IT!!'

He stares at me with such shock, such uncomprehending horror, that it's all I can do not to burst into tears.

'Ring Ian.' My hand shakes as I point at the phone. 'Ring your boss!'

My heart is beating so hard in my chest I can hear it in my ears.

'I'm sorry I screamed at you but you're better than this. Stronger than this. And I won't stand by and watch you destroy yourself and everything you've ever loved. I have already lost one son and I won't lose you too.'

'Jake?' I say as Mark walks silently out of the room. 'I need you to ring Ian and tell him you'll be back at work this week. Then I want you to ring Kira and apologize for shouting at her. Okay?'

'Okay.' His voice is no louder than a whisper.

*　*　*

Mark is in the bedroom, perched on the edge of the bed, his overnight case packed and zipped at his feet.

'Tell me to stay,' he says as I gently close the door behind me. 'Just say the word and I'll stay.'

The bed squeaks beneath me as I sit down next to him. 'No. You should go. And don't feel guilty.'

'I do though.' They're just three words but they're so laden with pain and sorrow he seems to bow under their weight.

'You need to go to work. We need to keep this house.'

'You're more important than this house. Jake's more important than this house.' His voice cracks as he says his son's name and I wrap my arms around him.

'I feel so awful,' I say as I press my face into the crook of his neck. 'I screamed at him like a banshee.'

'You were standing up for me. You've never done that before.'

I twist in his arms so I can see his face. 'Haven't I?'

He shakes his head. The sadness in his eyes is more than I can bear.

'I'm so sorry.'

'You put the kids first – that's the way it should be.'

'No.' I shake my head. 'It's not. We should have been a team. I should have supported you.'

'It doesn't matter.' He brushes a strand of hair out of my eyes. 'At least we're talking again. Properly talking, I mean.'

'Mark.' I pull away, the tiniest bit. 'I need to talk to you about Stephen.'

He stiffens. 'What about him?'

'I'm finished at Wilkinson & Son. I haven't told him yet. Not officially.'

Mark leans forward and tugs on the zip of his overnight bag, even though it's already shut. 'Right.'

'Don't you want to know why?'

'Not really.' He gives me a long searching look and my cheeks flush warm. He knows I'm hiding something but, like me, he doesn't want any more arguments. This is the closest we've been in months and neither of us wants to shatter our fragile truce. 'So what do you think you'll do now? Get another job or wait until after DS Forbes gets back to us with—'

A knock at the bedroom door interrupts him.

'Yes?'

The door opens slowly, revealing Jake in the doorway with the landline phone in his hand. He shifts his weight from one foot to the other.

'I rang Ian,' he says, looking directly at me. 'I'm going in later this week. I rang Kira too. She's sleeping on Amy's floor tonight. I said I'd pick her up in the morning.'

He looks so broken, so contrite, so deeply ashamed that my heart twists in my chest. One of my sons is missing and the other is falling apart in front of my eyes. I have never felt so powerless or so impotent in my life.

'Wait . . .' He holds up a hand, palm out, as I move

to stand up and hug him. 'There's something else I need to say. Dad. I . . . um . . . I just wanted to say sorry. I . . .' His gaze drops to the floor and he swallows. 'I was out of order. I'm sorry. I just . . . I was angry and . . .'

'It's okay, son.' Mark steps over the suitcase and crosses the bedroom. 'I understand.'

Hug him, I urge silently. Please just hug him. But only one of Mark's arms reaches for his son.

'You look after your mum,' he says as he grips Jake's upper arm and gives it a squeeze. 'I've got to go.'

He turns to look at me. 'I'll be back on Sunday night. Give me a ring if anything happens. I'm only in Gloucester.'

'Of course,' I say. 'We'll be fine. Won't we, Jake—'

But our son has already slipped away into the shadows.

Chapter 34

'So are we ready for a bit of vampire action then?'
Liz announces as she bursts into the living room, a
DVD under her right armpit, a bottle of Prosecco in
each hand and two glasses woven through her fingers.
One bottle is already open and the wine sploshes out
from the neck and runs down her hand as she throws
herself at the sofa. It's 6.30 p.m.

'You've started early.'

'Yeah, I know.' She pulls a face. 'Switched shifts
and I'm knackered. Oh, pizza!' She points at the open
box on the rug in front of the TV. 'Can I have a slice?'

'Sure. Jake's having his in his room and I'm not
hungry.'

'Is he not joining us then?'

'No. I think he's watching something on his laptop.'

'Kira?' She crams a slice of pizza into her mouth,
poking a stray piece of pepperoni between her lips
before it falls to the floor.

'Out.' I haven't told her about what happened earlier.

'Shame. Though she's probably seen it before.'

'How's Caleb?'

'Out with his boyfriend.' She smiles as she slips back onto the sofa. 'God, I need this.' She hands me the glasses, then tips in the wine so quickly the bubbles surge to the top and spill over down the sides. 'Sorry! I'll get a tea towel.'

'It's fine, don't worry.'

It's been a while since I've seen Liz this manic. It can only mean one thing. Lloyd's been in touch.

'You okay, Liz?'

'Great.' She places her glass on the table next to the sofa, then tries to insert a DVD into the player.

'What's Lloyd said now?'

'Oh God.' She sighs heavily and rocks back on her heels, holding on to the TV unit for support. 'You don't need to hear my crap.'

'Yes, I do. What did he want?'

'The mortgage paperwork. And his bank statements and pension stuff. I think he's going to ask for a divorce. He's an arsehole. What can I say? Anyway –' she waves a dismissive hand through the air – 'I'm not going to let him screw up tonight too. We have wine to drink and a film to watch and I'm not going to give him a second thought. How are you anyway?'

I take a sip of my wine. 'Let's just say I'm looking forward to the film.'

'Great.' She flashes a smile at me. 'I knew there was a reason I liked you.'

For thirty minutes we do nothing apart from sip wine and watch the screen as a young girl falls over a lot and a pasty-looking bloke and his equally pasty family act aloof and mysterious at every opportunity. When we've finished the first bottle Liz pauses the DVD so I can go to the kitchen to retrieve the other one from the fridge.

'He's gurt lush,' she says as I refill her glass.

'Who?'

'Robert Pattinson.' She gestures towards the screen where the freeze-frame has captured the actor looking wistful and conflicted.

'He's about twelve!'

'Actually, he was twenty-two when he filmed this.'

'But he's at school in the film, so he's supposed to be what, sixteen?'

'Seriously though, Claire.' She pauses the film, then digs in her handbag for her phone. She presses a few buttons and tilts the screen towards me. 'Look at this.'

'Is that Tinder? You installed it then!'

'Yep. And I have a point to prove. Now here –' she swipes at the screen – 'are some of the local men who are about the same age as me. Shout out if you see one you think is fit.'

She swipes through photo after photo, all of them of middle-aged men. Some are balding, some have a good head of hair, some are fat, some thin, some badly dressed, some in suits, some wearing very little at all. Apart from the half-naked man flexing a bicep in the bathroom mirror and scowling into the camera,

I'm surprised at how normal they all look. They're the sort of men you'd see down the pub, in the supermarket or at work.

'Still waiting for you to shout when you see a fit one,' Liz says.

She continues to flick through an encyclopedia of men.

'That one!' I say.

'Okay.' She peers at the man I've selected. He's sitting on a picnic blanket, a glass of beer in his hand and his head thrown back in laughter. His hair is peppered with grey above his ears but long and thick on top. He's got a strong jaw, a Roman nose and good skin. More than anything else, he looks as though he'd be a laugh.

'Okay, I'll give you him.' She swipes to the right and laughs. 'Or rather, I'll have him. Anyway, now I'll change the age range so it's eighteen to thirty. Shout if you see someone lush.'

A photo of a toned bloke standing by a swimming pool flashes up and Liz raises an eyebrow at me. 'Lush or not?'

'Well, yes, but—'

She swipes to the right. 'How about this one?'

'Yes, but—'

'And this one?'

'Okay, okay.' I hold up a hand. 'I get it. You think the younger blokes are fitter and maybe they are but you're forty-three, Liz – what are you going to talk to an eighteen-year-old about?'

She smirks. 'Who said anything about talking?

Claire, I was with Lloyd for twenty-two years. I think I deserve a bit of fun.'

'You do, but I still think *Twilight* guy is too young.'

'For you, maybe.' She laughs at the expression on my face and reaches for the remote. 'Right. On with the film.'

Liz weaves her way across the street and up the path to her house. She pauses to wave at me as she reaches her front door, then drops her key on the ground and swears loudly. It takes her four attempts to fit it into the lock. I glance at my watch as she closes the door behind her: 9.15 p.m. She fell asleep during the last fifteen minutes of the film, her wine glass still in her hand, her phone flashing on her lap each time she received a new Tinder notification. It took me for ever to wake her up. Saying her name had no effect so I gently agitated her shoulder which made her murmur, 'Leave me alone, I'm too tired to have sex.' My laughter woke her up.

I put our wine glasses in the dishwasher and the empty bottles in the recycling bin. Despite the amount of wine I've drunk I feel strangely clear-headed as I wipe down the kitchen surfaces and tidy up. When I've finished I go back into the living room. I haven't heard from Mark for several hours and I need to check he's okay.

My mobile's not where I thought I left it on the side table by the sofa so I get on my hands and knees and look underneath, just in case I knocked it under when I was getting up and down to fetch more wine.

I scramble back onto my feet. There's nothing under the sofa apart from a thick layer of dust and hair on the carpet and several of Kira's bobby pins. And it's not in my pocket either. Under one of the cushions, then?

The floorboards creak above me as Jake walks from his room to the bathroom. My fingernails fill with crumbs as I search down the side of the sofa but there's still no sign of my phone. That means it's either down the side of the armchair or it's in my handbag in the kitchen. I head for the armchair and yank at the cushion.

A phone flips onto the base of the armchair. It's an iPhone, but it's not mine. It's a newer model. I press the circular button at the base of the phone and the screen flashes to life revealing a preview of a new message. Even though the phone is locked I can still read every word of the short text:

I can keep a secret if you can.

Chapter 35

Where am I?

WHERE AM I?

It is dark. Pitch black. I can't see anything.

'Jake!' I scream his name. 'Mark!'

No one comes.

I shout again. 'Someone please help!'

The sound reverberates around me.

'Hello?' The word catches in my throat. 'Can anyone hear me?'

My hands shake as I lift them from my lap and tentatively extend my arms. I grope around in the darkness, swiping at the air. There's nothing, nothing, and then the fingers of my left hand graze something cold and solid and I snatch my hands back to my chest. As I do something sharp pricks at my stomach. It's in my lap! I swipe at it and jump away. My back smashes against a wall and my heels skitter on the ground.

There is a clattering sound, like metal hitting tile, and I freeze.

I want to shout for help but I can't. I can't speak. I can barely breathe.

My bottom feels cold and wet, as though liquid has soaked through the seat of my jeans and onto my skin. The air is thick with the scent of urine and iron.

I need to calm down. If I don't I'll pass out.

I concentrate on my breathing, sucking in air and filling my lungs before I blow it back out again.

In. Out. In. Out.

Slowly, slowly, my breathing quietens and my fingernails, gripping the wall I'm pressed into, cease their incessant tapping.

'Hello?' The word echoes off the walls. I am in a room, an empty room. I touch my fingertips to the ground beneath my feet. The walls and floors are tiled.

Okay. Okay. I'm in a room. I'm on my own. There has to be a door or a window, a way out.

As my heartbeat slows, the darkness surrounding me seems to fade and objects emerge from the gloom. There are two sinks to my right, two cubicles to my left and a metallic urine trough on the other side of the room. Beside it is a door, with a sliver of light at the bottom.

I haul myself up and step towards it. As I do my heel catches something on the floor. It skids away from me, spinning across the tiles towards the sinks. It makes a low clunking sound as it hits the wall and then lies still. I inch my way forward and peer under the sinks.

A knife.

I don't scream. I don't drop to my knees. And I don't run towards the door beyond the sinks.

I stand up.

I know where I am now. I know what's happening.

I'm dreaming. I'm asleep on the sofa at home and I'm looking for Billy. As soon as I find him the dream will end and I'll wake up. I step towards the nearest cubicle, one hand outstretched and push at the door, hard. The lock clatters against the wall as it swings open.

Empty.

Of course. Billy's never in the first place I look for him. I always have to search. I take three steps to my right and push at the second door.

Empty.

'Mum?'

I spin round, but the pale-skinned person staring back at me from the mirror above the sink has my eyes, not Billy's. I put a hand to my forehead and stroke the hair out of my face. Four smudged and bloodied fingerprints appear on my skin. A guilt dream. A nightmare in which I discover that I was responsible for Billy's disappearance.

I crouch down and reach for the knife under the sink. It's one of my kitchen knives. The handle is smeared in blood. I don't touch it. Instead I open my handbag, slung across my body, and pull out a tissue. I wrap it around the knife, tuck it carefully into my bag and then wash my hands. Blood swirls around the basin before disappearing down the plughole.

Billy is not here. I have to keep looking.

The second I step out of the door and into the light two figures rush towards me. A man and a woman; their faces are taut with worry. The woman has a phone pressed to her ear.

'Oh my God.' The man reaches me first and draws to a halt. 'What happened?'

The woman puffs towards us, still talking into her phone, her breath coming in short sharp bursts. 'I can see her . . . she's right in front of me . . . she's on her feet . . . she doesn't appear to be hurt . . .'

'Are you okay?' the man asks.

His fingers graze my arm and I snatch it away from him, smacking my hand against the door frame.

A sharp pain shoots up my wrist and I hug it to my chest. I try to speak but the words feel jumbled in my mouth as my legs give way beneath me.

'What did she say?' the woman asks, her phone hanging loosely in her hand, as the man grabs me round the shoulders and slowly lowers me to the floor.

'Something about how you can't feel pain in a nightmare and oh God, I'm awake.'

'What did you ring an ambulance for?'

'Because that guy sounded so worried about her.'

'Why didn't you wait until we got to her? As if the NHS hasn't got enough problems without their

261

ambulance crews being called out for no reason. She looks fine and she's not injured.'

'Malcolm, just because she's standing up again doesn't mean she's not hurt. She's only just stopped shaking.'

'She's probably a prostitute. Why else would she be hanging round the men's loos at ten o'clock at night?'

As they continue to argue in hushed tones, but not so quiet that I can't hear them, I look around. The walls are pale and grubby and there are grey stairs, the edges painted yellow that stretch above and below the small square of concrete where the three of us are standing. A black metal handrail runs the length of the stairs and, on the wall, is a blue sign that says, *Have you paid and displayed your ticket?*

I'm in a car park.

'Where is this place?' I touch the woman on the arm.

'Oh!' She leaps away from me and clutches at her husband's arm. He takes a step towards me, instinctively tucking her behind him, protecting her. From me.

'Bristol. You're in a multistorey car park in the centre.'

'Who sounded worried?'

'Sorry?' The man smiles sympathetically but there's a different emotion in his eyes now. He thinks I'm on drugs, or drunk.

'You said someone was worried. Were you talking about me?'

'There was a man,' the woman says. 'He ran past our car shouting that a woman had collapsed in the men's toilets.'

'Was he young?' My heart contracts with hope. 'Could he have been fifteen?'

'I don't know.' She glances up at her husband.

'He was wearing dark clothes, maybe a hoody, but I didn't see his face.'

'I need to ring my family,' I say. 'I need to tell them where I am.'

As I unzip my handbag I see something wrapped in my tissue and the ground seems to drop from beneath me. The knife is real. I didn't dream that either.

'She's gone very pale,' the woman says. 'I think she's going to pass out.'

'Do you want to sit down on the step?' The husband reaches out a tentative hand. 'My wife's rung an ambulance. It should be here soon.'

'Let me take your bag,' says the woman but I snatch it away before she can touch it. The sudden movement makes my legs give way. I grab at the handrail but I'm falling too quickly and I land heavily, smacking the base of my spine against the sharp line of the top step.

'Don't move,' the man says as he crouches beside me. 'You might have injured yourself.'

'It's okay.' I ease myself up into a sitting position and rub at my lower back. It spasms with pain.

'Listen . . . um . . .' The man pauses. 'Sorry, what's your name? I'm Malcolm and this is Mandy.'

He looks at me expectantly, waiting for me to say my name.

I try to pull myself up but my legs are too wobbly to hold my weight. 'I just need to get home. I think I might have a car here, somewhere.' I glance back towards the door that leads to the car park but I have no idea where my car is, or even if it's here at all. I could have walked, taken a taxi or got a lift with someone. It's a blank.

'You need to wait for the ambulance,' the woman says from behind us. 'You might have hit your head when you fell over in the toilet. Concussion can be very serious. My cousin Sarah fell down the stairs a few years ago and—'

'Mandy!' Malcolm shakes his head. 'Not now.'

'But she might—'

'You still haven't told us your name.' He looks back at me.

I clutch my bag to my chest. The knife may be wrapped in swathes of tissue paper and hidden beneath a fold of leather but I feel as though it's a flashing beacon. If the police turn up with the ambulance they're going to start asking questions I can't answer. Whose blood is on the knife? Who was stabbed? Where did the knife come from?

'My name is Kate,' I say. 'Kate Sawyer.'

'Great.' The man smiles. 'I shouldn't imagine the ambulance is going to be much longer Kate. We're happy to wait with you until it gets here.'

'No. No ambulance. Please, I just need to get home. Thank you for all your help.' I force myself onto my feet and, clinging on to the handrail, descend one step at a time.

'Wait!' Malcolm calls. 'At least let us give you a lift. Mandy can cancel the ambulance.'

'I'll get a taxi.'

'Let us walk you to the rank. I'm sure your family are very worried about you. Please, just let us do that.'

I'm too tired to say no again.

Chapter 36

'You're back!' Jake rushes into the kitchen as I stumble in through the front door. 'Oh my God. You look awful! You're limping. Why are you limping?'

His eyes are bloodshot as though he's been crying, there's a sheen of sweat on his forehead and his hair is dirty, slicked back with grease or hair product – I can't tell which. He's wearing a tatty jumper, pulled over his hands. It feels as though I haven't seen him for years and I'm shocked anew by how broken he looks.

'Mum?' he says again and his strong, handsome face seems to collapse in on itself. 'Say something, Mum.'

'I had another blackout.' It's all I can manage before I collapse into his arms.

He pulls me into him and I press my face to his chest, comforted by the familiar but musky scent of his skin through his T-shirt.

'Oh my God, another one?' he says. 'What happened? Tell me everything you can remember.'

'And then they walked me to a taxi rank and I came home,' I finish. 'And let myself in.'

I'm on the sofa and there is a cup of tea on the table beside me. Steam no longer rises from the surface of the mug. I haven't had more than two or three sips since we sat down.

'That's it?' Jake asks. 'That's all you can remember? Coming round in the toilets?'

'Jake, I . . .'

I want to tell him how terrified I was. How I thought I'd woken up in a coffin or been locked in a box. But I can't tell him how disorientating, how truly, truly frightening it is not to know where you are or even who you are, because I don't want to scare him. I don't want him to worry about me. He's falling apart as it is. 'Yes,' I say. 'That's all I can remember.'

My handbag is tucked between me and the arm of the sofa. I haven't told Jake about the knife. How can I when I don't know what it means? It looks like one of mine, one of the knives we use for steak, but there must be hundreds or thousands of people who own one. I bought it from B&M in the Broadwalk shopping centre, not somewhere fancy.

There are only two possibilities: either someone used the knife on me or I used it on them. But I'm not bleeding. There was blood on my fingertips but I'm not hurt. I surreptitiously checked myself for

267

injuries while I was sitting in the back of the cab.

Someone else's blood then.

'Mum?' Jake says. 'Aren't you going to answer that?'

'Sorry?'

'Your phone.' He points at my bag. 'It's ringing.'

I tilt the bag towards me, hiding the contents from Jake who's sitting in the armchair across the room, as I unzip it and carefully take out my phone.

It's Mark.

'Hello, darling.' His voice sounds muddied, as though he's tired or been drinking. 'I just wanted to check that you're okay and say goodnight before I turn in. I was thinking about you all the way from Bristol to Gloucester.'

'You're there then?'

'Yes, of course.' He laughs. 'Where did you think I was?'

'Nowhere. I . . . it's good to hear your voice.'

'And it's good to hear yours.' He laughs again. He's definitely drunk. He always used to get a bit soppy after a night out. Soppy and loving. 'It's been a while since I rang you to say goodnight, hasn't it? Remember when we were dating and I'd go on a night out with the boys and you'd go on a night out with the girls? I'd always give you a ring before I went to sleep. Well, it was more like passing out and we'd . . .'

He continues to talk, laughing at his one-sided reminiscences, his voice a low murmur in my ear as Jake reaches into the pocket of his tracksuit and pulls out his phone. He taps at the screen with his thumb.

I interrupt Mark, still in full flow. 'I'd better let you go. You've got a big day tomorrow.'

'Yeah.' He sighs. 'I have. Okay. Sleep well, Claire. I love you.'

'I . . .' I pause. It's been so long since I told Mark I love him that the words feel alien in my mouth. 'I love you too.'

'Bye then. Bye!'

The line goes dead and Jake looks up from his phone. 'Was that Dad?'

'Yeah.'

'You didn't tell him what happened.'

'No.' I shake my head. 'I didn't want to worry him and . . .' I pause as an image flashes across my mind. The last thing I saw before I blacked out.

'Mum?' Jake says. 'What's the matter?'

The room swims and the air grows thick and hot.

'Mum?' Jake tucks his phone back into his pocket as he moves to stand up. 'You're not having another blackout, are you? Should I ring someone?'

'No.'

'What do you want me to do?'

'Tell me the secret you're keeping from me.'

Jake shifts in his seat. 'Secret? I don't know what you're talking about.'

'Yes, you do.'

'No, I—'

'Give me your phone then.'

'What?' He blanches. 'No. It's . . . personal.'

I sit forward, my mind suddenly clear. 'I read one

269

of your messages. It said, "I can keep a secret if you can." Who sent it to you?'

'Uh . . .' His hand moves to his pocket, as though he's checking that the phone is still there. 'No one.'

'I read it. Tell me who sent it to you, Jake. Was it Billy? Do you know where he is?'

'Billy?' His eyes widen in surprise. 'God . . . no . . . no, of course it wasn't. How could Billy—'

'Then who? Who sent it? Tell me or I'll ring the police.' It's an idle threat but Jake doesn't know that. I can't ring the police, not until I've checked whether the knife is one of mine.

Jake looks across at the photograph of Billy on the mantelpiece. 'It's from a girl.'

'What girl?'

'A girl I know.'

'You haven't left the house in days. How could you have met a girl?'

'Well, I . . .' He rubs his palms against his thighs. 'I haven't exactly met her in person yet but . . . but I know her.'

'How?'

'Through –' he clears his throat – 'Tinder.'

'Tinder? The dating app?'

'Yeah.'

'But what about Kira? I thought you loved her.'

'I do. I do love her, more than anything in the world, but she won't let me near her. We haven't had sex in months.' The base of his throat flushes red as he stares at the carpet. 'I was just having a bit of fun, a bit of banter.'

270

I hold out a hand. 'Show me the phone.'

'No.'

'Show me the phone, Jake.'

'Mum, it's . . . the messages, they're . . . they're quite explicit.'

'Show me the phone.'

'Okay. But you're not going to like it.' It seems to take an age for him to cross the living room and join me on the sofa. He tilts the phone away from me and unlocks it, then shows me the screen. 'See, Tinder.'

He points at a white icon containing a red flame. It's the same app Liz showed me earlier.

'Show me the messages.'

He cringes away. 'Mum, please.'

'Now, Jake.'

'Okay.' He sighs as he taps the message icon and a list of his most recent messages fills the screen. The one at the top says:

I can keep a secret if you can.

It's the message I saw earlier. Below it is a message Jake sent:

I shouldn't be doing this. I'm really nervous someone will find out.

The one before that reads:

I can't wait to see you. Last night I fell asleep dreaming of your cock in my mouth and your fingers in my hair.

Beneath it, another message from Jake:

I really want you. I know I shouldn't but you're all I can think about. You make me feel things I haven't felt before. I want to fuck you really hard and—

'Okay.' I push the phone away. 'I've read enough.'

'I told you.' Jake can't bring himself to look me in the eye. 'I told you it was bad.'

'Bad?' Rage builds in my chest as I think of Kira, standing at the back door crying because of how much she loves him. 'Go!' I point at the living-room door. 'Get out of my sight before I do something I regret.'

Chapter 37

The second Jake's bedroom door slams shut I head for the kitchen and yank open the cutlery drawer. I rifle through the different compartments and count out the steak knives.

I find three and put them on the kitchen table, then pull open the door to the dishwasher. It's mid-cycle – Jake must have put it on shortly before I returned home – and a cloud of steam hits me full in the face. When the steam has dissipated I pull out the cutlery basket and pick through the spoons, forks and knives.

I pull out two steak knives by their handles and line them up with the others on the table. Five knives.

I go through the cutlery drawer again, lifting up the metal tray to see if a knife has found its way underneath but there's nothing there apart from a rusty bottle opener. I look in the dishwasher, both trays this time, then pull the bottom one out and feel around in the drum of the machine. Nothing.

The utensils pots near the oven are next. The missing knife isn't in with the wooden spoons or the spatulas, nor is it in the knife block. I rummage through the junk drawer beneath the microwave but there's no knife there either. The only other place to check is Jake's room.

I have to knock three times before my son responds.

When I open the door he is lying on his bed in his boxer shorts, his thick arms crossed over his chest, his hands tucked beneath his armpits. I can see the wariness in his eyes. He thinks I've come to have another go at him about cheating on Kira.

'What is it, Mum?'

'Just looking for dirty dishes.' Normally I'd find plates on the carpet, mugs on the chest of drawers and breakfast bowls stacked on top of each other on his bedside table, but his room appears to be completely free of either crockery or cutlery.

'I put the dishwasher on earlier.'

'Yes, I saw.'

'You don't need an excuse if you want to come and talk to me, you know.'

'I didn't . . . I wasn't . . .'

'I deserved it,' he says flatly. 'You screaming at me earlier. It's been a long time coming. I'm surprised you didn't hit me.'

'I'd never do that.'

'I know, and I've always found that weird. When me and Billy were at primary school the other kids would come in sometimes and they'd tell everyone

274

how they'd been walloped the night before because they'd stolen something or talked back to their parents or whatever. It wasn't just one kid – loads of kids in my class were hit by their parents and I didn't get it. Me and Billy answered you and Dad back all the time. We played up. We didn't do what we were told. Billy even nicked money out of your purse one time and—'

'I didn't know that!'

'He was sneaky like that.' He smiles. 'We both were. We were little shits, just like the kids in school who got smacked by their parents, but you two never touched us.'

'That's because our parents hit us and we swore we'd never do the same to our kids.'

'Me and Billy – neither of us were angels.'

'I know that,' I say softly, 'but I still love you. There's nothing either of you could do that I couldn't forgive.'

'Seriously? So if I told you that Billy had killed someone or I'd raped someone you'd still forgive that?'

I stare at him in horror. 'What are you trying to tell me?'

'Nothing that bad . . . but . . . I . . .' His chin drops to his chest. 'I said and did some horrible things the night Billy ran away.'

I put a hand on the door frame. 'Like what?'

'After Dad went to the pub and you went to Gran's, Billy started dicking about with his lighter, holding it under a cushion and saying he was going to burn

275

the house down to pay Dad back. I lost it. I told him that everything Dad had said was right. That he was a loser and an embarrassment to the family.'

'That's no worse than the things your dad said.'

'It gets worse. Billy told me I was going out with the town bike and that everyone was laughing at me behind my back. I lost it and I hit him. I punched him in the face. I split his lip.'

I try to cover my shock with my hand but I'm too slow and he hears me gasp.

'Kira heard the whole thing.' He turns to look at me. 'She was standing at the top of the stairs. I ran up to her, thinking she'd thank me for sticking up for her, but she just . . . she just sort of froze, so I asked her if it was true. She didn't say anything. She just stood there.

'I was so angry I went into my room and cracked open a bottle of whisky and necked it. Next thing I knew it was morning and Kira was in bed beside me and I was so hungover I could hardly open my eyes.'

I can't believe what I'm hearing. 'Why haven't you told me this before? Does Dad know? Did you tell the police?'

'I thought Billy would come back. I thought he'd done it to get attention and I wasn't going to play along.' He takes a deep breath. 'When we realized that he wasn't dicking about and the police interviewed us I told them the truth. They asked if anyone could corroborate my statement and I said that Kira could. They never talked to me about it again. I should have told you and Dad too but you were both so cut up and I didn't . . . I didn't want you to hate me.'

'Oh, Jake.'

'No, Mum. Don't hug me. I don't deserve it. If I hadn't hit him Billy wouldn't have left and Jason Davies wouldn't have got hold of him. My brother's been murdered and it's all my fault. It's my fucking fault!'

He moves in a blur. One second he's sitting on the bed, the next he's up on his knees. He swings back his right arm and smashes his fist into the bedroom wall, then follows it with a punch from his left hand.

'Stop! Jake, stop! Don't do this!'

I use all my body weight to try and pull him away but it's like wrestling a bull as he punches the wall again and again and again, driving his fists into it, smearing it with blood.

'Please! Stop! Please!'

Jake pauses, fist pulled back, and as quickly as his rage boiled to the surface it dies away and he slumps onto the bed and curls up in the foetal position, his knuckles raw and bleeding.

'Jake.' I press myself into the curve of his back and wrap my arms around him. 'Jake, it's not your fault. Listen to me, please. I could never blame you for what's happened. Never. Never.'

He howls with anguish and then bursts into tears. I hold him as he cries, his body juddering in my arms just the way it did when he was a toddler.

Chapter 38

Sonia gestures for me to take a seat and smiles warmly. The box of tissues that normally sits on the window-sill behind her has been relocated to the coffee table next to me. I don't know if that's because her last client was a crier or because she's expecting me to be.

'Thanks for seeing me,' I say. 'If you hadn't had a cancellation I don't know what I would have done.'

'No problem at all.' She tucks a strand of hair behind her ear and settles herself in the seat, neatly tucking one ankle over the other. 'Tell me what's going on with you, Claire.'

She listens silently as I tell her what happened after I read the message on Jake's phone. Almost everything. I don't mention the blood or the knife.

'Then,' I say, 'when Kira came home I managed to have a quick word with her before she went up to Jake's room. I told her he was in a bad way. That

278

he felt guilty about Billy's disappearance but that didn't give him the right to talk to her the way he had. I said that if he spoke to her like again she needed to tell me.'

'How did she respond?'

'She looked shocked.'

'Did you ask her about the night Billy disappeared?'

'Yes. She said it happened exactly as Jake had described. She said she'd been angry too, that Jake would believe that she'd cheat on him. That's why she wouldn't talk to him.'

'How do you feel, Claire? Knowing more about that night?'

'Confused.' I run a hand over my face. The window on the other side of the room is open a few inches but the air feels too thick to breathe. 'If Billy did run away there were a lot of reasons why, not just because he was in trouble with the police and us.'

'And how do you feel now, about spending that night at your mum's?'

'I don't know.' My head is pounding so I close my eyes.

'What is it, Claire? What's wrong?'

'I just . . . there are so many things going round in my head and none of it makes sense. I thought the fugues would stop after I started seeing you but the last one was terrifying.'

'Because of where you were?'

Do I tell her? I didn't tell Mark about my blackout when he came home. I don't know why. Maybe because there's a tiny part of me that's worried he's lying about the photo album? What if there is more evidence that links him with Billy's disappearance? But what? None of it makes sense. Mark loved Billy. He'd shout at him and come down on him hard but he's not a cruel or violent man. So why is part of me so suspicious? What is it that I don't know?

'Claire?' Sonia says. 'What is it?'

I look at her through my fingers. If I tell her about the knife will she inform the police? My GP? Could she have me sectioned if she thinks I'm dangerous?

'If I . . .' I falter. 'If I tell you there's a chance I've committed a crime will you tell the police?'

'A chance?'

I sit forward in my chair. 'Will you tell the police?'

For the first time since I sat down Sonia looks ruffled. 'I am not legally obliged to report any crimes that my clients may confess to but it does present me with an ethical dilemma.'

'So you would, then?'

'No.' She regains her composure. 'That's not what I said. I'd use my professional judgement to work out what to do, and what to advise you.'

'You'd tell me to go to the police?'

'Well, yes. I'd be more likely to advise you to go to the police than do it myself but if I did report the crime to the police it wouldn't be without your knowledge. And I would discuss it with my supervisor first.'

I weigh up my options. I could keep quiet and get rid of the knife. I could talk to Liz about it. Yes, that's what I should do. I should tell Liz. But if I have committed a crime that would make her an accomplice. And what could she do, anyway, other than tell me to go to the police, tell Mark or keep quiet about it – all possibilities I've already considered myself.

If I tell Sonia, I get a psychologist's insight into what happened. And if she can't help me maybe I should go to the police? The only way I'll find out whose blood is on the knife is for them to check it for DNA and ask the car-park company to look at the CCTV. But what if it reveals that I stabbed someone? I kicked a cyclist after I came round from my second fugue. What if I'm capable of worse? If I killed someone I'd be jailed for murder.

'Claire.' Sonia moves the box of tissues away from me. 'Claire, it's okay.'

There is a pile of torn tissues on the floor in front of me. I don't remember reaching for the box. How can I have shredded that many and not noticed?

'Whatever happened –' Sonia crouches on the floor beside me, her eyes soft and non-judgemental – 'it has obviously really upset you. Have you spoken to anyone about it? A member of your family, or a friend?'

I shake my head.

'You said you *might* have committed a crime, not that you *did*,' she says softly. 'There's a difference. Tell me what happened.'

'I can't.' I shake my head. 'I can't remember.'

'Then what makes you think that's a possibility?'

'There was a knife –' the word catches in my throat – 'on the floor next to me in the car-park toilet. It was covered in blood.'

She nods, gently urging me to continue.

'It was one of my steak knives. I checked the drawer when I got home. There are supposed to be six, but one is missing.'

'I see.' Her expression remains impassive. 'And when was the last time you counted the knives? When did you last check that there were six?'

'I don't think I ever have. I bought them years ago and put them in the drawer. I've never bothered counting them because we only ever needed five.'

'Are you the only person in your family with access to those knives?'

'No, of course not.'

'Claire,' she says softly, laying her hand on the table, 'what if you weren't the one to commit the crime? What if someone else took that knife?'

'But it can't have been anyone else,' I say. 'Jake was at home, Kira was at a friend's house and Mark was away.'

'That's not what I mean.' Sonia's knees click as she eases herself up from her crouched position and returns to her chair. 'The knife could have been taken from the drawer months ago and you wouldn't have noticed.'

'You think . . .' My heart double-beats in my chest. 'You think Billy could have taken it?'

'I think anyone could have. But what I'm most interested in is why you've jumped to the conclusion that you were the one who used the knife to commit a crime.'

'Because it was right next to me and I was alone.

Wait!' I jolt forward in my seat. 'The couple who found me saw a man running across the car park. He told them I'd collapsed. I thought it was Billy.'

'Why?'

'I don't know.'

'But it could have been someone else?'

'Yes, yes, it could.'

'Which means there's a possibility that you witnessed a crime. Claire, I'm going to be completely honest here. I think you should go to the police and tell them what happened. Do you still have the knife?'

Yesterday, before Mark came home, I wrapped the knife in a plastic bag and hid it in an old tote bag in the bottom of my wardrobe.

'But what if you're wrong? What if . . . I don't know . . . what if the man who was running away was a witness and I had stabbed someone?'

'Why would a witness run away? And why would he ask total strangers to help you?'

'I don't know.'

Neither of us says anything for several minutes.

If I contact the police I could be turning in someone I love without knowing what they did or why. Just yesterday Jake was asking me if I'd still love him and Billy if either of them did something awful. What if it was him? What if I caught him stabbing someone? But he wouldn't run away and leave me in such a confused state. Or would he? No, I won't let myself go there. I can't.

'Claire,' Sonia says. 'I have a suggestion. In our last session we tried to make sense of the causes of your fugues so we could work on preventing them from happening again. Unfortunately it seems that it didn't have enough of an effect so I have another suggestion.'

I eye her warily. 'What kind of suggestion?'

'Would you agree to be hypnotized by me?'

I make my decision in a split second. 'Yes, yes, I would.'

Chapter 39

My mind has retreated deep inside itself. Normally my thoughts are at the front of my brain, whizzing and whirling around each other, but those thoughts are a long way away now. It is dark, this place I have reached inside my head. It feels as though I'm in the depths of a tunnel. The sides are grey and cloud-like but they make me feel protected, not scared.

Sonia's voice surrounds me, telling me to relax, telling me to let myself go deeper with each breath. I do as I am told and my body becomes limp and heavy and my heart stops thudding in my chest. As Sonia continues to speak random thoughts pop into my head – thoughts telling me that I should be worried, that I need to stay in control. I acknowledge them and then, as Sonia tells me to, I let them drift away.

'I'm going to take you back,' she says, 'to the moments before your first fugue. You were in Liz's house and you went to the bathroom. Remember it now, remember what her bathroom looked like. Have a look around and tell me how you feel.'

I am so relaxed I have to work hard to form words in my throat but the urge to answer her question is stronger than my desire to remain silent. 'Liz just suggested that Billy might never come home and I feel sick.'

'Let that feeling go,' Sonia says. 'Let it go. You no longer feel sick. You are running the tap. Feel the sensation of the water on your face.'

I hear myself sigh.

'What happens now, Claire?'

'I see . . . I see a newspaper, sticking out of the bin. Billy's name is on the front page.'

'What else does it say?'

'There's a quote. Someone, a neighbour. They said . . . they said . . .'

'It's okay, Claire. You're safe here. You can tell me what it says.'

'Maybe someone in that family knows more about Billy's disappearance than they're letting on.'

'How do you feel now, Claire?'

Panic grips my chest and my breath catches in my throat.

'Relax. Relax and go deeper. Those memories cannot hurt you now. Listen to my voice and go deeper, Claire. Let your whole body relax. You are safe.'

'No. No, I'm not. They know.'

'Who? What do they know?'

'Everyone. They know what I fear.'

'What do you fear, Claire?'

I hear a low groan. It must be coming from me.

'That someone I know hurt Billy.'

'And why do you fear that?'

'I don't know.'

'I think you do. Let yourself go deeper, Claire. As you listen to my voice let yourself go deeper. Let your body and mind relax. You are safe. You have nothing to fear.'

The grey walls close in on me and I drift backwards, deeper into myself. It is dark but it is safe. I am safe. I want to stay here.

'Why do you think that someone in your family hurt Billy?'

'Gut. Gut feeling.'

'Is it something someone has done or said?'

I don't want to talk any more. I feel tired. I want to go to sleep.

'Claire? Was it something someone said or did?'

'I don't know.'

There is a pause, silence, and I drift around within it until Sonia's voice calls me back again. 'Okay. Okay, let's move on. To the next fugue. You found a photo album with images of Mark blacked out and abuse scrawled over the pages. You went looking for Mark, didn't you?'

I try to search my memory, to answer her question, to please her, but there's nothing there. 'I don't know.'

'What did you feel? When you saw those photos?'

'Scared. Shocked.'

'And did it occur to you that maybe Mark had hurt Billy? That he'd had something to do with his disappearance?'

'Mmm.'

'Is that a yes?'

'Yes.'

'And the next fugue. When you saw the message on Jake's mobile phone. What did you think?'

'Secret. About Billy.'

'You thought Jake and someone else knew what had happened to Billy?'

'Yes.'

'And who did you think sent the text to Jake?'

'I don't know.'

'Who could it have been, Claire?'

Faces flash at me through the darkness. Kira. Mark. Liz. Caleb. Stephen. Lloyd. Edie Christian. Caroline. Ian.

'Someone you know?' Sonia says and I don't know if I said those names aloud or if she can see inside my head. 'You think your friends and family are keeping secrets from you, don't you?'

'Yes.'

'I'm going to bring you out of your trance in a minute, Claire, but I've got one more question I'd like to ask you first. It's a difficult question but I want you to give me the first answer that comes into your head. Can you do that for me?'

I attempt to nod my head. It feels heavy and unwieldy. 'Yes.'

'Claire, do you think Billy is alive or dead?'

I don't want to speak. I don't want to say a word but the compulsion to answer her is too strong. My lips part and my tongue taps at the roof of my mouth. 'Dead.'

Chapter 40

We drive in silence through Bristol and up the Wells Road. The streets flash past. Mothers, bent double and panting, heave their buggies up the hill as school-children speed past them on scooters. Old men sit at bus stops staring vacantly into space as their wives natter, unheard, beside them. Weary shoppers pour out of the Co-op, heavy carrier bags cutting into their palms, and men stride out of the barber's, tapping at their hair. Everywhere I look there is life but mine has ended.

'Here we are, love,' Mum says as she turns off the engine and I am surprised to find myself outside her two-bed semi on the edge of Knowle. 'Let's get you in.'

She reaches over and unbuckles my seat belt, then gets out of the car and disappears from view. A second later she is beside me and I feel a rush of cool air on my face as she reaches for my hand. 'Come on, sweetheart, let's get you inside.'

She leads me towards the front door and I stumble after her like a child who's just learned to take its first steps. She turns the key in the lock and gently ushers me into the lounge. She angles me towards the sofa and I land heavily as my feet disappear from beneath me.

'Tea,' she says under her breath as she disappears back out through the living-room door.

Sounds drift towards me from the kitchen: a tap running, a kettle boiling, mugs clanking together and my mother speaking in a low voice.

'I've rung Mark and Jake,' she says as she reappears beside me, two steaming mugs of tea in her hands. 'I've told them you'll be staying with me for a bit. They were both concerned, of course. They want to come and see you but I told them you need a break, just for a few days.

'I put some sugar in yours,' she says as she presses the mug into my hands. 'Good for the shock.'

I don't know what Sonia said to her. She took Mum into another room when she came to collect me. When they reappeared my mother's eyes were red and shiny. Sonia had promised me that anything I told her was strictly confidential but, in that moment, I didn't care if she'd told Mum everything. I just wanted her to get me out of that room.

I drink my tea, draining every last drop as my mother sits beside me, her eyes never once leaving my face. She takes my empty mug away when I'm finished and places it on the floor in front of the sofa.

'Do you want to talk?' she asks. 'Would it help?'

I am so exhausted I can only manage a single word. 'Sleep.'

'Of course. I've got the spare room made up.' She reaches for my hand and helps me to my feet.

Together we walk up the stairs, Mum leading, me following, my hand drifting along the same banister I slid down as a child.

She pulls back the covers of the double bed that nearly fills my childhood room. Piles of cardboard boxes bursting with clothes, toys and ornaments take up the rest of the space. To get onto the bed I have to sit on the end and crawl up to the pillow.

'Let's get your sandals off,' Mum says as she fiddles with the straps, then pulls them off my feet.

She hovers at the end of the bed as I curl my knees up to my chest and pull the duvet over my shoulders.

'You sleep,' she says as my eyes close. 'You sleep, sweetheart, for as long as you need.'

Thursday 27th November 2014

Jackdaw44: *FUCK.*
ICE9: *What?*
Jackdaw44: *Busted.*
ICE9: *What?!!!*
Jackdaw44: *Mum found a bunch of tickets from the machines on Weston pier. She went through my jeans pockets when she was doing the washing. She knows I wasn't in town with mates when I skived school last week.*
ICE9: *Jesus! I thought you meant WE'D been busted. I nearly had a heart attack.*
Jackdaw44: *That's old age for you.*
ICE9: *You're an idiot.*
Jackdaw44: *And you're amazing at blow jobs. I can't stop thinking about last week. You're a fucking pro.*
ICE9: *Charming.*
Jackdaw44: *Not like that. You were fucking amazing. And it wasn't weird.*

ICE9: *You thought me sucking you off would be weird?*

Jackdaw44: *Well, duh. Seemed like you were enjoying yourself too.*

ICE9: *I can't believe we're having this conversation!*

Jackdaw44: *That means you did.*

ICE9: *I think you know the answer to that.*

Jackdaw44: 🏆🛏️🗳️

Chapter 41

When I wake it is dark, the only light a low glow from beneath the bedroom door. For one terrifying second I'm convinced that I've suffered another fugue but then I make out the shapes of the boxes beside the bed and the bundle of clothing hooked over the metal frame on the back of the door and I realize where I am. At the same time the memory of what happened in Sonia's office earlier comes flooding back. I rub my fist against my chest but the pain doesn't dissipate. It can't be soothed like a small child's bumped elbow or bruised knee. It is relentless.

Dead.

Billy is dead. I know it with the same level of certainty that I know my name is Claire Wilkinson.

My younger child has gone and he's never coming back. I'll never get to hold his angular body in my arms again, inhale his scent or hear his voice. I'll never watch him fall in love. I'll never see the look of adoration and terror on his face as his wife-to-be walks down the aisle. I'll never get to watch his face light up with love and fear as he holds his first child in his arms. My baby. My child. My beautiful son. I was there for every scratched knee, every playground fight, every monster in the dark, every nightmare, but I wasn't there when he needed me most.

I watched a documentary once, about a surfer whose arm was bitten off by a shark. He didn't feel any pain until he was hauled out of the sea by lifeguards. The doctor who treated him said that pain is a survival mechanism, and where pain would make survival even harder, we shouldn't be surprised that there is none. Is that why the pain is so unbearable now? Because Sonia tugged my true feelings out of my subconscious in the same way that the lifeguards hoisted the surfer out of the waves? But my ordeal isn't over. It isn't even remotely close.

'Hello, sweetheart.' Dad gives me a smile as he puts a mug and a pint glass away in the cupboard. 'Mum said you've had a bit of a day.'

'Yeah. It's been tough.'

Mum stops stirring the pot of brown gloop on the hob and gives me a smile too. 'Cup of tea?'

'I've had enough tea to last me a lifetime. I'll just have some water.'

'I'll get it.' They turn instantaneously but Dad reaches the sink first and fills a pint glass.

They watch as I drink the water. Dad grabs the empty

glass before I can put it in the sink. 'Why don't you go and put your feet up? Watch a bit of TV or something?'

'Maybe in a bit. There's something I need to talk to you both about first.'

They exchange a look and I catch the fear in Mum's eyes.

'There's no news,' I say quickly. 'DS Forbes hasn't been in touch. It's about me. There's something I need to tell you.'

'Why on earth didn't you tell us?' Mum says.

'Shh, Maggie.' Dad holds up a hand.

'I didn't want to worry you.' I adjust my chair, shifting myself closer to the kitchen table, and press the soles of my feet against the kitchen tiles. The coolness is soothing. 'I knew how upset you both were about the TV appeal going wrong.'

'We both were,' Dad says and this time Mum is the one to make a shushing sound.

'I thought the fugue to Weston was a one-off. So did my GP and counsellor. No one thought it would happen again.'

'But it's happened three times now,' Mum says. 'How many more are you going to have? Surely there's something they can give you for it. Some drugs or something.'

My mum, the pill popper. When I was a kid she'd demand antibiotics from the doctor if I so much as sniffed.

'What's causing them?' Dad asks. 'And why did you go to such weird places?'

Although I've told my parents about finding myself in Weston, Gloucester Road and a car park in the centre of town I haven't mentioned the photos I took of Mark or the knife I found. I'm not ready to tell them everything.

The knife.

At some point I have to go home and get it. I need to take it to the police – but not yet. Today has drained me and I couldn't cope with the fallout.

'Claire?' Dad says. 'Do you know what's causing the blackouts?'

'Yes, sorry. Sonia thinks they are caused by stress. She says I've been bottling up my feelings.'

'You were always like that as a girl,' Mum says, looking to my dad for a nod. 'Always keeping yourself to yourself. We didn't have the first clue that you were being bullied at school until we went in for parents' evening. Did we, Derek?'

My dad shakes his head.

'You know you can always talk to us, Claire.' Mum reaches for my hand and clamps it between hers. 'There's nothing you can't tell your dad and me. We're always here for you. Aren't we, Derek?'

'Anything you need, love, anything at all.'

'I got such a shock,' Mum says, 'when Sonia rang me using your phone. She said you were too upset to speak and could I come and collect you? What's wrong, love?' She gives me a searching look but I'm not sure if I can answer her. They're my parents. They love Billy as much as I do. I don't want to hurt them.

'Come on, love,' Dad says.

'Remember what your therapist said. You mustn't keep things to yourself, Claire. You'll make yourself ill. Tell us what made you so upset.'

I look down at my hand. It's starting to throb under the weight of her grip. 'I told her I thought Billy was dead.'

'Oh!' Mum's hands fly up to her face.

'Oh no, no, no.' Dad shakes his head. 'You mustn't be saying things like that, love. You need to stay positive. We're still hopeful. Aren't we, Maggie?'

Mum doesn't answer him. She's still staring at me, her fingers quivering against her lips.

Dad reaches round the table and puts a hand on my shoulder. 'I know you had a shock when that nasty piece of work came out with . . . with what he said . . . but if the police haven't confirmed it then . . .' He tails off, doubting the words he's saying even as they come out of his mouth.

I look at them, at my strong, feisty, determined parents, and a wave of sadness washes over me. They shouldn't be going through this. They should be enjoying their retirement, conquering the bridge club league and gossiping about who's having an affair with who and the fact that there are roadworks on the Wells Road again.

I try to read the look in my mum's eyes, to work out if she's horrified because she doesn't agree with what I just said or because she does, but I can't see beyond the film of tears.

'Mum. Please don't—'

I'm interrupted by the sound of the landline ringing in the living room. Dad disappears into the hallway. Seconds later he is back, the phone in his hand.

'It's for you,' he says. 'It's Mark.'

Chapter 42

'What's happened?' Mark shouts. I hear the roar of traffic down the phone. He must be parked somewhere.

'Your mum rang,' he says. 'She said you had some kind of breakdown at your counsellor's house? I said I'd come and get you but she told me not to. Is she there?'

'Yes. She's in the kitchen. So's Dad.'

'Good. That's good. So what happened?'

I push the living-room door closed, aware that my parents have suddenly gone quiet in the kitchen just a few metres away.

'I had a difficult session, that's all. Sonia hypnotized me. She said she wanted to discover the reason for my blackouts.'

'Did it work? What did you say?'

That I don't trust anyone apart from my parents.

'Sonia says I have a lot of fears that I haven't confronted.'

'What kind of fears?'

'Fears about what happened to Billy.'

There's a pause, long enough for me to wonder if we've been cut off.

'Mark, are you still there? Can you hear me?'

'Yes. I can hear you. I was just . . .' I hear the spark of a lighter and the sound of my husband inhaling deeply on a cigarette. 'Sorry. I know you hate me smoking but—'

'It's okay. It's fine.'

'So what –' he inhales on his cigarette again – 'what kind of fears are we talking about? Because we talked about this the other day. You can't assume anything until we hear back from DS Forbes, sweetheart. And if we hear the worst then we'll deal with it. We'll get through it.'

'Yes.'

'Is that what upset you?'

Now it's my turn to pause.

'Claire? Are you still there?'

'Yes.' I sit down on the sofa and reach for a cushion. I pull it close and bury my face in it. The soft material slips between my lips and stoppers my nostrils but I can still breathe. I press harder. I wait for panic to rise in my chest, for the compulsion to rip it away from my face to kick in, but none comes.

'Claire? What is it? What's the matter?'

I move the cushion away. 'Do you think Billy's alive or dead?'

'Sorry?'

'Billy. Do you think he's dead?'

302

There is no sharp intake of breath from the phone. No horrified gasp. Just a long, slow sigh.

'Mark?'

'I think this is a conversation we should have in person. Face to face.'

'I want to have it now.'

'Claire, is your mum there? Could you put her on the phone?'

'Why?'

'I'm worried about you.'

'I'm fine.'

'You're not. I'm coming over.'

'No!' The word comes out sharply. 'I need to think. I need to be here. Alone.'

Another pause. Another sigh. 'I don't understand. Have I done something? Has Jake? I rang him at work. He said you had words the other day. Why didn't you tell me? What did he say? Did he upset you?'

'It's not Jake and it's not you. I just . . . Mark, please, please, just answer my question. Do you think Billy is dead?'

I count the seconds.

One.

Two.

Three.

'Yes,' he says softly. 'Yes, Claire. I think Billy is probably dead.'

'Why? Why do you think that?'

'He's been missing for a long time. The appeal's been in the news, it's been in the newspapers. There aren't many people who haven't heard his name or seen his photo. If he was staying with someone they would have come forward. If he was injured someone would have found him. And if he was living rough he'd have been recognized. I'm sorry, sweetheart. I know that's not what you want to hear and I can't believe we're having this conversation over the phone. Please. Let me come and see you. Let me take you home. I need you. I need to see you.'

There are no words. My head is empty and full all at the same time.

'Claire? Please talk to me. I'm so worried about you.'

'I'll be fine.' I whisper the words. 'And I'll be home soon. I promise. I just need a few days.'

'Can I ring you? You didn't answer when I tried your mobile.'

'It's in my handbag. I didn't hear it.'

'Are you sure this isn't something I've done? Something I've said?'

'I'm sure.' I can't bear lying to him like this. There have been lies in our relationship before, of course there have, but they were small ones – the number of men I slept with before I met him, how well the boys behaved when he was away on a conference, how many bottles of wine I drank with Liz on a night out – but nothing like this. Nothing so monumental.

'I love you,' Mark whispers. 'You know that, don't you? I've never stopped loving you, no matter what we've been through, not even for a second.'

'I know,' I say.

'Do you still love me?' His words are loaded with fear.

I close my eyes and reach inside myself, searching for an answer to his question through the fear and the doubt and the nights spent lying silently in bed back to back.

'Yes,' I say. 'I do.'

Chapter 43

I am wearing a jumper that's so long the sleeves cover my hands, and a pair of jogging bottoms that are rolled up at the waist and above my ankles. After two days of wearing the same clothes I've been forced to raid my dad's wardrobe. Mum is several sizes smaller than me and there's no way I'd fit into her size 10 clothes without splitting something. It's been strange spending so much time with my parents with all their idiosyncrasies on show – Dad watching game shows back to back each afternoon, flicking between channels the second the closing theme music begins, whilst Mum tucks herself up on a kitchen chair and calls a seemingly endless number of friends for 'a quick catch-up'.

They tiptoed around me for the first twenty-four hours, asking if I was okay or if there was anything they could get me but now they largely leave me to my own devices. Not that there's anything to do other than watch TV. I've spent most of my time in the spare room, running over the events of the last few weeks trying, and failing, to make sense of it. Sonia would tell me that I should let myself grieve for Billy but I can't. Not yet.

When I woke up this morning the first thought that went through my head was, I'm going to the police today. The second thought was, I need to call Jake and Mark first.

I've rung Jake several times over the last couple of days. The first time I called I was worried that he'd be falling apart without me to keep an eye on him but he sounded more stable than he's seemed in a while. His main concern was the reason why I'd left home. He thought it was because he'd confessed to hitting Billy and was hugely relieved when I said it wasn't. He told me that he was back at work and that he'd made up with Kira. He didn't specifically mention his Tinder 'friend' but he did reassure me that he wouldn't be repeating his mistakes and that I didn't need to worry about him.

Mark seemed fine too. He said how strange it was to wake up and find an empty space where I should be and that he missed seeing my face when he got home from work. I asked if he'd been eating and he joked that, because Jake and Kira didn't even know how to turn on the oven, it had been left to him to feed everyone and could I please come home before he burnt the bottom out of every pan we own. He said he and Jake were getting on; that they were eating together and that Jake and

307

Kira had joined him to watch a film one evening.

'We even had a couple of conversations,' he said. 'And they didn't descend into arguments or mudslinging. Jake's not a bad kid. It's a lot for someone his age to deal with. For anyone to deal with.'

I could hear the tenderness in his voice when he said his son's name and it reassured me. Whatever happens to me they will be fine. Mark and Jake will pull together and look after each other. What's left of my family will remain intact.

Mark picks up the phone on the first ring.

'Hello, darling, how are you?'

'Good. I just wanted to say good morning to you before you go to work.'

'Good morning to you too!' I can hear the smile behind his words. Relief too. 'So, what are you up to today?'

I take a deep breath. This will be the last lie I tell him. There will be no more secrets once I've spoken to the police.

'I thought I'd go into town, maybe do a bit of shopping or have a coffee on the waterfront.'

'You're going out?' He sounds surprised. 'That's great news. I've got a few appointments in Cheltenham this afternoon. I don't imagine I'll be home until eight tonight. Will you be . . .' He tails off but I know what he wants to ask me.

'I'm not sure when I'll be home. Soon, hopefully.'

'Do you want to speak to Jake? I think he's up. Someone's in the bathroom anyway.'

'It's okay. I'll call him on his mobile.'

'All right then, sweetheart. Enjoy the shopping and coffee and I'll see you when I see you. Take care of yourself. I love you.'

'I will. Bye, Mark.' The call ends before I can tell him that I love him too.

I ring Jake next. Unlike Mark's phone Jake's mobile rings and rings and then goes to answerphone. I try again and finally it's answered.

'Mum,' he says, sounding out of breath. 'Sorry, I was in the shower. Kira didn't bother to tell me that my phone was ringing.'

I hear the irritation in his voice and worry who he'll confide in if I'm in prison. I'm not the only one in our family who bottles things up. 'What's the matter?'

'She said I can't go to her photography exhibition next week. She says it's too personal.'

'Maybe it's to do with her dad.'

He sighs. 'Maybe. Who knows?'

'Whatever her exhibition is about it obviously makes her feel vulnerable and you need to respect that.'

'But it feels like she's keeping secrets from me.'

'And you're not keeping secrets from her?'

'Fair enough.'

We both fall silent.

Then he says, 'You are going to come home, aren't you, Mum?'

I try not to think about the knife in my wardrobe and what will happen when I hand it in to the police. 'Yes, son. I am.'

Friday 19th December 2014

Jackdaw44: *I can't stop thinking about you.*
ICE9: *Me neither.*
ICE9: *I feel so guilty though. We shouldn't be doing this.*
Jackdaw44: *Stop then.*
ICE9: *Really?*
Jackdaw44: *Yeah. If you want to stop we stop.*
ICE9: *I thought you'd make it more difficult.*
Jackdaw44: *Not if you're not happy.*
ICE9: *But I am. That's the problem.*
Jackdaw44: *I don't think you really want to end it, do you?*
ICE9: *I know I should . . .*
Jackdaw44: *But?*
ICE9: *I like the way I feel when I'm with you.*
Jackdaw44: *And how's that?*
ICE9: *Happy. And free.*
Jackdaw44: *Me too. X*

Chapter 44

I drive past the house three times before parking outside. There's a gap on the street where Jake usually leaves his van and Mark's car isn't in the driveway. Liz's driveway is also empty. There are no lights on in our house but I watch the front and back doors for a few minutes anyway, just in case Kira suddenly appears, her hair unbrushed, her top slipping from her shoulder under the weight of her camera equipment, frazzled and running late.

When no one emerges from the house I look at my watch – 10.17 a.m. – then open the driver's-side door.

I'd expected to return home to a tower of plates in the sink, a bin full to overflowing and a pile of pizza boxes stacked up on the table, but the dishwasher is full, a fresh load of washing has been folded and stacked in the basket and there's food in the fridge.

The living room is similarly well kept; the rug has been hoovered, the blanket on the back of the sofa is straight and neat and there are no mugs or dishes on the side tables.

I'd imagined that my home would fall apart without me in it but somehow they've managed without me. It feels like for ever since I quizzed Jake in the garage about his relationship with Kira and he called me a control freak. I've been in control my whole life: of my family, of the office at work, of my mind. Over the last few months I've lost control of everything. There's only one more decision I have control of – whether or not I tell the police about the knife.

The tote bag is just where I left it, buried in the corner of the wardrobe under a pile of winter jumpers. I peer inside, to check the knife is still there, then snatch up the bag and hurry back down the stairs. My mobile rings as I reach the kitchen but I don't pause to answer it.

The ringing stops as I hurry out of the back door and sprint across the road to my car. My mobile starts up again as I open my handbag to retrieve the keys and I flip it open, certain I'll see *Mum*, *Jake* or *Mark* flashing on the screen. Instead it says *Withheld number*. Probably someone wanting to check if I've reclaimed PPI or ever been injured in a road traffic accident. I move my finger towards the end-call button, then change my mind. It could be DS Forbes.

'Hello?'

'Claire, it's Stephen. Please don't put the phone down. Please! It's urgent.'

Irritation rises in my chest. He withheld his number knowing I wouldn't have answered a call from him. 'Sorry. It's not a good time.'

'Caroline's left me.'

'What?'

'I just got home and all her stuff is gone.'

'Got home from where?'

'I . . . I went out last night. Slept on a friend's sofa. Please, Claire, I need your help.'

I stare out of the window, at the traffic rushing past my car and the neighbour three doors down struggling to pull her bin in from the street. I always knew that Stephen and Caroline's marriage was shaky, what with the stress of IVF and everything, but I'd assumed they'd managed to put all that behind them once they'd decided to stop trying for a baby.

'Please, Claire, she likes you. Would you ring her? Convince her to speak to me.'

'I'm not sure I'm the right person.'

'I can't ask anyone else. I'm just . . . I can't . . .' His voice cracks and he bursts into tears.

As he sobs down the phone I look across at the tote bag on the passenger seat beside me. I feel sorry for Stephen, I really do, but I can't put off going to the police. I've left it too long as it is.

'And . . . talked . . . Billy . . .' I can barely make out what Stephen is saying for the sobbing. 'It was my fault.'

'Sorry? What was that?'

313

'Billy told me he was in love with someone but I thought it was just a stupid crush. I told him to man up and move on.'

'Billy was in love with someone? Who?'

'I don't know,' he sniffs. 'Someone he couldn't be with, that's all he said, and I changed the subject. And I shouldn't have because then he disappeared and that fucking paedophile Jason Davies dragged him off the street and killed him.'

'You know about Jason Davies?'

'John told me. I can't . . . I can't believe I'm never going to see Billy again.'

His words run together as he speaks and it hits me. He's drunk. At 11.05 a.m.

'Stephen, Stephen, listen!' I hold up a hand, even though he can't see it. 'Slow down. Firstly, we don't know that Jason Davies had anything to do with Billy's disappearance. And secondly, why is it your fault that Billy disappeared?'

'I just said.' He sniffs noisily. 'He told me the day before that he was in love with someone and I told him to man up instead of talking to him about it.'

'And you think that's why he ran away? To be with someone he loved? Or because he couldn't be with them?'

'I don't know. Why else would he have disappeared in the middle of the night? I should have talked to him about it. I should have given him advice instead of telling him to—'

'Man up. Yes, you said.' My heart races as I process what he's just told me. This is new. Billy being in love with someone. This could give us answers. 'Stephen, think. Did Billy give you any clues about who this person might be? Did he mention a name? Say how he met her?'

'No. Nothing.' He blows his nose. 'And I keep thinking back to that day . . . when we had lunch at the Lodekka. It was my fault Billy got punched. I told him to tell Jake about Mark.'

'Tell Jake what about Mark? What are you talking about, Stephen?'

'I'm in the Ostrich pub. Meet me and call Caroline and then I'll tell you.'

The line goes dead and I stare at the phone, waiting for him to call me back. Minutes tick by but it continues to lie silently in my palm. When I ring him back it goes straight to voicemail. I try again. Same result. I look back at the bag on the passenger seat. If I take it to the police and they arrest me I'll never find out what Stephen knows. But what if it's got nothing to do with Billy's disappearance? What if he's just drunk and feeling sorry for himself and he's using Billy's memory to manipulate me into calling Caroline for him? I need to get to the police station. Now, while I'm still feeling brave.

I glance into the rear-view mirror, spot Jane Hargreaves from three doors down raising a hand in greeting, and make a decision.

Chapter 45

Stephen doesn't even attempt to stand up as he spots me striding across the pub towards him. He doesn't smile, wave or speak. Instead he reaches for his pint, wraps his thick fingers around the glass and sinks the whole thing in four or five messy gulps.

'I would ask you if you'd like another,' I say as he sets the empty glass on the table. 'But I think you've probably had enough already.'

'Yeah, right!' He runs a hand over his shiny forehead, then wipes it on his blue sweatshirt, leaving a sweaty stain. His eyes are dark-rimmed, his skin blotchy and lined. 'Go on then, if you're offering.'

I ignore the request. 'No work today then?'

He glances over my shoulder towards the bar, points at his empty pint glass and grins as the barman gives him a weary nod.

'I take it that's a no.'

He shrugs.

'Are you going to tell me why Caroline threw you out?'

'Fuck knows.' He pushes his mobile across the table towards me, sliding it through a puddle of beer. 'Ask her.'

I pick up the phone and wipe it on the hem of my cardi. 'I need you to tell me what happened last summer first.'

'Eh?' He looks confused.

'When Jake and Billy had a fight outside the Lodekka on my birthday. You said you told Billy to tell Jake something about Mark.'

'No. Ring Caroline first.' He folds his arms across his chest. He may be drunk but he's not drunk enough to forget the conversation we had fifteen minutes ago.

'Stephen, I'm supposed to be somewhere.'

'Ring Caroline.'

'Fine.' I push his phone back towards him. 'But I'll use my phone if she's ignoring your calls.'

She picks up on the third ring. 'Hello, stranger. I haven't heard from you for ages.'

'I'm with Stephen. He asked me to call you.'

She gives an exasperated sigh. 'Don't tell me, you're in the pub?'

Ask her, Stephen mouths as he lurches forward in his seat. I wave him away.

'He seems upset about an argument you've had recently. He said you've moved out.'

'Yes, I have. I don't know what he's told you, Claire, but I've had enough. A day doesn't go by when he doesn't have a drink and he's getting worse. He pissed in the wardrobe when he came home from the pub the other night and I'm pretty sure he's been drinking at work.'

I look at Stephen, with his flushed cheeks, puffy face and enormous gut, and it all makes sense – the reason his hands shook when he was making the coffee, why he seemed so jittery when I walked into the office. He had the DTs. God only knows if there was water or vodka in the bottle on his desk.

'I didn't know that, Caroline.'

'No, well, you wouldn't. You don't have to live with him.'

Please, Stephen mouths. 'Please.'

I lower my gaze but I can still feel his eyes boring into the top of my head. 'What if he agreed to go to AA or something? Or couple's counselling?'

'I don't know, Claire.' There's something in the way she sighs that reminds me of myself. She's exhausted. She can't take any more.

'I don't know if it's us not being able to have kids, or work, or Billy going missing,' she says after a pause, 'but he needs to sort himself out. I can't keep living like this, not knowing where he is or what he's doing. I've had enough of being woken up when he stumbles into the bedroom at all hours of the night. Why can't he be more like Mark? You don't see him falling apart, do you?'

We're all falling apart, I think, but not all of us show it.

As the barman places a pint of lager on the table I twist round in my chair, so Stephen can't see my lips, and lower my voice. 'Do you still love him?'

Caroline hesitates. 'I don't know. He's not the same man I married. He's changed, and not for the better. I think I'd be happier on my own.'

'It's not too late. He can change.' I look back at Stephen and he nods. 'He still loves you.'

I don't know why I'm acting as a marriage counsellor for a man who has insulted my husband, criticized my son's girlfriend and admitted to goading one of my son's into punching his brother. It goes beyond getting answers from Stephen. Maybe I'm tired of being surrounded by unhappiness. Maybe I see shades of myself in Caroline. Or maybe I can relate to their situation. They lost a child. They're still grieving.

Caroline sighs again. 'I'm sorry, Claire. I know you're just trying to help but it's not as if I'm overreacting to a couple of drunken nights. Things have been bad for a while. What happened last night was the last straw. I think it's over.'

My heart sinks, and not just because I know it's not the answer Stephen is hoping for.

'Are you okay?' Caroline asks. 'Stephen told me about Jason Davies and what he said. Have there been any developments? I gather you haven't been in to work for a while. Have the police said—'

'No. There's no news.' I glance towards the door as two men walk into the pub, laughing and punching the air. My car is parked in a dodgy one-way street nearby, the tote bag tucked under the passenger seat. I think I've hidden it well enough that anyone walking past won't see it and I don't imagine car thieves operate this early but I can't take the risk. 'I'm really sorry. I've got to go, Caroline.'

'Oh.' She sounds affronted. 'Okay then.'

'I'll give you a ring soon. Talk to you properly.'

'No worries. Take care of yourself, Claire. Bye.'

Stephen reaches for his pint and drains half of it in one gulp.

'Well?' he asks as I tuck my phone back into my handbag. 'What did she say?'

'She's still angry. You're going to have to work hard to win her round.'

'But she'll give me a chance?'

I want to lie. I want to tell him that she loves him and she's just a bit pissed off but I can't do that, to either of them.

'I don't know.'

'Oh, for fuck's sake! Fat lot of good you've been.'

'Stephen, I tried.'

'Bollocks.' He drains the pint and then signals to the barman. 'Another pint and a whisky chaser, please.'

Then he hitches up the sleeves of his sweatshirt, revealing his tattooed forearms. 'I don't know what you're looking so smug about,' he says.

'Me?'

'Yeah. You and Goldenballs. You can pity me all you like, Claire, but you haven't got the first clue about the man you married. You're the one who deserves pity, not me.'

'I'm not listening to this.' I push back my chair

and stand up. 'I tried to help you and now you're insulting my husband because you're feeling sorry for yourself. Stay here and drown your sorrows, Stephen. I've got more important things to do.'

I reach for my handbag and start walking away but I haven't taken more than three paces before he grabs my wrist.

'Wait!' He looms over me, stinking of fags, sweat and beer. 'You need to hear this.'

'No.' I wrench my arm away. 'I really don't.'

'There's something you don't know about Mark.'

I turn back. The barman, the two men in the corner of the room and a young lad playing the fruit machine all turn and stare.

'You need to hear this, Claire.'

I stalk back to him and push him down towards his seat. 'Keep your bloody voice down.'

'Mark kissed Billy's teacher.'

'What?' I sink into a chair.

'You heard me. That's why your boys came to blows in the garden of the Lodekka last summer. While you and Liz were in the loos Mark got a call from his boss. When he left to answer it Billy said he hoped his dad wasn't being bollocked again because Miss Christian wasn't here to kiss him better. He said it quietly, so only I could hear, and I laughed. Jake wanted to know what was so funny so I told Billy to tell him.'

Stephen falls silent as the barman approaches our table and places a pint and a glass of whisky in front of him, but the self-satisfied smirk on his lips stays in place. I want to tell him that he's drunk and he's talking shit but I can't.

'Why would Billy say that about Miss Christian?'

Stephen shakes his head. 'I've said enough.'

I stare at him in disgust. 'No, you haven't. Tell me what Billy meant.'

'No. I've changed my mind.'

As he reaches for his pint a wave of fury courses through me and I sweep it clean off the table. It hits the ground and explodes, showering my lower leg with glass and beer.

'Tell me. Now. Or I'll give Caroline a call later and convince her never to take you back.'

Stephen remains straight-backed in his chair, refusing to be intimidated, but as his gaze shifts from mine I know that I have won.

'I'll tell you,' he says. 'But you won't like it.'

The barman approaches with a brush and pan in his hands and a weary expression on his face. I sit back down.

Stephen waits until the barman has tidied away the mess, then sits forward in his seat, elbows on the table.

'I loved Billy,' he says. 'Really loved him. But we weren't always close, you know that. He used to hero-worship Mark but I noticed that changing when Billy hit his teens. I'd seen Jake do the same thing. It happens with boys, when they grow bigger and stronger. They feel like men, not little boys, and they question their dad's authority. Mark did it with his dad. I would have done it with mine too, if he hadn't fucked off.' He laughs drily. 'But

322

I kicked off at John a few times, even if he was just my stepdad. No one was more surprised than me when I ended up joining the firm instead of Mark.'

He stares off wistfully into the distance and I clear my throat.

'Yeah, yeah.' He reaches for his whisky and necks it. 'So I wasn't surprised when Billy came round my house one Sunday and said that his dad was a dick. He said Mark was coming down hard on him for doing badly at school. But then he started going on about how weak Mark was and how he had no respect for him.' He scratches the back of his neck. 'He said he was embarrassed by him.'

'Embarrassed? Why?'

He reaches for his empty whisky glass and raises it to his lips. A single drip trickles into his mouth. 'Because of what he saw.'

I don't like the way this conversation is going. I want to leave. I want to walk out of the pub before Stephen can say another word but I force myself to stay in my seat. 'Go on.'

'Billy went to the pub one night. It was some time last summer. He was meeting a mate who was going to smuggle a couple of bottles out so they could get pissed in the park. Billy spotted Mark and some of his teachers from school in the pub and he hid behind a skip so they wouldn't see him.'

'Mark was with Billy's teachers?'

'No. He was by himself. Anyway, he came out to take a call. It was his boss, Billy said. Mark sounded really pissed and he was trying to keep the conversation light-hearted but then he started pleading.'

'What for?'

'His job. Mark was saying that John had had a heart attack and he thought he was going to die and that was the reason he hadn't been meeting his targets, and that he was sorry. He begged his boss not to fire him. He said he had a wife and two kids to support and a mortgage to pay.'

I stare at him in horror. Mark's boss nearly fired him and he didn't tell me?

'That's not the worst of it,' Stephen says, misinterpreting the expression on my face. 'Mark started to cry then. Really blubbed down the phone to his boss, apparently. Billy said he'd never been so embarrassed in his life, listening to his dad sobbing down the phone. He said his dad was a hypocrite for the way he'd laid into Billy about the trouble he'd got into at school. His dad acted like he was the big "I am", like he was this strong, respectable pillar of the community that his sons should look up to, when really he was weak and spineless. A snivelling little shit, Billy said. He told me he couldn't respect a man like that – a man who'd rather beg than tell his boss to fuck off. According to Billy, Mark was still crying when he went back into the pub. That's when one of his teachers went over to him and he kissed her.'

'Mark kissed Edie Christian?'

Stephen glances away. 'Yeah. Billy didn't take it too well. First the begging and the crying, then his dad snogging his teacher. He put a brick through Mark's car window.'

'Billy did that? Mark said it was some random vandal.'

'Mark didn't know who did it. He didn't see him, did he? Billy said when he got back home afterwards he was so angry he wanted to smash up more of Mark's stuff but you were in bed so he destroyed a photo album or something.'

'He blacked out all the photos of Mark. I've seen it.'

'Oh, right. Well, there's something else you should know too.'

I grit my teeth. 'What?'

'The real reason Mark didn't get into the police.'

'When he was nineteen? Why the hell are you bringing that up now?'

'Because you need to know the truth.'

'I know the truth. He didn't get in because a couple of his uncles had criminal contacts. Mark told me.'

Stephen raises his eyebrows. 'He lied. You thought I was a twat for saying you should be careful about Mark and Kira living in the same house. You thought I was shit-stirring but I'm not the one with a record for having sex with an underage girl.' He shifts in his seat as I gasp and cover my mouth with my hands. 'Hmm . . . I thought it would feel good to get all that off my chest but I feel like shit.' He slumps forwards, head in his hands, and lets out a low moan. 'No wonder Caroline has left me. I'm a total cunt.'

I don't say a word. There isn't a shred of sympathy in my heart for the man sitting in the chair opposite me. How can there be when he's just ripped it apart?

Friday 2nd January 2015

Jackdaw44: *I saw you arguing last night.*

ICE9: *Where?*

Jackdaw44: *Outside the Southside pub.*

ICE9: *Are you stalking me?*

Jackdaw44: *I was going to meet Archie. I saw you from across the street.*

ICE9: *We need to stop this. I love being with you but I can't bear the deceit. I'm lying all the time and I can't do it any more. I feel like I'm being pulled in two directions. It's tearing me apart.*

Jackdaw44: *Make a choice then.*

ICE9: *I have.*

Jackdaw44: *So?*

ICE9: *I'm sorry.*

Jackdaw44: *You're dumping me?*

ICE9: *Don't put it like that. What we had was a bit of fun. It wasn't real.*

Jackdaw44: *Felt fucking real to me.*

ICE9: *I'm really sorry. I don't want to hurt you.*
Jackdaw44: *Well, I'm hurt. OK?*
ICE9: *You said we could end this at any time. You said I could stop it if I wasn't happy.*
Jackdaw44: *That was before you said it was just a bit of fun. I thought you had feelings for me.*
ICE9: *I did. I do. But we could never work. You're too young and we're too different.*
Jackdaw44: *Fuck YOUNG. You didn't complain about how young I am when my dick was in your arse.*
Jackdaw44: *I fucking LOVE YOU.*
Jackdaw44: *That's it? I tell you I love you and you ignore me???*
ICE9: *I'm not ignoring you. I just don't know what to say.*
Jackdaw44: *You could start by telling me that you love me too.*
ICE9: *You know I can't do that.*
Jackdaw44: *Why? Because you love someone else? People in love don't cheat!*
ICE9: *You're angry and you've got good reason to be and I'm sorry.*
Jackdaw44: *Meet me in the park at 8 tonight.*
ICE9: *I can't.*
Jackdaw44: *Please. You owe me that much. I just want to see you again. I need to say goodbye properly.*
ICE9: *I don't know.*
Jackdaw44: *I love you. Just let me say goodbye.*
ICE9: *OK. Tonight. But I can't stay long.*

Chapter 46

A sex offender? My husband is a sex offender and a cheat? What else don't I know about him?

I sit alone in the kitchen watching the back door. Six hours have passed since I walked out of the Ostrich, leaving Stephen with his head in his hands.

The first thing I did when I got home was to go through the pockets of all Mark's jackets and coats. Then I searched through his chest of drawers. I had no idea what I was looking for – a charge sheet, a love note from Edie Christian, a hotel receipt, a cinema ticket, a petrol receipt – something, anything, to explain what Stephen had told me. I found nothing incriminating. I called Billy's school but then put the phone down again when the receptionist answered. I did the same with DS Forbes's number.

I need to talk to my husband, not anyone else. I need to ask him face to face if what Stephen said is true. I'll know if he's lying. I can normally tell by the small half-smile that flickers at the edges of his lips.

After Lloyd left her Liz read up on the signs that someone is lying. Apparently all that stuff about people looking up and to the left is wrong. You can't tell whether someone is lying by filling out a check sheet of facial expressions; you look for differences from the way they normally behave. That's why I believed Mark when he said he didn't know why Billy had defaced the photos and—

No. That's not what happened. When I asked him if he could think of a reason why Billy would do that he didn't actually answer the question. He said something about fathers and sons clashing and reminded me that he hadn't got on with his own dad. Then he asked me if I was accusing him of doing something to Billy. He deflected me. Twice. I asked him twice and he changed the subject both times. He didn't actually lie.

A new thought occurs to me. Billy was doing an art project at school. That was why he'd borrowed it in the first place. When was that? I pull open the junk drawer and rummage around in the bottom where I keep the family calendars. I never knew what to say when the kids asked me what I wanted for Christmas so I'd always say a calendar because they were cheap and useful and it meant I wouldn't have to smuggle overpriced bath-bomb sets that brought me out in hives into the charity-shop bag on Boxing Day.

Mark's always teased me about keeping the old calendars. 'You're turning into a hoarder like your mum,' he'd joke as I'd slip another one into the drawer on 1st January after I'd copied everyone's birthdays and anniversaries onto the new calendar. I didn't pay him any attention. I liked looking back on all the things we'd done each year: the kids' swimming lessons, the birthday parties they attended, the holidays we took. They were all recorded in my small, neat handwriting. Billy and Jake hated it when I pumped them for information about exam dates and coursework deadlines.

'Stop being such a control freak, Mum,' they'd chorus.

That accusation again.

I pull out a wad of calendars. Last year's is on the top. I flick through it, find nothing and then start again, reading each entry carefully.

5th January – Mum's birthday.

16th January – Parents' evening (Billy).

21st January – Dentist appointment for Jake and Billy.

30th January – Car MOT (mine).

I flick over the page.

4th February – Caleb's birthday.

17th February – Doctor's appt (Mark).

24th February – Billy GCSE art DEADLINE.

There! There it is. The end of February. And we went to the pub to celebrate my birthday on . . .

I flip the pages over and stab the date with my finger. Sunday 31st August. At some point between 24th February and Sunday 31st August Mark went to the pub, nearly lost his job and kissed Billy's teacher. Stephen said it happened last summer but he didn't say when. I turn the page.

5th/6th July – Mark to London for annual general meeting

2nd/3rd August – Mark conference

13th/14th September – Mark training weekend

25th November – Mark sales team meeting

How many of those were real? Or was Mark shacked up in a hotel with Edie Christian, the fact that he was married and a father of two locked up in a box in his head and filed away?

My hands shake as I place the calendar and the photo album on the kitchen table.

It's nearly five o'clock. The knife is still stashed in the tote bag under the passenger seat in my car. I can't go to the police until I've found out the truth. God knows what time Mark will get home from work but I'm not going anywhere until he does.

Chapter 47

'Coo-ee! Just me! Claire, are you home? What are you doing sitting in the dark?'

Liz reaches around the door and flicks the light switch. I blink as the kitchen fills with fluorescent light.

'Claire?' She crosses the kitchen and pulls out the chair opposite me. 'Are you okay? I saw your car in the drive. You didn't tell me you were coming back today.'

I sent Liz a text from Mum and Dad's the day after my session with Sonia. I told her that things were stressful at home and that I needed a few days' peace and quiet. She responded immediately, asking if I needed to talk. I said no, but that I'd ring her in a couple of days.

'I didn't know I was coming back today either,' I say.

I want to tell her everything. I want to let every

last worry and fear spill out but I haven't got the energy. I need to save what little I have left for my conversation with Mark.

'Liz,' I say instead, 'did Caleb ever mention anything to you about Billy being in love with someone? Maybe Jake told him—'

I'm interrupted by the sound of the back door opening.

'Claire!' Kira says. 'You're back.'

'For now.' I keep the smile fixed on my face. 'How's college? It must be your exhibition soon.'

'Yeah.' She lowers the art folder she's carrying to the floor and wiggles the fingers of her left hand.

'Can we come and see it?' Liz asks. 'Is there any nudity? I can't remember the last time I saw a naked man.'

The base of Kira's throat turns red as Liz laughs raucously. 'No, not really,' she says.

'So what's it about then?'

Kira's tongue moves back and forward in her mouth as she clacks her piercing against her teeth. 'Tattoos.'

Tattoos? Jake told me Kira wouldn't let him go to her exhibition because it was too personal. What's so personal about photos of tattoos?

'Hey, Kira!' Liz lifts her top and flashes her tummy. 'You could have taken a photo of my dolphin. Although I'm such a fat fucker now it looks more like a whale.'

'Do you regret it?' Kira asks as she peers at it.

'Cheeky bitch!'

'No, no. That's what my project is about. Tattoos

334

and regrets. I've been taking photos of tattoos that people regret and then interviewing them. The project's a mixture of photos and words. It's all anonymous. There are no faces and no names.'

'Then you should have given Lloyd a ring. He's got a fuckload of tattoos, most of them grim. Apart from the one of my name. Obviously that's a beauty although I bet he bloody regrets it now! Oh, that reminds me, Claire. Guess who texted me yesterday?'

'Lloyd?'

'Yep. He's coming to Bristol this weekend.'

'To your house?' Kira asks. She looks as horrified as Liz does.

'Mmm-hmm.' Liz nods. 'I said I'd meet him in Charlie's Bar but he wouldn't have it. He's insisting on coming to the house.'

'Why?'

'Maybe he wants to get back with you?' Kira says.

'No chance. I wouldn't take him back even if he begged. No, my guess is that he wants to meet at home because he doesn't want a row in public. Or tears,' she adds quickly. 'I think he's going to ask for a divorce.'

'Why not tell you that over the phone?'

'Because he's a sadist?'

'Will he be coming round here?' Kira asks. Considering she normally takes the first opportunity to escape from the kitchen and go up to her room she seems unusually interested in this conversation.

'Yeah.' Liz laughs. 'I thought we'd throw a welcome-home celebration for him and parade him round the streets. The prodigal fuckhead returns! Why the hell would he come round here?'

Kira shrugs. 'To see Mark?'

'Yeah, like they're the best of friends. I think they only tolerated each other because Claire and I are such good mates.' She looks at me. 'Isn't that right?'

'Yes.' It's a lie, but only to spare her feelings. It took our husbands a while to warm to each other but they did get on and by the time Liz and Lloyd's marriage was on its last legs they were definitely friends. Not that Mark has heard much from Lloyd since he walked out on Liz; a couple of replies to his texts but never more than a terse *I'm good, mate* or *I'm living up north*.

'Kira, are you okay? You look a bit pale, sweetheart.' Liz pulls out a chair. 'Have a seat.'

'I do feel a bit light-headed.' She presses a hand to the side of her head. 'I think I'll have a lie-down upstairs.'

She makes a move towards the hallway but I move to intercept her.

'Kira, before you go. Could I talk to you about something?'

'Um . . .' She touches the side of her head again. 'I'm really not feeling very—'

'I know what happened in the Lodekka last year. I know why Jake hit Billy.'

She says nothing, but her gaze flicks from left to right as though she's looking at each of my eyes in turn. She's trying to work out how I'm feeling.

'It was about Mark, wasn't it?' I say. 'About him kissing Billy's form tutor.'

I hear Liz inhale sharply behind me but don't turn round.

Kira looks down at her feet. 'Yes,' she breathes.

'Jake told you?'

'Um . . . yeah. He said it was bullshit and Billy was shit-stirring because he had nothing better to do. He said Billy wanted to fuck everyone else's lives up because he couldn't stand anyone else being happy.'

'Did Jake ask Mark if it was true?'

She chews on the side of her lip and says nothing.

'Kira? Did Jake ask Mark if it was true?'

She nods, her eyes still downcast.

'And? Did Mark admit it?'

Her gaze flickers up and her eyes meet mine. 'Yes,' she whispers. 'Yes, he did but—'

'One more question,' I add quickly, before she can leave. 'Did Billy ever tell you that he was in love with someone?'

Her gaze flits towards Liz, still sitting at the kitchen table with a shocked expression on her face, then returns to me. 'I heard Caleb and Jake talking once, about a girl Billy liked. Jess, I think her name was. Is that who you mean?'

'Did he love her?'

She shrugs. 'I don't know.'

Chapter 48

'How are you feeling?' Liz asks for what feels like the hundredth time.

Physically I'm fine. I'm sitting on a wooden chair across the table from my best friend with my arms crossed. Emotionally I am numb. I can't process what Stephen told me earlier. Billy was in love with someone he couldn't be with and Mark's been prosecuted for sleeping with an underage girl. And he's cheated on me. More secrets. More bloody secrets.

Mark and I have been together for over twenty years and it's always been there, that fear that he might have strayed at some point in our relationship, but I never truly believed he was capable of that kind of deceit.

'Men are such shits,' Liz says. 'I swear. I'm going to delete Tinder and go celibate. Do you think there's an app that teaches you how to be a nun? How best to style your habit? How to get the no-make-up look?

That sort of thing.' She pushes her chair back from the table and sighs. 'It's not the actual shagging that's the problem, is it? It's all the lying and the sneaking around. I know they lie to their mistresses and say they're not getting any at home but Lloyd and I were still having sex until the month before he—'

'We didn't have sex for nine months.'

'Sorry?' She shuffles her chair closer to the table.

'By last summer Mark and I hadn't had sex for nine months. I remember thinking to myself at the time that it was the longest I'd gone without sex since I was a teenager.'

'Are you blaming yourself? Because if you are we're going to have words. It's totally normal for couples to have dry spots when they've been married as long as you two have. Some couples stop shagging completely. It's no excuse for an affair.'

'I know. And Mark didn't put any pressure on me to have sex. He didn't seem that bothered either, if I'm honest. He was tired, I was tired and suddenly nine months had gone by.'

'Well, it happens, doesn't it?' She shrugs. 'Sorry, that doesn't really help, does it?'

I force a smile. 'Talking to you does help but there's no point analysing it to death.' I glance at the kitchen clock.

'Shit.' Liz glances at the clock too. 'Caleb's motorbike is in the shop and I said I'd pick him up from work and give him a lift to the mechanic's. Are you going to be all right?'

When I nod she says, 'Whatever happens you've

always got me. Come and stay at mine if you want. The box room's a mess but you're welcome to share my bed if you don't fancy the sofa. I promise not to poke you in the back with a hard-on in the middle of the night.'

'Thank you.' I reach for her hand and squeeze it. 'I don't know what I'd do without you.'

'Well, you'd probably drink less,' she says and laughs. 'Seriously, Claire, if there's anything you—'

She's interrupted by the sound of a car drawing up outside the house. The familiar sound of late-nineties drum and bass drifts through the window and then stops.

We share a look.

'It's Mark,' I say.

Chapter 49

If my husband is surprised to see me sitting at the kitchen table after two nights at Mum's house he doesn't let on. He gives me a nod as he steps into the room. He is dressed in a dark blue suit with a white shirt and a grey-and-white striped tie. His black shoes are shiny. His hair is neatly brushed back from his face. The only thing out of place is the position of his laptop bag. Normally he wears it casually slung over one shoulder. Today he is clutching it to his chest.

Liz's eyes narrow as he walks into the kitchen.

'All right, Mark?' she says in a tight voice.

He doesn't acknowledge her. 'Claire, could I talk to you? Alone.'

Liz looks at me and raises an eyebrow. So many emotions in one look – irritation, anger, worry – one wrong word from my husband and she'll go off.

I reach for her hand. 'I'll come and see you later? Okay?'

She nods, her lips pressed tightly together and stands up.

She leaves the kitchen, deliberately taking a wide arc around Mark. He barely registers her departure. His eyes are fixed on me as he sits down stiffly at the table, hugging his laptop to his chest. 'Is he here?'

'Jake? No, but Kira's upstairs.'

'Right.' He looks from the hallway to the kitchen window. 'We can't talk here. Let's go to the garage.'

I am so stunned, so wrong-footed by the look on his face, that I do as I am told and follow him out of the house and into the garage. He turns on the light and then sits down on Jake's weight bench. He pats the space beside him and waits for me to sit down. He looks surprised when I shake my head.

'Claire –' he places the laptop bag on his knees and presses down on it with the heels of his hands – 'I don't know how to tell you this.'

'You're having an affair.' The words sound ridiculous as they come out of my mouth. I feel as though I'm playing the role of the wronged wife in a soap opera.

'What?'

'With Edie Christian.'

'Edie Chr—' He tips back his head and laughs.

Irritation bubbles inside me. 'Mark, I know. Stephen told me. Billy saw you kissing her in a pub last year.'

Mark's laughter stops as quickly as it started. 'What?'

'Billy was there. He was outside, waiting for Alfie. He saw you, he heard your phone conversation with your boss outside, he saw the kiss.'

'He . . .'

'He was hiding behind a skip. He heard and saw everything. That's why he defaced all the photos of you in the album. I checked the dates on the calendar. It happened last summer.'

Mark doesn't say a word. He stares at me dumbly, his bottom lip wet with spittle. He blinks several times, then looks down at the laptop on his knee.

'Mark?'

His Adam's apple bobs up and down as he swallows. 'I can't . . . I can't take it in. I came home to talk to you about something else. I wasn't expecting this.'

'When did the affair start?'

'Affair?' He frowns. 'I haven't had an affair.'

'There's no point denying it. I'll ask her.'

'Ask who?'

'Edie Christian.'

'Oh God.' He runs a hand over his hair. 'Claire, I'm not having an affair with Edie Christian, or anyone else for that matter.'

'So you're denying that you kissed her? You're saying Billy was lying.'

'No. He wasn't. But he didn't see what he thought he saw.'

'So tell me what happened then?'

'Oh God, Claire. It wasn't . . . it wasn't as bad as it sounds.'

343

'You kissed another woman.'

'I tried to.'

'And that's supposed to make me feel better?'

'We . . .' He puts the laptop down on the bench beside him and stands up so he's facing me. 'We hadn't been getting on for a while and—'

'So it's my fault, is it?'

'No! God, no! It was me, it was all me. I was stressed. Dad had been ringing me up to moan about how unreliable Stephen was but when I tried to ring Stephen he laid into me. He said they were over-worked and understaffed and if I gave a shit about Dad I'd do the right thing and join the firm. Then Dad had his heart attack and I was so scared. I thought he was going to die and it was my fault for being ambitious and thinking a builder's merchants was beneath me. Then there was work – my work – and the pressure I was under to hit my targets. The kids were fighting at home. You and I weren't getting on. And I couldn't deal with it, Claire. I didn't have anyone to talk to.'

'You've got friends.'

'I know. But no one wants to be the boring bastard bringing the mood down on a night out by complaining about how stressed they are.'

'You could have talked to me.'

'Could I? We were jumping down each other's throats every other day.'

'And you thought kissing another woman would help?'

'No!' He reaches me for but I shift back before he

can touch me. 'I was drunk. I was drinking alone and then Phil Jones called. He said I hadn't been performing well and my figures were shit and that he'd have to let me go. I begged him. I begged him not to and I told him everything – all the reasons why I'd been struggling – and he said he'd give me one last chance. A written warning and if I put one foot wrong I was out. I was a mess when I went back into the pub. Miss Christian was there with some of her friends and she came over to the bar to see if I was okay. She was so nice to me and I was drunk and I was so stupidly grateful that she gave a shit that I . . . I . . .'

'Tried to kiss her.'

'Yeah.' He briefly closes his eyes. 'She pushed me away. She was so shocked. Really embarrassed. I tried to smooth things over but she ran off to her friends and then someone over by the window stood up and asked if anyone had a Ford Focus because someone had just chucked a rock through the window.'

'It was Billy.'

'What?'

'Stephen told me.'

'Stephen knew all this and he didn't say anything?'

'He was protecting Billy. He'd been confiding in him. You should understand that.'

Mark shakes his head, his cheeks flushed red with anger. 'Why should I?'

'Because apparently you had no one to talk to either.'

'Claire?' He reaches for my hand. 'Please don't cry. Please. I can't bear it.'

'I'm not crying because I'm upset. I'm angry. I'm so bloody angry that—'

'It wasn't even a kiss, not really.'

'It's not that!' I throw his hand away from me. 'It's you. You and Billy and Stephen and Jake. Things go wrong in your lives but instead of talking about them you smash things up and drink and cheat and lie. What's wrong with you? What the hell is wrong with all of you?'

Mark stares at his feet as I scream in frustration.

'Why didn't any of you talk to me? I could have helped.'

'Could you?' Mark says softly.

'What's that supposed to mean?'

'There are some things you can't control, Claire – some things you can't fix. It might not make sense to you, the way we deal with our shit, but it's our way of coping.'

'So Billy was right to throw a rock at your car, was he? Graffitiing his school was a good thing? So was winding up his brother and insulting you?'

'I don't know.' He sinks back down onto the weight bench and rests his head in his hands. 'I don't know anything any more. I knew we were going to have a tough conversation tonight but not about this.'

'What did you want to talk to me about?'

'This.' He touches the laptop bag on the bench beside him.

'What are you talking about?'

'I found some photos on it,' he mumbles through his fingers. 'Photos of little boys. Naked photos.'

A cold chill runs through me. 'Whose laptop is that, Mark?'

He looks up at me. 'It's Jake's.'

Chapter 50

Neither of us speaks as we stare out from the garage. The laptop, resting on top of the bag, is on the floor in front of us. Neither of us want to touch it.

Mark told me he borrowed it from Jake's room this morning, after his own laptop had failed to boot up when he'd installed an update. Jake had already left for work and Kira was still asleep in bed. She stirred when Mark knocked on the door, then waved a hand towards the desk when he'd asked if he could borrow Jake's laptop.

Mark didn't try to log on until he reached a service station on the M4 on his way to Chippenham. We bought the laptops for both boys for Christmas two years ago. Mark set them up. He created their accounts and gave them both the same password – BRISTOLCITY123. Jake hadn't bothered to change his and Mark was able to log straight in. He downloaded some PowerPoint images he needed from

348

OneDrive. And that's when he discovered the pictures in Jake's downloads folder.

Boys. Loads and loads of images of boys in their early teens. Some standing casually in front of the camera with their arms crossed over their chests and erect dicks proudly on display. Others adopting different positions, bent over, on all fours, or else sucking on dildos or the erect penises of men or boys out of shot.

Mark showed me the search history:

How to meet young boys

Chat sites where young boys meet up

How to groom young boys

Social media for meeting kids

The list went on and on.

'Could it be someone else?' I asked. 'Maybe Jake lent the laptop to someone at work?'

But we could tell by the dates and times that Jake had been home when the searches were made. The majority of them were when he was off work with stress. When he was in his bedroom, me sitting downstairs with no idea what he was up to.

'Claire,' Mark hisses as a white van pulls up on the street outside, rap music blaring out of the open window. 'He's back.'

Jake laughs as he strolls up the driveway towards us.

'What are you two up to? His and hers workout?'

'Jake—' Mark begins but I interrupt him.

'Could we have a word?'

Jake draws to a halt outside the garage. 'In there?'

'Kira's in the house,' I say. 'And this discussion would be better in private.'

'So let's go to the pub then?' He inclines his head towards his van. 'Unless . . . has this got something to do with Billy? Is there news?'

'No,' Mark says. 'This is about you. Close the garage door please.'

Jake does as he's told then turns back to look at us. His eyes are wide and fearful.

'Dad borrowed your laptop this morning.' I point to the computer on the floor between us. 'He found some images.'

'Photos,' Mark says. 'Of young boys.'

All the colour drains from Jake's face. The garage door clangs as he stumbles back into it. 'It's not what you think.'

'What do we think, Jake?'

'That I'm a paedophile. And I'm not. I'm really not.'

'Jake.' I fight to keep the emotion out of my voice. 'Those messages you showed me on your phone. Were they between you and a young boy? Were you arranging to meet him?'

'What messages?' Mark gives me a sideways look. I asked Jake not to tell him what happened the night of my car-park fugue. And he obviously hasn't.

'No.' Jake holds out his hands. 'You've got it wrong. I was going to meet someone, but not a boy. I was the boy.'

Mark and I exchange a look.

'I was pretending to be a boy. Fuck.' Jake slaps himself

350

on the side of the head. 'Look, I was angry, okay. You told me about that bastard in jail and what he said he'd done to Billy and I couldn't . . . I couldn't deal with it. It was fucking with my head. I couldn't sleep. I kept . . . I had these horrible thoughts, about the things he'd done to my brother and I felt like it was my fault. If I hadn't hit Billy then he wouldn't have run away and the paedophile wouldn't have got him . . . he wouldn't have . . .' He twists to one side and pounds his clenched fist into the garage door.

'That doesn't make sense,' Mark says. 'Jason Davies is in prison and inmates don't have access to computers. Why would you pretend to be a young boy?'

'To trap one of them. I knew I couldn't get to Davies but I still wanted to hurt someone. To get revenge for Billy.'

'But we don't know if Jason Davies had anything to do with Billy going missing,' I say. 'The police are still investigating and—'

'They've been investigating for nearly seven months and found sod all!' Jake rubs his clenched fist. 'I had to do something.'

'You can't take the law into your own hands, son!' Mark says but if Jake hears him he blocks him out.

'I thought if I put a photo of me when I was thirteen or fourteen on Tinder then all the paedos would come running but they didn't. A few older women sent me messages to say that you have to be eighteen to be on Tinder and then suddenly my account was suspended. Someone must have reported me.

351

'So I did some research online. And I know how dodgy it looks –' he glares at Mark – 'but what was I supposed to do? I'm not a paedo. I don't know where they hang out or how they do their twisted shit but I had to read about it, didn't I? To find out, so I could pretend to be a kid.'

He wipes a hand over his brow. It's airless and hot in the garage and Jake isn't the only one sweating. 'I got obsessed with it. I kept dangling bait, waiting to see who'd bite, but they're really nervy. They won't agree to meet up with you just because you say you're fourteen. They need photos first, photos in lots of different poses to show you're who you say you are.'

'But those photos. Fucking hell, son.' Mark shakes his head as though he's trying to clear his brain of the images on Jake's hard drive.

'I know, I know. I couldn't look at them either but I had to do it. I had to reel one in.'

'But that's the police's job, Jake! Not yours!' I look to my husband for support. He rubs his hands over his face and peers at me over his fingertips. He looks as shocked, exasperated and exhausted as I feel.

'Yeah? Well, the police did a fucking great job with Jason Davies, didn't they, Mum? They let him get Billy.'

'We don't know that!' Mark says. 'We don't know what happened to Billy. No one does.'

'But what if he did do it, Dad? He said he did. He's abused other kids. That's why he's in jail. I looked him up on the Internet. I read about his court

352

cases. I couldn't get to Davies but I thought that if I took one out – one paedophile – if I fucked him up badly enough he'd be too scared to try it again. And I'd have saved a kid. I'd have saved someone else's child, someone else's brother but then . . .' He rubs a hand over his eyes and takes several deep breaths.

'What is it, Jake?'

'You followed me.'

'What?' Mark looks at me.

'To the car park?' I say. 'I followed you to the car park?'

'Claire?' Mark says. 'What are you talking about? What car park? What happened?'

'Mum followed me. I went to meet this guy, someone I'd reeled in, in the men's toilets in a car park in town and Mum turned up.'

All the hairs on my arms go up. He was there. Jake was there. And he ran off and left me.

'Oh God, Mum. I'm sorry. I'm so sorry.' Jake stalks from one side of the garage to the other, breathing heavily through his nose and staring at the ceiling.

'Tell us what happened!' Mark barks and Jake stops pacing and looks me in the eye.

'This guy, Graham, I met him in a chat room for teens. I called myself Jamie and said I was fourteen. We started chatting about football at first but it didn't take him long to ask me whether I had a girlfriend. I said no, I wasn't very interested in girls and I was feeling quite depressed because my family didn't understand me and—'

'Oh God.' Mark slumps forward, head in his hands again.

'Carry on, Jake,' I say.

'Graham said he understood. He said he hadn't got on with his parents either and he knew what it felt like to be a black sheep and blah, blah, blah. Anyway, he tried to groom me. He asked for photos so I sent him some of some kid I'd found on the Internet. He said I was a good-looking boy and that he really wished he could give me a hug to make me feel better about my life and –' he makes a winding motion with his hand – 'to cut a long story short, he asked if he could email me so I set up a fake email account. And that's when things started getting sexual.'

'He asked for naked photos?'

'Yeah. So I had to find some.'

Mark points at the laptop. 'You know you could go to prison for what's on there, don't you?'

'Yeah, but I was using them to catch paedophiles, not to jerk off to.'

'And you think the police would buy that, do you?'

'Enough!' I hold up a hand. 'Tell us what happened next, Jake.'

Mark sighs but says nothing. Jake looks relieved.

'So I sent the photos and he asked for my mobile number. That's when he suggested that we meet. He said he'd bring poppers and vodka. The plan was to meet in the loos at the car park and then go to the Downs in his car and have a little party, just the two of us. I took the van. I had no idea you were following

354

me. I thought you were in the loo when I slipped out. You must have been watching through the window or something.'

'And then what happened? When you got to the car park.'

'I went into the men's toilets, where I was supposed to meet him. And there he was, this scrawny little scrote with grey hair and a potbelly. He had a plastic bag with him. I could see there was a bottle of vodka in it. He pretended he was washing his hands when I went in but then I said, "Graham?" and he looked up. That's when I went for him.'

The image of the knife, bloodied and skidding across the tiles, flashes before my eyes. 'You stabbed him?'

'I hit him. The knife was in my back pocket. Just in case he was a psycho.'

'Jesus Christ,' Mark says under his breath.

Jake eyes his dad warily and then continues. 'I heard someone scream, while I was beating the shit out of Graham, and saw Mum standing by the door with the knife in her hand. It must have fallen out of my back pocket. I was so shocked to see her I just kind of froze. Graham tried to escape. He started shouting that he was going to call the police and he ran right at Mum, knocking her out of the way so he could get out the door. She hit one of the cubicles and dropped the knife. I picked it up and said I was going to get him but Mum wouldn't let me. She said she was scared the police were going to show up and I'd end up in prison. She told me to get myself home and she'd meet me there so I dropped the knife and ran.'

'It was you.' I stare at him incredulously. 'You were the person Malcolm and Mandy saw running away? The man in the hoody?'

'I didn't want to run. I swear. You were screaming at me that you'd lost one son and you weren't about to lose another. You seemed normal, Mum. If I'd known you were having one of your blackouts I never would have left you. Never.'

He is so big, so incredibly broad and strong, but I can see flashes of Jake as a child in his eyes. Jake who would cry the second I raised my voice because he was so desperate not to disappoint me or let me down. I've never seen him look so fearful.

'Why was there blood on the knife,' I ask, 'if it just fell out of your pocket?'

Jake doesn't meet my gaze. 'It was his,' he mumbles. 'I gave him a proper going over. Pretty sure I broke his nose and split his lip. His blood was all over my hands.'

I stare at him in horror. 'Do you have any idea how scared I was when I came round? I didn't know where I was or what had happened. When I saw the knife I thought I'd stabbed someone. And you knew. You knew what had happened but you didn't say a word when I got home. You pretended you'd been here the whole time. You even put the dishwasher on!'

'I didn't know what to do.' He wipes the back of his hand across his eyes. 'I was going to say something, I swear. But when I realized you couldn't remember anything I . . . I thought it would be better to keep quiet. I'm so sorry. I'm so, so sorry.'

As Jake sobs I look across at Mark. He is shaking with anger.

'Mark,' I say softly. 'Go back to the house for a bit. Let me deal with this.'

'No.' He shakes his head. 'I'm staying. We're a family. No more secrets, Claire. No more.'

Chapter 51

The light bulb above our head flickers and buzzes as Mark, Jake and I continue to talk. It is dark outside, a sliver of black beneath the garage door where just an hour ago there was daylight.

'Where's the knife now?' Mark asks.

'In a tote bag, underneath the passenger seat in my car.'

'What are you going to do with it?' Jake asks.

None of us has moved in over an hour and a half. Mark and I are still sitting side by side on the weights bench. Jake is sitting on the floor. The laptop separates us. 'If you want to take it to the police I'll understand. You've got to do what you've got to do.'

Jake looks deflated, as though every last drop of anger has been wrung out of him. Mark looks old. Tired and old. He hasn't raised his voice once since Jake started crying. It is as though his son's tears have disarmed him.

And me? I feel calmer than I have in a long time. Calm and empty. I've got answers but they aren't the ones I was hoping for. I thought they'd lead me to Billy but he's still as far away as he's ever been.

'What do you want to do?' Mark asks and I shake my head.

'I don't know. If this Graham person presses charges against Jake then we need to keep the knife, the laptop and the messages on Jake's phone. He'll need them to form his defence.'

'But the knife's probably got my blood on it too,' Jake says. 'My hands were pretty fucked up when I got home.'

'But I would have noticed if you'd hurt them . . .' I say and then stop. When I got home he was wearing a jumper that covered his hands and then he'd tucked them under his armpits when I went into his room. And then he'd punched the wall. Did he deliberately do that so I wouldn't question his torn knuckles or was he genuinely upset about Billy?

'I'm sorry, Mum,' he says again. 'I'm so, so sorry.'

Mark runs a hand over his jaw. His stubble makes a *scritch-scritch-scritch* sound against his palm. 'It's still a weapon. It could look like intent to kill.

'The chances are he won't press charges,' Mark continues. 'It's been, what, a few days since it happened? He knows Jake has copies of the emails and messages. It would be a hell of a risk on his part.'

What do we do? Tell the police or keep it to ourselves? Mark said no more secrets but at what cost? If DS Forbes finds out what happened Jake could go to jail and all because he couldn't deal with his own guilt about Billy's disappearance. Is that fair? The man he punched had hurt children, or was planning to hurt a child. Should my son be the one punished for that?

There's a tapping sound on the door and a soft voice drifts into the garage.

'Hello? Jake? Are you in there? Can I come in?'

Jake jumps to his feet as a pair of hands appears at the bottom of the door and Kira lifts it above her head.

'Oh!' She looks in surprise from her boyfriend to Mark and me. 'Sorry, I didn't realize—'

'It's okay.' Jake wraps an arm around her shoulder and pulls her in to him. 'We were just . . .'

'Having a chat,' I say. 'It's okay. You two go in. It's cold out here. We'll be in in a second.'

My son looks unsure but I wave him away. 'I'll come and say goodbye before I go back to Gran's.'

Jake's lips part but he doesn't say anything. Instead he angles Kira out to the driveway and back towards the house.

'Do you think he'll tell her?' Mark asks when they're out of earshot.

'No, their relationship's not stable enough to take something like that.'

'She's more resilient than you think.'

'In what way?'

'She's had a tough life. Her mum beat her up. Her dad killed himself.'

'I didn't know you knew about him.'

He shrugs. 'She told me after my dad's heart attack. I assumed you knew.'

He looks so different in the half-light of the garage. His hair looks thinner, his eyes darker and more beady, and there are lines that stretch from his nose to the edges of his mouth. I thought I knew every inch of my husband after twenty years but there's still so much of him that is a mystery to me.

'Mark,' I say. 'How many more lies are there?'

He shakes his head. 'I don't understand.'

'When were you going to tell me the real reason you didn't get into the police?'

'Oh God.' He slumps forward. 'Who told you?'

'It doesn't matter who told me. Is it true? Are you a sex offender?'

'No!' His eyes search mine, then he looks away. 'Technically, yes. But not like you're thinking. I didn't hurt anyone. I didn't force myself on someone. I was sixteen. I was going out with a girl in the year below. She was fifteen. Her mum was a religious nut job and when she found out she reported me to the police. And yes, I was cautioned. I didn't disclose it when I applied to the force and they found out. Of course they bloody found out. They terminated my application. I couldn't tell you that. You would have left me.'

'What else have you lied about, Mark?'

'Nothing. I swear.'

I sit in the gloom beside him, a hundred thoughts running through my head, and force myself to stand up. 'I should go and see Jake and say goodbye.'

'You're going back to your mum's then?'

'Yes. I think that's for the best, don't you?'

'Because of Jake?' he asks softly. 'Or because of me?'

'A bit of both.'

He doesn't say a word as I cross the garage but I can feel his eyes boring into my back. The weight of sadness in the air is more than I can bear.

When I turn back round Mark has his head in his hands.

'I need to talk to her,' I say. 'To Edie Christian. You understand why, don't you?'

'Yes.' He nods. 'Yes, I do.'

Chapter 52

Are you sure this is a good idea?

Yes, Mark knows. I told him.

Do you believe him?

I unwind the car window and reread Liz's text. Do I believe that nothing happened between my husband and Edie Christian?

My heart says yes, my head says I need to be sure.

That's fair enough. I'm here if you need to talk afterwards. You know that, don't you?

I do. Thanks, Liz. Xx

'Mrs Wilkinson!' Edie Christian raises a hand and waves. Her long blonde hair is tied back in a pony-tail and she's wearing a red flowery dress with black leggings and sensible shoes. Her lanyard swings from left to right as she bounces across reception towards me.

'Miss Christian.' I shake her outstretched hand and

363

force a smile, aware that the receptionist is watching.

'I've booked a private meeting room,' she says as she ushers me down a corridor. 'A lot of the year heads are in the office today and I know you wanted a private chat.'

I know her office well. I felt as though I spent half my life there last year, discussing Billy's various 'issues'. I'd mentally prepared myself for our chat to take place there and I'm thrown by her suggestion that we talk in private.

She opens the door to a small beige room, and gestures at the desk and six chairs in the centre. Does she know what I'm about to ask her? Is that why she wants me out of earshot of the other staff?

'Take a seat. Would you like a tea or coffee? Some water?'

She radiates a happy, enthusiastic energy but there's something strained about the smile that's been fixed to her face since she spotted me in reception.

'I'm fine. Thank you.' I take the chair nearest the door.

'How are you?' she asks, leaning towards me, all bright enthusiasm and curiosity. 'Is there any news about Billy? Anything I, or the school, could do to help?'

I shift in my chair, cross my ankles, then uncross them again. I can't believe I'm doing this. Two days have passed since my conversation with Mark. Forty-eight torturous hours of going back and forward in my mind about whether or not this is a good idea.

'Miss Christian.'

'Yes.'

'Have you been having an affair with my husband?'

She recoils, her chair creaking as she sits back. Her right hand flies to her chest. 'I'm sorry?'

'My husband. Mark Wilkinson. Have you been having an affair with him?'

'No.' Her hand drifts from her chest to her throat. 'God, no.'

'But you've kissed?'

'What? No.' She glances towards the window in the top of the closed office door as a student walks past. 'Whatever gave you that— Oh.' Her expression morphs from horror to understanding. 'This is about what happened last year, isn't it?'

I nod. 'My brother-in-law told me that Billy saw you kissing. He put a brick through Mark's car window.'

'I didn't know that.'

She sits forward in her chair again, her professional demeanour regained. 'Mrs Wilkinson. I'm not sure what your brother-in-law told you but I think he might have got the wrong end of the stick. Your husband was very upset that night. I recognized him and went up to the bar to check if he was okay. He was . . .' She glances towards the door again and lowers her voice. 'He was very drunk. Very upset.'

'And he tried to kiss you?'

'Yes. But I rebuffed him. There really wasn't anything to it. I left shortly afterwards.'

'Did he say anything? After he tried to kiss you?'

365

She shifts in her seat. 'I'm not sure it would be helpful if I—'

'Please. What did he say?'

'He said that you were the love of his life and he thought he was going to lose you. He said he knew you were unhappy but he didn't know how to make things right. He blamed himself. He said he'd been working so hard you'd barely seen each other and it had all been for nothing. I told him to talk to you, to tell you how he felt.' She gives me a long, lingering look.

'We didn't have that conversation.'

'I see.'

'And when you met him recently, at the doctor's, what did he say then?'

She looks surprised. 'He said how sorry he was. He was really very apologetic. I said it was okay, that I'd already forgotten about it.'

'And that's it? That's all the contact you've had since it happened?'

'Yes.' She runs a hand over her hair. A diamond glitters on the ring finger of her left hand. 'That's all the contact we've had, other than when the two of you were both here about Billy.'

'Did you see him?' I ask.

'Sorry?'

'Billy. You said you left the pub shortly after Mark . . . after the incident. Did you see Billy when you left?'

She gazes up at the ceiling as she tries to remember. 'I don't know. I couldn't say for sure. It was very

366

dark. I spotted a couple of people over by the bins. I was startled when I saw them. I remember walking faster but I couldn't tell you if one of them was Billy.'

'Were they male or female?'

She shakes her head. 'I don't know. As I said, it was dark. I'm sorry. Is there anything else I can—'

'No.' I stand up so quickly my chair tips backwards and I have to put out a hand to stop it from falling. 'No, that's it. Thank you so much for your time. I won't bother you again.'

'Mrs Wilkinson,' she says as I reach for the door handle. 'One more thing, before you go.'

'Yes.'

'I know it's not my place to give you advice but I do think it might help if you and your husband had a convers—'

'I don't think that's any of your business, do you?'

Saturday 3rd January 2015

ICE9: *He saw us! I can't believe he saw us.*

Jackdaw44: *It was dark. He won't have seen our faces.*

ICE9: *But he stopped! I saw him stop, right by the fence. He looked straight at me.*

Jackdaw44: *So he's a pervert who gets off on watching people fucking in the bushes. So what?*

ICE9: *You don't get it, do you? If he recognized us my life is over!*

Jackdaw44: *You're freaking out over nothing.*

ICE9: *Nothing?! You might have nothing to lose but I'd lose everything. My home, my relationship, everything. I knew it was a mistake to meet you last night. I knew it.*

Jackdaw44: *So it's my fault we shagged, is it? I forced you into it?*

ICE9: *You kissed me.*

Jackdaw44: *I kissed you goodbye and you kissed me back.*

ICE9: *I should have walked away.*
Jackdaw44: *You didn't though, did you? I knew you still had feelings for me. I knew it.*
ICE9: *I'm sorry. I can't do this any more. It's over. For good this time.*
Jackdaw44: *I've heard that before.*

Chapter 53

I drive straight to Liz's house without stopping. She takes one look at my face and wraps her arms around me.

'Oh, sweetheart. I'm so sorry. He's such a fucking bastard.'

I let her lead me into the kitchen and sit down on the chair she pulls out. She pushes a box of tissues towards me but I shake my head. I cried all the way from the school to her house but, now I'm here, the tears have dried up.

'How long has it been going on?' she asks. 'Since last year?'

I shake my head. 'They haven't been having an affair.'

'What? But you've been crying. I assumed—'

'He tried to kiss her and she pushed him away.'

'Did she now?' She raises an eyebrow.

'I believe her. She said he was really upset. He told

her he loved me and he was scared he was going to lose me—'

'And so he kissed her. Way to rescue your relationship, Mark! For fuck's sake.'

'But he was right. Things weren't great between us and—'

'No.' Liz crosses her arms. 'I am not going to let you blame yourself for this. This is about Mark, not you. You were going through a bad patch but you didn't throw yourself at one of your kids' teachers. Did you?'

'No.'

'No, you fucking didn't. Honestly.' She opens the fridge and takes out a bottle of wine. 'I could swing for him. I really could. Men and their fucking dicks.

'Sorry.' She takes a deep breath. 'I'm making this about me. Lloyd is coming over tomorrow and I'm really bloody nervous.'

'Has he told you why he wants to talk to you yet?'

'No.' She takes two glasses out of the cupboard. 'I guess I'll find out soon enough. So, what about you? What are you going to do?'

'I don't know.'

'You could leave him.'

'For a kiss? For lying about something he's ashamed of? We've been married for twenty years.'

'That's not a reason to stay together.'

'But . . .' The same images repeat themselves in my head: Mark tenderly checking me over after my first blackout, holding hands during DS Forbes's visit, ringing to wish me a drunken goodnight, kissing in the kitchen. 'Things have been different between us recently. We've felt closer. We've been talking.'

'Well, that's something.' She plonks a glass of rosé in front of me and sits down.

'What would you do?' I ask. 'If you were me?

'She takes a sip of her wine. 'But I'm not you, am I? I could tell you that there's no way you can trust him now he's lied to you about something this big and that you'll be happier without him but that's a decision you need to make.'

'Are you happier without Lloyd?'

'I've got Tinder, haven't I? And a nine-inch dildo?' Her smile slips as she looks up from her glass. 'I'm fine. I wouldn't say I'm happy but it's early days. I miss being in love, I miss curling up with someone on the sofa and I miss having someone to talk to. But maybe it was for the best that Lloyd left. We didn't love each other any more.'

She sighs. 'What I'm saying is that it's better to be on your own than with someone who doesn't love you. I'm not the right person to ask for advice, Claire. The way I feel about men at the moment I want to tell you to fuck Mark off. But if you still love him and he loves you, and you can put what happened behind you, then maybe it's not too late for you two to put things right.'

'Maybe.'

'Don't make any big decisions yet. Give yourself some time to—'

She's interrupted by the sound of my mobile ringing.

'Sorry.' I fish it out of my bag. An unknown number flashes on the screen. 'Hello?'

'Hello, Mrs Wilkinson. It's DS Forbes. I was wondering if there's any way I can get together with you and Mark at some point today? There's been a development.'

Chapter 54

We sit as we did the last time he visited: DS Forbes in the armchair and Mark and I on the sofa. We're holding hands, our damp palms pressed together, fingers entwined. Mark launched himself at me the moment I walked through the back door. We clung to each other. When I pulled away from him he had tears in his eyes.

'It's bad news, isn't it?' I whispered.

Mark shook his head. 'I don't know.'

'DS Forbes said there'd been a development. That word scares me.'

'Me too.'

'Oh God, Mark. I don't think I can do this.'

He smoothed a hair back from my cheek. His hand lingered there, then fell away awkwardly. He was thinking about the conversation we'd had two days earlier, the one that ended with me telling him that I was going to see Edie Christian.

The image of my husband pressing his lips to hers had haunted me for days but, compared with what we might be about to face, it felt like nothing. It felt utterly insignificant.

'It might be good news,' he said. 'There's always that possibility.'

I didn't tell him that I don't believe in good news any more. Or that, for me, it was no longer a matter of if we were told that Billy was dead but when. But I didn't want it to be now. I didn't feel ready. I would never feel ready.

'Mr and Mrs Wilkinson.' DS Forbes gives us the same look he gave us last time, professional but sympathetic. 'I'm so sorry it's taken so long to give you an update into Jason Davies's claims but the investigation had to be thorough, given the nature of those claims.'

'Claims?' I say.

'He confessed to the abduction and murder of multiple children.'

'Oh my God.' The horror I feel is reflected on Mark's face.

'The process for investigating claims of this type is extensive. We've had to liaise with the prison warden in order to take a statement from the cellmate and then we had to match dates with the known movements of—'

'Just tell us.' Mark's grip on my hand tightens. 'It's bad news, isn't it?'

DS Forbes shuffles forward in his seat and presses his palms to his thighs. 'I'll cut to the chase. There is no evidence to support the claim that Jason Davies was responsible for Billy's disappearance. The dates don't match up. He was nowhere near Bristol on the fifth of February. He was in Aberdeen the week before and after that date. We have several sources that corroborate that fact.'

'Oh, thank God.' Mark's hand slips from mine as he slumps forward. 'Oh, thank God.'

He takes a minute to compose himself, then looks at me. 'It's good news, Claire.'

'Yes.'

'Are you okay?'

I nod but the motion does little to shake the dark cloud that has engulfed me. I should be as relieved as my husband that Jason Davies isn't responsible for abducting Billy but then I never thought he was. So why do I feel so numb and disappointed?

'Are there any other leads?' Mark asks DS Forbes.

He shakes his head. 'Not at this time, although we are still following up on some possible sightings that were reported after the television appeal.'

Possible sightings. We've been there before. Sightings of kids going to a skate park, graffitiing a bridge or sleeping on a street corner. Sightings of children who look nothing like my son. Children who are not my son.

And there's my answer.

That's why a cloud of despair has descended. We are still no closer to finding out what happened to my Billy. The torturous limbo we've existed in for the last seven months continues. I no longer believe that my son is alive but every day that passes feels like a week. Every week a month. Every month a year. I want Billy to be returned to me. Alive or dead. I just want him to come home.

'We're doing everything we can,' DS Forbes says.

Mark and I both nod but mine is as automated as that stupid dog in the insurance commercial.

'Do you have any other questions?' DS Forbes asks.

'Yeah.' Mark leans back on the sofa and crosses his arms over his chest. 'Why would that fucker admit to abducting our son if he didn't do it? We've been tearing ourselves apart for weeks now and for what? So some twisted bastard can get his kicks? Men like him don't deserve to live. If we still had the death penalty I'd be first in line to watch him hang.'

DS Forbes nods minutely. Whether to placate my husband or because he agrees with him I can't tell. 'I understand why you're angry, Mr Wilkinson. This individual has done more than waste police time and he will be punished for it. He'll go to court, most likely be awarded extra time to his sentence—'

'But why?' Mark says. 'Why would he admit to something like that if he knew he'd be found out and get more time?'

'We may never know. Maybe he saw the appeal on TV and fancied a share of the limelight? Maybe he thought it would impress his new cellmate? Maybe it was some kind of twisted wish fulfilment. I really can't say.'

'Jesus Christ. And people wonder why these paedophile hunters go after them?' Mark presses his lips together and glances at me. It's been two days since Jake confessed to what he'd done and we haven't discussed it since. I've rung Jake to check how he's doing and each time he's spent the majority of the conversation apologizing over and over again.

We'll have to tell him about this latest development. Kira too. God knows what the fallout will be like.

'We need to tell Jake and Kira,' I say. 'And Mum and Dad and John and Stephen.'

Mark frowns. 'Stephen?'

'I need to talk to you about him,' I say softly. 'He's been drinking a lot. Caroline has left him.'

Mark's eyes widen. 'Seriously? When?'

DS Forbes clears his throat.

'If there's nothing else.' He moves to stand up and when neither of us says anything he gets to his feet.

'Thank you.' I cross the room, my hand outstretched.

DS Forbes shakes it firmly, then holds out his hand to Mark.

'Yes,' Mark says. 'Thank you.'

The tension in DS Forbes's face softens as the two men shake hands. Sometimes I forget that there's a regular bloke, probably with a wife and family, hidden behind the suit and the solemn expression. How did he feel as he walked up to our front door? Tired? Fed up? Bracing himself for an emotional outburst from one or both of us? I wonder where he'll go after he's said goodbye. Back to the station or to some other family? God knows how he does this job day after day.

'I'll be in touch,' he says.

Friday 16th January 2015

Jackdaw44: *I miss what we had.*
Jackdaw44: *It's not even about the sex.*
Jackdaw44: *What we had was special. You know that. I know that. You made the wrong choice. Deep down you know that.*

Chapter 55

We watch from the kitchen window as DS Forbes gets into his car.

'You need to sort things out with Stephen,' I say as the black Volvo disappears down the street.

'Why should I?' Mark's tone is defensive, but I can hear the pain behind it.

It's a good question. I've been thinking about Stephen for days. I was so, so angry with him after I met him in the pub. I felt as though he was deliberately trying to destroy what little life I have left by getting his own back on Mark. Only he wasn't, was he? Not completely. He was telling me things other people had kept from me. Wherever I look I unearth another lie or another secret and Stephen is one of the few people who's been straight with me – or as straight as a broken drunk can be.

'He's your brother, Mark.'

'Stepbrother.'

'You used to be close.'

'That was a long time ago.'

'He needs you. And you need him.'

Mark yanks at the handle on the dishwasher door and pulls out the tray at the top. There's a saucepan and baking tray jammed in with the mugs and glasses instead of down at the bottom where the jets are stronger.

'Stephen's in a bad place,' I say. 'He's drinking too much. His marriage is on its last legs and he's torn up about Billy.'

Mark hooks his thick fingers through the handles of several mugs and transfers them to the mug tree by the kettle.

'I think he'd talk if you reached out to him.'

'And why would I want to do that?'

'Because you miss him. Because you both need someone to talk to. And because your argument is eating away at you as much as it's eating away at him. Don't you think Jake would go back and sort things out with Billy if he could? He'd do it in a heartbeat. Don't leave it too late to talk to Stephen. That's all I'm saying.'

He reaches for the saucepan, then rests his hand on top of it.

'I'm just so tired, Claire. I'm tired of fights and tension and not knowing from one day to the next what shitty thing is going to be thrown at us next. I just . . . I just want to rewind time and go back to when things were good. You know?'

'Yes, I do.'

'Remember that time?' He looks at me, his eyes lighting up. 'When the kids were little and they wanted to go camping but we couldn't afford it so we borrowed a tent off Dad and set it up in the garden. The boys said they were going to stay in it all night but we knew they were both secretly scared and neither of them wanted to be the one to admit it and come in?'

'We threw marbles at the tent through our bedroom window!'

'They couldn't get out fast enough!'

'They were good times.' His smile disappears and sadness fills his eyes. 'When did it all go wrong?'

'They grew up. We did too. We were so young when they were born, not much more than kids ourselves.'

'You haven't changed at all.'

'Haven't I?'

'I meant it as a compliment.'

'I know.'

'Claire.' Mark takes a step towards me and his fingers brush the skin on the back of my hand. 'I never wanted to hurt you. Not then, not now. I've only ever wanted you to be happy and what—'

'All right, Mum? Dad.' Jake steps into the kitchen, followed by Kira who raises her hand in a half-hearted wave.

'Hello, sweetheart.' I take a step towards him and give him a hug.

'Kira.' I reach for her too but her shoulders twitch away so I plant a kiss on her cheek instead.

'DS Forbes just left,' Mark says and they both stiffen. 'Jason Davies wasn't responsible for Billy's disappearance. It was all bullshit. He made it up to get attention.'

Jake stares at him. 'What?'

'It's true,' I say. 'The police looked into it and he was nowhere near Bristol the day Billy vanished. He was in Aberdeen. He was there for the two weeks.'

'Do they know that for sure? Maybe he travelled down here? You hear about it all the time, murderers randomly driving somewhere just to kill someone and then—'

'Jake.' Kira pulls on his arm. 'Jake, please don't—'

'Don't what? Don't get angry? My God. I could have . . . I nearly . . .' He looks at me and shakes his head. 'I'm so sorry, Mum.'

He walks back out the back door without saying another word. Kira runs after him.

'Should we go after him?' Mark asks.

I shake my head. 'No, let him go.'

Tuesday 27th January 2015

Jackdaw44: *You can't ignore me for ever you know.*

Chapter 56

It is the morning after DS Forbes's visit. I didn't stay long after Jake left. The decision to go back to Mum's didn't come easy. I wanted to wait for him to return, to check he was okay, but that would have meant more time alone with Mark and I knew he'd ask me questions that I'm not ready to answer yet. Questions about the future. Questions about us.

Seven months ago there's no way I would have left my home when my family needed me. My place was in the heart of the family. I had to know where everyone was, what they were doing and why. Nothing got past me.

At least that's what I thought.

The kids called me a control freak. Mark did too but only ever in a jokey way. I'm no psychotherapist but I can't help wondering if I'm like that because of my childhood. Mum's crap was everywhere, life was chaotic and I lived in a constant state of insecurity, never quite sure when the next argument would be or if it would all get too much for Dad and he'd leave us. I promised myself that my kids would never feel like that. Their mum and dad were going to stick around, no matter what. *I'd* stick around, no matter what.

My first fugue, when I went to Weston, was the first time I'd gone anywhere alone for a long, long time. Sometimes, when the kids were fighting and screaming and Mark was hiding away in the garage, I'd fantasize about running away. About how I'd go to the train station and buy a ticket to St Ives or Brighton or Weymouth, and book a room in a hotel with a double bed just for me and spend the weekend walking along the seafront, drinking coffee in quaint cafés and lying on the beach reading books. I'd breathe in the sea air and I'd daydream about my other life, the one where I turned left instead of right. Me, single and childless, training as a nurse and then going to work for the Red Cross or Médecins Sans Frontières.

I never did jump on a train to St Ives but I did let myself daydream about a different kind of life. I never told anyone about those daydreams, not even Liz, because I didn't want to appear ungrateful for the life I had. We all have secrets. Most are guilty, a few are wretched and some are too precious to share.

My mobile bleeps, snapping me back into my childhood bedroom where piles of boxes and bags are stacked up beside the bed and a floral duvet that smells of lavender washing powder is pulled up to my chin. It's 8.05 a.m. and Mum and Dad are moving around in the kitchen. Mum's singing along to a tinny tune on the radio.

Two text messages. One from Stephen. One from Kira.

Stephen: *I had a text from Mark asking me to go to the pub with him tonight. Do you know what he wants?*

Kira: *Hi Claire. I hope you're OK. Just to let you know that Jake's all right. He's gone to work. Only trouble is Ian has asked him to work on a job in Cheltenham so he's had to take his van and he was going to let me borrow it to help my friend bring in her sculptures for the exhibition, ready for the opening on Monday. I don't suppose you know where we could rent one for cheap? K x*

I text them back:

Hi Stephen. I think Mark wants to sort things out between the two of you. You should call him. Life's too short. C.

Hi Kira. Glad to hear Jake is OK.

I pause. Has he told her what happened in the car park that night? He can't have. She wouldn't have stuck around if she knew, not when her own mum is so violent. Jake must have decided not to tell her until after her exhibition.

More secrets. Will they never end?

You can borrow my car, I tap out. *I'm not planning on going anywhere today. Pop round to my mum's and I'll give you the keys.*

A text from Stephen appears the second I press 'send'.

Is he angry? I'm not going to meet him if he's angry.

He's not angry, I type back. *He wants to put things right.*

Another text from Kira.

That's very kind but I don't know how long I'll need it for and I wouldn't want to put you out. K x

It's fine. Honestly. It's insured for other drivers. Come round.

Will you be there? Stephen types back. *I'd prefer it if you were.*

'Claire!' Mum calls up the stairs. 'Dad's making some bacon sandwiches. Would you like one?'

I am up to my elbows in bubbles, scrubbing at an oven tray shiny with bacon fat, when there's a knock at the front door.

'I'll get it.' Dad shuffles out of the kitchen in his slippers. At the same time Mum appears from the living room with her laptop in her hands. She joins me at the sink and lifts it up so it's at eye level.

'Claire, I know you said you didn't want to hear about any more psychics but someone called Athena Larkin has been in touch. She said she's helped the police in a number of high-profile cases and—'

'Claire! It's Kira. She says she's come to collect the car.'

'One second, Dad!'

Mum paws at my shoulder. 'At least read the email she sent. She says that—'

'Are those the keys?' Dad shuffles back into the

389

room and points towards the kitchen table where my car keys are lying on top of my handbag.

'Yes. Hang on a second, though, because there's something I need to— Mum, could you get the laptop out of my face? It's going to get wet and anyway, I told you I'm not interested in—'

'Got them.'

'But we're back at square one now, aren't we? And it's not like the police have got any new leads. Not from what you said last night, anyway. Look at this part.' Mum takes one hand off the base and points to the screen.

'Careful!' I reach for the laptop as it lurches towards the sink. The oven tray I've been holding drops back into the washing-up bowl, spraying me with soapy water.

I'm vaguely aware of the front door closing with a click and the sound of Dad walking back to the kitchen but I'm distracted by my T-shirt clinging damply to my stomach.

'Claire!' Mum whips the laptop away from me. 'You nearly knocked it into the water.'

'I was trying to stop you from dropping it!'

'What the hell's going on in here?' Dad stops in the doorway to the kitchen. 'Claire, there's half a swimming pool on the kitchen floor! Bloody hell, girl. That's what happens when you get a dishwasher. You forget how to do the washing-up.'

'Dad.' I look from the kitchen table to my dad's empty hands.

'Yes, love.'

'Did you just give Kira the keys to my car?'

'Yeah. She said you'd given her the okay to borrow it.' He glances back towards the front door.

'Claire!' he shouts as I sprint down the hall. 'Claire? What's the matter?'

I wrench the door open and stare out onto the street but my red Polo is no longer parked behind Dad's blue Peugeot. It's gone. Along with Kira, the tote bag tucked under the passenger seat, and the knife.

Tuesday 27th January 2015

ICE9: *Don't you EVER do that again.*
Jackdaw44: *What?* 😠
ICE9: *You know damned well what.*
Jackdaw44: *Twat now, am I? You changed your tune quickly enough.*
ICE9: *You were out of order and you know it.*
Jackdaw44: *You were ignoring me. How else was I supposed to get your attention?*
ICE9: *Someone could have seen.*
Jackdaw44: *They didn't though, did they? I like touching you up when other people are around. Turns me on that they have no idea what I'm doing.*
ICE9: *You're the only one it turns on.*
Jawdaw44: *Liar.*
ICE9: *I'm not talking about this any more. You obviously don't think you did anything wrong.*
Jackdaw44: *So you're going to start ignoring me again?*

ICE9: No *shit*.

Jackdaw44: *Let's see how well that works out for you.*

ICE9: *What's that supposed to mean?*

Jackdaw44: 😈

ICE9: *You'd better not be talking about what I think you're talking about.*

Jackdaw44: 📷 🛏 🖤

ICE9: *You're lying. I looked through your phone after you said you'd deleted them and they were gone.*

Jackdaw44: *You didn't look in all the folders though, did you? You didn't look in the one called Graffiti?*

{file uploading . . .}

ICE9: *You fucking arsehole. Delete that photo NOW.*

Jackdaw44: *OK. Deleted. Do you like this one better?*

{file uploading . . .}

Jackdaw44: *Still planning on ignoring me?*

ICE9: *I fucking hate you.*

Jackdaw44: *No, you don't. Tell me you love me.*

ICE9: *No.*

Jackdaw44: *Looks like I'll have to press 'send' then . . .*

ICE9: *I love you, OK. There. I said it. Now delete the photos.*

Jackdaw44: *You're such a bad liar. Good fuck, bad liar.*

ICE9: *What do you want?*

Jackdaw44: *Sleep with me. There's some stuff I want to try out.*

393

ICE9: *What kind of stuff?*

Jackdaw44: *Stuff in videos on the Internet. Hardcore shit. Looks fun.*

ICE9: *No.*

Jackdaw44: *OK. *presses send**

ICE9: *Stop!*

Jackdaw44: *Changed your mind?*

ICE9: *If I do what you say how do I know you'll delete the photos? How do I know you haven't got them backed up on a memory disk or something?*

Jackdaw44: *You don't. You'll have to trust me.*

ICE9: *That worked out well last time.*

Jackdaw44: *That's because I wanted to keep the photos to look at when we weren't together. I don't need them any more. I've got the Internet.*

ICE9: *I don't trust you.*

Jackdaw44: *I'll delete the photos in front of you and let you take a photo of me.*

ICE9: *Naked?*

Jackdaw44: *Yeah. Keep it on your phone. Call it collateral.*

ICE9: *You'd let me do that?*

Jackdaw44: *I told you. I want to see you again. I want to touch you. I want to fuck you. Let's do it one more time then I'll leave you alone. I promise.*

ICE9: *Just once? You swear? And you'll delete the photos in front of me and let me go through your phone?*

Jackdaw44: *Yes.*

ICE9: *I'm not doing anything involving shit or piss.*

Jackdaw44: *How twisted do you think I am? (Don't answer that.* 😈 *)*

Chapter 57

I call Kira's number over and over again but each time it goes straight to voicemail.

I type her a text.

Hi Kira. There's something I need to get from the car. Where are you?

Then I delete what I've written. If I tell her there's something I need in the car she might look for it. The tote bag is tucked out of sight beneath the passenger seat and the chances are she won't even notice it's there. But what if she gives someone a lift? What if they shift the seat forwards or backwards and notice it? They wouldn't open it. Kira would assume it was mine and tell them to put it back. But what if they left it in view when they got out of the car and an opportunist thief walked past and spotted it?

I lay the phone down on the duvet and take a deep breath. I'm over-thinking this and there's no need to.

The bag will be fine. It's been under the seat for days and nothing bad has happened. But no one else has been in the car other than me. Oh God. Why didn't I just leave it in the wardrobe? Why didn't I throw it away when I had the chance?

I'll wait. Yes, that's what I'll do. I'll just wait here at Mum and Dad's until Kira brings the car back and then I'll get the bag and I'll drive to Chew Valley and throw it in the lake.

It's fine. I can do this. I can wait it out. Nothing bad's going to happen.

'Jake,' I say into my mobile as the taxi pulls up outside Bristol School of Art. 'I've been trying to get hold of Kira and she's not answering her phone. Have you spoken to her this morning?'

'One second, Mum. Scott needs me to . . . What?' His voice becomes muffled. 'Yeah. Tell Ian I'll give him a ring in a second. I'm just on the phone. Hi, Mum. I can't be long. Ian needs to talk to me. What's up?'

'It's Kira. I'm trying to get in touch with her but she's not answering.'

He sighs. 'Her phone's shit. She's had it so bloody long the battery only holds a charge for a couple of hours before it dies. I keep telling her I'll get her a new one but she won't have it. She says she'd rather have the money and buy it herself.'

'I've been trying to ring you too, all morning. I was getting worried.'

Four hours. That's how long I managed to hold

out at Mum and Dad's. Four long, torturous hours while a hundred different scenarios ran through my head, including one where Kira wasn't answering her phone because she was in the police station, handing over the knife. That's when I rang the taxi cab.

'Signal's shit here,' Jake says. 'I've got like one bar worth of reception. Sounds like Ian's been shitting a brick because he couldn't get hold of any of us. Look, I'm going to have to go now, Mum. Are you all right? You sound stressed. Is it because of what DS Forbes said? I'm sorry I freaked out. I just . . . I can't talk right now. I'll come round to Gran's after work. Okay?'

'No,' I say quickly. 'No, don't do that. Uncle Stephen and Dad are going to the pub to sort things out tonight. I'd like you to be there. You can be the peacekeeper.'

'Me?' He laughs. 'You're kidding me, right? That's your job!'

'Not any more. I need you to do this, Jake, for your dad, for our family. It's important.'

He falls silent for a couple of seconds, then says, 'All right. If that's what you want. I'll go along but don't be surprised if they come to blows. Kidding!' he adds quickly. 'It'll be fine. Don't worry.'

The taxi driver coughs and glances meaningfully at the meter.

'I've got to go,' I say. 'I love you, Jake.'

'I love you too, Mum. See you later.'

I'd expected to be met at the entrance by a receptionist

or a security guard but it's remarkably easy to stroll into the School of Art building and no one gives me so much as a second look. I don't know if it's because it's a Saturday or if it's always this quiet. After five minutes in the lobby I approach an Asian girl in a headscarf who's walking past carrying an armful of fabric.

'I'm looking for Kira Simmons. Do you know where I might find her?'

'Is she staff or a student?'

'A student. She does photography.'

The girl shrugs. 'Sorry, can't help. I'm textiles.'

'She's putting on an exhibition,' I add as she turns to leave. 'Do you know where that might be?'

'There's a gallery through there.' She tilts her head to the right. 'Looks like it's being set up for an exhibition. Someone in there might know.'

'Thank you.' I flash her a smile. 'You've been very helpful.'

'I dunno about that.' The girl laughs as she ascends the stairs and disappears.

The gallery is a hive of activity with students hanging artwork on the walls and arranging ceramics; craning their heads this way and that to check that the paintings and photographs are straight and altering the positions of sculptures by half-inch turns. As I walk through the gallery, scanning faces in search of Kira, a couple of students turn to look at me but no one stops me to ask who I am or what I'm doing there. I pass by several photography exhibits, pausing by one of pregnant women dressed in different uniforms and outfits. There's a pregnant policewoman, a pregnant fisherwoman, a pregnant clown. I smile at the photograph of the pregnant chef, her whites gaping over her belly as though she's eaten one too many of the pastries stacked up beside her. Next to her is a pregnant stripper. That makes me feel sad.

I hurry on. Kira told Liz that her project was about tattoos and regrets.

I've nearly reached the far end of the cavernous room when I finally spot Kira's small patch of wall. There are hooks for lots of canvases but she's only hung six. Each one is a close-up of a tattoo with a small white card mounted on wood underneath.

The first canvas I look at is of a Nazi symbol on a man's forearm. On the card underneath it says:

My mate did this tattoo for me with a compass and some ink when we were fifteen. I thought it was cool. I didn't even really know what it stood for, just that it pissed off old people. I'm sixteen now and I'm saving to get it covered up. I wear a lot of long-sleeved T-shirts.

The second canvas shows the name *Nadia* tattooed under a rose.

Nadia was my first wife, says the description on the card. We were together for twenty years. I thought we'd be together for ever but I cheated on her and we split up. My new girlfriend hates it. She keeps telling me to get it covered up and

*get her name instead but I won't be making the
same mistake twice.*

The third canvas shows a clenched fist with a
triangle, a circle, a cross and a square tattooed onto
the figures.

*When I got this tattoo done I loved my PlayStation
more than anything else in the world, says the
card. Now I feel like a bit of a dick.*

As I move towards the fourth canvas I sense
someone behind me and turn around. It's a young
bloke with a piercing through his nose and dark hair
cut into a teddy-boy style.

'All right?' He gives me a curt nod.

'I'm Claire. Kira lives with my son Jake.'

'Mason.' He holds out a slender hand. 'I'm Kira's
tutor.'

'Nice to meet you. I don't suppose you know where
she is, do you?'

'One minute.' He ducks round the partition wall
that separates Kira's exhibition from the one beside
it. A couple of seconds later he reappears.

'She's gone out for coffee.'

'Yeah.' A young woman with pink hair twisted into
a messy topknot pokes her head around the partition.
'She said she was meeting someone. Didn't say who.'

'Do you know which café?'

She shakes her head. 'Sorry, no. Somewhere on
Queen's Road probably. I don't imagine she'll have

gone far. She's got to get this finished before we open on Monday.'

She gestures towards the row of canvases propped up against the base of the wall. I half-glance at them, then do a double-take.

'What's this?' I crouch down by the canvas at the far end of the row.

'Careful!' Mason says as I reach for it. 'You shouldn't be touching—'

'Billy.' I point at the black inky image in the centre of the canvas. The word is almost lost in the abstract spikiness of the design but I know what it says. *DStroy*. 'Billy drew this.'

'What?' He tilts his head to one side. 'I'm not sure I—'

'It's one of my son's graffiti designs. I'm sure it is. I've seen it before, in the sketchpad he kept by his bed. Did Kira say whose tattoo it is?' I look from Mason to Pink Hair who is standing beside me, arms spread wide as though readying herself to protect Kira's exhibition. They both shake their heads.

I scoot across to the other end of the row where a pile of cardboard descriptions is stacked neatly and sort through them, flicking them to the floor as I read.

Me and my best mate thought it would be fun to . . .
It was my stag night and I was drunk . . .
I really liked My Little Pony as a kid and . . .

'Whoa!' Mason grabs holds of my wrist as Pink Hair dips down to gather up the discarded cards. 'I don't know what you think you're doing but you're damaging private property. Kira's worked really hard to—'

'It's not here.' I snatch my wrist away from him. 'The card that describes that tattoo. It's not here. Where is it?'

I spot a black art folder propped up against the partition but Pink Hair gets there first. She whips it up by the handle and holds it away from me.

'Can we get security?' She looks at Mason who nods.

'You don't understand,' I say. 'I know Kira. She's my son's girlfriend. And this tattoo. This DStroy symbol. My son drew that. My son Billy. He's been missing for over six months.'

Pink Hair takes a step back, into the crowd of students who have congregated around us. They are all staring at me as though I'm one of the exhibits.

'Anyone?' I scan their faces. 'Does anyone know anything about this photo?'

'I'm sorry.' Mason places his hand on my elbow and guides me to my feet. 'But I think you should leave.'

Wednesday 28th January 2015

Jackdaw44: *So last night was fun.*

ICE9: *I fucking hate you. I'm never doing that again.*

Jackdaw44: *Yes, you are.*

ICE9: *I knew you had backups of the photos. I'm not an idiot.*

Jackdaw44: *I've got screenshots of our Snapchat conversations too, including the one where you said how much you enjoyed sucking my cock.*

ICE9: *And I've got a photo of your erect dick.*

Jackdaw44: *And?*

ICE9: *The photo includes your face.*

Jackdaw44: *So?*

ICE9: *If you try and blackmail me again I'll send it to all your mates and post it on your Facebook page.*

Jackdaw44: *Got the numbers for my mates, have you? And if you post on my FB page it'll have your name attached. And you can't post to my page unless you're a friend.*

ICE9: *I'll find a way.*

Jackdaw44: *Cool.*

ICE9: *You're calling my bluff.*

Jackdaw44: *Am I? Or maybe I don't give a shit that you've got a photo of me and my massive cock. It would prove Liv's a fucking liar for one.*

ICE9: *You'd be humiliated if I made this photo public.*

Jackdaw44: *Would I? Kids my age don't give a shit about that kind of thing, not if they're well hung. Look up Dappy, look up Arg from TOWIE, that bloke from Made in Chelsea. It's not a big deal. But YOUR photos on the other hand . . . shit would hit the fan and then some.*

ICE9: *I'm not doing what we did last night again.*

Jackdaw44: *I don't want you to do that again. It was a bit of a disappointment if I'm honest.*

ICE9: *Then what do you want?*

Jackdaw44: *Nothing you haven't done before.*

ICE9: *Sex.*

Jackdaw44: *Something else.*

ICE9: *Like what?*

Jackdaw44: *Oh, the suspense! Beg and I'll tell you.*

Jackdaw44: *Still waiting for the begging . . .*

ICE9: *I don't know what kind of twisted game you're playing but it stops now.*

Jackdaw44: *Your call. Oh, is that the sound of photos whooshing out of my phone I hear?*

ICE9: *Do it. I don't care any more.*

Jackdaw44: *Now who's bluffing?*

ICE9: *Do it.*

405

Jackdaw44: *You'll lose everything.*

ICE9: *Do it.*

Jackdaw44: *Hope you enjoy jail.*

ICE9: *What?*

Jackdaw44: *I'm 15, remember?*

ICE9: *And?*

Jackdaw44: *You're over 18. That makes you a paedophile.*

ICE9: *Don't be fucking stupid.*

Jackdaw44: *You slept with someone under 16. PAEDOPHILE.*

ICE9: *You started this.*

Jackdaw44: *Did I? You were the one that kissed me. I'll tell the police you groomed me.*

ICE9: *They'll laugh you out of the police station.*

Jackdaw44: *Not if I say you raped me.*

ICE9: *They won't believe you.*

Jackdaw44: *Won't they? I have photos, remember. You'll be locked away for a very, very long time. Do you know what they do to people like you in jail?*

ICE9: *What do you want?*

Jackdaw44: *I just want you to do one more thing for me and then I'll leave you alone.*

ICE9: *I don't believe you.*

Jackdaw44: *I'll write something, a letter. I'll say we had consensual sex, that I was in love with you, that I started it.*

ICE9: *I don't believe you. You'll come up with something else.*

Jackdaw44: *I swear. Just one more thing. Something*

406

that will always be our little secret. Then we're over,
I promise. It's not sex.
ICE9: *What is it?*
Jackdaw44: *It's something you've done before. And*
it might hurt.

Chapter 58

The street is awash with people doing their weekend shopping: students, mothers, fathers, children, shoppers, browsers and dawdlers. They spill out of the shops, congregate in front of windows and fill the pavement, forcing me to step into the road to overtake them.

'Excuse me, excuse me, excuse me.' I hurry down Queen's Road, past supermarkets, banks, letting agents and record stores. Pink Hair said Kira was meeting someone in a café, but which one? There are so many.

I dart in and out of each café I find as I follow Queen's Road all the way down to Bristol Museum. I am vaguely aware of bells chiming above doors as I enter, staff asking if they can help me and customers turning and staring but I ignore them all as I scan every face looking for Kira.

I feel breathless, manic and strangely elated. I am

certain that the tattoo somehow holds the answer to Billy's disappearance.

When I reach Bristol Museum I cross the road and go back up Queen's Road, checking all the cafés on the other side. My pace slows as I get halfway up and not simply because I am out of breath.

It's just a tattoo. It doesn't mean anything. It's not a clue.

I stop walking and rest a hand against the window of a shop as the adrenalin that propelled me out of the School of Art and down the street is replaced by an overwhelming feeling of exhaustion.

The answer is obvious. Billy got a tattoo he didn't tell me about – another secret that's been kept from me. I don't know why I'm even surprised. He skived off school so many times he could easily have got a tattoo without us knowing. He's always looked older than he is. He would have blagged being eighteen if the tattoo artist had asked. He was always able to wriggle out of an awkward situation. And not just with me.

Ever since we've known her, Kira has been snapping away, taking photographs. She did a project last year called 'The Face of Terror' where she made us watch scary films while she took photos. She even went round to Liz and Lloyd's to do the same. Billy must have confided in her that he regretted getting his tattoo done and she took a photo as part of her project. That's why she told Jake she didn't want him to come to her exhibition. She didn't want him to see it and get upset.

End of mystery. End of story. There's nothing more to it than that.

I feel flat and drained as I continue to trudge up the street. It starts to rain and I pull the hood of my jacket up over my head as I continue to stare into the windows of cafés and restaurants but I do it half-heartedly. All sense of urgency has gone. I still need to get my car keys so I can retrieve my tote bag and get rid of the knife but—

I double-back and take a second look through the window of Mama Valerie's. Kira is inside, sitting at a table near the door. I nearly missed her because the rain is falling heavily now and her hair is gathered up on the top of her head in a messy bun. She almost always wears it down. She's sitting opposite a man but I can't make out his face from this angle. I take another step back down the hill and see a flash of auburn hair, a russet-coloured goatee, a long-sleeved black top, a pair of long khaki shorts and a tribal tattoo on a hairy calf.

'Lloyd?' His name catches in my throat.

What is Liz's husband doing having coffee with my son's girlfriend?

A group of teenaged girls push past me and I'm buffeted towards the open door of the café. I can still see Lloyd's face and a sliver of Kira's profile. He hunches forward in his seat, staring at her intently as she swipes at her eyes. What is she saying? And why is she crying?

Lloyd says something, then reaches a hand across the table as though inviting her to take it. As he moves, the sleeve of his top slides up revealing a flash of black ink on his forearm. Kira snatches her hands from the table and shakes her head. She fans at her face with both hands as though trying to stop herself from crying. After a couple of seconds she stops fanning herself and fumbles with the button of her cardigan instead. She pushes the grey material from her shoulders, then leans across the table towards Lloyd.

He says something else that I can't make out but I lip-read the very last word he says.

'Liz.'

A group of young men surround around me and I'm buffeted into the café. Two of the men block my view of Kira but I still hear her reply. I hear every word.

Chapter 59

Where am I?

WHERE AM I?

Oh God, not again. Please God, not again.

My fingers graze something cold and rough. A tree root. I am outside, surrounded by bushes and trees. Beneath my feet is mud, carpeted with leaves. The sky is grey, striped with the orange glow of street lights and pollution.

The *stomp-stomp-stomp* of heavy footsteps on concrete startles me and I curl up, making myself as small as possible. The sound gets louder and then fades. When it is completely quiet again I uncurl, part the bushes to my right and ease myself onto my knees. A wide expanse of grass. Trees. Houses, loads of them, clustered together with rolling hills in the distance. The Downs. I'm in Bristol. I'm still in South Bristol. Oh, thank God. I part the bushes to my left. Railings. Beyond that pavement and a road and then . . . my heart double-beats in my chest as I look at the house opposite. My house. I'm in the park opposite my house. There's Jake's van parked outside. Mark's Ford Focus, Liz's Mini, Stephen's Zafira, Caleb's motorbike and Lloyd's black Alfa Romeo.

I can see two figures in my kitchen, standing close together, both of them with their arms folded over their chests. It's Mark and Stephen. Jake appears beside them. He raises his arms in the air as though remonstrating and Mark shakes his head. There is movement on the first floor as Kira passes the landing window. She must have heard the argument downstairs and come out of her room. Back in the kitchen Stephen has disappeared from view. Now Mark and Jake are talking. I wait for Kira to walk in but she doesn't appear. She must be standing at the top of the stairs, listening.

I shift my weight from my knees onto the balls of my feet as I try to stand up but I'm so dizzy I lose my balance and tip backwards. I put out my hands to break my fall and my right hand knocks against something. My handbag is beside me but that isn't what I touched. It's something on top of the handbag. I reach under the bush and feel about. I find leaves, tree roots, an empty crisp packet and then, finally, something solid. I pull it out carefully. It's an old-style phone, thick and chunky with sturdy buttons.

The screen glows blue as I press on the keypad. At the top of the screen is a mobile phone number. I have no idea whose it is – I don't know anyone's mobile number off by heart. Beneath it is a text message, unsent:

I know you were sleeping with Billy. I know about the tattoo. I know you were responsible for his disappearance. And so do the police.

I am so shocked I drop the phone.

I pick it back up again and turn it over in my hands, being careful not to accidentally hit the send button. Whoever wrote the text didn't send it. It's still in compose mode. The mobile is a Samsung. Black. Basic. I don't know anyone who owns a phone like this.

Where has it come from? Did someone give it to me? Did I steal it?

I tip the contents of my handbag onto my skirt. I find my phone and use the light to go through my belongings. I find my usual house keys, purse, tissues, make-up compact and something else, something that wasn't in my bag when I left Mum and Dad's this afternoon. A crumpled Carphone Warehouse plastic bag. In the very corner of the bag is a receipt. I angle the phone towards it so I can read the faint text.

Sim Free Samsung E1200 Mob – £14.99

Virgin Sim Pack – £1.00

And beneath it are the last four digits of my bank card.

I bought the phone.

Sonia told me that my fugues are caused by things that arouse my suspicions. What was the last thing I saw? Images flash up in my mind – Queen's Road,

Mama Valerie's café, Lloyd, Kira – but the pictures are dark and indistinct and the harder I try to bring them into focus the more they blur together.

Whatever I saw on Queen's Road it was enough to convince me to buy a pay-as-you-go mobile phone and compose an anonymous text. But who to? I must have copied the number from my mobile. I press the wake-up button on the side of my iPhone but nothing happens.

I press it again.

Nothing.

I press the button harder and the phone vibrates in my hand as a white swirl appears on the screen and then disappears.

The screen goes black again.

Using the light has drained the last of the battery.

It's all I can do not to hurl it into the bushes. There are seven people in the two houses on the other side of the road: Mark, Jake, Stephen, Kira, Lloyd, Liz and Caleb. If you'd asked me a year ago to name the people I trusted more than anyone else in the world I would have said their names along with Mum and Dad, Caroline and Billy.

When I stopped outside the Mama Valerie's I was convinced that Billy had secretly had a tattoo of his design inked somewhere on his body but I must have seen or heard something that made me change my mind.

I know you were sleeping with Billy. I know about the tattoo. I know you were responsible for his disappearance. And so do the police.

Mark, Jake, Stephen, Kira, Lloyd, Liz and Caleb.

Do I really believe one of them would have hurt my son? Seven months ago I wouldn't have. But now?

I move my thumb over the thick, clunky buttons and hit 'send'.

Chapter 60

20.16.

20.17.

20.18.

In my house Mark, Jake and Stephen are still in the kitchen. They drift into view, then out again. Mark and Stephen's arms are still crossed. Their expressions are strained. As I watch, Jake walks past the landing window towards the bedrooms. Seconds later he walks back the other way and reappears in the kitchen. Liz's front door remains closed.

20.19.

20.20.

20.21.

My heart catches in my throat as the door to Liz's house flies open and Lloyd storms out, his palms pressed to his temples. A split second later Liz appears behind him with Caleb at her side.

'A baby?' she screams as Lloyd marches down the

garden path. Caleb grabs her arm and tries to wrestle her back into the house but she shakes him off and runs after her husband.

'You want me to sell the house so you can have a baby with some slag you met at work?' she shouts as Lloyd heads for the Alfa Romeo. The sidelights flash as he points his key fob at it.

'Melissa,' he shouts back. 'She has a name and she's more of a lady than you'll ever be.'

'What about him?' Liz turns and points towards Caleb. 'He's your child too. Or have you forgotten that?'

She launches herself at Lloyd, arms whirling. One of her hands makes contact with the side of his head and he twists away, an arm raised to protect himself as he wrenches at the car door.

'Mum, don't! He's not worth it.' Caleb appears at her side and tries to pull her away but she shakes him off and lunges at Lloyd again.

'Listen to Caleb,' Lloyd shouts as his son wraps his arms around his angry, squirming mother and lifts her clean off her feet. 'You're embarrassing yourself.'

Liz howls with rage but Caleb is too strong and she can only watch as Lloyd slips into the driver's seat, slams the door and starts the engine. As the car pulls away Liz's howls turn to sobs. My heart twists in my chest as Caleb gently sets her back on her feet, then turns her back towards the path and half-leads, half-carries her back into the house.

As the front door of number 10 closes I look back at the phone.

20.25. No reply to the text I sent.

20.26.

20.27.

The door to my house opens and Stephen appears on the step with his phone in his hand. He raises it to eye level. Moments later he tucks the phone into the pocket of his jacket and stares out into the fading light. For one terrible second I think he can see me but then Mark appears behind him and puts his hand on his shoulder.

Stephen glances round, nods and then takes a step onto the path. Mark follows, then Jake. Mark says something I can't hear before all three men walk down the path in single file. When they reach the pavement Stephen looks back at Mark. He indicates that he should turn left. Stephen nods and sets off again, with Mark and Jake following behind him. As they disappear down the road in the direction of the pub Jake says something to Mark who laughs and puts his arm around his son's shoulders. Kira appears briefly in the kitchen then disappears from view.

20.29.

I pull my coat tighter around me and shiver, but not because I'm cold. I feel tired, confused and embarrassed. I don't know what I was expecting to happen when I sent that text. A reply? A confession? For the person who was responsible for Billy's disappearance to come flying out of one of the houses, jump into a car and speed away?

What if someone walked past and spotted me here; crouched in the bushes, spying on my own family? I need to go back to Dr Evans and ask her if there's any way she can speed up the request for a CAT scan. Or beg for medication. Valium or something. There must be a drug I can take to prevent this from happening again. I can't live like this any more. It needs to stop.

I open my handbag and drop both phones into it, check that the coast is clear and then step out from the bushes. The park is still empty.

I make my way towards the gate a few feet away. The park is supposed to be locked at night but the gate has been broken for months. I make a mental note to ring the council about it in the morning as I head towards the house. I step onto the path, stop and look up at the first-floor windows. The landing light is still on and Kira is standing at the top of the stairs. There is something in her hands. Something long and white like a looped dressing-gown cord. She lifts it into the air and then, almost in slow motion, lowers it over her head.

Chapter 61

I twist my key in the lock.

Nothing happens.

I twist it again but the back door doesn't budge. It's been double-locked from the inside.

'Kira!' I pound on the door with both fists, then run round to the front of the house and stare up at the landing window. She's vanished.

'Kira!' I run back to the door, twist the key in the lock and barge against the door with my shoulder. It doesn't give an inch but the glass panel at the top rattles.

There are two small bay trees in ornate pots on either side of the door. Liz gave them to me for Christmas. I pick up the slightly smaller one and hurl it at the panel, then press my handbag against the jagged glass at the bottom and reach my arm through the hole.

I fumble at the catch as I search blindly for the button that releases the double-lock.

'Come on, come on, come on.'

I flick it to the side, turn the key in the lock and press my shoulder into the door. It swings open and I fall inside.

'Kira!' I scream as I run through the kitchen. 'Kira, no! Don't! Don't!'

My heart is in my mouth as I reach the bottom of the stairs.

'I'm so sorry, Claire.'

Kira is balancing awkwardly on the wrong side of the landing banister. There's a noose around her neck made from the belt of my white towelling dressing gown. She's holding on to the railing but her toes hang over the ledge. One step forward and she'll drop at least ten feet.

'Kira,' I say as her eyes fill with tears. 'Don't do this. Whatever you've done, whatever's happened, we can talk about it.'

She closes her eyes.

'Please don't do this, Kira. Let me ring Jake and—'

She moves to takes a step into the void and I scream.

The sound makes her draw back again. The skin stretches over her knuckles as she tightens her grip on the banister. It's not just her legs that are shaking. It's her whole body.

'Okay, okay. No Jake. No one else. Just you and me. Just you and me, Kira.'

She doesn't move or open her eyes. She doesn't speak or react in any way but I know she's listening.

'You can talk to me,' I say. 'You can talk to me

about anything. I want to make things better. I want to help you.'

A low moan escapes from her throat.

'It's true.' I place a foot on the bottom step of the stairs. Kira's eyes fly open as it creaks under my weight.

'I'll jump,' she says. 'If you come upstairs I swear I'll jump.'

'Okay, okay.' I hold out my hands in surrender and take a step back. 'I'm not going to try anything. I'm not going to touch you. I promise. All right?'

She doesn't reply. Instead she continues to stare at me as I take another step backwards. She doesn't look afraid. Her large blue eyes are completely devoid of any emotion. I've never been more scared in my life.

'I'll stay back here,' I say. 'But I need you to promise me you won't do anything silly. Whatever's happened, whatever it is that you're worried about, we can deal with it. I love you. We all do. You know that, don't you?'

She doesn't reply but I see something spark behind her eyes. Relief? Is that what it is? She's relieved because I've said the right thing. Oh, thank God. Thank—

'No!' I scream as she mouths the word, Sorry, and steps free from the ledge.

Chapter 62

'NO!'

I lurch forwards and reach for Kira's legs as she drops through the air. I manage to grab hold of her calves and try desperately to hoist her upwards but she's too heavy and she oscillates wildly above me, tipping from left to right as one outstretched hand smacks against the banister, the wall, the banister. Her fingernails scratch at wood and then paint as she tries and fails to grab hold of either. Her other hand is up by her neck, tugging at the dressing-gown cord that bites into her skin. A terrible gasping, choking sound fills the air as she fights to breathe.

'Help!' I scream. 'Help! Somebody help me!'

I try to change position, to move the heel of my hand from under the sole of Kira's foot so I can get a better grip but as I do she kicks out, thumping me in the side of the head. I fight to keep my balance, to keep her leg up in the air, but my ankle twists beneath me and I fall.

'What the fuck?'

Caleb thunders up the stairs and suddenly Liz is beside me. She grabs Kira's foot as it slips from my fingers and hoists it into the air. She reaches up for the other foot and, as she grabs it, Kira's head smacks against the corner of the banister. Her hand falls from her throat and she closes her eyes. She is deathly pale.

'Claire!' Liz shouts as Kira's legs go limp in her arms but I'm already beside her. I reach up and grab hold of Kira's hips and heave them up in the air. My arms shake. She's too heavy. I'm going to drop her.

'I've nearly done it,' Caleb shouts from above us as his clumsy fingers pick at the white cord wrapped around the banister. 'Have you got her? As soon as this is undone she's going to fall.'

Liz and I adjust our positions so that, between us, we are holding Kira's near-horizontal body above our heads. Her head lolls on her neck, eyes closed, and her arms dangle at her sides.

Please let her be okay, I repeat over and over in my head. Please, please God, let her be okay.

'There!' Caleb shouts and the dressing-gown cord drifts down from the banister and lands on Kira's chest.

'Ring nine-nine-nine!' Liz screams as we lower Kira's limp body to the carpet, but Caleb already has the phone pressed against his cheek.

'Ambulance,' he barks. 'Number eleven Whitehart Road. Kira Simmons, nineteen. She's just tried to hang herself. I don't think she's breathing.'

Chapter 63

Jake's face is white as he walks back into the waiting area. We're back in the hospital after returning home just after eleven last night. None of us has slept.

'Kira wouldn't say why she did it,' Jake says, his voice thick with emotion, as he approaches the plastic chairs where I'm sitting beside Mark. 'She didn't say anything. Not a word. She wouldn't even look at me. I don't know why she'd do something like that, Mum. I don't . . .' The muscle in his jaw pulses as he stares at the ceiling, fighting back tears.

'Oh, sweetheart.' I wrap my arms around him and pull him in to me. There are other families in the waiting area with us. I can feel their eyes on us but I don't care.

'I don't get it.' Jake gently removes my hands from his shoulders and slumps into a chair beside Mark. 'I just don't get it.'

'She seemed fine.' My husband sits forward in his

426

seat and rests his forearms on his thighs. 'I spoke to her yesterday morning and she seemed really excited about the exhibition. She was really quiet when she got back from college, but she so often is . . .' He tails off.

Everything happened very quickly when I arrived at A&E in the ambulance with Kira last night. She regained consciousness en route but was groggy and confused when the medic asked her name and whether she was in any pain. She was lying on a stretcher, packed into a vacuum mattress with an oxygen mask over her face. Once at A&E she was wheeled into a booth and immediately seen by a doctor who asked me a series of questions about what I'd seen – how far she'd fallen and how long she was suspended from the banister before the ligature was untied. As I answered he checked her breathing and hooked her up to a heart monitor. Kira passed out as he was attending to her and he shouted something about intubation and asked me to leave the cubicle. That's when I called Jake.

'How is she physically?' Mark asks.

Jake shrugs. 'The doctor said she's okay. She's breathing on her own and he doesn't think she's done any damage to her brain, heart or spine but –' he touches his throat – 'she's got a red speckled mark that goes all the way round her neck. I couldn't look at it.'

'Thank God you came home when you did,' Mark says, looking at me. 'If you'd have stayed at your mum's like you were supposed to . . .' He shakes his head. 'It doesn't bear thinking about.'

'No, it doesn't.'

'Are you going to text Liz again and let her know that Kira's woken up?'

I nod but, as I do, a cold, sick feeling twists in my stomach. I still haven't told them everything that happened yesterday. When Jake arrived at the hospital with Mark last night he was in a terrible state, demanding that the doctors let him see Kira, begging them not to let her die. It tore me up, seeing him like that. I tried to convince myself that it wasn't my fault she'd tried to hang herself, that I still didn't know for sure whether she was the one I'd sent the text to. I kept telling myself that, all the way home after a nurse told us that Kira had been stabilized but we wouldn't be able to see her until visiting hours today.

The second I got in I plugged my phone charger into the wall. It took for ever to flicker back to life and my hand shook as I scrolled through my list of contacts.

The number on the new phone matched a number in mine.

I'd sent the text to Kira.

Before I could decide what to do next Liz popped in to see how we were. She told me what had happened after I'd shouted at her to ring Mark and then clambered into the front of the ambulance with the driver.

She'd called him straight away and told him to get to the hospital with Jake. A couple of minutes later the police arrived. They spoke to Liz and Caleb at length about what had happened. Liz told them that she'd heard glass breaking and she'd come round with Caleb to see what was going on. She described what she'd seen and said it was definitely a suicide attempt. The police seemed convinced and told her they'd contact the hospital to check Kira had survived and would be in touch if they had any concerns. After they left she locked up the house with her spare key and Caleb nailed some wood over the broken panel in the door.

'How's Jake?' she asked as I slipped the new phone off the kitchen counter and into my pocket.

'Not good. Mark's with him in the living room.'

'Wine.' It was more of an order than a question so I pointed her in the direction of a bottle of red and two glasses.

'That poor girl,' she said as she handed me one. 'I had no idea she was that unhappy. Did you?' She looked at me, as though waiting for a response, then continued. 'I wonder if it was the stress of her exhibition. Or something to do with Jake? Had they been arguing?'

I shook my head.

'Had her mum been in touch? Fucking bitch. Who treats their child like that? Didn't you tell me that her dad killed himself? It wasn't the anniversary or anything, was it?' She pulled out a chair and topped up her glass. 'Did I tell you that Lloyd came round tonight? He's only bloody knocked up the woman he left me for. Someone from work. Melissa he said her name was. Never heard of her. Anyway, he wants to get a divorce and sell the house so he can buy somewhere for her and the baby. Can you fucking believe it? I know he doesn't give two shits about me but you'd have thought he wouldn't want Caleb turfed out on the street. Wouldn't you, Claire? Wouldn't you think—

'Oh Jesus!' She jumped up as my glass shattered on the floor and a blood-red stain puddled around my feet. 'Claire, your wine! Are you okay? Don't worry. I'll mop it up.'

'Claire. Claire, love.' Mark taps me on the knee. 'I think we should go in now.'

It takes me a couple of seconds to register where I am. 'I'm sorry?'

'To see Kira,' he says. 'Jake said he wants to get off home soon but we haven't seen Kira yet. You ready?'

I shake my head. I still feel as though I'm hovering six feet above my body.

'I'd like to see her alone for a bit.' The words sound as though someone else is speaking them. 'Is that okay?'

Chapter 64

She has her back to me. Her long blonde hair is a mass of tangles and a thin white hospital blanket has been pulled up and over her shoulders. The curtain has been pulled around her bed to give her some privacy but the ward is alive with the sound of other patients coughing and sniffing and talking in low voices.

'Kira? Kira, it's Claire.'

I sit down in the chair at the head of her bed. There is a jug of water and a glass on the small table beside me. Kira's back rises and falls soundlessly as she breathes in and out. I spoke to her doctor on my way into the ward. She told me that apart from the marks on her neck which will take a few weeks to fade, Kira has no other injuries. Her heart and brain function are fine. There are no injuries to her spine and, despite intubation after she was admitted, there are no problems with her respiration.

'She was very, very lucky,' the doctor said.

'Kira,' I say again. 'Kira, can you hear me?'

Now that I am here and I can see how small, vulnerable and silent she is I no longer feel numb and disconnected. I feel solid, strong and calm.

A nurse pokes her head through the curtain. 'Sorry to interrupt but someone from the psychiatric assessment team will be here to see Kira in a bit. So if you could keep it short that would be good.'

'Of course.'

I wait until she's disappeared again, then walk round to the other side of the bed.

'Kira,' I say as I crouch beside it. 'I can't begin to imagine how you're feeling. You must have been in a very dark place to do what you did yesterday.'

Her hands are pressed up against her face, covering it. She doesn't move a muscle as I talk. She doesn't respond in any way but I know she's not asleep. She's listening to every word I say.

'I saw you in Queen's Road,' I say. 'You were in Mama Valerie's café with Lloyd. I heard your conversation.'

Her fingers twitch. She knows exactly what I heard.

'Billy was in love with you, wasn't he?'

Her fingers part just a couple of millimetres and I catch a glimpse of a pale blue iris and large black pupil staring out at me.

'I'm right, aren't I?'

Her eyelids shutter back down.

'Please,' I say softly. 'Please, Kira. Just tell me where he is.'

Chapter 65

KIRA
Wednesday 4th February 2015

Billy's going on about the next place he wants to tag. He's planning on going to Avonmouth to graffiti the bridge. He's standing behind me, pressing himself up against me with so much force that the window ledge is digging into my legs. His breath is hot and damp in my ear.

'By the time I'm done there won't be a bit of Bristol that I haven't tagged,' he says. 'Fuck what I did at school – that's amateur shit. I want people pointing and going, "Who the fuck is DStroy?" I want to be everywhere, on every building, every train, every bridge. Half the kids in my year want to be famous. I'd rather be infamous.'

I don't say anything. I'm watching the street, waiting for Jake's white van to pull up. I've started to spend longer and longer at college so I don't have to spend time alone with Billy but I was caught out today. I thought the others would be back but Mark's not here, Jake texted to say he's working late and Claire popped round to Liz's half an hour ago. It's just me and Billy, alone in the house.

'Let me see it again.'

I feel him lift up my hair. 'Fuck off.' I try to swipe his hand away but he catches me by the wrist and glares down at me.

'Don't you ever tell me to fuck off. I can look at that tattoo whenever I want. Hey!' My skin stings as he rips the plaster from the back of my neck. 'What the hell's this?'

'What do you think it is?'

'Oh, no.' He shakes his head slowly from side to side and his eyes narrow. 'Oh, no, no, no, no. That wasn't part of the deal, Kira. You don't get to cover it up. Or is this your sick little way of telling me you've changed your mind about ending things?' He slips a hand under my armpit and squeezes my boob.

I knock his hand away and try to twist free but he holds me fast.

'Kira,' he says as he nuzzles his face against mine, his stubble scraping my cheek. 'You were the best fuck I've ever had.'

I want to close my eyes and block him out, just as I have every time he's forced me to have sex with him, but I'm scared Jake will pull up in the van and see us at the window.

I thought the shit was going to hit the fan when Lloyd saw us in the park in January. I was in the kitchen the next day, Googling how to hitchhike from Bristol to Edinburgh on my phone, when Liz came bursting in saying that Lloyd had walked out on her. He'd left the night before after telling her that their marriage was over. He wasn't going to the pub when he stopped and stared at us, he was walking to his car at the end of the street. I didn't believe Liz when she said he was gone for good. I thought he'd be back. Each time a black car parks outside Liz's house I feel sick. But he hasn't come back. He hasn't even rung her. Not according to the conversations I've overheard between Claire and Liz. But what if he does? What if he tells her what he saw? My life will be over. I can't keep living like this, waking up each day wondering if today is the day that Jake finds out what I've done.

I was an idiot for agreeing to the tattoo. I knew it wouldn't stop Billy from hassling me but I thought it would buy me more time. I'm totally skint. My next student loan doesn't come through until next term and Jake's been paying for everything. I've been trying to save the £30 he gives me each week for bus fare and food but it's impossible. It's £168 to get the train up to Granddad's house in Edinburgh. When I was Googling how to hitchhike from Bristol I read loads of horror stories about women getting raped or killed and I can't risk it. I'm going to have to nick some money. Claire's always leaving her bag lying around and Jake chucks his wallet on the floor when we get back from the pub. I don't want to steal from them but what choice do I have?

Amy offered to let me sleep on her floor but she lives with her parents and I need to get out of Bristol. If Billy puts the photos up on Facebook they'll go viral and people round here think I'm a slag as it is. That's if I don't get arrested for sleeping with someone underage. No. I need to disappear. To vanish in the middle of the night. Billy can't threaten me any more if I'm gone. He can't blackmail me.

But what about Jake? I can't let myself think about him. It's going to kill me to leave him. It'll kill him too. And he'll never know why.

Why did I have sex with Billy? Why? I wish I could rewind time. If I'd taken a different route back from Amy's last August, I never would have bumped into Billy outside the pub. He wouldn't have confided in me about his dad kissing Miss Christian. He wouldn't have started texting me all the time. We wouldn't have gone for a drink. I wouldn't have kissed him. None of this would have happened if I'd turned left instead of right.

Chapter 66

We can hear them arguing downstairs; Claire and Mark shouting at Billy for getting nicked by the police for stealing spray paint from B&Q. He texted me earlier, saying I should prepare for his impending death. He must have sent it from Claire's car after she picked him up from the police station. He knew his dad would kill him when he found out what he'd done.

'Beer?' Jake twists over on the bed and hands me a can of lager. His eyes are half-closed and he's grinning like a lunatic. He only had to do a half-day at work today so he and some of his workmates went to the pub at lunch. They stayed there all afternoon and when I got back from college he was so pissed he couldn't stand up straight. Mark had a go at him and told him to stay in his room until he sobered up so I went with him.

It's ten past seven now and he can hardly keep his eyes open.

'No thanks, hon.'

Jake shrugs as I wave the can away. He cracks it open, takes a long, deep swig and then moves to put it down on the bedside table but there are a stack of my photography books and other bits and bobs on the top and the can tips to one side. Beer froths all over the carpet.

'Oh, fuck.' I try to clamber over him so I can mop it up but he grabs me as I throw a leg over him and pulls me close.

'Well, hello, Kira Simmons!' He grins up at me. 'Fancy seeing you here.'

'Jake.' I can't help but smile at his stupid, drunken grin but I stiffen as his hands move up to my shoulders and he tries to ease my cardigan away from my body. 'Jake, don't.'

'Kira!' He says my name in that playful, sing-song way he uses whenever he wants to have sex. 'I just want a kiss.'

'Jake, your mum's going to go spare if the beer soaks into—'

'Oh, for fuck's sake.' He lets go of me and I slide off him and onto the floor. 'We never have sex any more. And don't tell me it's because you feel weird that Mum and Dad might hear because that never stopped you when you moved in!'

My eyes fill with tears but I don't want him to see

438

so I turn away and grab a towel from the chair, then dab at the beer stain on the floor. My phone bleeps in my pocket as I drop the towel into the laundry basket at the foot of the bed. I duck down, so Jake can't see what I'm doing, and slip it out of my pocket. My first thought is that it's Billy, taunting me with a text, but then I hear his voice ring out from downstairs as he swears at his dad.

As I turn the phone over in my hand and read the message the back door slams shut, shaking the bedroom wall.

'This fucking family.' Jake hauls himself out of bed and slams a hand against the window as he peers outside. 'Oh, look, Dad's fucked off to the pub.' The bedroom wall shakes again. 'Oh, and Mum's off too. Jesus Christ, Billy's such a dick. Little twat. He can't get away with this bullshit.'

'Jake!' I put out a hand to try and stop him from leaving the bedroom but he's too drunk and angry to notice and charges out onto the landing.

'Billy, you twat!' he shouts as the stairs creak under his weight. 'Oi! What the fuck are you playing at?'

I shove the phone into my jeans pocket, scramble out of the bedroom and crouch down by the banisters. I can't see Jake or Billy but I can hear every word they're saying in the living room.

'Give me that!' Jake shouts. 'Arsonist, are you now?'

'Well, it would teach Dad right if this house went up in smoke,' Billy shouts back. 'He's an arsehole and a loser.'

'No, Billy, you're the loser. You want to know why Dad gives you a hard time? Because you're an embarrassment. You think you're the hard man with your spray cans and your stupid scribble, but you're just a kid. Anyone with half a brain can see you just want attention.'

'Is that right, golden boy?' Billy laughs. It's such a venomous sound all the hairs on my arms go up.

'You need to grow the hell up, Billy, and stop being such a jealous brat.'

I pull myself to my feet and hurry to the top of the stairs. I need to stop this. I need to stop Billy saying one more word before—

'Why would I be jealous of you, Jake? You're going out with the town bike. Everyone's laughing at you because she's sleeping around behind your back and you're too much of a mug to realize. She's been fucked more times than a porn star.'

There's an almighty crack, then a thump as something or someone hits the floor, and then Jake thunders up the stairs towards me. He stops right in front of me and stares, waiting for me to say something, but I'm so scared my mind has gone blank. Any second now Billy is going to shout up at him that we've been fucking and that'll be it, game over.

'Well?' Jake leans in so close I can smell beer on his breath. 'Is it true? Are you sleeping around behind my back?'

I want to tell him that it's not true, that Billy's a liar and that I'd never, ever do anything to hurt him. But it is true. It's awful and it's dirty and it's true.

440

But if I admit it he'll never look at me the same way again. He'll look at me like I'm worthless and a slag and a liar. He'll look at me the way my mum looks at me and I won't . . . I can't . . . deal with that. I'd rather be dead.

Jake looks at me for the longest time, not saying a word, then he shakes his head, steps around me and crosses the landing to the bedroom. The door clicks shut behind him.

'Hey!' Billy shouts as I walk through the living room and head for the kitchen. 'Hey! Kira!'

I ignore him and go over to the coat hook by the back door. Jake's navy work jacket is hanging next to my fake-fur coat and the small black rucksack Billy takes to school. I slip my hand into one of Jake's pockets and pull out his keys.

'Kira!' Billy grabs the back of my cardigan as I slip on my shoes. I don't bother to try and shake him off. Instead I take a step forward, letting the cardigan slip from my shoulders, and step outside. It's dark, the only light the orange glow of the street light at the end of the path. All of the lights are off in Liz's house. She must be out. Or asleep.

'Where are you going?' Billy grabs my wrist, forcing me to look at him. His bottom lip is split, his chin sticky with blood. His rucksack is slung over one shoulder.

'For a drive.'

'Great. I'll come.'

He grins at me, as though expecting me to put up

441

a fight, then raises an eyebrow when I say okay.

He keeps hold of my wrist as we walk towards Jake's van, then insists I get in through the passenger door so I can't drive off without him.

It takes me three attempts to get the keys in the ignition but then we're off, the van jolting and bumping along as I drive away from the house and towards the Wells Road.

'Where are we going?' Billy asks as I turn the van onto the A417.

I say nothing. Instead I press my foot down on the accelerator which makes Billy lean back in his seat.

'Fucking women drivers,' he jokes but I can hear fear in his voice too. For months he's been the one in control and now I am.

I slow down as we approach the ring road at the bottom of Callington Road, then speed up again as I spot signs for the A4 to Bath. As I continue to drive – through suburban Bristol and out into the industrial estate on the Bath Road – the scenery changes. Houses and breeze-block buildings gradually fade away, replaced by rolling fields and tall trees, bushes and thick, wiry undergrowth that flanks the road on both sides. It's darker out here, in the depths of the countryside, the only light the flash of headlights from the occasional passing car.

We continue to travel through the countryside in silence for ten, maybe fifteen, minutes before Billy turns on the radio. He turns it off again. He winds down the window and shouts, 'Fuck you, world!' into the darkness. He puts a hand on my knee and

442

squeezes it. When he doesn't get a reaction, he does the same to my boob.

'Jake's got a mean right hook,' he says, then he lets go of me and presses his hand to his jaw. 'Wanker.' He glances at me. 'You do realize I'm going to have to tell him about us now, don't you?'

'Okay.'

'You're bluffing.'

'Tell him. I don't care any more.'

'Well, well, well.' He reaches into his bag and pulls out a plastic lunch box. He opens it and takes out his mobile phone. 'Just in case I drop my bag in the river when I'm tagging bridges,' he says when he notices me watching. 'My phone's not insured, is it? Bollocks!' He jabs at his mobile with his index finger. 'Fucking battery's dead. Ah, well –' he drops it back into the lunch box and re-seals the lid – 'looks like I'll have to tell Jake when we get back. More fun if he has to look me in the eye.'

Trees loom over us as the road narrows and fields streak past, bleak stretches of grey under the dark sky. I can't see the moon – it's hidden behind thick clouds. There's a light rain. It drifts through the open window onto my face and arms but I don't wipe it away.

'I reckon Jake'll move out when I tell him. We could have his room. It's bigger than mine,' Billy says.

I say nothing.

'What?' He twists round in his seat. 'Is that such a bad idea? Seriously? You seem to have forgotten what a laugh we had, but I haven't. I know you like me, Kira. And you won't have to feel guilty about it once Jake's gone.'

Normally I'd laugh – at him, at how ridiculous the suggestion is – or else I'd get angry. But his words wash over me. They don't matter any more. Nothing does.

I turn on the wipers as the windscreen mists with rain. 'My granddad's dead,' I say. 'My mum sent me a text earlier.'

When I was in the bedroom with Jake. When I still thought I had an escape route.

Granddad's dead, the text said. Not, how are you, Kira? Or, I know you loved him. Or, I know it's a bit of a shock.

Just *Granddad's dead*. She might as well have written, it's over. It's all over now, Kira.

'Oh.' Billy shrugs. 'Sorry about that.'

'Yeah.'

I move down a gear and indicate right, then turn into a small country lane. There is a building and small patch of well-kept grass hidden in the depths of the countryside. You'd miss it if you didn't know what you were looking for.

'Where the hell are we?' Billy says as the tyres crunch on gravel and I pull in to the car park.

'The boules club.' I turn off the engine and undo my seat belt.

'In the middle of nowhere?'

'My dad worked here. He was a handyman. He cut the green.'

'So?'

I open the van door and step outside. I take a deep breath of cool, crisp air, then set off along the path between the green and the clubhouse. There are no houses nearby, no street lights, no pavement. Billy was right: the place I've driven us to is in the middle of nowhere, nestled between fields and woodland.

'You want to play with balls in the middle of the night? I'd have let you have a go on mine if you'd asked nicely.' Billy laughs as he runs to catch up. 'Hey! Where are you going?'

I reach the wood – tall, dense and imposing – that separates the clubhouse from the fields that surround it. It's at least an acre in size and belongs to the farmer who owns the fields. My dad used to say what a shame it was that he'd let it get so overgrown and unkempt. It was an eyesore, he said, compared to the neatly trimmed lawn of the boules club. I told him I thought a witch lived in it, and that was why the farmer stayed away.

There's a wire fence that runs all the way around the wood – a fence that's been put up since Dad killed himself – and, for a second, I'm terrified that there's no way in, but then I find a place where it's come away from the base of the fence post, unnoticeable unless you look carefully. I peel it back. Not enough space for Billy to get through but I'm smaller than him.

'What the hell?' I feel Billy grab at my right trainer as I squeeze through the gap, but my shoe is slippery from the rain and his hand falls away as I kick out at him.

And then I'm in.

A train rumbles on the tracks, deep and bassy in the distance as I stumble through the dense wood. A bird squawks as it flies out of a bush, then falls silent as it soars into the air. I hear Billy swear loudly. He's managed to get in. I quicken my pace, crashing through the bushes and swerving around trees. It's pitch black away from the headlights of the road and I can barely make out my hands as I swipe at branches and leaves. The wood seems to go on for ever but the fear that Billy will catch and stop me propels me on. And then I break through the trees and my left foot slips as the ground drops away and I fall, tumbling into a bracken-covered ditch between the wood and rail track. The undergrowth is so tall it reaches up to my throat and scratches at my hands, arms and legs as I scramble up the bank and into the bushes that separate the ditch from the train track.

'Shit!' Billy shouts and I hear the sound of branches snapping and leaves rustling as he escapes from the wood. 'Bloody bag, caught in the bloody . . . someone needs to cut this shit. It's a jungle.'

The rain is falling heavier now and my hair is clinging to my cheeks.

I can still remember the day I found out that Dad had killed himself like it was yesterday. I was in maths and Miss Ramdas from student support knocked on the door and asked Mr Price if she could talk to me. I was really pleased – any excuse to get out of algebra – but I freaked out when I saw the look on her face.

446

It wasn't a 'you're about to get a bollocking' look. It was an 'I feel really sorry for you' grimace.

When I got to her office Mum was standing by the window with her best mate Sharon. They were hugging and Mum was crying. She opened her eyes when I walked in and she gave this huge gasp and started crying even harder. That's when Miss Ramdas sat me down and said she had some bad news.

She didn't say much, just that my dad had died. When I asked how she looked at my mum who nodded and Miss Ramdas said he'd killed himself by walking in front of a train. It wasn't until a few months later, when Mum was pissed, that I got the whole story. Dad had been on his ride-on mower at the boules club. Someone in the clubhouse saw him stop it suddenly, right in the middle of the green with the grass half cut, and get off. They thought he'd run out of petrol or something but he didn't go back to it. It was half an hour before anyone thought to find out where he'd gone. An hour or so after that the police arrived. Dad had cut through the wood and walked several miles up the railway line and then lain down on the tracks as the train drew closer. There was no way the driver could have stopped in time.

'Kira?' Billy grabs hold of my wrist. His hair is plastered to his face and there's a scratch on his cheek. 'This isn't funny any more. We're going back.'

'To what?' The rumble of the train is louder now, more like a rushing sound, accompanied by the high-pitched noise of the horn. The rain lashes down and the wind whips my hair around my face. It's so dark I can't see more than a few feet in front of me but I can make out the train track: a dark stripe beyond the bushes just six or seven feet ahead of me.

'Home.'

'That's not my home.'

'Don't be stupid. Come on.' He yanks at my arm, pulling me back towards the ditch. The train sounds its horn again, louder this time and I swipe blindly at Billy. I won't let him take me back to Bristol. My fingernails connect with his skin as I scrape them down the side of his face.

He shouts in pain and lets go of my wrist. The train clanks on the tracks, louder and louder, roaring and whistling, and I spot the cab through the branches, speeding towards us.

I plough through the bushes, away from the wood and towards the track. The train is so close I can see the windscreen wipers swiping from left to right. The wheels *clank-clank-clank* on the tracks. The beams from the headlights temporarily stun me and I close my eyes, just for a split second. I need to do it. I need to do it now.

I can't move.

I'm frozen to the spot.

The train rushes closer and closer. One more step. One more step and I'll be out of the bushes and in front of the train. But I can't move. I feel frozen to the spot.

The engine roars past me. The wheels pound the tracks. The noise is overwhelming. It's not too late.

I take a step forward. I can do it. I can still—

'No!' I hear a scream above the roar of the train, then there's a weight against my shoulder and I'm knocked from my feet. There's a dull thump, a rush of air hits me in the face then there's a crashing sound as though something has been thrown into the woods from a great height. And then everything goes quiet.

Chapter 67

CLAIRE
Sunday 30th August 2015

I do not feel relieved or angry or shocked. I do not feel sad or vengeful or scared.

I feel nothing.

I am aware that I should react, that I should cry or scream or shout, but I feel no compulsion to do so.

I feel nothing.

It is as though someone has scooped out my heart and replaced it with sand. There is nothing inside me apart from a strange, dull ache in the centre of my chest.

Kira's face is still hidden behind her hands but the cotton pillow beneath her head is wet with tears. I didn't think she was going to talk to me but once she started she couldn't stop. The words poured out of her; the words, the pain, the fear.

'Billy saved you,' I say. 'He pushed you out of the way to save your life.'

Kira says nothing. So talkative and now so silent.

'And you left him there, dead or dying in the wood, and you drove back home. And then you crawled into bed with his brother as though nothing had happened.'

She sobs, audibly this time, and pulls the blanket up and over her head. I gaze down at her, at the slender figure shrouded beneath the blanket. Seven months. For seven months she's watched me lose my job, my marriage, even my sanity and she hasn't said a word. All this time she's idly stood by as Jake and Mark have torn themselves apart.

'You could have told me. If you'd said that Billy was blackmailing you I would have done something. I would have made him stop.'

The shape beneath the blanket moves as she shakes her head.

'You don't believe me?'

The sheet shifts as she pulls it away from her face and looks up at me with red-rimmed eyes.

'You'd have thrown me out.'

'How can you be so sure?'

'Because you thought Billy was perfect.'

Did I? Doesn't every parent? I wasn't blind to Billy's faults. I knew there was a reason he was acting up at school and getting into trouble for graffitiing. Something was making him unhappy but I didn't know what because he wouldn't let me in. He could have told me what he'd seen outside the pub that night but he kept it to himself. Did he do that to protect me? Or did he think I thought Mark was perfect? There's a twisted irony there that I can't deal with right now.

'How could you do it?' I say. 'How could you carry on living in our house? You saw how upset we were. How could you watch that, knowing what you did? We were searching for our son, we were desperate and all along you knew . . . you knew where Billy was.'

'I didn't know he was dead.' She glances away.

'I don't believe you.'

'I didn't. I swear. I heard him hit the side of the train when he tripped, but when I got up I couldn't see him. He wasn't by the tracks. And I got scared. I ran back to the van. I thought he'd come after me.'

'You can't have been that scared. You went back to our house and got into bed with Jake.'

She shakes her head. 'Not straight away. I sat up in the kitchen. Granddad was dead. I couldn't go to Mum's. And I told myself . . . I convinced myself . . . that there was another way out. I decided that if Billy came back . . . when Billy came back . . . I'd tell him that I'd keep having sex with him. I'd have told him anything to stop him from telling Jake what we'd done. I love Jake. I love him so much.'

'Maybe you should have thought about that before you slept with his brother.'

'I know.' She closes her eyes tightly.

'Kira, you went back to our house! You sat in our kitchen like nothing was wrong when Billy was lying in the undergrowth *dying*. You could have rung an ambulance. You could have saved him!'

'I was scared. I thought he'd hurt me.'

'Hurt you?'

'You don't know what he did, Claire.' Her eyes glisten with tears. 'The things he'd seen on the Internet . . . the things he made me do—'

'No.' I hold up a hand. 'You could have stopped that, Kira. You had a choice.'

'Did I?' She looks at me, her eyes lifeless.

'You must have realized that Billy was dead when you woke up the next morning and he hadn't come back.'

'I . . .' She runs her hands over her face. 'I went along with what Mark said – that Billy had run away because of the argument. Jake said he was doing it for attention. I let myself believe that. I told myself that he'd got up after the train hit him but was staying away to freak everyone out, to freak me out. And then when the police got involved I made up new stories in my head – Billy was staying with mates, he had amnesia and didn't know who he was, he'd hitchhiked somewhere.'

'You saw us, Kira! You saw how distraught and scared we were.'

'I know. And it tore me apart. I couldn't sleep. I couldn't eat. The only way I could live with it was to tell myself that what had happened was an awful accident but it wasn't my fault. I didn't force Billy to come with me. I didn't push him in front of the train.'

453

'So why didn't you tell anyone? If you really believed that it wasn't your fault why didn't you tell me?'

'I couldn't do it. I couldn't look you in the eye and tell you that he was dead. Not when you were so hopeful. Not when you kept telling everyone that you'd find him.'

'So you knew he was dead then.'

'I don't know.' She curls into herself and begins to cry again. 'I don't know.'

'*Don't tell Liz that I was fucking Billy.*'

That's what I heard Kira say to Lloyd when I was pushed into the café.

I only remembered when Liz came round and was talking to me about Lloyd. That's why I dropped my wine glass. It all came rushing back – the conversation I'd overheard and the tattoo on the back of Kira's neck when she'd taken off her cardigan. I'd seen it before – when I'd interrupted a private moment between her and Jake in the kitchen – but I'd mistaken it for a bruise. Everything suddenly made sense – why Kira had freaked out when Jake had pulled her dressing gown away from her neck, why she wouldn't sleep with him any more, why she always kept her hair down.

'Kira, how did Lloyd know you were having sex with Billy?'

'He saw us, in the park one night. We thought he was going to the pub and he'd tell Liz when he got home. But he didn't. That was the night he left her.'

'And when Liz mentioned that he was coming back to see her . . .'

'I panicked. I thought he'd watched the appeal on the TV and he wanted to tell her what he'd seen. I had his number from when I'd photographed him so I asked him to meet me. We always got on. He's a nice man.' She starts to cry again.

'Just me!' The nurse pops her head round the curtain, making me jump. 'The psych team are here so if you could say your goodbyes now, please.' She gives me a small nod.

'Please.' Kira looks imploringly at her. 'Just one minute.'

'Thirty seconds.' The nurse pulls the curtain back over.

'Claire.' Kira's eyes well with tears as she looks back at me. 'I'm sorry. I'm so sorry. I hate myself for what's happened. I wish you hadn't found me. If you hadn't then now I'd be dead.'

I give her a long look but say nothing. I don't trust myself to speak.

Chapter 68

Sonia glances at her notes. 'Am I right in thinking you got the results of your CAT scan last week?'

I nod. 'Yes. It was clear.'

'That must be hugely reassuring.'

'It is, yes.'

Eight months ago I would have been terrified, being slid into a small, claustrophobic space. Eight months ago I was a different person.

'And is it tomorrow that you're going to hold the memorial for Billy?' She crosses one leg over the other and rests a hand on her calf.

'It's not a memorial as such.' I reach for the glass of water on the table in front of me and take a sip. 'It's a family thing. Just me, Jake and Mark. We're driving over to the rail tracks to lay some flowers. The boules club have said it's okay.'

'Good. I think that's important.' She eyes the box of tissues beside the water jug; tissues I have left

456

untouched since I walked into her office fifteen minutes ago. 'And how are you feeling, Claire, now the investigation has been closed?'

'Relieved. It means we can start planning the funeral.'

'Of course. Will you be taking that on yourself or—'

'We're going to do it together,' I say. 'Jake's spoken to some of Billy's friends about the sort of songs he might like and Mark will give a reading. Stephen asked if he could deliver the eulogy.'

'And how does Mark feel about that?'

'He's okay.' I nod. 'They've been spending a lot of time together recently. There's still some . . . tension . . . between them but they're working through it. Stephen has started going to AA and Caroline's moved back in.'

Mark and Stephen had several heart-to-hearts after we found out what had happened to Billy. Stephen admitted to being jealous of Mark for forging his own career and having a family. He said he couldn't bear how ungrateful he seemed, despite having so much and that he wanted to take him down a peg or two. Mark is still angry but I think he'll forgive him, eventually. It's not as though he hasn't said and done things he regrets.

'And Jake?' Sonia asks, 'How is he?'

I look down at my hands. 'He's very quiet. He was really angry when it all came out, when he found out what had happened between Kira and Billy. He threw out all her stuff. He was going to burn everything in

457

the garden but Mark stopped him. That first week was . . . it was awful.'

'I can imagine.'

I twist my wedding ring round and round the finger of my left hand. 'He hates her but there's a part of him that misses her. He won't admit it but he does.'

'Where is Kira?'

'Living with a distant relative on the outskirts of Bristol according to DS Forbes. He said they're considering prosecuting her for perverting the course of justice.'

'And how do you feel?'

'About Kira or the verdict?'

'Both.'

'Misadventure.' I pull my wedding ring clean off my finger, then push it back on. 'It's such a strange word to describe a death, isn't it? It sounds like something fun that went horribly wrong. Although –' I look across at Sonia – 'maybe there's some truth in that. Neither Billy nor Kira really knew what they were getting themselves into.'

'Is that how you see it – that they were mutually responsible for what happened?'

I shrug. 'I've thought a lot about that. At first I was too angry with Kira to think straight. I kept remembering all the times we'd talked alone since Billy's disappearance, all the opportunities she'd had to open up to me about what had happened and all the times she'd lied. I wanted to charge back into the hospital and shake her and scream in her face that she'd destroyed all our lives . . .'

'But?'

'Then I started thinking about what Billy had done, the messages he'd sent to her. The police found his phone. Did I tell you that?'

She shakes her head.

'It was in a Tupperware container in his bag, in the undergrowth. They found his . . .' I take a deep breath '. . . body in the wood next to the boules club. The land belonged to a farmer but it was overgrown and neglected. He never set foot in the wood he said, he only ever went into the field on the other side to see to his sheep. The police told us the brambles and bracken were six foot high. Billy's body . . . it . . . it crashed through the undergrowth. He was completely hidden.'

'And the train driver didn't see them? He didn't –' she pauses – 'feel any impact?'

I shake my head. 'It was dark and raining heavily and they were both wearing black and hiding in the bushes. It was a goods train, one of those huge great things. The driver didn't feel a thing.'

'Oh, gosh.'

'Billy might have been found if the railway company had cut back all the bushes and hedgerows. They do it every six months according to DS Forbes but there was some kind of dispute with the company they use and it was delayed. Billy could have been found months ago.'

'And no one from the boules club thought to investigate the hole in the fence?'

I shake my head. 'There wasn't one. When Kira

climbed back through she bent it back so it looked like no one had ever been there.'

Sonia presses her fingers to her lips, momentarily stunned. 'Gosh,' she breathes when she finds her voice again.

'I know.'

A silence falls between us and then Sonia says, 'You mentioned something about messages . . .'

'Yes, on Billy's phone. Because it was sealed in Tupperware the police were able to retrieve some data. Images. Pornographic ones of Kira. And some of their Snapchat conversations. He'd saved screen-shots.'

'You saw them?'

'No, but DS Forbes told me about them. They were pretty bad. He was blackmailing her. It started off as a harmless flirtation but it went too far and when she put an end to it he began blackmailing her. He made her act out some things he'd seen in hardcore porn videos and filmed it.' I drain the last of my water before reaching for the jug and topping up the glass. 'It's been hard, trying to reconcile the boy I thought I knew with who Billy actually was. He said and did all those horrible things but then he died trying to save her life. That has to count for something, doesn't it?'

'I'd say that was quite noble.'

Noble. I turn the word over in my mind. Kira told the police she thought Billy had tripped when he'd tried to push her out of the way of the train. He'd tried to stop her from killing herself but he hadn't meant to die in her place.

'The thing I don't understand,' I say, 'is why Kira would take a photo of the tattoo. Why would she put it in an exhibition for everyone to see?'

Sonia shifts in her seat. 'A cry for help? Guilt? She must have been carrying quite a weight around with her every day. I imagine that was almost impossible to bear. It's why people confess to crimes on their deathbeds. Guilt is a cage they want to be free from.'

'So it was a subconscious thing, like my fugues?'

'Maybe. She'll have made a conscious decision to get that tattoo printed onto the canvas. Whether she'd ever have hung it up –' she shrugs – 'we'll never know.'

'No.' I tip the glass from side to side, watching as the water sloshes up the side and then runs back again. 'I don't suppose we will.'

Sonia glances up at the clock. 'Is there anything else you'd like to talk about? We've got ten minutes left.'

I shake my head but then change my mind as a thought occurs to me. 'Yes. I want to ask you about my fugues.'

'You haven't had another one?'

'No. Nothing like that. But I don't understand why I didn't follow someone during the first one, to Weston. I did for all the others but why not that one? I still don't know what I did there, or why.'

'Okay.' She rubs her hands together and stares at a spot just above my head as though considering the question. 'I think the first fugue occurred because you were trying to escape. You read in the newspaper

461

that there were suspicions about your family and you didn't want to confront that possibility. Admitting to yourself that someone you loved might be responsible would have had far-reaching consequences.'

'They'd be arrested?'

'Psychological consequences, I mean. For you. You love your family. They make you feel safe. They're one of the foundations upon which you build your sense of self. If you'd admitted to yourself that you didn't trust them it would have had a devastating psychological effect. So you suppressed that thought and escaped.'

'But I couldn't because Jake and Mark came after me.'

'Exactly. And then your condition took a different turn. You began to confront your fears rather than try and escape from them.'

'But they've definitely stopped now, haven't they? I won't have any more?'

'Why would you?' she says, her brow creasing with sympathy. 'When your worst fear has come true?'

Chapter 69

Mark's fingers brush mine but we don't hold hands. It is enough that he's beside me, enough that we're talking. The house has been on the market for three weeks. I don't know what we'll do when it sells. We might buy a smaller place together. We might choose to live apart. I might go to nursing college. I might not. Billy's disappearance revealed a lot about my relationship with my husband – good and bad – and I need to decide what I can live with and what I can't. I'm certain Mark was telling me the truth when he said he had no idea why Billy had defaced the photo album and that he didn't have the strength for another argument, not when there were so many other things stressing him out. But he did lie when I asked him if he knew where it was. And he tried to kiss another woman. I need to decide whether I can forgive him for that and whether I would be happier with or without him. But there's no hurry to make that kind of decision. There are some things you can't force. Some things only time will reveal.

'Do you think Jake will be okay?' Mark asks as we walk past a faded sign offering one donkey ride for £3, two for a fiver.

'Just a second.' I dip down to undo my shoes. When I shake them out there's half a sandcastle's worth of sand in each one.

'Jake will be fine,' I say as we continue to walk. Mark in his trainers, me barefoot, despite the biting November wind. 'Living with mates will be good for him. They won't let him wallow.'

It's a new start for him. A clean slate. I drove to Chew Valley the day after we saw Kira in the hospital and I threw the tote and knife into the lake. There are days when I wonder whether it was the right decision, whether I should have told DS Forbes about the paedophile Jake met. He might have been jailed, taken off the streets so he couldn't go looking for other boys. Or Jake might have been the one that ended up behind bars. It was a risk I couldn't take. Not after everything he'd been through.

'Practically, I mean.' Mark says. 'He's never so much as boiled an egg. You'll have to give him lessons.'

'He'd love that –' I smile – 'his mum popping round in her pinny! Honestly, Mark, he'll be fine. He's made of stern stuff.'

He gives me a sideways glance. 'Like you.'

I felt anything but stern stuff at Billy's funeral. I managed to keep it together all the way through the ceremony but my knees buckled at the graveside and

464

Jake and Mark had to prop me up. There was no holding back the tears as Billy's coffin was lowered into the ground. We all cried as we said our final goodbyes. No one cared who saw, least of all me.

Billy's friends had asked us if they could graffiti his coffin. We talked about it for a long time. Mark said no, immediately. He wanted our son to have a normal funeral, he wanted to have his death taken seriously, not marred by strange and obscure tags and designs on his final resting place. I was torn. Billy wanted to be remembered. In one of the text messages the police found on his phone he'd told Kira that he wanted to be infamous, that he wanted the world to see his tags and know that Billy Wilkinson had existed. But the world does know that Billy existed, at least our small part of it. We deliberately avoided the papers when the police released the news of his death. We closed our doors to the reporters and photographers who turned up on our doorstep. We hid ourselves away from the world, the world that knew that our younger child was dead, and we grieved in private. Billy wanted to tag buildings but it is our brains that his name is inscribed upon, our lives that have been transformed through knowing him, our hearts that have been for ever changed.

Finally we said no to the coffin being graffitied. We wanted it to be new, untainted, untouched by the world, just as Billy was when he was born. He was such a beautiful baby. The moment he was in my arms I pressed my nose into his hair and inhaled the heady softness of him and my heart swelled with love. My child, my second child. We had created him – me and Mark. We had produced another perfect little boy. I felt blessed. I knew enough women who'd suffered miscarriages to know how very, very blessed I was to have conceived, carried and birthed a healthy child. I don't believe in God but doing it twice in a row felt like a miracle. He was a miracle. And he had his whole life ahead of him. A life of joy and fun, love and adventure. He could have been anything, done anything but all I ever wanted was for him to be happy.

We tried to be good parents. We did everything we could for our children. We clothed them, fed them, played with them and loved them but one of them slipped from our fingers. One of them let go when we told him to hang on.

Why did that happen? Where did we go wrong?

That was the question we asked ourselves, over and over again, in the days that followed the funeral. We hid behind closed curtains, side by side on the sofa, sheltering in the dimly lit living room as we tore ourselves apart. Had we been too hard on him? Too soft? Too judgemental? Too lenient? Mark blamed himself. It was his fault, he said. His fault for letting Billy down, for letting him see a moment of weakness instead of setting him an example. If he hadn't cried, he kept saying, if he hadn't tried to kiss Edie Christian, then Billy never would have done what he did. He wouldn't have thrown a rock at Mark's car, fought with his brother or taken his anger out on Kira. He wouldn't have died.

Billy was his own person.

That's what I told Mark. Our son had already made some bad decisions before he overheard the conversation in the car park, before he saw the kiss through the pub window. He'd already rebelled against us and his school. And that came from nowhere, or from hormones, or from growing up and realizing that actually the world doesn't hand you your dreams on a plate. You need to work for your dreams and even then, sometimes they still don't come true. That's a hard thing to wrap your head around when you're fifteen and you've been told as a child that you can be, or do, anything you want in life. The one thing Billy's death has taught me is that happiness doesn't always lie in the future and in any success you hope might come your way. It's in the here and now. It's in your children throwing their arms around your neck and pressing wet lips to your cheek. It's in the laughter of friends. In a walk or a run or just breathing in and out. It's in surprises, in day-to-day comforts, in a voice on the telephone, the warmth of an embrace, the soft gaze of someone who loves you. You never know how much you have, you never realize how much you've got to be grateful for, until it's snatched away from you. Cherish every moment. Cherish your life and all its ups and downs. Cherish the lives of those you love. We're only here for a short time, so much shorter than you might think.

'Has Jake heard from Kira?' Mark tenses ever so slightly as he says her name, unsure how I'll react.

I shake my head. 'Not recently. They exchanged a

467

few texts but he found it too upsetting. He asked her not to contact him again.'

'Right.' Mark digs the toes of his shoes into the sand as he walks, leaving small ridges behind him as we head towards the pier. 'Have you heard from her?'

'Not since the card.'

'The one asking us to forgive her?'

'Yeah.'

'Can you? Forgive her, I mean?'

A cloud passes over the sun and I wrap my arms around my body as the wind bites at my thin cardigan.

'I already have. Billy too.'

We pass silently under the thick metal struts of the pier. By the time we come out the other side the sun has reappeared from behind the clouds.

'Look at that!' Mark points into the distance where two young boys, bundled up in coats and hats, are running along the beach side by side trying, and failing, to launch their kites into the air. 'Reminds me of our two.'

'I remember that holiday.' I catch his eye and smile. 'We kept telling them to just buy one kite and take it in turns to be the one that ran with it and the one that threw it up in the air, but they insisted on having one each.'

'And neither of them could get their kites into the air.'

'Until we stepped in to help.'

Now we watch as the boys charge up and down the sand laughing and shouting and tripping over their own feet as their parents point and smile and take photos.

One day those boys will be teenagers and they won't look to their parents for reassurance any more. They'll make their own decisions and come up with their own definitions of right and wrong. I blamed myself for Billy's disappearance for far too long. For not understanding what was going on in his head. For not knowing what he was up to. For not being there when he needed me. But you can't hold your children for ever. You have to let them choose their own path and hope that, if they choose the wrong one, they'll come back to you and reach for your hand.

As I gaze across the sand, one hand raised to shield my eyes from the sun, it's Billy and Jake racing across the beach and throwing their kites up into the air. They play until they get bored and then Jake points out to sea and Billy nods excitedly. The sea is further than it looks, maybe a quarter of a mile from where we're standing. The kids will have to wade through thick mud before they reach it. But they don't care. They whoop with delight, their faces tipped up to the sun as they speed towards the sea without looking back. I could call them back. I could tell them the mud is dangerous. I could tell them they won't make it.

I let them run.

ACKNOWLEDGEMENTS

Huge thanks to Caroline Kirkpatrick for her support, help and insightful editorial skills. Caz, you helped shape *The Missing* into a book I'm truly proud of. A big cheer for everyone else at Avon, HarperCollins for all their hard work behind the scenes, particularly the sales and digital marketing teams, and to LightBrigade for their PR brilliance. A massive hug to Maddy, Thérèse and Cara at the Madeleine Milburn agency for your guidance, support and expertise. I'm so proud to work with such a fabulous group of women.

I'm indebted to the people who gave up their time so willingly to help me with my research. It's important to me that my books are as accurate and realistic as possible and I couldn't have written *The Missing* without you. Thanks to Stuart Gib for answering my enormous list of questions about police procedures, Dr Jez Phillips for kindly giving up so much of his time to help me understand dissociative amnesia, DK Green for talking to me about counselling and ethics, Torie Collinge for giving me the low-down on life as a pharmaceutical sales rep, Andrew Parsons for pharmaceutical advice, Lee Stone for his train expertise, Dr Charlotte McCreadie for answering my GP questions, Michael Jones for explaining paramedic procedure and to Joanna Purdue for being a mobile phone guru. Thank you Ray Wingate for answering my questions about CCTV – unfortunately those scenes didn't make the final cut but I'm still very grateful for your time. I'd also like to thank Susannah Thomson who ferried me around in her car so I could research some of the Bristol settings in the book. The black bag we saw floating in the river made it into the Avonmouth scene!

A special mention goes to Pierre L'allier who won a mention in the acknowledgements as a result of his very generous bid in the Authors for Nepal Auction. Thank you too to Clare Christian who was equally as generous in supporting the Clic Sargent auction. She named the character Edie Christian. I hope your daughter enjoys the book, Clare.

So much love to my parents Reg and Jenny Taylor whose never-ending support (and babysitting help!) make it possible for me escape from my desk so I can go out and about and meet my readers and other authors. You're the best! Love too to my sister Bec and brother Dave for amusing me on WhatsApp and keeping me grounded. A massive hug to my extended family – Sophie, Rose, Leah, Suz, LouBag, Ana, Angela, Guin, Steve, Nan, Ali, Margaret, Sam and all my lovely uncles, aunties and cousins (there are a lot of us). Big kisses to my amazing friends – Rowan, Julie, Kate, Miranda and Tamsyn – for always being there. Love you girls. There are so many other people I'd like to thank but I'm running out of space so thank you to the CAN ladies, the Bristol SWANS, the Brighton mob (past and present), the Ellerslie Girls, Knowle Book (Wine) Club and all my lovely writer friends.

And finally . . . all the love in the world to Chris and Seth. You have my heart.

AUTHOR NOTE

Three things inspired *The Missing* – my mother and grandmothers, my son, and my love of abnormal psychology. My late grandmother Milbrough (Millie) had eleven children, a husband and a haulage business in the Worcestershire countryside. My other late grandmother, Olivia, had six children, a husband and lived in a mining community in Northumbria. They were matriarchs, the person family life revolved around, and they were loved and respected in equal measure. It's only now that I have a small family of my own that I realize what incredible women they were. How strong must they have been to juggle that many children, a home, a marriage and a business. How tired must they have felt when they fell into bed every night. How stressed.

My mum continued the tradition of strong women in our family – an army wife with three children who set up her own florist business, and then re-trained to be a teacher in her forties – but she's not alone. There are millions of women in this country, in the world, juggling home, family, ailing parents and work. As women we often put the needs of others before ourselves. We give up our time, our dreams and sometimes our food to provide for our children. We want everyone to be happy and, often, we put our own happiness last. I wanted to write a novel about a woman who was desperately trying to keep her family together, who had chosen to remain in an ailing marriage rather than break up their home and who no longer knew the minutiae of her children's lives. I was struck by how quickly your children can change when my son went to pre-school earlier this year. Within months he was using words and phrases he hadn't used before. He had friends I hadn't met. He seemed to leap from toddler to young boy overnight and I found it quite disconcerting. I no longer had any control over what he heard, what he saw or what he did. I realized that my influence would continue to diminish as he continued to grow up, particularly when he hit his teenaged years.

That's why I made Billy fifteen. I wanted him to be young enough to be vulnerable but old enough to be somewhat independent. I wanted him to have dreams and ambitions that his parents didn't share and secrets that he'd never tell his mother. I wanted to explore what would happen when Claire, a control freak by nature, realized she no longer knew the son she'd nurtured for so many years. I wanted to see how she'd react when her family began to fall apart.

I decided to give Claire dissociative amnesia because I've always been fascinated by abnormal psychology and because I think our subconscious can have a powerful influence on our mind and body. We can say 'I'm not scared' but our hands will still shake or we'll rush to the toilet. We can lie but our deceit can be read in micro expressions. Claire doesn't believe that her family is responsible for Billy's disappearance but her subconscious believes otherwise and, as a result of the stress of the situation, she suffers from fugues. I did a lot of research into dissociative amnesia before I started writing *The Missing* and Dr Jez Phillips was particularly helpful in answering my questions. I tried to be as faithful as I could to the information I unearthed but I did have to make a few tweaks to make the story more intense and unnerving. Firstly, people suffering from dissociative amnesia normally flee from a situation they find stressful. I had Claire escape to Weston for her first fugue but then, instead of her subconscious forcing her to run from her fears, it makes her confront them. That's why she then follows various members of her family. The second aspect of the condition that I wasn't faithful to was the frequency with which the fugues occur. They normally occur just once. On the rare occasion that someone suffers more than one fugue it won't happen until months, or years, have passed. I didn't want the pace of the story to flag so Claire's fugues happen more frequently.

I do hope you enjoyed reading *The Missing*. I'd

love to hear from you if so. You can write to me via my agent Madeleine Milburn or you can contact me on social media or via the form on my website.

http://www.facebook.com/CallyTaylorAuthor
http://www.twitter.com/callytaylor
http://www.cltaylorauthor.com

A *conversation with* C.L. Taylor

1. Where did you get the idea for *The Missing*?

Most of my novels begin with a 'what if…?' question and *The Missing* was no different. My initial thought was, 'What if a child disappeared in the middle of the night?' My second thought was, 'What if everyone in that child's family felt guilty about the disappearance?' As I was brainstorming the idea I read about Agatha Christie's fugue to Harrogate and that sparked new ideas – what if Claire was responsible for her son's disappearance but couldn't remember what happened? What if she'd suffered a fugue and started a new life with him somewhere and left him behind? I considered lots of different possibilities but the one I kept coming back to was – what if Claire couldn't accept that someone in her family was responsible for Billy's disappearance? How would that affect her subconsciously? What if it triggered a psychological disorder? I wanted to write a novel that explored family dynamics, the pressures of motherhood and the lies we tell ourselves and each other. *The Missing* was the result.

2. Did you include any real-life experiences in the novel?

This is the first psychological thriller I've written that doesn't include any of my real-life experiences but it does explore one of my fears, and a fear a lot of parents have – the loss of a child. There's something very cathartic about writing through your fear, but it's also very difficult as you have to put yourself in the main character's shoes and let yourself feel every emotion she's feeling. It took me about five months to write the first draft of *The Missing* and there were at least two months when I felt constantly tense and unsettled. I couldn't understand why I felt so odd but then I realised it was because I was so immersed in Claire's feelings that they'd become enmeshed with my own. As soon as Claire came to terms with her feelings in the book it was as though a huge weight had been lifted from my shoulders.

3. Your main character, Claire, is a very unreliable narrator. Did you find her difficult to write?

She was quite difficult to write as I wanted her to be a strong character who was a bit of a control freak but she had to be likeable too. I needed the reader to identify with her, care about her and feel her confusion each time she suffered a fugue. But

I also needed the reader to mistrust her and question whether she had anything to do with Billy's disappearance.

4. Did you always know how the novel would end? Did elements change during the writing process?

I always knew that Billy would be found and that he would be dead. I did play around with a couple of scenarios where he was found alive but that would have watered down the emotional journeys that all the other characters go through. They, and their lives, needed to be changed forever by Billy's death.

5. As a mother yourself, did you find that the writing process and subject matter affected you emotionally?

It did, yes. The subject matter really affected me emotionally as I was writing *The Missing* and much earlier than that, when I was researching the subject of missing children and read books about Madeleine McCann and James Bulger. I found those books utterly harrowing. I cried, I couldn't sleep and I couldn't get certain images out of my mind. I knew there was no way I could write a book about a very young child going missing (my son is four) so I chose to make Billy a teenager. I also made him quite unlikeable. It worked for the storyline and it also allowed me more emotional distance than writing about a toddler or pre-schooler would have.

6. What advice would you give to aspiring authors?

It's hard to give blanket advice because each author's journey to publication is so different. I started by writing short stories. I entered them into competitions and submitted them to women's magazines and, once I felt I could craft a good short story, I turned my hand to novels. But lots of authors have never written a short story, or have no interest in writing one. I learnt about writing novels by reading 'how to' books. I read everything I could get my hands on – books about crafting characters, creating plots, the three act structure, the hero's journey, writing a 'blockbuster' – everything. I also read, and continue to read, books on writing screenplays as a lot of what you can learn from a gripping film you can also apply to novel writing. But the best way to learn how to write a novel is to read. Read everything and anything, within your chosen genre and outside it. Read with a critical eye. What makes one book good and another bad? Analyse a book you found compelling. Why did you keep turning the pages? When you've finished writing your book get a second opinion from someone who isn't a friend or related to you. Join a local or online writing group or befriend another aspiring writer online and swap manuscripts. Learn from feedback. The chances are it will sting and you might be tempted never to write another book but if you can learn from it and bounce back you'll become a better writer and your book will become a better book. Rejection and criticism are something all writers experience and it doesn't end when you get an agent or a publisher. You need to be thin skinned to be a writer, but thick skinned to get published. To get a book published you need to write a damned good book and you need to be determined. Keep going!

Book club questions for
The Missing by C.L. Taylor

1. As Claire searches for Billy, she realises she didn't really know her youngest son at all. Was that Claire's fault, or is this typical of the dynamic between mother and teenage son?

2. The novel is interspersed with WhatsApp messages. How effective did you find this very modern literary device?

3. There are several clues that Mark might have something to do with Billy's disappearance. When did you pick up on the signs?

4. What did you think of the character of Kira? And when did her behaviour make you suspicious?

5. The novel tackles the growing problem of online hard-core pornography and its implications. Did

you find this added a very topical element to the story?

6. How does Claire change over the course of the book? What would you do if you began to suffer such terrifying episodes of amnesia?

7. Did the subject matter make you think more closely about your own family, and the secrets and lies that can be harboured?

8. What did you think of the ending? Would you have liked it to end differently?

9. What do you think the future holds for Claire and her family?

10. What other similar books would you recommend to people who enjoyed *The Missing*?

Discover more from *Sunday Times*
bestselling author

C.L. Taylor . . .

Sue Jackson has the perfect family but when her teenage daughter Charlotte deliberately steps in front of a bus and ends up in a coma she is forced to face a very dark reality.

Retracing her daughter's steps she finds a horrifying entry in Charlotte's diary and is forced to head deep into her private world. In her hunt for evidence, Sue begins to mistrust everyone close to her daughter and she's forced to look further, into the depths of her own past.

Sue will do anything to protect her daughter. But what if she is the reason that Charlotte is in danger?

Jane Hughes has a loving partner, a job in an animal sanctuary and a tiny cottage in rural Wales. She's happier than she's ever been but her life is a lie. Jane Hughes does not really exist.

Five years earlier Jane and her then best friends went on holiday but what should have been the trip of a lifetime rapidly descended into a nightmare that claimed the lives of two of the women.

Jane has tried to put the past behind her but someone knows the truth about what happened.

Someone who won't stop until they've destroyed Jane and everything she loves . . .